YOUNG FLAME

BOOK THREE

YOUNG FLAME

BOOK THREE

J. B. Oro

Podium

Published in 2025 by Podium Publishing
www.podiumentertainment.com

YOUNG FLAME

BOOK THREE

The
Titan Alps
Pact
Nation
Joiak
Zad
Wastelands
Ve
Vetus
(Ursu Homeland)

RIPARIA
HENOSIS
HEOCRACY
WARRING
ISLES

CHAPTER ONE

Tense Alliance

I hate rain. It's impossible to avoid, makes the air hard to breathe and worst of all, it hurts no matter the energy I have.

Regardless of the strength I've gained, water is still as terrifying as it was when I was a child, freshly separated from my tribe. A lot of things that I was once scared of now hardly faze me. But there are two things that I'll never lose my fear of: Titans and water. Now, I get to experience both.

I clutch to Grímr's chest, suspended as he cuts through the downpour. So close to the wall of water, I have no choice but to focus on the only other thing I can see, the buzzard Titan. Peeking past Grímr's metallic tail trailing behind us, I can make out the outline of the impossibly massive bird resting upon the horizon.

The creature is hard to make out through the rain, but I'd much rather focus on the terror that is leagues away than that which surrounds me. Without my outfit, every little splash that hits me, feels like I've been whipped. Grímr has done an amazing job of covering me, but every now and then, a drop makes its way onto my fiery plumage.

After being trapped for months underground, I thought I'd be fine with anything as long as I wasn't stuck under stone and rock, but this is definitely worse than being down there. I'm trapped clinging to Grímr. The only thing I can do is hope the rain lets up soon.

We still need to meet up with the mermineae before I can get my outfit back and have at least basic protection against the weather. Hopefully, Jav will snap out of the funk he's in and fix up my snowsuit soon.

Placing my focus on the giant bird behind us might not be the smartest thing, but it's easier to keep my mind off the water than following the land below. There is nothing interesting down there, so my focus always returns to the water's proximity.

Water and Titans. Why do they have to exist? What would life be like if neither were around? I'd probably still be with my tribe back in the wasteland. A weak child slowly increasing the heat of her flame in the comfort of family.

If I had the chance to join another tribe, would I? Should the option present itself, would I return to the life of wandering the deserts with a new family?

Sometimes I feel nostalgic about those quiet moments with those close to me, and I realize how far away those memories are. Not only are they years in the past now, but I'm physically far from the wasteland now. An impossible distance, considering I'd have to pass the Alps to return there.

But . . . while the idea of a new tribe and the simplistic life I might have with them is appealing, I don't think I could. I'm not even really sure why. The outside world is filled with dangers far exceeding what we faced in the wasteland. Birds that can cut me clean in half with a simple swing of their wing. Mystical disasters that create worlds with the things they consume and twist them in excessive ways. The extensive list of entrapping threats.

Even without considering water and Titans, the lands outside the wasteland are horrifying. And yet . . . I don't want to go back.

My tribe is already dead. I accepted that years ago now. If I was to go back, adopt the same lifestyle I did all that time ago, it would feel like everything I've done since has been pointless. Er . . . maybe not pointless, but it'd definitely be like feigning ignorance of the changes both around me and to myself.

I've gained far more strength than I'd thought possible when I joined Luis-Eight. So much more, yet it is lacking compared to the beasts we face. When will it be enough? I joined them to gain enough strength to avoid being trapped again, but the entire action of joining this team was what landed me under the Alps. So is it better for me to back off and stay away from what is dangerous, like most áed tribes do? Or should I continue to push head-on into danger, risking my freedom and life for the chance of greater strength?

So which is better, a conservative attitude avoiding all risk, or an aggressive push to gain better defense?

The question itself is flawed.

Without sight of the future, it is impossible to determine which is better.

The former worked for my tribe until a risk too great tore everything apart. Henosis mages shook us out of our comfort. The Titan tore us apart, and no preparation could have readied us for that.

The latter has already bitten me. If I hadn't been so willing to push for more strength, I'd have never been trapped. I never would have ended up over here, separated from friends. But, then again, I also never would have gained this much energy.

A gust of wind brushes a few raindrops over my back and I flinch away, hugging myself closer to Grímr. The rest of my team is riding on the alicanto's back. Unlike me, they can stay out in the rain without care. The water not eating away at their bodies like it does mine.

I can hear them talking, but the wind's strength is too great for me to distinguish any words. It didn't take long to get Bunny talking again, simply asking what weapon she'd want to make first set her off on a spiral of ideas and weapon names that sound like gibberish to me.

We're currently looking for the burrow that we agreed to meet at after freeing our team. We should have reached it hours ago, but the rain has made it all but impossible to find in the dark.

It was an hour after we dropped below the Lower Elevation into the Stepps that the rain hit. The crevasse on this side of the mountain is almost nonexistent. Much of the glacier had fallen into its depths, leaving only the sudden shift from ice to earth as the only sign it was there in the first place.

It's actually crazy how fast the mermineae can move. From what I can tell, they can reach nearly triple my maximum flying speed while entirely on the ground. Of course, once Grímr gets moving, he far surpasses that, but it doesn't help that we have such a great distance to cover.

In an attempt to hide from the rain, I decrease the size of my body. Literally shrinking away from the water. I'm able to cut the size of my bird form in half, leaving me marginally smaller than Bunny's head, but larger than Jav. Any further, and I hit a wall. The energy within me doesn't want to compress beyond a certain density.

My chest aches when I push it too far, so I have to settle with this size. It's better, but the odd gust of wind still whips a few drops of water over me.

The angle of Grímr's wings notably drops, and we descend. I look down, trying to find if he's found the meeting point. The weather interferes with my heat sense, so it is impossible to feel if any mermineae are below.

There, far ahead of us, are the landmarks we've been looking for. A curved crater dug in the ground and three boulders stacked on top of each other, both separated by a hundred meters.

As Grímr slows down, he curves us off to the right of the landmarks. The two iconic formations pointing toward our meeting point with Aana and Muuro.

Grímr comes in to land three hundred meters from the boulders. The well-hidden burrow only comes into view as Grímr's talons slam into the earth. It's a much better landing attempt than when we were trying to free the others, but he still has some work to do.

His wing closes around me. I'm thankful for the cover as he trots forward before diving into the hole. It's far too small for him, but it takes almost no effort for him to widen the opening and worm his way inside.

I, along with Remus, Jav, and Bunny, fall into the burrow while Grímr carves out a side of the wall for himself. Immediately, I fly to the back corner of the small space, keeping far away from the puddle of water near the entrance.

Once I'm certain there's no threat of the water reaching me here, I notice the four heat signatures hiding along the walls of the burrow. One of them is crawling away from where Grímr just took out a chunk of the wall.

I was only expecting Aana and Muuro, so I'm immediately put on edge. Do they plan to ambush us here? They know I can see them when they stay hidden, though, so why wouldn't they attack as soon as we entered? Regardless, I need to warn my team that there are more than expected.

"Aana? Muuro? Who are the other two hiding?" I demand, readying my flames to strike at any suspicious movement.

Thankfully, Remus and Tetsu are quick to guard, standing ready.

They take longer to respond than I'm happy to forgive, so I flare my flame in warning. The walls char under the sudden lick of flames. I spread a flicker toward each of the hiding mermineae, both showing my team where they are and telling the mermineae that they cannot hide.

"Whoa, whoa. There's no need for that. We helped you, did we not?" Muuro finally drops his camouflage and walks away from the wall. Aana follows not long after.

It's the other two that remain hidden that I worry about. I'm about to snap at them that this isn't the time for games and maybe shorten their fur a bit, but Remus jumps in before I can.

"There's no need for us to be hostile. We have the same goal." With a casual smile in his eyes, he gestures for me to calm down.

Jav isn't with him as usual. He's still with Grímr near the entrance. Remus must have set him aside before speaking. I guess he isn't ready to face those that have tormented them for so long. In fact, as I glance over at Bunny, I can tell she is barely holding back the fury in her eyes.

"We want to work together, but we can hardly do that if you refuse to show yourself." Remus gives an intentional look to the places I pointed out.

Aana bites her lip as she looks between us and the hidden mermineae. She's obviously nervous about something. I focus on the heat given off by the two creatures, trying to get any more information about them without igniting them where they stand.

The silence stretches as the two mermineae still refuse to show themselves.

Muuro speaks up for them. "If you could please just treat the—"

"I guess there is no point, then. Come, Saad. There's no point if they know we are here," a gruff voice speaks.

The two mermineae finally show themselves. Both have a wiry coat of fur with so many patches missing that I'm surprised they could even hide themselves. The speaker has a large scar running the length of his body, with an ear missing and one of his sharp teeth exposed by the damage. Saad, the other, has loose skin over much of his face in contrast to the usual tautness mermineae have.

They are obviously far older than the norm. They stand more assured of themselves than even the arrogant Muuro. The most notable aspect is the entirely gray eyes they share. Forvaal, but the cloudiness of their eyes has spread to leave no white nor pupil left.

Neither seems to look in any particular direction, but they have no trouble approaching Remus. Muuro lowers his head and steps out of their path.

I'm annoyed they ignore me and head straight for Remus. I mean, I was the one who'd done all the talking with the mermineae until now. Most of the work was done by me and they should know it, unless these Forvaal never talk. There's no way it wasn't intentional. I was the one that pointed them out and spoke first, after all.

Even if I'm annoyed at their obvious slight toward me, I shouldn't care this much. It's better that Remus take over the discussion. Not only because he is likely far better at negotiating than I am, but I'll probably let my agitation get the better of me if I have to deal with them directly.

I note my bag on the ground by Aana's side. I quickly grab it and fly back between Grímr and Bunny. Not so close to the water, but also not near the mermineae.

I gave a moment of consideration to whether I should stay in my bird form for a quick escape, but the heavy thrum of the downpour outside makes the decision easy. I have Grímr to carry me away if things go badly, anyway.

"So, you will talk to the outsiders on our behalf?" the old Forvaal with the scar asks.

Both Aana and Muuro act far more restrained in the presence of these two elderly mermineae. They bow their heads and hesitate to speak.

"Like I said, we have the same goal." Remus's eyes, while cheery, hold steadfast on the Forvaal before him. "I need to have a chat with them myself. You see, the mermineae traveling to our homeland would be problematic. So, assuming you want to keep them here as my team members have told me, our partnership should be natural."

The tension is near tangible as the elderly duo remain motionless, unspeaking in response. Bunny's fists clench and the two younger Forvaal's eyes dart between their elders and our group.

Saad grunts, and the scarred merminea bares his fangs. I'm not sure if he's trying to grin or threaten us.

"Yes, natural," he says. "May the great Kalma not curse our collaboration, and shall we achieve our mission without her knowledge." He clasps his hands in front of the patchy fur of his chest.

"Welcome to the Euroclydon's hunting ground."

CHAPTER TWO

Pointless Games

Remus and Taanoraa, the scarred merminea, keep most of the discussion between themselves. Once a common ground had been determined, they moved onto confirming the lesser important terms of our cooperation and information trade.

I don't believe for a second they are being entirely open with us, but it isn't something I can do anything about.

The other elder, Saad, has backed off from the talks, grunting only a few times at comments of his fellow. The merminea is even less approachable than the others of his kind. A sneer almost permanently affixed across his face.

The Beith mercenaries we chase are apparently only a few days' travel southeast of here. The Forvaal clergy have tails attached to them, so it shouldn't be hard to find them. Whether Remus can convince them to help us is the greatest concern at the moment. Of course, only if you ignore the risk working with these merminea poses.

Why did the Beith mercenaries come across the Alps in the first place? For so many of them to abandon their posts as defenders of the pact nations, they must have a reason. If that reason is important enough to travel so far into unknown lands, then will they even put it aside to help us? Will they listen?

There's no point worrying about it for now. We need to find them first, and we can't even start traveling until this damn rain lets up.

Seated by Grímr's side, I look down at my arms. The damage from my time beneath the Alps has left my sleeves in tatters. Now that I have time and don't have to worry about hiding my flames, I can try out some alterations to my form. The lack of sleeves means that the outfit is almost worthless as a protection against the rain. I should look at the bright side; it gives me the opportunity to see if any of the ideas floating around in my head to improve my spearmanship would work.

Slowly, from beneath my original arms, I grow a second pair. It feels . . . strange. Unlike when I grew wings, it isn't completely alien, but more like I'm feeling an echo of my first pair. I move my arms and find the lower pair following the movements of my main limbs. There is a fair bit of mental strain I have to put into manipulating them independently, but the more actions I take, the easier it becomes.

A bellow from Remus gains my attention. I don't know if he's just trying to get along with the mermineae or if something they said was actually funny, but it isn't important. As I'm lowering my eyes, I can't help my attention falling on the hyper-flexible tentacles he has.

Without a moment of hesitation, my four arms mimic the dohrni's limbs. As with every time I try a different form for the first time, it is an odd feeling. The long appendages are particularly difficult to grasp at things. The lack of dexterous fingers really interferes with how I'm accustomed to holding things. Even the talons of a bird are far easier.

I hear another chuckle from Remus and almost ignore it, but from the corner of my eye, I see him watching me. I tilt my head at him before I realize he's laughing at me. Indignance fills my chest from his obvious misunderstanding. I don't know exactly what he's thinking, but he's definitely confused.

My arms return to normal as quick as they can and I avoid eye contact.

I've lost my motivation for exploring, so I fall back into practicing my control. A ball of cinders appears in my hand and I toss it in the air. The weight I give it lets it fall back into my hand without issue. Throwing it again, it hits the ceiling and bounces back.

I have to keep a bit more focus on retaining the mass with the flames than I would sustaining a normal fire, but it actually acts like a real ball now. I'd spent so long back in that furnace trying to figure this out. Now I can do it without faking it. As long as I keep a tiny portion of my focus on having the ball retain its shape, it doesn't splatter across the dirt ceiling.

As the ball rises and falls, I try to push as much of my control through it. I want to compress the flame. Not only shrink the flame, but keep the heat and intensity of a larger flame in a smaller space. Unfortunately, just like my body has a block to how small I can become, my flame refuses to compress any further without me removing some of the energy.

I know there should be a way to push past this blockage. Well, I don't know for sure, but why wouldn't there be? I'm certain Elder Cyrus could do it. The heat of his flames was always far greater than every other áed. I just need to figure out how.

Movement from my side has me turning to Jav, who, for the first time since we freed him, seems to move with intent. He walks up to me and stands there, unable to look up at me. It's an awful comparison to the self-assured volan he used to be.

His wingsuit is in as bad of a condition as my outfit; the wings obviously torn to prevent him flying off after he was captured. Jav's downcast gaze makes me realize just how small the volan is. His attitude always seemed larger than his body. Now that it's gone, I realize he's like a jerboa amongst giants.

I recall the feeling of intimidation I struggled with when I was living amongst the ursu.

"Solvei," he starts, scratching at his hand resting against his chest. "I'm sorry for abandoning you back then." He still cannot look up at me.

What does he mean? The time when he got caught? But he's the only one who suffered from that mistake.

He's visibly struggling to speak any further.

A pang of guilt hits me. He's obviously been through a lot, and still, he thought about how he left us. And I was harsh enough to consider it a just punishment.

I don't know if I can forgive the betrayal yet, but I don't hate him. I don't hate any of them. Never should I have wished this sort of treatment on them. He is not in a condition for me to keep any grudge against him over what happened months ago.

"Jav . . . there is nothing for you to apologize for. It was unfortunate what happened. That's it. Grímr and I survived just fine on our own. You were just trying to save your friends. There's nothing wrong with what you did." I lay down so I'm closer to his level. "We are out now. You can move on from what happened down in those tunnels."

Jav finally raises his head. Our eyes catch for a split second before he averts them. He hesitantly nods.

Oh, I will not be so forgiving the next time I come across mermineae. I turn my head to glare at the four across the burrow from us. But no, they aren't the ones who did this. I'll focus my anger on the next group of 'traitors' we meet.

It seems Remus and the scarred merminea, Taanoraa, have finalized their discussions. Both of the elderly Forvaal move toward the entrance beside Grímr. Aana and Muuro close behind.

"Well, there's no reason to delay," Taanoraa says. "Shall we meet your old comrades?"

He wants to head out? In this downpour? Thankfully, Remus doesn't even need to look my way to know how much I'm against that idea.

"No. We need to wait until the rain stops."

Taanoraa narrows his eyes at Remus, before pivoting to me.

"Suit yourself." He squeezes past Grímr, who blocks most of the exit. The other Forvaal follow close behind. "Catch up to us when you can." And with that, the mermineae are gone.

It is just our team again, and I'm thankful for it. I just can't get comfortable around them. Except for Aana, they all come across as duplicitous. It's the same feeling I got from Gloria, like poorly hidden contempt, disguised with a smile. Well, the two elderly ones weren't smiling, but it still felt the same.

Remus lets out a sigh. "This will be rough. Those grumpy old farts remind me far too much of the bureaucrats back home."

"Are we still going to work with them?" I ask.

"For now, we will. Though I'm uncomfortable leaving the task of halting the mermineae's encroach entirely in this clergy's hands, we shouldn't oppose them. At least until we know more."

"These Beith mercenaries we are going to find, how well do you know them?"

"I'm not sure who we will find, but I've worked with most on the roster over the years. It'll be hard to tell if we can convince them until I know who we are dealing with."

Hopefully, the Beith mercs will be more than willing to help once they realize the danger the nations face in their absence.

The rain continues its downpour for hours. As we wait for it to let up, the five of us relax together for the first time in what must be forever. We have the urgent task of protecting the pact nations, but none are willing to put me in danger. I appreciate their consideration.

Even before we found ourselves stuck beneath the Alps, it had been hectic. I can't remember the last time I just sat down and talked about nothing like this.

Bunny must be desperate for some form of weapon. She tugs out a worrying amount of her own hair that had grown rather long in her captivity. Binding it into rope, she somehow straps a bundle of jagged stones to her fist. She calls it a caestus. Well, I assume the actual weapon would look better than the wrap of hair and stone she keeps readjusting.

It's good to know she hasn't changed.

Jav, on the other hand, mostly keeps to himself. The apology to me being the only moment I've seen him interacting with the outside world. Remus is paying close attention to him, staying by his side and giving him words of reassurance and comfort.

As we climb out of the burrow after the rain, I stick to Grímr's back. I know my boots should keep the water soaking the ground off my feet, but I will take no chances.

The sky seems clear, not a bird in sight. Well, except the Titan. Grímr's body seems to be an effective deterrent to those dangerous creatures. Hopefully, they stay away from us.

Hmm. Now that we are all together, could we take on that four-winged eagle I'd faced? I'm curious, but there's no point asking for a fight we don't need to take. Especially with no certainty of victory.

Grímr stretches his wings with improved coordination and the others join me on his back. He takes to the skies, heading for the next meeting point.

Half the day passes traveling at the incredible speeds the alicanto reaches. We make it to the agreed meeting point, but I can't feel any mermineae around me at all. It looks like we got here quicker than them. They should be here already. I cast my sight over the horizon, but that hardly tells me where they are.

I've seen how fast they can run. Even accounting for Grímr's flight being faster than their running, they left hours before us, so why aren't they here?

"Where do you think they've gone?" I ask.

"Who can say," Remus says. "They might not have gone anywhere and are just trying to pressure us. I've seen tactics like this a million times."

Pressure us by . . . not showing up on time? I'm not sure I understand.

My confusion must have been clear on my face as Remus lets out a chuckle.

"It's a politician's tactic. Rather pointless and annoying, but they are trying to show to us we aren't important to them. Also, considering they've yet to tell us where the Beith's are, I'm sure it's their way of saying we can't work without them."

He casts his gaze over the horizon before continuing. "But if this is a political game, it's rather otiose. More likely, they've stopped somewhere along the way. They may report to their clergy, but if that was the case, a single one of them would have been capable of delivering the information."

They aren't planning another ambush for us, are they? I look around while simultaneously feeling for any out-of-place heat signatures. But I find nothing.

I guess we're going to be waiting for them.

CHAPTER THREE

Beith

When the four mermineae finally arrive, they run in from the west. I guess they aren't even trying to hide that they went somewhere.

"Come." Taanoraa announces their presence without visibly showing himself. "We have no time to delay."

And just like that, the four of them run off again, this time heading south. Would saying *hi* hurt?

We all mount Grímr once more and head after the hurrying Forvaal. They are quick enough to escape the range of my senses by the time we rise to the air, but it doesn't take long for us to find them again. I keep Grímr informed of the whereabouts of our guides. He keeps his altitude low enough to keep them within range of my senses.

A full day of nonstop travel. We cross an incredible distance before the mermineae stop for a rest. Good timing too; the Ember Moon will burn the sky in a few minutes and we'll get to see that strange reaction Grímr's body has.

We drop to the earth and I balk as the mermineae put space between us. They seriously don't even want to try getting along with us? Whatever. At least Remus should understand what I was talking about now.

Red slowly devours the sky and the dark moon reappears. I watch Grímr closely this time, not wanting to miss the changes as they occur.

Even ready for them, I almost miss the transition. Most of the changes are subtle, but fast. Razor feathers split into jagged saw-blades. The tail peels outward, curving in on itself until it becomes a ball of protruding spikes. The crimson glister of his metallic coating has no hint of the green and gold from moments before.

His beak opens to reveal two rows of vicious, predatory teeth. A growl rumbles out of his chest, a deep oscillating whirr. The teeth begin moving, spinning along his maw to add a buzzing noise to the creature's growl.

Its wings slam into the earth and it rises to its feet, ready to pounce forward. Before I have the chance to worry that Grímr might have lost control, its joints lock and it topples beak first into the ground, stiff. The buzzing teeth cut through the stone with ease, almost like the hard rock is nothing but paper.

Hmm . . . we'll need to be careful not to fly on Grímr during the Ember Moon. He's obviously not got control of it, so I'd hate to see what would happen if we're a thousand meters in the air when the change comes on.

The Ember Moon eventually recedes and Grímr can relax his body from the toppled metal statue he'd become. Tail, feathers, and beak return to their original shape. It's pitch black for a minute, but soon a trickle of moonlight returns the glow to his feathers.

"That . . . is strange," Grímr says as he inspects his wings. "It's usually only metals that this body craves. But under the midnight light, it becomes a ravenous carnivore."

"Is there no way for you to stop the change from initiating?" Remus asks as he passes a limb along the flat tip of Grímr's tail.

"Not unless I hide from the light. The process is completely separate from the nervous system, so it's not something I can influence. The movements it makes under the influence of the midnight light aren't orders from the brain, so I can't control it."

"So we should keep away from danger at midnight. Or do you think it would be better to look for something better? Something without such a flaw?" Remus asks.

"No, no. I could hardly hope for a better body than this." Grímr curves his tail and the grinding sound starts up again as his feathers weave through each other. "It might take me a while, and a lot of energy, but I think I could put something in place to give me control in the altered form. This might be rash, but I think I want to commit to this body."

"You sure? There are probably plenty of species out this side that we have yet to discover."

Grímr nods. The movement looks much smoother now that his head isn't completely deformed. Feasting on metals has done wonders. "Yes. We aren't here to explore and I think it'll be hard to find something with more utility and combat potential than this that wouldn't be impossible to defeat. Besides, I can be helpful to both Bunny and Solvei with this."

"Splendid." Remus turns his smile to me. "Then, Solvei, if you are okay with remaining as our mage, Grímr will join us in the ritual from now on."

Well, it's fine for now, but if they plan to head back through the tunnels, we'll have to part ways. There's no chance I'll be going down there again.

"Do we have time to worry about the ritual, though?" I ask.

"You're right, there are more important things to focus on, but if the opportunity presents, we won't miss it."

Too bad they can't just go underground for a while and eat glow-bugs. That worked pretty well for me.

We've been following the mermineae for a few days now and finally, we are closing in on where the Beith mercs should be camped out. The landscape is as consistent as always. The only discrepancy is the wide, shallow river cutting down the Stepps.

Now that we've come down the Alps far enough, there is plenty of plant- and tree-life around, but none are tall. On the other side of the Alps, it was common to see tall trees that rose far above my head. But here? I've yet to see a plant taller than myself.

Far ahead of us, the recognizable four-winged shape of an enantiorn eagle is visible. It is almost too far to see, but I watch as the large bird nose dives toward the earth. It must have found something to prey on.

I wait for it to return to the air with whatever it has caught, but it doesn't. A handful of seconds pass and it still fails to rise.

"Huh," Remus says but doesn't elaborate.

The mermineae below spread, separating from each other as their pace slows to a crawl. I tell my team about their actions, but they are just as curious about what happened to the enantiorn. We fly a few hundred meters ahead of the lagging mermineae before I can make out the shape of the eagle.

Or, what's left of it.

The bird is in halves, bisected right down the middle and now lies dead. There's a dot moving between the two pieces, but we are still too far away to see.

"Well, looks like we've found them," Remus says.

Really? Already? "I kinda thought it would be harder," I admit.

"Welp, I've yet to talk to them. There's still time."

That Beith mercenary cut the enantiorn in half in moments. The same bird that gave me so much trouble, beaten just like that. I know they are supposed to be strong, but as Remus said, they were his old comrades. I thought they'd only be a touch stronger, not this much.

It makes sense. After all, the mermineae could not touch them, and they've been out here for months at the very least. I doubt the first thing that attacked me out in these plains is the most dangerous thing around. The eagle is probably one of the most common creatures . . . which is pretty concerning now that I think about it. We're lucky to have made it so far without being attacked ourselves.

It's a surprise we've found them so quick. The mermineae have been leading us out this direction, but have refused to give any information and only tell us to follow them. On one hand, I'm happy about the separation between us, but on the other, we'd be able to work far more effectively if we properly cooperated.

We know what our role is, so we move ahead without discussing with the Forvaal. Not wanting Grímr to be mistaken for a normal predator of the sky, we drop to the ground a few hundred meters from the enantiorn corpse. From here, I'm finally able to see the Beith mercenaries. There are three; two dohrni and one khirig.

Remus takes the lead, Bunny following close behind with two holstered knives she'd crafted from the metals Grímr found. Both the handles and the sheaths were made from sapling wood. Not the best materials, but she seemed to make it work. Unfortunately, we've yet to come across anything she can use to make a spear shaft for me.

I walk alongside Grímr with Jav on my shoulder. The volan has opened up somewhat, enough that we don't have to worry about him getting caught lost in his mind mid-fight. Though, participating will probably be a ways off from now, and not only because his wingsuit still needs repair.

As I look over the team, I realize just how unprepared we are if a fight is to break out. Only Grímr and I are at full fighting potential. Remus says he knows most of the Beiths, but they came across the mountains for a reason. What if they don't like the idea of being followed?

I'm suddenly reminded of the Fearn team that went missing, and a pit of dread wells up within me. Did the Beith mercenaries kill them because they were caught making their way up the Alps? Nobody knew that they had been sneaking across, so they must have been actively hiding it. Did they murder members of their own organization just so they wouldn't be found out?

The Beiths ahead of us stand awaiting us. They aren't too far off now, but they stand relaxed, confident of their strength, despite our unannounced appearance.

"Remus," I hiss. I keep my voice quiet as I'm unsure how good their hearing is. His eyes spin in his head and lock me with a questioning gaze. "The Fearn team."

He nods with an understanding look before turning ahead, his pace unfaltering.

I guess he'd already considered that. It's a relief to know he's not blindly assuming they are his friends. Hopefully they are, and they have nothing to do with the death of the scouts from back then, but we need to keep our guard up.

"Remus?" one of the dohrni asks with surprise marring his face.

The man is huge. He stands a head taller than Remus, and each of his tentacles are twice as thick. Two massive war-hammers rest in a curled limb, each about as long as he is tall. The weapons look quite dangerous, but he holds them in a non-aggressive manner near the heads.

At his side, equally relaxed, is a khirig. Unlike the others of her kind, her antlers are sharp and sleek. They don't branch like normal. Her cage exposes much of her chest, but each of her antler limbs looks like a sharp blade in and of themselves.

Both have the iconic markings that out them as mages. But while they have a fair number of the lines wrapping around their limbs—or antlers in the khirig's case—neither come close to the other dohrni.

The last of the group is tiny. Well, not as short as me, but still tiny for a dohrni. While the others have the markings of mages, they look more like fighters. This one cannot be confused as anything else. Her markings leave not a speck of unblemished skin. In many places, the markings overlap one another. From what Leal taught me, I thought that was impossible.

"What are you doing out here?" the tall dohrni asks.

"I could ask you the same, Hëki," Remus says with apparent cheer. "Last I heard, you were on defense standby in Boreen. Did the Order give you leave?"

Before Hëki can respond, Remus addresses the other two with a dip of his head that almost looks like a bow. "Imiha, Cairin, a pleasure."

The khirig responds with a nod, but the short dohrni looks annoyed.

"I see you've already made friends with the locals." Hëki glances behind us where I can feel the mermineae lingering. So he can see them even while they're hiding? "That's so very like you, Remus." He laughs, his eyes snapping over the rest of my team before returning to Remus. "I don't know why you bother."

"Yes, you know me well. I'm an appreciator of unique cultures, and that's why I've come here, to preserve our own." Remus's words sharpen as he finishes.

The smaller dohrni huffs and crosses a pair of tentacles. "Have you come to take us back? I'm sorry you had to come so far, but we have no plans to return."

"What is so important for you to leave the nations defenseless? Why come all this way?"

Hëki chuckles. "Defenseless? Hardly. The Order has more Beiths waiting around than ever before and all we do is get called for creatures the average Luis team could manage. A few of us leaving for a year or two won't hurt when we haven't been needed for five decades. It'll be good for the growth of the Luis teams to deal with some greater challenges."

"These lands are incredible hunting grounds," the khirig speaks up. "We don't need to prepare anywhere near as much as the Mid Elevation to grow the same amount. Leave us here for a while and we'll come back stronger than ever."

"Oh? That sounds great. I'm sure that abandoning your posts is worth the extra growth." Remus's tone sounds jovial, but I can tell he's pissed. "Did you know that these locals have flooded down the path you opened and are ready to invade?"

"What?" The small dohrni stands shocked, but the other two seem unfazed.

"Hey, we weren't the ones to open the way. We arrived months after the first Beith."

Remus sighs. "Regardless, I need your help to stop them. We've already met with some mermineae willing to help us, but it wou—"

"No."

Remus is silent. Even the short dohrni turns to Hëki, incredulous.

"Forgive me, my hearing must be failing me. I thought you just refused." Remus's voice is calm, but there's no mistaking the furious undertone.

"Why should I sacrifice my gains when there are plenty of others out here? Unlike you, I have no intent to let myself fall behind."

"I can understand wanting more strength," Remus says calmly. "But you would abandon your oath to protect the people?"

"What are they gonna do? The Order's lapdogs weren't invited, so by the time we return, they won't be able to do shit. Besides, that oath is only for public opinion. The Order only ever cares about the deepest pockets."

"I see." Remus turns to the other two. "And you both will make the same mistake?"

"Yes." The khirig nods with a bored expression.

"How could you?" The small dohrni turns on Hëki. "There's a limit to how thoughtless you can be," she says and storms over to Remus's side.

"Thank you, Imiha."

"Shut it," she snaps at Remus.

"What are you doing?" My body goes rigid at his words. The Beith mercenary's presence floods the area as his eyes narrow.

I grit my teeth and push down the instinctual fear that rises within me. The dohrni's power floods the air the same way the arachnid monstrosity's growl would.

I feel Jav flinch, and Grímr lowers his chest to the ground while flaring his wings. Bunny unsheathes her weapons but Remus remains still, undaunted by the intimidating aura billowing off Hëki. Only barely can I hold myself back from attacking. My flames churn within, ready to strike. I shouldn't attack until Remus acts.

"You are not welcome to leave." Power laces Hëki's voice, directed at Imiha.

An intricate pattern illuminates along her skin, far more complex than anything I've seen before. Hëki's presence recedes, only to be replaced with another just as intense.

"Try me."

CHAPTER FOUR

Imiha

You're going to leave us after all we've done for you?" Hëki sneers. "We've given you priority on all hunts for years and now you're just going to leave? We had a deal."

"Our deal never incorporated leaving my people defenseless. I'm not about to abandon them."

Hëki lets out a short sharp laugh. "Your people already abandoned you. They didn't care when they cast you out, so why do you?"

A rush of amber light spreads through Imiha's markings and a swarm of stone spikes rise out of the ground, surrounding the two opposing Beiths. I'm reminded of the dahu's abilities, but these spikes are thinner. The spikes surround the two but don't attack. While I watch, the recognizable silvery-gray of iron seeps out of the rock and coats each spike.

"You know not what you speak!" The glowing amber light swirls around her body. "They were fooled by Listis. He killed mother, I'm sure of it!"

Hëki uncurls the limb holding his war-hammers and holds them out to his sides. His own single-layered markings come to life in a deep purple glow, lighting a spiraling pattern down the limbs toward the weapons. Nothing obvious changes about the hammers, but I don't doubt it'll be dangerous.

"I don't care what you think happened back in Meja. We have a deal and you have a duty to fulfill your end."

"The only duty I have is to my people. I'll finish the deal once I know they're safe."

"I'm not falling behind again."

Before I realize what's happening, I'm stumbling back from the sudden wave of his presence. It explodes over Imiha's and hits me almost like a physical wall. An unnatural panic runs through my body, only suppressed because of my familiarity with the feeling.

Hëki's hammer shatters through a wall of stone in front of Imiha. I hadn't seen him move, nor the rock that rose from the ground to block his attack.

Despite his hammer moving at incredible speeds into the stone, only a few of the shrapnel shards come our way. Most of the stone flies toward where he came from. The khirig behind him almost lazily dodges the speeding projectiles.

Hëki must have come in at an intense speed, but something strange happens.

For a brief second, he hangs suspended in the air before he falls backward. He tumbles through the air, accelerating until he is thrown back as fast as he came in.

Hëki slams his hammers into the ground, halting his momentum immediately. The surrounding spikes all angle toward him and shoot out of the ground. Each does not differ from a heavy iron spear. Hëki jumps to avoid the flying javelins, but I watch each of them slow in midair before accelerating toward him, where he has nowhere to dodge.

I thought it was supposed to be impossible for mages to control their element when they weren't connected to it. So how is this possible? Is it the double-layered markings?

A slight disturbance in the air is my only hint that something odd is happening. Imiha sends many more stone spears up into the air around Hëki, but instead of trying to pierce the dohrni immediately, they spin around him. The longer they move through the air, the faster they become. I can't see any individual projectile anymore, only the blurry haze where hundreds of them pass.

Hëki isn't falling. I take far too long to realize, but he's suspended in the air. He spins around, fending off the many spears shooting at him while the ring continues to grow. The same odd disturbance holds both him and the javelins aloft.

I'm prepared to ignite the dohrni, as I'm sure both Grímr and Bunny are tensed to jump forward, but Remus signals us to hold back.

Ivory and amber markings illuminate across Imiha's body and I almost miss the sudden pattern that lights up beneath the others. All the stones spinning at an unbelievable speed immediately snap toward the center, toward Hëki.

His own markings flare. Hëki blurs, moving too fast for me to follow, but the stone projectiles that miss fly off to the horizons in every direction. Each javelin is out of sight before they can crash to the earth.

Somehow, Hëki is unharmed. He stands on the earth below where he was suspended and glowers at Imiha. She takes a step back, apparently unnerved that he's without a scratch.

He lifts his hammers, ready to fly forward in an attack, but Cairin appears at his side and whispers something in his ear. I don't know what she says, but it stops him from attacking. His glare switches from Imiha to Cairin, but relaxes his stance.

Hëki tsks. "Fine. Do what you will, but I expect you back in six months. That should be more than generous to wipe out those uncivilized creatures. Not a day late. I don't think you'd like the consequences if I have to come looking."

"Thank you," Imiha says, the glow receding from her markings.

Hëki huffs and returns his glare to Cairin before walking away. His own markings continue their deep purple glow as he storms off.

Cairin doesn't follow immediately. She smirks at Imiha. "Like mother, like daughter. No wonder the Meja Matriarchy doesn't want to be a matriarchy."

Amber markings light up along Imiha once more and stone spears pierce the ground around Cairin, ready to pincushion her. Before any of us can react, the khirig appears in front of Imiha, too fast for the stone spikes to touch. She slams the flat of her blade antlers into Imiha and sends her crashing along the ground.

"Don't forget you only reached where you are because of our pity. Without us, you'd still be a powerless child with aspirations greater than you deserve." Cairin looks down on Imiha with a calm expression. "It still shocks me you think you have a chance, *princess*," she sneers.

A flash of her markings and the khirig is besides Hëki, walking away without a glance back.

Imiha stands with many shallow cuts and a large bruise across her head bleeding through the tattoos. She watches the two other Beith mercenaries moving away with fury in her eyes, but doesn't give chase. A marking with a dark green hue illuminates across her body and before my eyes, the cuts close and the purple bruise returns to unblemished skin.

I've never seen mage healing before, but this must be it. Remus's eyes widen at the sight, so it must be an impressive feat.

"Thank you, Imiha," Remus says only for her to turn her glare to him.

"I'm not doing this for you," she snaps and walks past him to Bunny. "It's a pleasure to meet the daughter of the former Grand Champion of the Vanguard. I hope your father's recovery is coming along well?" Her tone is completely different talking to Bunny. What did Remus do to gain her ire?

Bunny bows her head. "Unfortunately not. The last I saw him, there was no improvement."

"Well, that's too bad." She glances over Bunny's shoulder to the rest of us. "You have quite the interesting team here," she says, pointedly ignoring Remus. "A wingless volan, an unadjusted portian, and . . . an albanic child?"

Imiha steps past Bunny and approaches me. She is strong, so I don't want to anger her, but my flames churn beneath the surface in case she tries anything. We need her help, so I don't step away, even as she gets close to my face.

"Did you bring your niece with you? Isn't that rather reckless? This isn't a playground, you know." She reaches a tentacle and brushes my cheek. Her eyes widen at the touch. "Oh! No wonder. She has so much energy for one her age. She's no albanic, she's an áinfean."

I open my mouth to correct her, but she pushes the tip of her limb over my lips to stop me. "No, no. I haven't had a puzzle like this in ages. Let me have this," she says and I can't do anything but stare at her, perplexed. "You're not an áinfean either, your hyle is similar, but it's not the same. Oh! You're an áed, right?"

I hesitantly nod to her and she lets out a cheer, apparently forgetting her anger at Remus and the two Beiths. She wraps her tentacles around me and pulls me into a hug.

"Oh, it's so great to meet you. For such an interesting race, it's a shame how isolated you keep yourselves. And for such a cute kid to be the first áed I meet." She squeezes me tight and I struggle in her grasp.

Jav has already abandoned me to this torture. I cast a pleading gaze to Remus, Bunny, and Grímr, but the best I get is a look of pity from Bunny. Remus looks amused, and I still don't know how to parse the expressions of Grímr's bird body.

It is uncomfortable, but I'm glad I don't panic anymore. "Can you let me go?" I ask as calmly as I can.

"Oh sorry. It's been such a long time since I've seen a child, I couldn't help myself. My teacher's enthusiasm for áed and áinfean has rubbed off on me," she says with grinning eyes, but as she looks at me, her smile withers into a grimace. "I heard it's rare, but some áinfean can change their shape. You wouldn't happen to just be pretending to be a kid, right?"

She's loosened her grip enough that I can break out and put a few paces between us. I hear a laugh from Remus, but I don't get it. "Why would anyone pretend to be young?"

"To make people underestimate them," she says almost too quickly, her eyes smiling as if her expression never changed.

"Does that work?" I ask.

"Not really. Those on an equal standing with someone who can morph aren't likely to care about appearances."

"You don't need to worry about Solvei. While she can morph, I'm quite certain she's the age she says she is."

The sour look returns to her face as she turns to Remus. "Don't think I've forgotten how you walked away. I'll work with you to stop the invasion of Meja, but don't try that buddy-buddy act with me."

Remus sighs. "There was a vote. The people decided what they wanted."

"The vote was sabotaged from the start. Listis would never have succeeded if the Mercenary Order didn't take his side."

"It's been ten years. Don't you think it's time to accept that the people wanted something more than the old monarchy?"

"If that were all, then I would. But that bastard killed my mother. I can't leave Meja in his bloody hands."

"Let's not worry about that for now," Bunny interrupts. "Do you know where any of the other Beith teams are?"

"No. We came across one a while back, but these plains are immense. I haven't the faintest where they might be," Imiha says.

"That's not ideal. We need to close off the path soon or the pact nations will be overwhelmed."

"It's not all bad just yet," Remus says. "We have at least a month to search before we need to make our move. But before we get ahead of ourselves, we should introduce you to the mermineae we'll be working with, Imiha."

"That's 'your highness' to you, or at the very least, address me as Princess Imiha."

"Oh, come now, don't be so stiff," Remus complains.

Imiha wraps a limb around my shoulders again. I hadn't been paying attention to her creeping close to me. "Only you. The rest of your team can call me by my name. Only you I want addressing me properly."

"It's hardly proper, you're not a princess anymore," Remus says, but at her intense glare, he quickly backtracks. "Of course, that'll be no issue, Princess."

Remus waves for the mermineae to come, but they don't approach immediately. They creep toward us, remaining wary and hidden.

"I'm curious, Princess Imiha. How did you convince the Lu-lum family to teach you?" Remus asks.

"That's private." She eyes him up and down before laughing. "Oh, I see why you're asking," she says, but doesn't move.

Remus lets out a disappointed sigh. "Yeah, I thought that might be too much to hope." His eyes linger on the stump of a limb.

Aana and Muuro come out of hiding. The two older mermineae remain a distance away.

"Everything is settled now, yes? No more fighting?" Aana asks, keeping her distance from Imiha. That show of power must have concerned her.

"Yes, everything is sorted. This is Imi . . . Princess Imiha." Remus corrects himself at the slight presence she lets out. "She'll be helping us out for the next while."

"Uh, just her?" Aana asks.

"Yes, just me." Imiha approaches Aana, seeming to tower over the mermineae despite not being all that much taller. "Am I not good enough for you?" she asks while leaking her presence.

"N-no, you're good," she squeaks.

"The other two that were with you are gone, where?" Muuro steps forward, expressing far more confidence in Imiha's presence.

"They've gone to hunt. They won't be helping."

"Do you know the location of any others?" Remus asks.

"Yes, there are two within a month's travel, but we had been hoping this one would be enough." Muuro glances at Imiha. "Going after the other outsiders would be cutting it rather close. Most should reach the path in just under two months."

"Unless your plan doesn't involve us fighting at all, I think it's best we go in as prepared as possible."

Muuro glances between the two dohrni before looking over his shoulder where I can still feel the elderly mermineae. "Let us talk it over," he says and disappears back into the fields behind us.

Now that everyone's attention is on the fleeing mermineae, I back away from the dohrni that seems far too comfortable grabbing me.

"Hey, where are you going? I've never worked with an áed, I have some experiments I want to try."

Damn, she's just like Leal. What's with mages' obsession with áed?

CHAPTER FIVE

Heavy-Handed Diplomacy

Come on, please? It's not like it hurts you." Imiha follows me as I run off.

"No!" Why doesn't she just leave me alone?

She's only been with us for half an hour, but I'm already sick of her attention. It was fine to start off with, being nothing more than the curiosity Leal had with what I could do. Very quickly, that harmless curiosity has grown to a dangerous fascination.

She chases me now with a knife she grew from the ground, intent to cut me open and watch the transition of my physical flames into incorporeal. It might be true that it won't hurt, but I'm not letting her cut me up simply because she wants to.

The mermineae are still discussing between themselves what to do. I don't know what the issue is. If they just tell us how to find the other Beith mercs, we could fly there and be back far quicker than it would take them to lead us.

I know what their game is. They don't want us to become self-sufficient. They want our help, but they also don't want to give us too much freedom. My biggest concern at the moment is that they might plan to have us killed during the tunnel entrance offensive. Why else would they be so hesitant to let us find more of our strong 'friends'?

If I was to guess, they want us to have the strength to close the tunnel, but not enough to fight against their own Forvaal. Gaining too many of the Beith mercs to our side might be a concern for them.

"Please?" Imiha pleads. "It's incredibly rare for a mage to risk taking fire markings, so we never get to research it in great depth. You don't understand how great this opportunity is."

"No!" I dodge her grasping tentacles. "And what do you mean risky? I've seen plenty of inscriptions using fire."

"Inscriptions and markings are two completely separate sciences. They may be based on the same principals, but their canvases require immensely different considerations." Thankfully, she slows to a halt as she goes into her explanation.

I consider running off while she's distracted, but there's no way she'll let me get off that easily. Unlike Bunny, Imiha never seems to lose track of her surroundings when talking about her interests.

"Fire and more recently, lightning, are used for inscriptions because of their efficiency. Not only do their hyle forms experience less loss in physical mediums, but they are also far easier to create without a living being. Both elements naturally occur in a state closer to their hyle forms than other types, which makes the conversion easier."

Amber markings light up across her body and a stone chair rises beneath her. Something presses against the back of my legs and trips me into a chair of my own.

"These elements also exhibit far more of their natural characteristics while in their hyle form than other elements. We aren't sure what the reason for this is exactly—I could go on all day with theories—but it makes them rather volatile when passing through living bodies. Stone and water, in comparison, don't take on physical properties in their hyle form, so they flow through skin with more ease than our own blood. That's why you'll find them to be the most common."

"What about the other two elements you used? One healed you, but I'm not sure what the other was. What are they?" If she's being open, I might as well find out where her strengths lay.

"Oh, that was nature . . . or life . . . or growth. Nobody can really agree on what it is. I was taught how to use a couple of nature markings, but even those who spend their whole lives researching it don't truly understand it. The other is a secret." She smiles and her body glows amber again.

The chair I'm sitting in moves toward her and before I can jump out, she has me in her grasp again.

"Now I don't want to force you, but I really want to see how your body reacts." She waves the dagger in front of my face. "So tell me what you want in exchange and I'll do my best."

I'm not getting out of this, am I? A quick glance around reveals each of my teammates pretending to not be paying attention. Seriously, Grímr, couldn't you think of a better way to look busy than drawing circles in the dirt? After how pissed Imiha has been with him, I can understand why Remus is keeping his distance. But why won't anyone else take her attention?

I glance at the knife in front of me. The iron blade crafted entirely from the earth. It's not that being cut by it would be all too bad, I'd hardly feel it after all. If I let her get away with doing so, she is going to raise the stakes for the next thing she wants. Where will it end? With her wanting to see how well I can swim? No thanks.

But . . . if I can get something out of it, then just this once would be fine.

"Can you make me a spear?" I point to the knife in her hand.

"Oh? Sure." After a flare of her markings, an iron spear rises from the ground. "I'll make you a better one once we're in an area with better metals than iron. Unfortunately, I haven't figured the marking to create steel yet, so it'll have to do."

I lift the spear and find its weight far too great. I try to push my strength, but it still feels too unwieldy.

"Could you make it lighter?"

She touches the spear and a good amount of iron falls out of one end. It is much better now; far heavier than the wooden shaft spear I had before, but still not so heavy as to slow me down.

From the corner of my eye, I swear a disappointed expression passes over Bunny's face, but as I turn toward her, she's as impassive as ever.

"Well? It's my turn."

Imiha waves the knife in front of me, and I snatch it from her hand. If I'm going to get cut, I'll do it myself. I bring up my arm to where the dohrni could see, pull my sleeve back, and slam the knife through it.

My amputated arm reverts to flames, as does the stub. Tongues of fire reconnect the separated parts of my arm as soon as the blade has passed through. Hardly a second passes before my arm is whole again, and only a couple more before my flames are hidden.

Imiha watches on with curiosity. Her gaze is intense, and I feel a sudden regret about my choice. Maybe I shouldn't have given this to her.

She turns away from my arm and looks me in the eye. "That doesn't hurt?"

I shake my head, but that just seems to excite her further. She looks about ready to pile on more requests when I feel the mermineae finally return to us. This time, it looks like their elders have joined.

"We have decided to lead you to the closest known outsider. Any more would mean leaving the offensive far too late," Taanoraa says as he reveals himself.

"Excellent! We appreciate your help." Remus is quick to take the reins. I can see why he did; Imiha seems ready to leap in his stead. After the aggression she has shown, I can't imagine it remaining civil should she speak. I'm having enough trouble myself holding back criticisms.

". . . But if you simply told us where to go, we could accrue enough people to be sure the path can be closed. Not just temporarily, but for good. With flight and our new friend, we can make that distance in a fraction of the time."

That is a nice way to say we'd do better without them. I mean, I agree completely, but there's no chance they'll accept.

"No. That will not do. You will not find your way with directions alone," Taanoraa growls.

I expected it, but it's still annoying to hear them deny us. You could almost pin them as our enemies rather than allies, considering how much they are trying to limit us.

I notice Remus's subtle warning too late. Imiha steps past me, striding toward the elderly mermineae with a near unnoticeable application of her presence. She is expressionless. Neither anger nor curiosity mar her features as she stands tall.

Aana and Muuro take a step back and bow their heads, but the two cloudy eyed elders stand their ground.

After leaving them to stoke in her presence for an extended time, she finally speaks. "You know, it has been a while since I've had to deal with these games. I am always amused by the ploys of the weak and will often humor them, but right now, I am not in the mood. Do not think I am unable to find our targets on my own. Out of respect for this alliance we have, I shall let you show your worth."

She pauses a moment, looking each merminea in the eye. "Tell us what you know and I'll consider you comrades." She turns and walks back to my side before twisting her eyes back to them, unleashing the full force of her presence. "Do remember: if you are not comrades, you are enemies."

Her suffocating presence disappears in an instant, like it was never there.

I've really got to learn how to do that.

The two older mermineae growl at each other. They speak far too quietly to hear, but it is clear they are frustrated. Imiha stands tall and proud, as if she already knows the outcome.

Sure enough, Taanoraa speaks up, disgruntled. "So be it, we shall tell you, but you must take one of our own. Aana, join them."

"What?" Aana squeaks. "But, Forvaal . . ."

"Do what is required of you, jill."

". . . Okay." With a defeated look, she hesitantly approaches us.

The other Forvaal only wait around long enough to tell us where they have tracked the other Beith mercenaries. As soon as they are done, they run off, leaving a nervous Aana to watch as they leave.

They still only tell us the location of two more. If they've been monitoring three groups, then there's no reason to believe they don't know where more are. I guess this is their last attempt to limit our strength. Fortunately, Imiha has a way to find more without the mermineae.

"How are you able to track the other mercenaries?" I ask Imiha out of curiosity. Maybe we'll be able to find more that will help us in the time before we return.

She gives me an eye smile and leans down to whisper. "That was a bluff."

"Huh?" I say dumbly. It makes sense, though. I didn't even consider her to be lying about something like that with how strong she seemed, and the mermineae have shown little diversification in their abilities, so it would be easy for them to make the same mistake.

"They had little choice but to do as I say, even if they saw through it. The only asset they had was those locations, but they stretched that advantage more than they should have. So I gave them an ultimatum; either let it go, or become our enemies. Considering their position, they can't afford to risk the latter. Actually, this is something Remus should have done himself."

Imiha spins her eyes away from me and raises her voice. "Dotard, why didn't you push them from the start? Now is hardly the time to be obsequious to those primitives."

Aana flinches. Whether because of the intensity of Imiha's tone or the insult to her race, I don't know.

Remus gives out an exaggerated sigh. "What ever happened to that polite young girl you used to be?" Upon seeing her unamused expression, he cuts the jokes. "We are in their land, completely cut off from backup and resources we would have back home. The last thing I wanted to do was strain our relations with the only ones we have to help us. I think your threat was hasty."

"Letting them step all over you was hardly a better alternative. Besides, I've dealt with their type; they never had any intention of retaining diplomacy. They see us as nothing but tools at their disposal," she says and turns her gaze to the only merminea left. "Isn't that right?"

Aana squeaks at the attention but wriggles out an answer. "I couldn't hope to understand what the High Clergy Forvaal are thinking."

"Sure, sure. Pleading ignorance is fine, just as long as you understand that those superiors of yours have left you with us as a sacrifice. They don't expect you to survive. If they did, one of your superiors would have come themselves."

Aana lowers her head, neither agreeing nor protesting. She's probably fretting over her new role as is. Imiha's words would do nothing to help that.

Not wasting the daylight we have, we climb Grímr's back and take to the air. Even as big as his body is, there's not much room for any more people. Hopefully, the next Beiths we find have their own way to fly.

Imiha's markings light up once more. Ivory this time. Suddenly, even without beating his wings, Grímr accelerates at an alarming rate. We reach his top speed and surpass it in only a few seconds.

I look up at Imiha, who's sat uncomfortably close to me. She returns my gaze with a wink.

I guess we'll be traveling far faster than expected.

CHAPTER SIX

New Weapons

Our first target was last seen to the west, near what was described as a dead forest. The information given by the Forvaal clergy is dated. We'd be lucky if it's within two months old. The mermineae who'd followed the Beith mercs would have had to run near a month to reach the Forvaal we've associated. That's assuming the ones who collected the information didn't go somewhere else to share, as is more likely.

It has taken us two weeks of flight to make the distance, so it's hard to say if the Beith mercs will be anywhere near. Considering the delay of information, we'd be lucky if they are still within a week's travel.

The trip had been uneventful. Birds of prey mostly left us alone, even when we found ourselves close enough to see them. Those that didn't, quickly dropped out of the sky from a rain of stone spikes. The amber glow of Imiha's markings flowing out the tips of her tentacles and forming rock before her.

It was the same with those Henosis water mages. Hyle allows them to store their elements in their bodies without repercussion.

Anyway, it turns out that Imiha has access to a ritual version with far greater efficiency than what I learned, so I've essentially lost my job. She can even create the inscription with her rock, which is something I remember Remus saying most couldn't do. Was he just giving me false compliments, or is Imiha just one of those rare existences? Well, she's a Beith mercenary for a reason, so I'll assume it's the latter.

I'm not too concerned about not being the one to do it any longer. Maybe if she'd joined us before we'd fallen into the Alps, I'd have felt bad, unneeded or unwanted. But now? My motivations are different. I know I can hold my weight in a fight beside them. I don't think I would care if they didn't want me either, I'd just accept it and move on.

Grímr lowers us over what can only be the mentioned Dead Forest. The name is apt. Thousands of stumps are all that remain of what must have once been an impressive forest. Most of the stumps look like they're wider than I am tall, but none rise much higher than the same height.

We land amongst the Dead Forest and, despite the name, there is plenty of life. From the base of each stump, a ring of saplings grows, blooming wide foliage that I'd mistaken for dried grass from the air. While I can't see any sign of small wildlife, there are plenty of bugs flying and crawling around. On closer inspection, even the thick stumps themselves are alive. The points where the trunks had fallen from have grown over and healed.

I shake my head. We're not here to look at the environment, no matter how curious I might be.

"So, where were these friends of ours last seen?" Remus asks.

"It should be somewhere nearby. They said on the eastern border of the Dead Forest."

"And how big is this forest?" I ask.

"Um, I'm not sure. It usually takes about two weeks of running to go from one side to the other. I don't know how long it'll take to fly."

I groan a little inside. Many of those around me obviously feeling the same annoyance. We're already so late, and we have such a large search area. How are we supposed to find them without some immense luck?

"We rarely go near the northern side either, as a centzon dwelling is near there," Aana rambles.

"Centzon?" Imiha asks.

"Huh? Oh. They are horrible creatures. Unlike most dangers of the Euroclydon Hunting Grounds, they don't kill. No, what they do is far worse. If they catch you, they cut the fur off your back, skinning you alive before leaving. If blood loss doesn't kill you, it won't be long before the birds do." Aana involuntarily shivers.

Ugh. That sounds horrible. I've seen how much they rely on their camouflage capabilities. If they lose that, they have no chance out on these plains.

Imiha glances to the north as if she'd be able to see them and hums in consideration.

"What was your plan to find them once we arrived?" Remus asks. "I couldn't imagine attempting a blind search two weeks later than this and returning with any haste."

"In that case, we would have been able to remain in contact with their tails. Flying as we have has made that impossible," Aana says. "If we can find any of my kind in the area, they should direct us toward them."

Aana has become more comfortable with us over the past weeks. We placated her initial fear after doing nothing to harm her. Though she's still terrified of Imiha, especially when her temper is tested.

"Then it looks like we better split up. I'll take our little mermineae here and the rest of you will go for a flight."

I'm no longer the only one who can detect the mermineae. Imiha can sense them through the earth, which means our search will be much easier. Well, it is still just the two of us in this vast expanse, so we have to be lucky to come across one by chance.

"Before you leave, Imiha." Bunny steps forward. "Could you help me with something first?"

"Of course, Tetsu. What is it?"

* * *

I should have known it would be about weapons. Bunny plans to make weapons. She has Imiha pull up a large amount of rock, which soon has iron seeping to the top. Bunny collects it and sorts the iron next to various other minerals, including a type of coal you would usually only find in the deepest mines.

If only the áed back in the wasteland knew how to do what Imiha can do, we'd never go hungry.

As Imiha forms odd-shaped tools for Bunny, I ask her about it. "Do you think it would be possible for me to learn to raise a meal out of the ground like this?"

Imiha shakes her head as she works. "No, that's impossible, as far as I'm aware. For two reasons: first, the higher your binding with a particular element, the more difficult it is to use another. Both you áed and áinfean have surpassed the threshold for your bodies to exhibit aspects of your respective element. The second reason is far more simple; the marking ink cannot survive in your body."

Ah, damn. That would have been convenient if it was possible.

"Solvei, come here." Bunny calls me. She places much of the iron in a large, thick pot.

"Could you melt what's inside without melting the container? If we had the equipment from back home, we could make better quality steel, but this will have to do. Also, if it's possible, try to cycle the flow of air into the mix."

I place my hands on the rim of the pot and push my flames into the mixture. Immediately, I realize why she specified not to melt the pot. It's well within my abilities to turn it to sludge along with the iron if I'm not careful.

As my fire licks over the metal, I notice she's put in a small amount of coal and limestone alongside the iron. The iron itself, like the spear Imiha made, is . . . unclean, for a lack of better term.

The mixture quickly melts from my heat, and I have to hold myself back from consuming it. I've been spoiled for choice in snacks lately. This small amount of iron is not something I need.

My flames cup at the air and try to push them into the pot, but I just burn through the air instead. How am I supposed to mix air in? I don't have any better idea, so I lean over and push my arm into the molten metal, careful to keep physical.

The thick liquid doesn't flow easily, but I can fold it over itself, trapping pockets of air inside. It's probably not at all effective, but it's the best idea I have, as Bunny proposes nothing better.

It's only my arm submerged, but it reminds me of the comfort of the magma I'd experienced in the Void Fog. One day, I want to make a pool of molten rock. I can't imagine something more relaxing.

Imiha, crouched at my side, watches with interest. "You know, it's really strange to see a kid throw their hands into such heat."

I look at her oddly. "What's strange about it? I'm sure you could do the same without issue."

"Well, I could, but it's not at all comfortable. No matter how much you enhance your body, the conditions it favors never change." One of her tentacles joins my arm in mixing before she pulls it out and shakes it. "What's hot is still hot. I can push through it, but my body still screams at me, even if there is no damage."

"Wait, so you feel pain from this?" I've not cared about engulfing my team in flames because they don't get hurt, but what if they've been pushing through agony this entire time?

"Hmm, no. It's no longer painful in the normal sense. More like our nerves think they should be in pain, so they let us know."

The ivory markings light up along her body and a thin stream of air pushes down on the molten metal, making it spin even without effort from me.

"There, that should mix in air far better than your labor."

"What is that?" I ask, pulling my arm out of the spinning liquid.

It looks like she's controlling the air, but the effect seems different from what the enantiorn eagle or the general's sword demonstrated. She could throw heavy stones with those ivory markings, so is the wind just that strong? Still, it doesn't have that same clear distortion in the air that I'd seen from the other two.

"I told you. It's a secret."

She stops the stream of air and the swirling liquid slows. A lot of iron falls to the bottom of the pot. It feels a lot cleaner than when we started. Above the iron is a layer of mixed materials.

"Hey, Bunny?" I call. "It's only the iron you want, right?"

"Yes. We'll pour out the slag before the next step," she says.

"Don't worry."

I burn at the top layer. It doesn't taste all too great, as it's a lot of the stuff I'd find in rocks rather than anything that would give much nutrition, but it's easy enough to remove it from the iron.

"Huh. That makes this easier." She tosses a handful of powder into the iron and motions for Imiha to start her air gun once more.

Once we let the iron stop spinning once more, I eat through another, thinner layer of slag.

The process continues for quite a while. We pour the iron, now steel, into molds, and I keep them warm while Bunny hammers them into shape. It takes a lot longer to make weapons than I thought it would, but we replace the weapons we've lost, so it's worth it.

She gives me a spear far heavier than the last she'd made me, but like the one Imiha created, the heft should help me. I just need to get used to it. It's still not anywhere near the weight of the spear Bunny made for herself.

Besides the large array of weapons for her own use, she also recreated the gauntlets Remus used to have and a pair of tiny knives that could only be for Jav.

"That was surely worth it, but we've already wasted enough time," Imiha says as she moves toward the mermineae. "I'll see you lot once I find our target."

Aana squeaks as Imiha wraps a limb around her and jumps away, accelerating through the air. I feel bad for her, but it's better her than me.

"For someone who still considers herself a princess, she doesn't act like it," Remus says now that Imiha is far out of hearing range. "She's changed a lot since I last saw her."

I climb up Grímr after Bunny, but she lifts me up and holds me before her. I tilt my head back and look at her curiously. She looks away before our eyes can lock.

"Thanks for the spear, Bunny. This is much better than the one Imiha made," I say.

She nods, still not looking down at me, but the corners of her mouth rise ever so slightly.

"How do you even know her, Remus?" Grímr asks as he slams a gust of wind into the earth below and takes to the skies. "And why does she hate you?"

"Well, after the last queen became bedridden, the princess had her entire guard replaced. I was only meant to be a temporary part of her entourage, but once her mother passed, Imiha became inconsolable. Despite the idea of a reformation being desired by the populace for a good thirty years at that stage, she thought everything was a ploy. When she lost her position, she felt betrayed by everyone. It's worrying to see she still hasn't moved on, but at least she's no longer the mental wreck she was."

Remus's summary of past events puts everyone in a reticent mood. But there's one thing that's been concerning me since we met Imiha.

"I understand a little from the context," I start. "But what is a princess?"

Everyone turns and stares at me. Even Jav, who's been mostly withheld, and Grímr, who should look where he's flying, turn with stunned expressions.

Remus is the first to speak. "How have you gone so long without knowing?"

CHAPTER SEVEN

Euroclydon

Okay, so Imiha is the child of the previous leader of the Meja Matriarchy. Turns out, in Meja, being the daughter of the previous ruler meant you would be the one to lead. Or, at least, that's how it used to be.

The leader of áed tribes was usually the oldest or strongest, but not always. Elder Cyrus was both, and everyone trusted his judgment. There were other tribes where the leader was neither, but the tribe trusted them enough to make decisions.

Though, comparing the way our tribes considered leadership to any nation I've been to would be hard. A leader in our tribe never had absolute power. They were simply the ones everyone listened to during high-intensity moments. When time was not of the essence, everyone's thoughts could be heard.

The chairman of New Vetus had no blood relation to the previous ones, as far as I'm aware. I might be wrong. I never learned much about how he came to power while I was there.

Now that I think about it, I never really paid much attention to the structure of the nations I wandered through. Everything was so strange that I just accepted things as they were. But as we pass through the lands that the mermineae reside in, I have to wonder if they have their own governing structure.

They have no buildings of their own. Weapons and clothing seem like obscure concepts to them. They can make those horrible cloaks from sap and their own fur, so it's not like it is impossible for them, more like they choose not to.

Are the Forvaal clergy their leaders, with the god Kalma as the ruler on top? Or are they only a faction amongst the mermineae? Despite the clergy being immensely opposed to their escape from the Euroclydon's Hunting Grounds, the mermineae seem to have the coordination to organize so many of their race to move toward the Alps.

The Forvaal we are working with have not mentioned any group besides themselves. But is it even possible for such a large number of people to unite spontaneously like that? The clergy simply call them traitors, never going into detail about our enemies more than that. Are they hiding the existence of another group from us? Why?

I snap out of my thoughts as I feel the familiar thermal shape of a merminea below. They stand rock still, as the mermineae tend to when they feel threatened.

"There's one below," I call and direct Grímr down.

The merminea remains frozen stiff as we land ten meters before it. Grímr's landings have improved immensely, his talons no longer leaving gouges through the earth.

It is only when Grímr takes a few steps toward the merminea that it bolts. The camouflage of its fur remains intact as it weaves through the old stumps.

"Wait, we only want to talk." It seems that the sudden movement was enough for Remus to spot despite their camouflage.

Grímr takes to the air again and I point out where our fleeing target is. Bunny jumps off and tackles the merminea out of its sprint. Remus follows close behind.

"Stop squirming, we won't hurt you." I don't know whether it was Remus's words, or just the merminea freezing in a panic, but they comply.

Bunny loosens her grip, but doesn't let go.

"Now, we are looking for some outsiders. You wouldn't happen to know where they are, would you?"

"N-no." The merminea's eyes dart between each of us surrounding him. "You're the first I've seen."

"None of the other mermineae around here mentioned seeing anyone?" Bunny asks, her grip tightening.

"There was one a month ago, but they've long since left."

"Where did they go?"

"I don't know." The merminea lets out a panicked yelp as Bunny squeezes him. "I really don't, I swear on Kalma's fury."

Remus sighs and waves for Bunny to let him go. The merminea doesn't wait a moment and dashes out of sight.

"Welp, I guess we need to keep looking," Remus says and we climb up Grímr's back once more.

Before Grímr can beat his wings, we spot Imiha speeding toward us, flying a meter above the stumps. Her ivory markings change pattern and she slows to a stop beside us. Aana tumbles out of her grasp and trips on her own feet. On all fours, she scampers around Grímr, using him as cover.

"Oh, come on, it wasn't that bad," Imiha says to the cowering merminea.

"Why did you have to attract them like that?" Aana shouts around the thick metal body.

"Why not? It's not like those overgrown birds could hurt me."

"They'd be able to hurt me!"

"Oh, nonsense. I'd never let them through." Imiha focuses her attention on us. "Anyway, we've found where our target has gone. There's a lake a little way southwest from here. Apparently, that's where they've been the past few weeks."

Damn, why did it have to be a lake? I would have taken the snow-covered Alps over this. I know a lake is a large body of water. Every time I've been near large bodies of water, things have never gone well. The first, with the Titan, and then later when I was shipped across the sea as a captive of the Henosis army.

Hopefully, the Beith mercs are only near it and we don't have to go too close.

As I look over Grímr's head, I can only barely see the lake at the edge of the horizon, so it should take at least fifteen minutes to reach it, even with the boost Imiha gives Grímr's flight speed.

The wind whips against my face, and it's only with the help of Bunny holding me steady I don't fly off. It might make it easier on me if I reverted to incorporeal . . . but this is fine.

"Shit! Land! Now!" Imiha's hurried voice cuts through my thoughts.

"What?" Grímr asks as we all look back at her.

Imiha is not looking our way. Her eyes have spun around and watch directly behind us. It doesn't take long to notice what has her so alarmed. The impossibly large buzzard, Euroclydon, has spread its wings. Despite the distance, the creature still looks massive. Its brown and black feathered wings twist the light in a spectacular manner that is captivating to observe.

Then, the wings beat.

They don't make a sound, but the light twists around each wing. The image of the Titan disappears within a sphere of immensely distorted air.

"Land right now, you moron! We don't have time!" Imiha screams and before he has a chance to bring us down, she's already using that strange element of hers to rocket us into the ground.

Grímr slams headfirst into the earth and sends us all flying. I feel a pull around my chest and see Imiha has a tentacle around Jav and Bunny as well. We speed through the air, her ivory markings glowing with intensity, before we slam into a stump.

"Lay yourselves flat or hide behind a stump!" she yells to the other two.

What is going on? Why is she so panicked? I try to lift my head to look at the Titan again, but Imiha holds me down. Frustration wells in me, and I'm about to push out of her grasp when it hits.

The bang is earth-shattering. My ears involuntarily drop out of corporeality as the rest of my body shakes. Intense wind, stronger than any I've felt, slams into me. A visible barrier of wind rushes overhead, distorting light as it moves.

Grímr holds himself flat to the earth, doing as Imiha said. It isn't enough. His wings catch in the gust despite his best efforts to keep them bolted at his side, and he's sent flying. His body slams into a stump, bending around it in a way that would be excruciating for anyone but Grímr.

The stump stops him from flying off, but I note how many of the nearby stumps seem to edge upward together.

A cloud of dirt and debris blows overhead, blocking light and raining loose rock down on us. Day turns to night in moments, lacking even moonlight to see. I light up our surroundings, but it doesn't help the haze flying past in the wind.

We huddle together in the cover of the stump. Both Remus and Aana have found their own.

Soon, the wind eases and my hearing returns. Chunks of stone, dirt, and wood splinters rain down from above. A cloud of dust lingers in the sky, but without the intense wind, we can finally relax.

What in Eldest Ember's name was that? We'd have to be hundreds of leagues away from the Titan at the very least. Sure, the wind was strong, but it couldn't possibly cross such distances so quickly, right?

Gusts thread through the tree-stumps around us, creating a low humming whistle, but no longer is it strong enough to be near as dangerous. Grímr, no longer pinned, rolls to the earth and remains motionless. His spine must have snapped on impact. There's no other way his body could have bent like that. Hopefully, he'll be able to fix himself up without issue.

The saplings that previously grew from the base of the stumps have all ripped clean off and shredded in the wind. The foliage is no more.

Imiha's limb still wraps around me tightly, but considering the circumstances, I'm not too worried. It's strange to think about, but not long ago, I wouldn't have been able to deal with her hold, even under the threat of a Titan attack.

It's nice to know I have more freedom of thought than before.

A sudden, terrible migraine rips through my mind. I hold my head and the pain recedes. What was that? Did the Titan cause that somehow?

I look around, but nobody else seems in pain. Imiha peeks over the trunk toward where the Titan was resting. It's impossible to see through the cloud of dust, but she is intent on not moving her eyes.

The winds continue to slow as the dust storm falls around us, layering our bodies with dirt. I burn anything that lands on my outfit.

What would have happened if we'd still been in the air when that hit? I can't imagine a pleasant landing, assuming in the first place that we aren't torn to pieces by the intense blast.

We wait in silence until the dust thins enough to see the horizon again. The Titan's massive body soars to the north. As the buzzard descends the Alps, a tempest accrues beneath it. The storm spreads down the slope far ahead of the Titan, enshrouding everything in clouds and dust.

Imiha sighs in relief as the incomprehensible being flies past the horizon, out of sight, and away from us. The winds still whip past us, but they are closer to natural gusts than the unbelievable crushing force its wing-beats triggered.

"Wow. That was . . . incredible," Remus says, rising from behind his stump.

I can only agree. Incredible . . . and terrifying. What would that have been like if we were still near the entrance to the tunnels? Could the Titan have dealt with all the mermineae for us? One can hope.

"Thankfully, it's not coming our way," Imiha says. "We can relax."

"Have you experienced that before?" Bunny asks.

"Thrice. The initial wind is bad, but you don't want to get stuck anywhere near where it flies."

I head over to Grímr's side. He's rolled to his chest and I hear a sickening crack as his spine realigns itself.

"Are you all right?" I ask as I pass a cool flame over his plumage, cleaning off the accumulating dirt.

"No problem," he says. "Just going to be stuck here for a few hours until my body's spine is healed."

"Your bones are metal, right? Would heating until malleable make them easier to fix?"

Grímr eyes me for a moment. I don't know if he's considering my words, or has a problem with my proposition. "That might work, but it would definitely damage the muscles and tendons. Those are surprisingly harder to heal than an alicanto's bones."

I settle in by his side and stare into the sky. We're in a hurry to find the Beiths, but there is nothing to be done when our ride can't move. Such a tragic event will halt our search.

I'm not at all ecstatic that we have put the trip to the lake on hold. Nope.

Clouds roll in from over the horizon, approaching at incredible speeds. It's not thick cover, but the gray blobs roll above, threatening to drop their payload. Flashes of light spark out from many. Each cloud its own small thunderstorm.

Unlike normal lightning, the flashes of light don't travel to the ground. They stay entirely isolated within their dark blotches.

I watch each one as it moves toward us, ready to dive under Grímr's wing should they decide to be less self-contained and pelt me with their concerning liquid.

I'm trying to ignore the fact that the Titan is actively wandering around. The sheer presence of the other one was enough to nearly put an end to my tribe. Only due to fortune did I survive myself. If that monumental bird comes anywhere near us, I can't imagine being so lucky twice.

Even if we saw the Titan coming toward us, is there anything we can do? I doubt we'd be able to run out of its path before it reaches us. The being had to have traveled a hundred leagues in only a few minutes. There's no chance of outrunning it.

I shake my head and pull my head from the clouds. The Titans are natural disasters, there is no avoiding it if it comes. Not even the Beith mercenaries could survive the proximity of a creature like that.

Jav seems far more alert than he's been in a while. He holds an incredibly thin needle in his hands and works on his suit. Did Bunny make that for him when she was making all the other weapons? Or did Imiha?

Remus appears pleased as he watches over the volan's shoulder. I guess the shock the Titan gave his system was enough to wake him. Hopefully he'll be able to return to himself soon.

Imiha walks up beside Grímr and rests a couple of tentacles on his back. Green markings glow, and within a minute, Grímr is standing up and shaking his plumage. The feathers spin around one another like tiny weaving saws.

I guess we'll be heading to the lake immediately.

Damn.

CHAPTER EIGHT

Áinfean

Hey, can we skip this one?" I ask. "I'm sure we'll be fine with whatever Beith we find at the next search point."

As we approach the expanse of water, I lose my nerve. Just the sight of it is enough to make me want to run. The water sways back and forth. Waves crash against the shore, climbing a dozen meters across the earth before receding.

"Come now, there's hardly anything to fea—" Remus cuts himself off before reconsidering. "All right, you, Grímr and Jav stay back. The rest of us will head on."

I didn't actually expect him to agree, but I'm not about to complain. Even if he knows I fear the water, it didn't stop him from forcing me onward the last time I was terrified.

It's good to know he's reflected on what he's done. But it's not like he needs all of us to talk with whatever Beith mercenary they find. Imiha is strong enough to at least put up a fight. In a stressful situation or when he decides something is important, I don't think I could ever trust his decisions.

I don't hate my team for what they did, nor can I hold a grudge after what they experienced, even if I haven't forgiven them.

Hardly any time passed after I told them of my fear when they forced me down into those tunnels. I understand their reasons now, but how can I know their own ideas of what is good for me won't conflict once more in the future?

I can never truly trust Remus, Jav, or Bunny again.

Grímr is the only one who stood up for me at the time. The one to stay by my side throughout those entrapping tunnels. Only he I would trust with my life.

That's not to say I plan to pointlessly throw myself into a position where my life or freedom would be threatened. But should the day come where I have to choose, I'll rely on Grímr over anyone else.

We land a good few hundred meters from the lake and the others head on without us. Jav is quick to pull out his thin needle and work on his wingsuit. I watch as he works to fix the wings with thread scraps salvaged from other parts of his clothes. His tiny digits move with rapid precision to reform the material between his arms and torso.

"Will you have enough to remake them?" I ask.

He startles at my voice but quickly calms. "Uh . . . I need to dismantle much of the suit to get the wings to basic functionality. My sisters have always been better at this, but it should let me fly again."

Despite his timidness, it's great to see him getting better. I'm not sure if there's anything I could do to help him recover, but that he has something he's working toward is a good thing.

I shouldn't mention that he won't get much of an opportunity. If he flies without Grímr by his side, he's likely to get torn apart by an enantiorn or any of the other massive birds we've seen scouring the plains. There's a reason I've stayed in my default form the past few weeks.

The scattered clouds still speed overhead. The winds from the Titan must be blowing far stronger at higher altitudes for them to cross the sky this quickly. Brief flashes of light within each continue with regularity. They are concerning when directly overhead, but the phenomenon is oddly soothing to watch.

A blinding flash of light fills my vision, followed momentarily by the thrumming crack of thunder. From many of those small, isolated thunderclouds originates a series of forked lightning that snaps together in a mighty bolt that strikes the lake.

I jump to my feet. I'm not the only one startled; Jav flinches, sending the tiny needle flying out of his grasp.

That lightning strike was brighter than any other I've seen. As I look over the lake, a plume of vapor rises from the area of impact. The clouds above no longer flash with energy. It must have all been unloaded into the lake.

It can't be a coincidence that the lightning hit as soon as our team approached the lake.

Against my better judgment, I get Grímr to take me closer. I don't want to go anywhere near all that water, but I need to make sure the others are safe.

We retrieve Jav's needle and walk toward the shore. I stick to Grímr's back, keeping as far away from the wet ground as I can despite the boots that should keep me dry. The wind blowing over the lake keeps the waves rough. Every time they crash against the bank, I worry that it'll come all that much closer.

"We don't have to do this, Solvei. They'll be fine by themselves," Grímr reassures me.

"I just want to get close enough to see them. No more."

There, along the water's edge a few hundred meters away, I spot them. Thankfully, they all appear fine. They've moved fast to get so far around the lake. Grímr stops and we watch them travel along the shore.

It's good to know they're okay. That lightning bolt must have been coincidental after all.

I'm about to ask Grímr to take me away from the water again when a spark of lightning chains out across the lake. Unlike before, it doesn't drop from the storm clouds above. It originates at a point ahead of our team and lasts for multiple seconds. Enough time to see that beside the bright white core of the lightning, it tinges the air with a hint of violet.

The thunder rolls through us like a series of chuckles, before abruptly cutting off with the end of the light-show. None of the arcs came close to us, but I can still feel the tingle of electricity in the air.

"Shit," Grímr breathes beneath me. It's not like him to swear.

"What?"

"That's Spenne. No doubt in my mind."

Grímr seems concerned, but that name means nothing to me. "Who?"

"He's one of the few áinfean in the Mercenary Order. Easily the strongest."

"So, what's the problem?"

Grímr struggles to answer immediately. "I don't like saying this, because his nieces and nephews are close friends, but he's a lunatic." He pauses. "I'll tell you this now; don't trust him. He has an outgoing and cheerful exterior, but he won't think twice about tearing you apart if he thinks he'll find amusement in it."

I look closer toward where the lightning originated and spot a white figure just as it dives into the water.

"I should also mention he is probably the only áinfean to fear nothing."

My team reaches the shore, but doesn't follow. Soon, a disturbance in the water announces the áinfean's return. He trudges out of the water with a massive flat, scaled tail in his grasp. Each step he takes out of the water only shows how large the creature is. It's at least fifteen meters long, and he drags it out like it's nothing.

A chuckle, like rumbling thunder, echoes through the area. It's kinda creepy how far his voice rolls. The sleek creature he pulls from the lake is already dead. It's a strange-looking animal. Lacking legs or arms. Instead, flat growths appear in odd areas of its gray, scaled skin.

It's longer, and more snake-like, but the creature is very similar to the fish Jav caught back near the pact nations. The fins—I remember them being called—and tail are similar enough to make the comparison.

Spenne, the áinfean, approaches my team. His booming voice audible even this far, but the words aren't clear.

"How strong is he?" I ask. Unlike the last Beiths we found, Grímr could recognize who it was simply by the power shown. I want to know what we're dealing with before I rejoin my team, especially if the áinfean is a lunatic.

"He's the strongest of his race. There is no contest, nobody comes close. Amongst the Beith mercs, he's probably one of the top that aren't a part of the Order's trusted Inner Circle."

"With Imiha on our side, how do we fare if a fight starts?"

Grímr gives me a concerned look.

Hey! There's no need for that! I'm not planning to fight. I just want to be prepared in case it comes down to it.

"Imiha is strong, but she's young and unrefined, as are you." I give him a glare, but he continues on. "Spenne is older than Remus. To put it simply, we don't stand a chance if he turns against us."

So what? He's comparable to Hund? I hope not.

"Should we join them?" I ask. I'm unsure if we should hide from such a person.

"Yes. He already knows we're here, so there's no point waiting around."

I'd like to say I'm surprised that he would know we're here, but considering I can already feel heat from a hundred meters away, I have no doubt someone so much stronger would have their own methods. That, and we haven't really been hiding ourselves. Grímr is pretty big.

As we skirt our way to them, I glance up at the tumbling clouds above. In the short time since the áinfean pulled at their energy, they have charged once more. Brief flashes light up within them as they coast through the air.

It feels like it's been far too short a time, but here we are. I'd hoped Grímr would take a slower route. For some reason, I'm nervous about meeting this áinfean. Did Grímr's talk of him being a lunatic get to me? I've got to shake that thought from my mind. Treat him as I would any other on our first meet.

"Ah, finally! Everyone's arrived." His voice still thrums through my chest like thunder. Not every áinfean is like this, right? It's just because he's strong.

Spenne is strange. The most noticeable thing is the slick, white wraps that wind around each part of his body like bandages. In the small areas of his body left open to air, like his eyes, mouth, and some places along his arms where the wraps have loosened, arcing electricity thrums.

As an áinfean, he is similar to áed in that his body is formed completely by the element he is bound. But he doesn't seem to have any intent on controlling and hiding his electricity as we do our flame. Every few seconds, an arc zaps out through the wraps and winds down his arms or along his spine.

He stands on two legs that protrude from the torso that continues into a thick tail, not unlike that of the fish he pulled from the lake. His upper body is hunched and long, thin spikes poke through the white wraps along his spine. The face of the áinfean is wide, flat and pointy, like the edge of a dull axe. His eyes, small beady things that glow with power, lie on the top half of his head, while a wide, tooth filled maw spans the bottom.

Spenne fixes the three of us with a glance before he returns to Remus. He shows no interest in us.

"Of course, old friend, I will definitely help. How could we ever let these creatures attack our homes?"

Simply being in the áinfean's presence, I can hear a constant humming of electricity. Each time he speaks, the humming amplifies, giving his voice a strange frenetic tone.

"But, more importantly, who wants some fried fish? I'm not great at making the crumb from back home, but you wouldn't believe how great these whoppers taste."

Spenne slaps his hand on the belly of the fish, and lightning cracks, forking over the corpse. Thunder booms and I have to clamp down on my urge to back away.

The power that fills the air really is like nothing I've felt from anyone but Hund. And I'm almost certain he hasn't used his presence.

The bolt of electricity was brief, but the body of the fish falls apart in cubes, as if cut by a knife. He must do this often; the fillets are all perfectly cooked with branch-like patterns through the meat.

I glance over at Remus, who seems concerned, but resigned. If what Grímr was saying is true, this áinfean might be more than helpful when we have to face the mermineae. But he might also be too big a risk to keep around. There's probably a reason he's out here alone, without a team.

I'm just glad he isn't another Imiha, determined to open me up like a research subject.

Wait, he's an áinfean, why isn't she trying to cut him open? What bias. I send a glare at her, but she just looks back in confusion. She's oddly quiet, and I notice she's backed off to let Remus take the lead. Is she afraid of Spenne?

The áinfean swallows a chunk of fish about the size of my body in a single gulp.

Yeah, okay. I don't blame her.

CHAPTER NINE

Siege

The third Beith location was a bust. They were long gone by the time we arrived and so were any of the tails meant to be following them. We spent a week to search, but by then it was already falling far too close to our deadline.

It would have been great if we'd found a few more, but it can't be helped. Spenne is strong enough that we probably won't need to worry about any of the mermineae getting in our way. Preferably, we would have had more strength backing us in case Spenne proves Grímr's warning true.

It's hard to see, though. The áinfean seems like a rather jovial man, if brutal in a fight. Despite being overwhelmingly stronger than the creatures around, he is more than willing to go all out to obliterate from existence and tear the skies with lightning.

I've taken to muffling my hearing any time he runs off for a fight.

Thankfully, Spenne spends most of his time talking to Remus about old times and recent battles, leaving me out of it.

We arrive back at the mermineae's meeting point and, despite their usual reluctance to show themselves, Caavaa and Muuro approach us unhidden. I wonder where the two elderly ones are? I can't feel their heat anywhere nearby.

"You succeeded in finding another," Caavaa says. "There will be no issue fulfilling your upcoming task, I hope?"

"Yeah, rodent extermination is kiddie work. No issue." Spenne then turns to me. "Oh! No offense."

Really? I can't help but stare at him. Was there really a need for that? We have hardly even spoken this whole time, and now he calls me a kid. I hold back the irritation from showing on my face.

Caavaa has no intention of doing the same. His eyes narrow at Spenne's words. "Your task is to close the path. Nothing more. Clear the way to the tunnels, but kill no more. I don't want you murdering the clergy members hiding amongst them."

"Oh right, of course." Spenne pats his chest. "We'll follow your orders to the letter." He finishes with a wide grin, showing off the sparks that make up his teeth.

Of course, the áinfean's words do nothing to assure Caavaa, so Remus steps forward to mediate. "Don't worry, we plan to commit to our side. We have no reason to kill those of you trying to stop the invasion."

Caavaa's glare flicks between Spenne and Remus before he waves an arm at

Muuro, who sprints off. "Good. The attack will happen soon. For now, rest." He turns and crawls back into his burrow.

I'm assuming that Muuro has run off to tell the rest of their clergy that we are ready to move. We are within a day's travel of the entrance, so it shouldn't be long before we proceed with the attack. I'm concerned about the details of the siege. The Forvaal have been reluctantly cooperative at best, and have a nasty record of laying the entire risk on us. Will they do the same in the next few days?

Once Caavaa is out of sight, Remus turns to Spenne. "Just this once, hold back until we seal the path."

The áinfean hums, acting oblivious.

"I've known you for well over a century," Remus says. "Don't think your plan isn't abundantly clear. I won't stop you. Just let us seal it off and get out of the way before you have your fun."

Spenne remains frozen. Is he pissed? I glance around to see everyone as tense as I am. All eyes are on Spenne. We aren't all about to be attacked, right?

The áinfean's jaw drops. "Remus?" He turns away, gesturing to the dohrni. "This isn't Remus, is it? I'm being fooled."

I'm not sure why he's having this reaction, but at least he's not attacking.

Spenne snaps back to Remus. "You're serious? What did they do to you?"

"Right now, the safety of my team is most important. I would rather you don't go overboard, but I can't stop you," Remus says. "So I need to stress this: will you wait until they are safe?"

"Yeah, no problem," Spenne agrees without delay. "It's good to see you not so pacifistic, Remus. Do you want to join me?"

"No."

"Ah, that's too bad. It's gonna be fun." I swear the zapping grows louder as he grins.

There are a lot of mermineae. By a lot, I don't mean a couple hundred or thousand. No, there have to be tens of thousands moving along the slope ahead of us. Most still keep their camouflage up, but the sheer number of them removes any hope they might have had of remaining hidden.

We all sit on Grímr's back and wait for the attack to begin. The Forvaal clergy will make the first move. We just need to stay out of sight until then. You'd think that would be hard considering the size of Grímr's alicanto body, but we aren't the only ones to have noticed the immense merminea presence.

Birds of prey swarm the skies. Each looking for an easy meal offering itself up to them.

For the first time since I've been to this side of the Alps, I can truly see the desperation the mermineae have to leave these plains. They continue to push toward the tunnel entrance, despite the birds diving from above.

One of the enantiorn eagles dives toward some unfortunate soul, but before it can reach its prey, it screeches and pulls back into the clouds.

The Forvaal amongst the mermineae put a lot of effort into protecting their people, but for every bird they successfully turn away, two more take off with someone clutched in their talons.

Many die every minute, but the mermineae still march forward.

"This Kalma must be quite the character," Spenne ponders. "I don't think I've ever seen fear cause such solidarity before. Most creatures I've seen will stab their best friend to get away from what terrorizes them."

We watch as another merminea is plucked from the surface, screaming until the bird's talons end its existence. The merminea's neighbors move on with little more than a glance after their fallen brethren.

Spenne hums in curiosity. "Have they told you where one might find this Kalma?"

He's not planning to meet her, is he? I'm sure he's strong, but I struggle to believe it's even close to what these people consider a god.

"No," Remus says. "But if you go looking, please don't give her any reason to cross the Alps. There are some creatures that should be left alone."

We are supposed to wait for the signal before we attack. Once we hear it, we are to do whatever we can to get to the tunnel. As usual, the Forvaal don't share their plans with us. All we know is that there should be enough of a distraction to allow us ease of passage.

Well, that's what they claim. I don't believe for a second that it'll be that simple. There are so many of them clambering around the Titan's path that I can't help but doubt the mermineae we're working with.

Unfortunately, the buzzard Titan didn't wipe out these mermineae when it went on its hunt. While the Titan's resting place is still an immense distance away, near the top of the Alps, I thought the damage here would be far more intense considering how strong it was hundreds of leagues away.

Though, looking around, I see that there isn't much *to* damage. The slope is already as flat as can be. Any greater detail is hidden beneath snow. Is that why this side of the Alps looks like this? The winds of Euroclydon have worn away the mountains that were once here?

"Are we too late?" I ask. Considering the number of mermineae swarming as far as I can see, there can't be any more coming, right?

"We shouldn't be," Imiha says. "But these numbers are concerning. If there's more . . . "

"How do they feed this many?" Grímr asks. "For them to travel together like this, it can't be sustainable."

"It probably isn't," Bunny says. "They'll have to split and hunt within the tunnels. The deaths they accrue against the birds up here will be nothing to the losses they expect to take down there."

The mermineae must treat the death of their own kind like an assured thing to go through with this. What is their life like for them to feel this is their best option? It's not like the tunnels will be the only difficulty they will face.

I almost feel sympathetic toward them.

Almost. They're still threatening my friends' home.

A low, droning bellow rolls over the slopes. The mermineae freeze at the out-of-place noise. It's a strange sight. One moment they are easily visible due to the sheer number of them moving. The next, they have all disappeared.

Then, chaos erupts.

Amongst the thousands, many throw themselves on their neighbors. Claws tear through chests and teeth rip out throats. In moments, the white landscape drowns in crimson.

The coordinated assassinations devolve into frenzied brawls as the ambushers leap from their first kills into the crowd. Most don't survive, immediately retaliated upon by the surrounding mermineae, but they have achieved the chaos that was promised us.

Mermineae lash out, not knowing who is friend or foe.

"Well, that's one way to start a fight," Spenne says as he tugs at the bindings around his arms. "What are you waiting for? Let's get down there."

Grímr tilts his wings and we fall into a dive. We can't attack the tunnel entrance directly. It would put us in a direct sight line of the Forvaal defenders. If we don't want Grímr to be torn apart before we make it to the crevice, we need to approach from the ground.

Some opportunistic birds have taken to diving alongside us, so our approach couldn't be any better hidden. Our choice to not attack the tunnel directly is proven to be for the best. The birds diving near the path die in moments, each one decaying to dust before they have a chance to pull away.

They must have the strongest of the Forvaal defending that position. It's going to be hard to break through if they move their attention to us. The clergy should deal with them soon, but relying on them for anything leaves a foul taste in my mouth.

I wait until Grímr scrapes along the surface at full speed before I let free my flames. They spread to engulf everything, but struggle to keep up with the pace of this metal bird. Grímr glides barely a meter above the ground. His heavy wings crush heads of any unaware mermineae.

We tear through hundreds before one throws itself at Grímr's beak, angling his body just enough for Grímr to face-plant into the earth at speed.

We are all flung off his back. Thankfully, Bunny grabs me in midair, so I don't have to worry about a face full of frozen water. She sets me down, and I send a nervous glance down at my boots, buried in snow. It's fine, it will not leak through.

The mermineae that pulled us to the ground didn't survive the crash, squashed between Grímr and the earth.

The earth ripples, rises, and propels the snow away from us. The wall of stone now circling us also blocks the sight of any Forvaal. I give Imiha a nod of gratitude now that I have environmental conditions that I don't have to tiptoe around. She grins back before turning to the mermineae now flooding over her wall.

I don't give them any time to attack, igniting everything in the area. The fur burns off their backs before they can even scream. They don't last long enough for my flames to burn much further. A booming crack of thunder accompanies a flash of light and every mermineae in my flames drop dead.

The energy of the áinfean's lightning felt . . . oddly good. It didn't impede my flames. Instead, for a brief instant, I felt heat and intensity I couldn't hope to replicate. Despite the power behind it, it didn't hurt or hinder my flames. In fact, I'd say it enhanced them.

I turn back to Spenne and we lock eyes. A toothy grin grows along his face, arcs of electricity zapping around him almost seeming to grasp at my flames. "Oh, kid, I was wrong about you. This really is gonna be fun."

I'm not sure what he means, but I can't help but agree.

A bolt of lightning snaps out, covering an incredible distance past the walls that surround us. I'm surprised to find out my flames follow with it, letting me control fire far further than I normally could. The intense bolt cuts through several mermineae, killing them instantly. My flames burst out from the path of lightning and engulf many of those surrounding.

"Hey, kid, can you make as much smoke as possible?"

Smoke? I nod in agreement, even though I'm unsure why he wants that. If I want to make a lot of smoke, that means I can't use my flames to eat the energy out of things, nor can I add mass to my flames from the surrounding material. I need to let things burn naturally.

He better have a good reason for this. It's a waste to throw away resources.

I notice Spenne's wraps around his hands have loosened, leaving his electricity to arc out into my flames with little control. He no longer sends bolts beyond the sphere of my fire, so I don't have that easy method to spread my flames, but fire is nothing if not insistent.

It is a fire's nature to burn and grow. Extinguishing a flame is far more difficult than nudging it into an inferno, even for my own flames. Just the tiniest influence has the fire beyond Imiha's walls spreading between mermineae. I don't even need to mix my inner flame amongst the fire and risk touching the snow. With how many mermineae surround us, it's actually quite worrying how fast it spreads with only the tiniest of nudges.

Grímr finally digs himself out of the earth and we move forward. Imiha's walls follow along, keeping us surrounded. The seven of us push forward, slicing through any mermineae between us and the tunnel.

The real challenge still lies ahead.

CHAPTER TEN

Tetsu

Tetsu lunged forward, her falchion piercing the neck of her opponent. She twisted and jerked the blade out as her body flowed forward. In her other hand, a second blade swung through the chest of a merminea scrambling at the flames scorching its fur.

She didn't like to admit it, but the dual short swords had always been her best weapons. It just allowed for so much freedom in a fight. Of course, the downsides often made them unusable, especially in contests of strength, but when she could dance around her opponents like this, there was little she was as skilled at.

It was a point of pride to be well-trained in all weapons. She didn't want all her hard-earned skill to be hidden behind one in particular. Her father was once a master of every weapon in the family storage, but nobody ever mentioned anything but his immense talent for the halberd. As much as she wanted to be like her father, she did not want people to see her the same.

But right now, pride had to take a step back. She needed to perform her best. She'd already lost to them once, she wasn't about to let that happen again. Each merminea was naturally strong—likely due to the environment of their growth— but they were not skilled in combat against other sapients.

It was still frustrating how they got the jump on her. If so many hadn't ambushed them, Tetsu was sure that she could beat them in a grapple.

They were running forward at a decent pace. With Imiha's walls leading the way, it wouldn't be long before they reached the entrance to the tunnels. There was no doubt in her mind she needed to be prepared for the opposition they would face.

A merminea rushed through the surrounding fire with a crazed focus on the young girl beside Tetsu. She stepped into the path of the creature's attack and swung a falchion at its neck. The merminea was dead before it could register the sharp edge of steel.

The blade sliced through with ease. Tetsu forced every fiber of strength she could manage into her strike. The merminea fell to the ground, its head rolling by its side. The corpse left to burn behind them. It was likely an unnecessary level of effort directed at the creature; it would have died regardless and Tetsu doubted the áed would have been in danger, anyway.

But Tetsu couldn't help the anger she felt when she saw the girl in danger. She knew she shouldn't. It was an insult to Solvei after everything she'd been through.

With how much the girl has grown since they met, she doubted there was much that Tetsu could defend her from that the áed couldn't fight herself.

Why did Tetsu have this feeling of wanting to protect the girl now? Why didn't it show itself back when she committed the act that would ruin the trust the girl had placed in them?

As much as she regretted the past, it could never be changed. She could only work toward making it right.

A second horn blared, scarcely audible over the rolling earth, roaring fire, and crackling thunder already muting much of the outside chaos. Only a few seconds after the horn ended, a massive plume of dust rose ahead of them.

The group didn't stop, but they each looked to the ash spreading through the sky. Something happened near the guarded entrance. Tetsu knew the clergy were planning something, but from everything else they'd seen, she never expected it to be this big. Well, whatever it was, it would have distracted the defenders.

The resistance they faced loosened. Whatever caused all that dust must be far more concerning than Tetsu's small group.

Solvei's flames wrapped around Tetsu like a warm blanket rather than the inferno it was for their enemies. Her ability to hold back against her allies had improved tremendously, even considering her flames burned far hotter than they used to.

Between the áed's flames, the áinfean's aggressive shocks and the mage's earth piercing those who passed the walls, there wasn't much for Tetsu to do. Only the luckiest and most incensed merminea made it close enough for her to enjoy the thrill of the fight.

Months had passed since she could use her weapons. The makeshift blades she'd made were . . . decent, but she missed the proper craftsmen-made ones back home. Steel weapons just didn't last long against creatures with strong defenses.

"There's a crevice ahead," Imiha shouted over the cacophony of battle.

"All right. Be ready to face intense opposition," Remus said.

With little fanfare, the group dove into the tunnel as soon as Imiha's walls passed over.

Tetsu's feet slammed into some unfortunate soul. She felt several ribs shatter beneath her boots, but paid it only an instant of her attention. Tensing her legs, Tetsu pounced on the first Forvaal she saw. The creature had no time to activate its eyes, one blade pierced its chest, the other right between the eyes.

She kicked out at the next Forvaal, whipping its head away from her. It wasn't enough to do much damage, but it stopped the creature's eyes burning her. Two swipes with her blades were enough to end it before it could regain its senses.

Five mermineae stood before her, two of which were Forvaal. Their eyes glowed, ready to burn into her. Tetsu bounced forward, intent on stabbing both before they could.

Spikes shred out of the walls, pincushioning each mermineae before she could reach them. Tetsu looked back at the others, who had cleaned up the rest of the defenders of this crevice. All in all, a rather clean entry despite the number of Forvaal amongst them.

Spenne, Grímr, and Solvei would remain above, defending their entry point. Tetsu disliked the idea of leaving Solvei and Grímr. The mermineae were bad enough, but she'd heard plenty of stories about Spenne's predilection toward collateral damage and fratricide.

She didn't want to leave Solvei up there, but Tetsu wouldn't force her again, even if she thought it would be safer.

They pushed forward through the tube beneath the Titan's path, searching for the transition to ranked stone and the tunnel within it. Imiha crushed and pierced mermineae with ease. The environment made the mage's magic unbeatable even for the stronger Forvaal.

Despite the number of mermineae down in these tunnels, they held a less fierce defense than they'd been expecting. After only a few minutes of tearing through the wide tunnel, they found their target: a four-meter-wide hole bearing down through a three-meter-thick layer of ranked stone.

Things had gone worryingly well. Too many things had gone better than expected and now Tetsu was waiting for the one thing to go horribly wrong. Plans with this many unknowns never went this well.

Walls rose around them, blocking off any path except for below. Imiha sat before the hole, amber markings lighting the otherwise dark tunnel.

"Once I start, I won't be able to defend. Directing ranked stone is too difficult for me to be splitting my focus." Imiha's eyes dropped to the stub that was Remus's limb and let out an annoyed grunt. "Come here."

Imiha really should have healed Remus earlier, but at least she was doing so now. Tetsu didn't know what the history was between the two, at least deeper than the surface, so she didn't think it was her place to judge. It was good that Imiha was finally putting aside her reservations.

Remus smiled down at the younger dohrni. "Thanks, Your Highness."

Tetsu had been a part of his team for years now, and she still couldn't tell if Remus was joking at times. Imiha just ignored the possible sarcasm and got to work.

The ranked stone ever so slowly crept forward. Tetsu knew Imiha was an incredibly talented mage, and yet this was still as much as she could do with the near indestructible stone. It raised questions of how the mermineae knew it could be done. There was an immense difference between destruction and creation.

Remus, with his newly regained limb, took to the tunnel below to fight the mermineae clambering to rise. Tetsu would join him, but the walls erected by Imiha wouldn't last.

As expected, the walls crumbled, decaying to dust from the strange visual power of the Forvaal. The clergy had done their job of causing a distraction far better than she'd expected, but it looked like things were about to get difficult.

Tetsu prepared her weapons, waiting for the moment the first of them stepped through the new opening. She pounced as soon as the opportunity presented, flying past the first with a swipe at its jugular. It was imperative to keep moving. She couldn't stop to confirm her kill, lest her advantage be wasted.

There was no merminea behind the one passing through the opening, so her momentum took her to the rock face of the wide tunnel. With power in her legs gained from many years of training and enhanced by plentiful hunts, she sprung to the rearmost of the ten mermineae.

The wide tunnel was almost the perfect battlefield for her favorite type of fighting. That style also happened to be the cause of that infernal nickname bestowed upon her.

She would never tell them she secretly enjoyed the name.

The target she flew toward was one of the oldest Forvaal. Like Saad and Taanoraa, their eyes were entirely gray. They were blind, but that seemed to matter little to them. The old Forvaal must have some other sense, as they twisted out of the path of her blade. Her strike connected, but not deep enough to be fatal.

The Forvaal held its bleeding neck and shouted a command to the others around. In the brief moment Tetsu slammed into the wall, she inspected each of her opponents. There were only three Forvaal amongst them besides the old one. She could only hope to succeed if she took them out first. The foggy-eyed's reactions were too fast to waste time on.

Tetsu launched forward again, her blade swiping the eyes of one and her boot cracking the jaw of another Forvaal before they slammed into the tunnel wall. Before her feet touched ground and she could pick up speed again, Tetsu felt a blaze of agony across her back. It was as though tiny, hot hooks pulled at every muscle and nerve she had.

In a motion trained by countless hours of effort, she threw the sword at the last Forvaal. Relying only on her memory to aim.

She stumbled to her hands and knees, blood pouring down her arms as she tried to bite down the pain. This was no time to be tending to her injuries. Tetsu kicked out beneath her. Her thrown falchion rested a few meters off the third Forvaal, who clutched at their bleeding arm.

She needed that weapon back. More importantly, she had to kill that Forvaal before it could focus its eyes on her once more.

Tetsu sprung forward, eyes only for the Forvaal. Her tunnel vision was a mistake. The other mermineae, now realizing they couldn't keep up with her explosive movement, moved to intercept.

Claws dug into her side, the disturbance redirected her trajectory. Tetsu, no longer in a position to swing her blade, turned to body slam into the Forvaal.

Before the Forvaal could lower its eyes to her, Tetsu thrust her blade through its jaw and out its snout, holding its head up while she punched its exposed neck. She wailed on the mermineae until, with a snap, its neck twisted unnaturally.

Through the agony of her back and side, she pushed off the dead Forvaal. Not quick enough. A pair of mermineae plowed through her. Tetsu let out a gasp as her back ground along the earth. It was excruciating. Like hundreds of molten razorblades slicing through her skin.

She swung her short sword, but a merminea blocked her arm. Her blade failed to pull blood, but the strength of her blow stunned the creature. Its partner lunged forward, biting into the flesh of her arm. She refused to let her weapon go, but she could not pull her arm free.

Tetsu wasn't about to lose to these fucking creatures again.

She punched the throat of the merminea biting her arm. She winced in pain as its teeth sunk deeper, but so did her enemy. The moment the merminea's eyes shut, she dropped the blade from her pinned hand to the other and thrust it into the side of its head.

She couldn't fight anymore. There were still too many for her to take on and there wasn't a chance that elderly Forvaal would be weak. She could only praise her luck that it didn't burn her with his eyes. Whether that was by choice or because it couldn't, she didn't know.

It was stupid to push her advantage as hard as she had. She would have had a better chance if she kept the defensive advantage.

The first merminea sitting on top of her regained its senses and grabbed her beneath the chin, claws sinking into the skin of her cheek and neck. She tried to swing her arm, but it caught her wrist, stopping the blade only centimeters from the side of its head.

Tetsu pushed with all her might to kill this creature. She only had moments to deal with it before the others of its kind would be all over her. Her muscles bulged under the pressure, slowly edging the sharp tip closer.

The claws dug deeper into Tetsu's face and the merminea quivered as the blade sliced through the fur of its neck. Just a little further.

Suddenly, the resistance to her blade arm died and her falchion slid through her opponent's head with ease. She rolled out of the way, expecting the remaining mermineae to dive upon her, but it didn't come.

She looked up to see Jav spinning a thousand rotations around the first two mermineae, deepening wounds to their throats and tendons with each pass. Slowly rising to her feet, it became apparent that Jav wasn't the only one to come to her aid. Remus fought against the elderly Forvaal.

The dohrni danced around his target, only attacking when the opportunity presented itself, but mostly stayed out of retaliation range. His quick, strike and escape fighting style was one intended for those of far greater enhancement. Particularly those who didn't have the skill or talent to use that strength to its fullest capabilities. Warriors that did. . . well, in that case, it wouldn't be a fight.

Enhancement level was the great equalizer, but if they didn't have the skills to use those immense energy reserves, then they were nothing more than a tough punching bag to those who had spent years training.

Of course, that would still be made difficult due to the mermineae around them. Tetsu forced herself to her feet, ready to jump into the brawl despite the immense pain assaulting her body.

Before she could even reach her first target, it was taken from her. A pillar of earth crushed each merminea. Even the elderly Forvaal.

Imiha was done.

"I've closed it just enough for Grímr to pass through," Imiha said. "I've amassed a ball of enhanced earth we can drop after us and I'll be able to seal the tunnel in moments."

The dohrni walked up to Tetsu and rested a tentacle on her upper back. She winced, but attempted to ignore the pain as green markings glowed over Imiha's body.

"Now, how about we go get the other two before Spenne tires of waiting?"

CHAPTER ELEVEN

Thunderstorm

The clergy have something terrifyingly strong rushing around outside our walled area. Every few seconds, a plume of dust rises through the air. Whatever is causing all that damage, they are quick. One moment, a cloud of dust forms in front of us, the next, behind us.

The majority of mermineae seem completely unfazed by our presence. They either rush toward whatever it is they are fighting, or flee. Most flee.

I'm surprised the clergy is even holding up their end of the deal. It's almost suspicious how effective their distraction has been. Between Spenne and me, none of the few mermineae that still try to rush toward us survive. Grímr hasn't even needed to lift a talon.

Despite how effective it is at spreading my flames, Spenne has stopped casting bolts of lightning out into the crowds beyond. The wraps around his hands now tightened and hiding away the volatile electricity within.

Instead, he rushes around, fast as lightning himself. With his wide jaw, he bites into the poor victims that clamber into my inferno. Branch-like patterns glow beneath their skin before inviting me in. My flames run through the forking burns in their bodies and incinerate the mermineae from the inside out.

I would have liked to practice my spear against them, but Spenne doesn't give me the opportunity. He throws himself after each like a ravenous beast.

Outside our stone circle, the fire has spread rather far, but it won't be moving much further. The thinning crowds of mermineae make it nearly impossible for my flames to spread from fur to fur without direct control. The small nudges I've given the fire have been enough to spread a good few hundred meters, which is incredible considering the only sources of fuel are corpses half-submerged in melted snow.

Dark clouds of smoke hover above, spreading far over the surrounding slope. I can't help but look up at it mournfully. So many wasted resources. Uncle Rivin would be disappointed. Whatever reason the áinfean has for the smoke, it better be good.

A loud crash has me turning to the wall behind us, only to watch as it crumbles to rubble. Another massive plume explodes out of the new crater formed just outside our ring. It looks like whatever the clergy brought with them accidentally destroyed our defenses. Well, hopefully it's that, and not them attacking us.

I prepare myself anyway. Something that can cause that much damage so quickly would be at least at Imiha's level.

Through the obscured air, a merminea climbs out of the crater. Well, it has the shape of a merminea, but it is impossible to see it directly. A cloak of ash and dust flows off its body. It jerks its neck to something unseen; the motion accompanied by a wave of dust blowing away from its head.

On both forelegs and hind legs, it tenses before disappearing from sight. Another plume rises a few hundred meters away, likely the creature landing.

Was that really a merminea? Its movements are far too wild and feral to consider it as one despite the similar shape. If they had this creature hidden, then why are we even here? Couldn't it just kill any that tried to pass the Alps as Hund did with the army invading his land?

"Solvei, Grímr. It's time to go." Remus climbs out of the crevice.

They're done already? Well, I'm not about to complain. I climb up Grímr's back, ready to take to the air again and leave this place.

Spenne lets out a rumbling chuckle and unwinds the wraps around his arms. "About time!"

My team climbs out from the ground, but doesn't move away. Within my flames, I feel Remus has regrown his limb. Did Imiha finally forgive him?

Well, if we're all done, then there's no reason to stay around.

Grímr tilts his head back at me in a way I've learned to associate with him being perplexed. I'm unsure what the look is for, but he finally starts moving.

Only . . . toward the crevice.

I finally realize why my team hasn't moved away from the hole; they plan to go back through those tunnels.

No. There's no way. I jump off Grímr and backpedal. "No. I'm not going back down there."

I may not feel that terror of being trapped anymore, but I will still do everything I can to keep my freedom. Sealing myself beneath stone again is just asking for problems. Not only will my knot prevent me from going through with it, but I'll have to tell them of my mental rope. About how likely I'll be to stab them in the back.

I can't.

"I'm staying here."

Frustration crosses Imiha's face, but the others show resignation and concern, like they expected this, but hoped otherwise. Well, they shouldn't have expected any different. I've made my plan to stay on this side of the Alps abundantly clear. If they expected I'd want to go back through the tunnels once we were above them, they are sorely mistaken.

So what now? Is this where they betray my trust for a second time and drag me through?

Grímr walks up to my side and turns back to the others. "I have no reason to go home anytime soon. I'll stay by her side. You all have a job to do. Make sure the nations are prepared. There are surely still enough mermineae down in those tunnels to threaten our homes." Grímr brushes my side with the edge of his wing. "We'll find another way around, eventually."

"I'll stay too." Bunny steps forward.

"No, you won't." Imiha immediately rebukes her. "Your influence in Vanguard is far too important to let you stay here."

Bunny stops her advance toward me, obviously conflicted.

"Are you lot leaving or not?" Spenne asks. "I'm getting agitated."

His white wraps now dangle from his elbows, exposing the intense energy of his arms to the world. Wild electric arcs spark out through my flames, many zapping along the ground. Static empowers the air. Like his sparks moved through my flames with ease, I find my flames energized by the intensity in the air. What is he doing?

While my attention is elsewhere, Bunny slams into me, pulling me into a hug. I panic, thinking she's trying to drag me down with her again. As soon as I flinch, she lets go.

"Please come back safe." With that, she backs up to the rest of the team.

"We'll meet again," Remus says with a rueful smile.

Jav waves from Remus's head as they descend back into the depths of the Alps. I am . . . sad to see them go. It is too bad the only way back is through the Alps. Hopefully, there's another way . . . but if there is, the mermineae should have already found it.

"Finally!" Spenne raises his exposed arms above his head. Rapid sparks spread out from him, striking at anything they can find: burning corpses, stone, Grímr.

Grímr doesn't seem to mind, though.

Spenne shouts and I feel the thunder rolling through my chest. An explosion of light blinds me and a body shaking crack almost deafens me. I feel it before I see it. My flames rocket up into the air, following a thicker lightning arc than I've ever thought possible. Even as my eyes readjust and confirm what I feel, I struggle to believe it.

Two thick, continuous, forking beams of lightning strike the dark smoke clouds above with such ferocity I can scarcely believe it. Thunderous laughter rolls off the áinfean with each pulse of energy he thrusts into the sky.

The electricity seems to find a home amongst the sky overcast with smoke. Lightning spreads further, zapping the air outside the cloud of ash and smoke.

I can't turn my eyes away from the sight. Each second Spenne pumps more energy above, the darker the world seems to become. Despite the blinding arc of electricity right before me, the blue sky around the smoke darkens into a black thunderstorm. I don't know where these clouds are coming from, but before long there is no clear sky to be seen.

The áinfean's beams abruptly cut off, forcing me to squint to readjust my sight now that everything is so dark. The daylight has gone, but the sky is still lit by uncountable lightning strikes arcing through the storm above.

Spenne casually rewinds the wraps over his hands. I still can't take my eyes from the sky above. I can feel the energy thrumming through the air. My flames hijacking the lightning each time an arc crosses the sky.

I'm confused by his purpose. It's incredible, but what does creating this immense lightning storm help?

The áinfean turns to us with arms raised, gesturing to the sky he created. "I hope you two are ready." He grins as his voice thrums through me.

I can't help but feel we should have long left already.

The sky suddenly quietens. Lightning stops and thunder abates.

Spenne clenches his fist as if grasping the air and tugs downward. At his command, the world erupts in chaos and noise.

The sky ignites with a thousand bolts striking the earth at once. Some lightning strikes combine into major arcs of electricity, bridging the sky to the ground. These arcs tear through the slope, frying thousands in seconds.

The sound is constant. Loud booming overwhelms everything else.

I can intimately feel each strike around me. I can't control the electricity, but it wouldn't be hard to just reach out and ignite everything around it. Even a league away, far further than I've ever been able to feel, the lightning almost begs me to use its power.

A bolt crashes into Grímr, but he just stands there, unfazed. The energy simply passes around his metal plumage before flowing into the ground. The same cannot be said for any other bird still in the skies or the mermineae running along the earth. Vermilions, enantiorns and all other avian hunters fry in midair faster than even the ground creatures are obliterated.

Grímr nudges me, snapping me from my daze. "We should leave."

I nod to him wordlessly and climb onto his back. I circle my flames around us, preparing to give him a boost once he takes off.

We barely gain any air when an explosion of dust slams us into a wall of earth. I tumble off Grímr's back and a cloud of particles obscures my vision. It doesn't burn. I try to clear the dust and ash from the air, but I can't consume any of it.

Wait, no. That's wrong. The dust is burning, but I can't feel anything from it. It's like the particles have no energy at all, which can't be right. I've never felt something without energy. I didn't think it was possible.

The dust quickly disperses, my flames burning it away despite the contrary sensation. A vast swathe of earth is now gone and at the center, a massive concentration of dust keeps my flames at bay. Once the cloud clears enough for me to see, the frenzied mermineae becomes visible.

The energy deficient particles pour off the creature's body faster than my fire can burn through. I can't see the being through the mass billowing off it.

The creature shrieks. A guttural howl like nothing a living creature should produce. With all four legs tensed against the ground, it leaps at Spenne.

The áinfean lets out a thunderous laugh. "Yes! Come!"

Spenne twists a moment before the mermineae reaches him, his thick, finned tail slamming the creature to the ground. Much of the earth disperses in dust as the mermineae descends beneath the surface. The áinfean doesn't leave it at that. Hundreds of arcs of lightning tear into the crater before joining into one colossal beam unleashing untold power from the skies.

When the lightning stops, I have only an instant to see what this mermineae looks like before the dust covers it again, and what I see is horrifying. Hollow sockets are all that remain of any eyes it might have had, but that isn't even bad compared to the rest of its body. There isn't a touch of skin. Muscle, bone, and organs are all exposed, and each are in a decrepit state. Almost like they are falling apart.

The dust is its very body decaying at an accelerated rate.

How can it even move like that? There's no way it isn't excruciating.

Spenne cares little for my horrified concerns. His grin grows wider and he drops his arms into a stance that makes him look like he's ready to charge. "You survived that? Great! I was starting to think coming here was a waste of time."

"Murderer!" The mermineae's voice comes out in a raspy struggle.

Sparks rush out of Spenne's tail as he rests it back along the ground. The occurrence must surprise him as he lifts it to show a large section where the white wraps have decayed.

"Well, that's annoying," he says. "But no matter."

He lowers his tail, but doesn't let it drag along the ground as he usually would. It hangs suspended behind him.

The mermineae doesn't wait any longer, lunging at the áinfean. Spenne grabs the creature by the arms near the shoulder, stopping its offense dead in its tracks. The wraps around his hands immediately decay, exposing the electric arcs of his body to the open air.

He flings the mermineae away to give himself space and unwinds the white bindings from his arms and head. The mermineae charges once more, a blind attack on his enemy. Spenne just waits for it to get close and then strikes out. He snaps his maw over the head of the mermineae, biting it clear off. Before it falls over, Spenne swings an open palm into its chest. A lightning bolt strikes from the storm above at the same instant, and he sends the mermineae flying. It crashes through Imiha's wall of stone and obliterates it.

It all happens so quick that I forget we are trying to get out. Grímr digs the tips of his wings into the wall and uses them like fingers to pull himself up. I blast a burst of solid flames beneath me and join him on top of the wall. A little trick I'm happy to have learned.

I'm just about to help Grímr take off again when two rather concerning events happen. The dust mermineae climbs out of the wreckage, headless, but still moving. While that is bad in itself, the two new mermineae standing on the wall opposite me are far more worrying. Both exude as much dust and ash as their friend below.

CHAPTER TWELVE

Viisin

The headless mermineae walks out from the remains of the wall. A gash through the land shows exactly where Spenne sent him flying. As I watch, the dusty silhouette of its head regrows. It starts as a nub and slowly regenerates into the pointed snout shape unique to the mermineae.

I thought flesh creatures had brains in their head which they couldn't live without. Or was that just a few races? Each of Grímr's possessed bodies has been like that, but maybe the mermineae are different.

It's hard to tell if it's hurt because of the shroud, but it walks without issue despite taking a direct hit from Spenne's powerful lightning. Unlike what I expect, it doesn't rush in for the attack immediately. Instead, the creature's new head points up toward the duo of new arrivals.

"This is what you want?" it gasps out with its gravelly voice. "You are so opposed to our people finding a better home that you would rather an outsider slaughter the lot?" The mermineae spits, but the action does nothing but blow out a plume of dust. "You refuse to bear the weight of their deaths yourselves."

One of the two standing on the wall speaks up, his voice a similar hoarse croak. "Former Viisin Noriis, we did not bring the outsiders here to murder our brethren." It turns toward Spenne, who is being surprisingly patient as they talk. I can't tell if the creature is angry or not, because dust shrouds its face, but I'd say it's pretty likely.

"We only intended your death," it says, turning back to the first dust mermineae.

"Former Viisin?" The creature below chuckles, a harrowing and painful sounding laugh. "I am Viisin until the day Kalma takes back her *gift*." It says the word as if chewing on something foul.

Is that why their bodies are like this? Some gift from Kalma? If it causes your body to be in a constant state of decay, how could it be anything but a curse?

"And if you didn't bring them for the slaughter of our kind, then why?"

The two . . . Viisin? They don't reply. Rather, they attack immediately. Noriis is already looking down at the crevice. It's too late to blind the Viisin from our purpose. A massive explosion of dust obscures the three as the duo sends the lone creature sprawling.

Spenne looks around confused, as if he never expected to be ignored while his rain of lightning continued in the background. A frown crosses his face and he looks after the trio of Viisin as if he's been slighted.

We've already held around long enough. I nudge Grímr to take off again just as a heavy crack of thunder blows through me. Spenne is gone. Looks like he's chasing after the Viisin.

In no time, we are speeding through the skies. We face no opposition. No birds of prey fly around, nor are there any Forvaal waiting to burn us from below. The vast thunderstorm has left the land a horrorscape.

The sky is dark, only illuminated by the constant flashes. Below, all that remains are corpses. Some are charred, some lay in pieces, some still burn from the fire. There is not much snow remaining. Instead, the ground is a muddy quagmire of dirt, water, and blood.

I grip Grímr's feathers tighter. Beyond the slaughter beneath us are numerous gouges through the land, likely a consequence of the fight between Viisin.

I don't care for these beings. They've caused nothing but pain, worry, and stress for us. I don't like the mermineae, but this is still a hard sight to take in. Thousands of bodies lay dead, and we are leaving without returning their energy to the cycle.

I'm sure they'll be fine. They aren't buried after all. Once the storm clears, the avian hunters will have a feast for a good while.

Sudden, intense energy rushes through my body, down into Grímr. It is both incredible and painful. Too much heat even for me crashes through my body for an instant before it's gone. The flash of light and rumbling thunder tell me I was just hit by lightning.

It's different, feeling it directly rather than through my inner flame. I feel myself trying to reach for that intensity and take it for myself. I yearn for that heat, but I know I'm far from that capability myself. Like magma when I was a child, any more than an instant of that heat would be excruciating.

The lightning passed through Grímr as well, but he seems to have barely felt it. Or maybe he's just putting on an act. I know he pushes his bodies further than they should naturally go. I hope he doesn't hide his problems from me. It is only the two of us now.

It's not likely Spenne will follow along with us. Even if he wants to, I don't know if I'd want that. The áinfean is strong, immensely so. But if we meet anyone that might not have the same resistance to his electricity, he's already proven the concerns of my teammates.

Maybe that's being cruel. He did wait until the others were gone, as was asked of him, after all. There might be a way to work with him by giving him battles with no allies around.

Well, it's not like we need to worry about that anymore. The path is closed and my team is on their way to kick-start the nations' defense. Assuming they aren't already aware of the threat. All Grímr and I need to do now, is find another way back.

The only options I can think of are to follow the Alps to the south and eventually out west, near where the wasteland should be. The other option is to follow the trail of mountains north. I don't doubt it'll be a long travel, but we can fly; it'll be far quicker than it otherwise might have been.

The constant zapping in the thunderclouds above and lightning strikes halt. I turn my head back curiously. Is Spenne finished? Did he kill the trio or did they kill him?

A massive dust plume rises from right above where the tunnel should be. A pit of dread rises in my chest at the sight. Ranked stone can resist the Viisin's decay, right? It was mentioned a Forvaal's sight wouldn't be able to reopen it, but these Viisin are on a completely different level. Will it still hold them off?

Without warning, the storm unleashes a single, incomparable lightning arc down into the cloud of dust. A gust of air slams into us along with a deafening boom of thunder, sending us hurtling away. The beam continues to burn down on the earth for nearly ten seconds before it cuts off.

The air feels empty. The static that has accompanied us for a while now is simply gone.

There are no more dust clouds, nor are there more arcs of lightning. I hope that means the Viisin are dead. As concerning as Spenne is, I'd much rather have him around than the mermineae that just saw the death of many of their people at the hands of an 'outsider.'

I don't want to think about the scenario where the fighting hasn't concluded and it's simply fallen into the cavern below the surface. If they've reopened the tunnel in their brawl, my team will soon have more to worry about than the mermineae already down there.

If that's the case, Grímr and I will have to figure something out before we can even consider wandering off on a blind search.

I don't know what to do.

We've come back to the burrow we used as a meeting point with the mermineae, but there is no sign of the clergy members. Even after waiting a full night, no one shows up.

I hoped to find them again to learn if the tunnel has reopened, but it doesn't look like they're coming. Are they dead? Or are they simply wiping their hands of us?

Not everyone on the slope died. As we flew further away from the center of chaos, we passed by many mermineae fleeing down the Alps. It would have been great if we could just swoop down and question one of them, but there was no chance any of those running away would know.

If the Viisin broke through the tunnel, I hope the others made it far enough away before then.

I . . . wish we could have stayed together longer. It is obviously because of my resistance that we have been forced to split. I selfishly hoped they would stay with me despite the current concerns. It is unreasonable of me, I know, but I didn't want them to leave me.

Grímr has stayed with me, and I'm grateful, but it also makes me feel guilty. He won't be able to see his home for a long time because of me. How can I make it up to him?

"Solvei, we can't wait around here any longer," Grímr says.

"Then where do we go?" I ask. "How could we stop the rest of the mermineae from passing into the Alps?"

"I don't know." Grímr shakes his heavy head. "But we shouldn't stay here. If any of those Viisin follow us . . . well, I don't like our chances."

My flames churn in my chest. If they act logically, then there's no reason for them to come for us. We weren't the ones to kill all those mermineae. We aren't a threat to them. But I can't help but feel they won't see it the same way.

A lot of this whole situation doesn't make sense to me. What was the purpose of sending us in at the same time as the attack by the Viisin? I'm assuming I understand this right; the Viisin duo that I didn't hear the names of are part of the clergy, while the other, Noriis, is with the traitors.

For the closure of the tunnel to succeed, Noriis would have to be dead. So why didn't they send in the other two to kill the Viisin first? Maybe they were so assured of themselves that they could kill Noriis before they could realize the tunnel was being sealed, but that is incredibly foolish.

The alternative is that they didn't care about whether the path was closed or not, they just sent us in as a distraction or maybe in an effort to have us killed. But even that seems strange, the Viisin have enough strength that our presence—before Spenne—would mean nothing to them. Why not just kill us before any of this happened?

The clergy has shown they have the strength, so why don't they simply take control of the entrance themselves?

No matter which way I twist their actions and motivations, there always seems to be a piece missing. I don't know what to do now, but Grímr is right; we shouldn't stay any longer.

"All right, let's go." I climb to his back, and he spreads his long metal wings. "I want to know if the path is still open, but we can't go back. Let's go have a look at the mass migration of mermineae. They'll be the first to learn if the tunnel is permanently closed."

I'd hoped to put all this behind me. Once we did our part to stop the mermineae invasion on my friends' home, I'd wanted to just enjoy the experience of searching new lands. But my friends are still in danger. I can't relax until I'm certain the threat is gone.

If I was strong enough, I would cross the Alps and stop the mermineae myself. But I'm not. I've gained a lot recently, but taking on an army would be too much. I'm still nowhere close to the level of Hund.

Even if I was strong enough, I couldn't cross the Alps anyway. My mind won't let me. My decisions, limited by nothing other than my nous.

An intense, stabbing pain assaults me. I clutch my hands over my eyes and nearly tumble right off Grímr's back. Knives twist through my mind for an agonizingly long few seconds. When it finally abates, my mind is blank and I do nothing but stare into the sky.

"Are you okay?" Grímr's concerned voice brings me back to focus.

I shake my head. "Yeah, I am now."

"What was that?"

"I don't know."

This isn't the first time experiencing this pain. It's hit a few times, but never this bad. Hopefully, it's nothing to worry about. We already have too much to focus on.

First, let's find out if the mermineae are still moving to the Alps, then I can worry about lesser issues.

CHAPTER THIRTEEN

Pivot

It's troubling, but there was never any lie about the threat of mass migration. The first mermineae are far closer to reaching the tunnel than we were told; only a day's travel at most. The only respite was the separation between their numbers.

Grímr flies low, keeping the ground just within the range of my thermal sense. The mermineae hold an almost constant fifty-meter separation from one another as they travel. At first, I thought this was a good thing; if they aren't densely packed, then there can't be too many of them, right?

That couldn't be any further from the truth.

We travel above for an hour, but they just never seem to end. By the time we reach the other end of their numbers, we must have traveled almost ten leagues. How many hundreds of thousands are there?

I was worried Forvaal amongst them would burn us out of the sky, but other than freezing at our presence, they never reacted to us. We dove and snatched three mermineae during our flight, but not once did their surrounding kin attempt to help them.

It is fortunate for us, but it's still shocking to see the lack of effort they put into saving their brethren. How is a race like this, that cares so little for one another, able to unite enough to travel such a long distance together?

None we interrogated knew anything about the tunnel being sealed. Either the information didn't travel fast enough, or they have been given no reason to stop moving. It would be nice if it has remained sealed. I'm not about to be complacent, though. Until we get some form of confirmation that they have lost their route through the mountains, I'm going to assume the path is open.

But . . . what do we do?

I doubt flying along and burning any mermineae I see will be an effective use of my time. I'm more likely to bring those Viisin down on me than I am to put a dent in their advance.

Should we go looking for the other Beith mercenaries that are supposed to be wandering around the Euroclydon's Hunting Grounds? But we have no idea where to start. Even when we had the directions from the clergy, it had still been tremendously time consuming to find them. One group we still weren't able to find.

Even if we had more strength at our side, we would need to hold the tunnel so that it couldn't be reopened. I doubt Spenne or any of the other Beiths we find would sit still on guard duty for long. There's a reason they're not waiting around back in the pact nations.

I cast my gaze over the plains, hoping for some idea to hit me. My eyes fall on the Titan, resting in the heights of the Alps. I shake my head. Reasonable ideas, not suicidal ones.

We fly without purpose for a few more minutes before I give in and voice my idea.

"What if we lead the Titan to the tunnel?"

Grímr jerks, hard. His wings tilt upward and catch enough drag that I'm sent rolling over his head. A swift jet of flame halts my momentum and I pull myself back on top of Grímr. It's surprising how quick I can stop myself when I'm incorporeal.

He readjusts his flight before he can fall into a downward spiral. "Are you mad? We were lucky the creatures down in that cavern didn't crush us the last time I went along with your plan."

"It worked then, didn't it?" I ask. I don't mean to sound arrogant, but I really don't have a better plan right now.

"The Titans are on a level far beyond anything comparable. An attempt to manipulate one would be insanity."

I know that. I know how devastatingly dangerous the Titans can be. But I'm just trying to throw ideas out there. Everything else we've come up with is simply a variation of 'find more Beith' or 'massacre the mermineae.' Neither of which is all that helpful now that we know the existence of the Viisin.

Spenne, apparently one of the strongest Beiths, couldn't kill one, despite the unbelievable power he'd thrown into his attack. How many more of these are hiding amongst the mermineae? The only relieving aspect of the Viisin is that they can't hide like the rest of the mermineae.

I assume.

Eldest Ember, I hope they can't pretend to be normal mermineae.

"Then what can we do?" I snap. "Would you rather we go find their god and say her believers are trying to run?"

That's a far worse idea than trying to bait the Titan. I'd much rather deal with something that pays me the same attention one would a bug than the being venerated out of fear.

I huff in annoyance, lay back, and stare up at the sky. The line between the moon and horizon hasn't changed. Much to my relief, it seems my first assumption that the line was a tear created by some Titan was wrong. Well, I don't know it isn't for sure, but it hasn't opened wider in the time I've been in these plains.

The line distracts me every time I look at the moon. I've never really noticed, but the orb approaches far too close to the Eternal Inferno to be normal. I swear it used to be twice the distance at its closest. Is the moon getting closer? What happens when it hits the Eternal Inferno? Will Eldest Ember be okay?

If she joins the Eternal Inferno, then who will look over the lands? Who will burn away the darkness? If that were to happen, I can't imagine what horrific future awaits.

It's taken something like three or four whole years to get this close. If we have the same time until they collide, then that is ages. I'm sure Eldest Ember will save herself in time.

I snap my head away from the moon. Enough with thoughts of terrifying possible futures.

Huh. What else besides Kalma are the mermineae scared of? Revontulet and centzon.

"Grímr!" I jump to my feet, nearly tumbling off his back again. I really should get back around to practicing my balance. "Go back to the Dead Forest."

"Why?" he tilts his head back at me.

"The centzon! The mermineae are absolutely terrified of them. Almost as much as they are of Kalma. If we can talk to them, it's possible we could have them fight for the tunnel."

"And let another race learn to reach our side of the Alps? A race that scares the one we already have a problem with?"

I drop again. I hadn't considered that. Of course, we can't just tell them there is a way across the mountains. How do we know they won't do the same as the mermineae and add another problem for the people back home to deal with?

Do we even have a reason to believe they'll want to attack the mermineae? They might even consider them leaving the plains a good thing.

No, we still know nothing about them. The only thing we know is they enjoy skinning mermineae alive, but who knows if that's actually true. What we need now is information. With little other option, finding where they live and learning anything we can about them might be our best bet.

"I still think we should go," I say. "We don't have to tell them about the tunnel, but gauging their thoughts might give us something to work with."

Grímr hums, unconvinced.

"It's this or the Titan idea." If he's going to be this resistant, I just have to force him to agree.

He tilts his head back at me, giving me a dirty glare, but he changes direction regardless.

I hate forcing him like this, but we'll get nowhere otherwise. Grímr lets indecision cloud his judgment too often. I noticed it back in the caverns, and it's showing itself now. When there are no good options, he becomes overly passive, like waiting around will solve everything.

Actually, that's unreasonably harsh of me. He wasn't indecisive when it came to staying by my side. He hardly took a moment before he gave up the opportunity to return home. Without Grímr's speed, it might take me years to find a way back across the Alps.

I still need to test whether the avian hunters will attack me if I make my bird form look bigger.

It'll be at least a week before we reach the Dead Forest. By the time we return, the entire swarm of mermineae will have entered the tunnels. It's frustrating, but we have no way to prevent that. We can only try to limit any more passing afterward. If the centzon turn out to be trustworthy, it might even be worth sending them down. If they wipe each other out, all the better.

For now, I have a lot of time on my hands. I need to get back to improving my control. My physical flames have been an incredible asset so far. They aren't all too strong. Any decent application of strength will break through them, but the utility they provide is impressive.

I can throw myself around with jets, carry things, and make an adequate wall against the decay eyes of the Forvaal. More physical creations like the cinder chains were all right for tripping mermineae up, but they break far too easily for my liking.

I'd like to improve my control, as I'm sure it'll increase the solidity of my flame, but like my efforts to compress my fire, I've hit a wall. Nothing I seem to do or practice seems to allow any progress. There's something I'm missing and until I find out what that is, I'll be stuck.

So, instead of wasting my time, I turn my attention to the odd effects I've noticed recently. Primarily, how my flames still help Grímr gain air quicker even without bound mass.

I thought by pelting the underside of his wings with my solid flames, it would be like throwing a thousand tiny rocks at him. Not enough to hurt, but enough to push him upward. But there was still some effect pushing him upward after they'd lost their tangibility.

I take a loose strip of cloth from my pocket. Remnants of the gloves my outfit used to connect with. During our travel, Jav was nice enough to repair much of the torso, but the full sleeves and hood were irreparable.

Immediately, the cloth tries to fly off in the intense wind. I twist in my seat, trying to block the breeze with my body, but that makes very little difference.

I huff in annoyance and cast a spherical shell of physical fire around me. It's not totally effective, but it blocks enough of the wind that my little strip of cloth doesn't immediately fly off when I open my palm.

Despite my less than optimal testing conditions, I'm ready to see if I can replicate that unexplained lift effect.

First, I apply a tiny stream of physical flame to the underside of the cloth. As usual, I prevent the flame from eating at the threads of the cloth. It takes barely a thought these days to prevent things I don't want from burning.

The cloth flutters in my grip, trying to fly off. Not at all surprising. It's the same thing as pushing it with my finger, but testing it doesn't hurt. I let the fabric settle before the next trial.

Stripping my inner flame to its normal state, I push it against the remains of my glove. At first, it blows up, away from the flame, but after the initial rush upward, it falls limp. Strangely, completely entrapped in my flame, it droops faster than in normal air.

What is going on? I'm sure I replicated exactly what I did. Using both types of fire, I try again, but get the same result. I groan in frustration as I try to remember exactly what conditions pushed Grímr higher.

"You all right back there?" the very object of my confusion asks.

I pocket the cloth, and twist to Grímr's head, dispersing the shell as I do.

"Grímr, do you mind if I wrap you in fire?" I might as well make sure the conditions are as close as possible.

". . . Sure?" he says, but the hesitance and confusion are clear.

I don't hesitate, sending out a massive ball of fire beneath us. My inner flame rockets upward, consuming all of Grímr's impressive wingspan in a blazing pillar. There is some lift at the start, but it doesn't give us much height.

"Uh . . . why are you doing this?" Grímr asks.

Was it just luck the first time it happened? I'm about to pull back on the flames when I notice Grímr isn't flying straight anymore. He's gradually angling downward despite his wings remaining horizontal.

Grímr notices after I do and, in a panic, beats his massive wings. That seems to let him balance out his flight, making space from my flame at the same time, but as soon as the fire engulfs his wings once more, he's falling again. He is forced to flap his wings to stop from losing altitude.

Grímr gives me an annoyed glance, and I quickly extinguish the pillar. This isn't the same effect as I witnessed back during our escape, but it is definitely interesting. Could I drop birds out of the sky by covering their wings? It'll at least make their flight difficult.

Now that I think about it, I wasn't consuming the air when I gave Grímr a boost. Could that make a difference?

I cover myself once more and hold the cloth out in front of me. This time, I prevent my inner flame from eating the air as it blows over the fabric. It actually flutters this time.

I check the shell in case there is a gust from outside causing it, but even a third try shows I don't need to create the taxing physical flames to give Grímr a boost anymore.

Experimenting further, I find my flames don't even need to touch the cloth to move it. A small application of heat below forces the air up and the cloth flutters almost as much as it does in the midst of my fire.

It seems almost contradictory that my flames seem to be more effective when they aren't consuming the air.

What could I do with this?

"Hey, Grímr, can I cover you in fire again?"

I receive a groan in response, but that isn't a no.

CHAPTER FOURTEEN

Minefield

It took a while of flying, but finally we're getting close. I'm sure of it.

Once we reached the Dead Forest again, Grímr and I headed to the north. We had no idea exactly where they might be other than the general direction, but neither of us could think of a better idea.

We definitely had plenty of thoughts on what might go wrong, though. They might attack without so much as a greeting; maybe they'll listen to us but do nothing other than waste our time, or even trap us. We don't even know if they are actually sapient. I've only assumed they are because the way Aana described them made them seem methodically cruel rather than just savage as a normal beast would be.

I let out a breath. Unsupported thoughts like these do nothing but make me stressed. We'll find out whether we can work with them soon enough. We actually have a reason to believe they are nearby now.

The forest of stumps ended a while ago. But instead of a natural end, it was an immediate transition into an area where the earth had been flipped upside down. Exposed to open air lay a dense underground expanse of roots. The clear cut marks and missing wooden stumps screamed a logging zone.

We have seen no mermineae with a need for wood, so it is a good sign that these centzon are close by. It also shows they have intelligence, which is a relief.

The roots below the surface were interesting to see. The base of each stump intertwining to create a carpet of wood buried beneath the ground. It explains how the stumps survived despite everything else being blown away; each one has the support of the entire forest to keep it grounded.

In near no time at all, we come across a long, narrow canyon, which is a unique sight in the otherwise flat plains. Considering the timing, there's no doubt in my mind these centzon reside somewhere along this gorge.

We coast along, searching down in the slot canyon for any sign of movement. Its narrow walls block much of our sight, but I can't help the groan that escapes me when I see what is at the bottom. Water rapids rush along the chasm depths. The intense flow sends water as high as halfway up the vertical walls when it slams against rock.

I take it back. The timing means nothing. This is just a place they get the water they need, not a place for them to live.

My hope is immediately crushed as Grímr speaks up.

"Look, there's a tower ahead."

Unfortunately, he's right. About half a league ahead of us is a structure positioned on the edge of the narrow canyon. No other structures surround it.

It's a good indication if they can build, but the sign of a single building means there will be more. Considering I can't see any, I know I'm not going to like where they are.

In no time, my fears are confirmed. We fly high over the tower and beneath it, within the narrow canyon, is a vast number of structures bridging the huge earth walls.

A city suspended over water. How much worse could it be?

It's okay. There isn't anything I need to worry about. I can fly even without wings now. It may be nowhere near as efficient or controllable as using wings, but shooting out bursts of physical flame would be enough to stop me falling to my death.

It would still be better if I didn't have that thought looming over me for my entire time here. And hey, maybe there will be no need to enter the city, anyway.

Inspecting the city from this height doesn't give us much more information other than the knowledge that they are intelligent enough to build hanging structures. Even the tower anchors to the inner wall, rather than using the surface as a base.

I'd like to get lower and look over the city from closer, but considering Grímr's body, I'd rather they don't think we are a beast looking for a meal. Instead, we are going to have to approach from land. That's the only way I can think of that will give them the impression we aren't here to attack.

As soon as we land, a few hundred meters from the tower, I feel the heat of a few creatures rushing to surround us. At first, I think they are mermineae. They are invisible to sight and have a similar form. But a few things differentiate them from the creatures I've seen until now.

These beings are slow. They don't even reach half the average merminea's speed. Their shape is wrong too. While they seem similar, their bodies are definitely bulkier and taller. They don't have that distinct flowing run that only the lithe merminea bodies can produce.

"They're surrounding us," I inform Grímr.

"Don't point them out this time. It'll be easier to talk if they think they have one up on us."

I nod and take the lead. Grímr is controlling a creature that they would already be familiar with, one that usually lacks intelligence, so he follows behind with his beak to the ground. I need their attention on me, the one completely unique to them. It'll be better for us if their thoughts are curious rather than defensive.

Forgive me, Uncle Rivin. I let go of my controlled body and leave the flames of my form visible to all. I wouldn't go against my tribe's teachings if it weren't necessary. Emphasis on how different I am than anything else they've seen is the best chance we have of them not opening with hostility. Whether that's out of paranoia or curiosity, it matters little.

The bulky, hidden shapes I assume are centzon keep their distance as I approach the tower. It's a strange structure. The main support pillars are a whole piece, like they've been cut right out of the side of a cliff. Long metal hooks protrude from the front. Massive platforms of stone rest on its top and back; the side facing the canyon.

How it would ever survive the Euroclydon's wind, I do not know.

More centzon surround the two of us as we continue our walk. None yet show themselves, but that might be because they don't know we're here to talk. Time to fix that.

"Hello," I call out, forcing myself not to look directly at any of them. "We would like to talk."

None show themselves, but they creep forward. Some are as close as thirty meters away now and yet they still don't announce their presence.

I cast a concerned glance back, but Grímr just returns my gaze. So much for hoping he'd speak up too.

Upon taking my next step, the ground opens around me. Pointy teeth slam into me before I can even blink. They pierce my head and disperse it into flame without resistance.

What is this? Some giant earth monster? Is this similar to a colossal worm? I try to figure out what's going on while my head and sight reform. The familiar taste of metal runs through another point in my chest and in my hand.

I hear a grinding clank too late to react and I suddenly feel myself jerked downward, beneath the earth. Something heavy slams down from above, jolting both me and the metal teeth down. The jaw gripping me clamps down harder.

I'm trapped? My flames lash out around me, burning anything I can touch. Another bang rocks the earth and the stone above presses down with far more force than before.

This isn't the time to be panicking. I've already moved beyond that. I can work through this.

The first thing I notice is that this isn't some creature. The teeth are metal and arrayed far too disorganized to be some monster's maw.

It's lucky my body can revert to incorporeal; the crushing pressure pushing down on me right now is immense. Far more than I could ever hope to survive if not for my unique body.

First, I set to eating away the metal spears through my chest. I could simply walk out of it, but I'd like to keep my outfit intact. The metal is something I've never tasted before. It's like steel or iron, but there is something else added.

Regardless of what it is, it melts just as fast as iron.

I move my flames on to everything else around me, burning my way back to the surface. Now that I can inspect my surroundings properly, I realize that this whole thing is a contraption. The metal teeth attach to two stone frames that clamped closed around my sides. Both sections bind to a complicated mess of metal. Above me is a massive slab of stone. The centzon must have slammed it over me, to block my escape.

Once I burn through the stone, I realize it isn't the only layer. Above is another, thicker slab. How did they even move these massive pieces in such a short time? They definitely weren't carrying them.

The stone, metal, and earth all mix in a molten pool around me. The flames in my chest churn. I don't think I've been this incensed in a long while. Who do they think they are to trap me when I'm trying to greet them?

I wasn't planning to fight, even if they attacked us. Just running and trying another approach later was the plan. But I can't do that now.

I'm never going to let anyone who tries to trap me get off without the burns to remember their mistake.

The last of the stone above crumbles away and the sounds from above filter in. Grímr is screeching in rage. I don't think I've heard him like this, but the buzzing and grinding of his body amplifies his hateful squawks. Only some shouted words are coherent, focus on making himself understandable lost in his rage.

Flames erupt around me, blasting out of the molten earth pooling around me and spreading as far as I can push them. Grímr is trapped under a contraption not dissimilar from what dragged me underground. Long metal teeth pierce his wings, locking them to the ground with the weight of heavy cubic stone blocks.

As my flames spread over the four centzon standing around Grímr, I make them burn. I care nothing for asking their help any longer. All that matters is the incineration of the beings that dare attempt to trap us.

Their fur coats pulverize, stripping them of their camouflage. Beneath the color changing fur is another layer, a thin cover of fur that is far harder to burn. My flames don't let up even as they sprint away. I incinerate through this second layer and dig into their skin.

My flames spread toward the further centzon, but they back away before I can attempt to immolate them.

I direct my focus to the contraption pinning Grímr. The joints are all made with that strange metal, which makes tearing it apart simple. Once each joint is soft enough, Grímr jerks his wings free from their prisons. With leverage regained, he shoves the stone clamping down on his back off to the side.

Each of my enemies has backed up outside my range, most able to extinguish the flames coating their hides despite my intent to keep them burning. I clench my fist in irritation. I hadn't even been able to kill one of them.

With a short jet beneath me, I launch out of my molten hole and return to Grímr's side.

Now that my flames cover everything around us, I can see that the ground isn't as simple as it appears. Beneath the flat earth visibly indistinguishable from the rest of the plains is a frightening collection of contraptions. Traps. There are only a few paths forward that don't lead one through another snare.

As my flames burn into the small cracks between these heavy contraptions hidden under the surface, I feel an array of moving parts. Massive axles and gears constantly rotate meters beneath the static surface traps.

I look down at the tear right through the chest of my outfit. Jav just fixed this.

The fire twists around me, roiling in anger and wanting to scorch through everything. I know I'm unreasonably infuriated right now. But I can't help it. Everything has just been stacking on top of me in these past months. The mermineae that treat us with barely disguised contempt. The stress of constant danger. But worst of all, the rage from my betrayal that I've had no way to vent. I'd wanted to burn them alive, but I couldn't do that. I still care for them.

Now, these centzon, these beings that I have no attachment to, dare attempt to trap me? I need to keep on good terms with them, but right now, I do not care. I just want to scream at the world that it can't mess with me anymore. I won't let it.

My flames stop eating the air. Like with my small experiment, they let the air move with it. I fuel the flames with my energy and allow the air to carry them naturally.

The change isn't obvious immediately. The widespread fire slowly continues to spread toward the centzon near two hundred meters away. I halt its onward march and wait to see the changes for myself.

Gradually, the wind picks up. The grass and other small flora flutter, bending toward my flames as the wind rushes in. The centzon I can see soon feel the effect. Their fur quivers as the air blasts past them.

The effect on my fire is far greater than I'd even hoped. The rushing air carries my flames hundreds of meters into the air without so much as a push from me. With a small nudge, the flames spin around me. It's slow at first, but the wind picks up again and the firestorm grows.

Twisting and rising, the firestorm grows another few hundred meters. The spiraling twister blazes hotter over my centralized body than should be possible.

The base of the firestorm melts away rock. I make sure each and every trap I find is properly reduced to molten slag.

The centzon watch on from a distance as I obliterate their contraptions, though most tilt their heads up toward the towering flames.

Most of the centzon that lost their camouflage coats have run off into hiding, but I can still sense the rest of them. Do they think they are hidden?

I tilt the twisting pillar of flame toward the largest group, hoping to drop the firestorm on their heads. Cinders rain down on them, but most of my burning storm disperses before it tilts enough to engulf them.

For a moment, I'm disappointed, but that last only until I notice the new effect created. My flames rotate in several horizontal columns that jettison an enormous amount of flame out over the land between us. It takes almost no time until the air caught beneath this rush of fire heats to the point of ignition.

I hardly have to put in any effort at all. The airflow and fuel along the ground allow the fire to spread at an incredible pace. It takes no time for the massive fire to consume every patch of grass between me and the centzon, engulfing them in my inferno.

Never again. I'll forgive no one that tries to take my freedom.

CHAPTER FIFTEEN

Centzon

The centzon scramble to escape the flames, but there's no avoiding it this time. The blaze spreads astonishingly quickly. What distance they had is swallowed in seconds, leaving them with nowhere to escape.

Their camouflage coats burn off their backs as the centzon attempt to flee. I now realize it is a cloth made from merminea fur rather than their own hide.

I relish in the feeling of just letting go for once. Fire is meant to spread and burn. Holding back for the sake of 'civility' or 'cooperation,' what's the point of that? These beings are likely just going to work against our interests, just like the mermineae did when they should've had every reason to collaborate.

A whistle-like siren blares through the roar of my firestorm. I turn toward the tower now adding to the dissonance, and push the flames toward it. We're getting well out of my range of control now, but the firestorm is still all too willing to spread.

Grímr nudges me with his beak, but I ignore him. He wants me to pull back, but I won't. They don't deserve mercy. I was willing to be friendly at first, but these creatures need to be shown that I'm not to be messed with.

I belatedly note that the centzon are collecting around a few openings in the earth. They pile in one after the other. Do they really think that will be enough to escape? I simply direct the flame down the narrow stone tube after them.

As the last of the centzon close a heavy hatch behind them, I'm suddenly cut off from the fire down with them. I can still feel it—barely—but without a direct connection, I cannot control it.

The centzon beneath the surface are quick to extinguish my flames, but they don't get away without some serious muscle-deep burns. It'll only take a few seconds to melt through the hatch . . . is what I think until I actually attempt to melt the stone. I can't even feel it heating.

I try burning around the hatch. The earth melts with ease, but as soon as I reach the shaft, I find it made of the same heat-resistant stone. It's like the suits my Henosis captors wore. The reminder really doesn't help my mood.

I want to burn after them, but that irritating siren still blares in my ears. The firestorm is just about to reach the tower when the sound cuts out. Heavy banging takes its place. A rhythmic clanging of stone and metal colliding.

All along the edge of the canyon, running hundreds of meters to both sides of the tower, rises a massive stone wall. Sections rise without uniformity, but once they slam into place, a daunting bulwark stands as one. Intricate contraptions of metal line the stone.

If the field of traps is any indication, it will be better to destroy them before their purpose is revealed. I don't dare think that all their defenses are as ineffective as the ones I destroyed effortlessly.

I push forward, intending to melt the structures as fast as possible, but I'm too slow. From the top of the walls, flowing streams of water shower the stone. Fortunately, I spot the action fast enough to strip the inferno of my inner flame. It's not instant, but I take them away from the point of impact to get off safely.

The firestorm slams into the wet wall and blasts over it. An immense amount of steam rises, but the wall takes no damage. I consider for a moment pushing my inner flame back into the inferno and forcing it up and over the wall.

Before I can proceed with my plan, huge, meter wide vents slide open along the walls. Powerful torrents of water blow out of each new hole in the walls.

I'm immensely grateful for my hesitation to act. If I'd still had a part of myself in that, I can't imagine the pain that would follow.

Strangely enough, the firestorm isn't put out as quickly as I thought it would at the touch of water. A phantom ache stings my chest as I feel the flames at my peripheral dying off, facing opposition to its previously unhampered growth.

I want to take control, to send my flames up the tower and down the shafts, but I can't. As much as I want to punish these creatures for their attempt at snatching my freedom, the gushing water is far too great of a threat.

Why did it have to be water?

So much of the liquid is blasted out along the wall. In no time at all, the pools of water grow into a flood. I have to climb Grímr's back as, even hundreds of meters away, the water flows over the land.

They must be pumping an ocean's worth of water up into the plains. Their stone walls block it from falling back into the canyon, leaving the entirety to spread and fill the pits where their old traps once rested. Lava cools as an immense amount of steam rises.

Soon, the firestorm has no ground to stand on. Only the air burns as the wind continues to feed it, but with nothing to grasp onto, it eventually weakens and disperses.

"Solvei! Are you with me?"

"What?" I ask dumbly. What does he mean? I've been here the whole time.

"You need to stop. Remember why we're here."

No. I can't. It's happened far too many times now. I will let no one get away with treating me like shit anymore. If I let them go, then nobody will ever get it through their heads that I'm not going to let them get away with messing with me.

"Take me over their wall," I tell him.

"No, you can't kill them. We still need them."

"If you won't help, then I'll go myself."

I immediately start growing wings. It'll be hard to get past their walls with the rising steam, but I'll do what I must.

"Stop this! Do you really want to leave the merminea invasion unopposed? What about the people who can't defend themselves?"

Grímr could stop me easily if he truly wanted. The water is flowing past his talon as we speak, after all. But he doesn't, so I continue my change.

"These creatures have already shown their colors. They wouldn't help us, regardless."

Grímr slumps. "Is that really what you want? You won't put aside this slight for the sake of those back home?"

Why are you looking at me like that? I'm not the one that started our interaction with an attempt to entrap the other side. Why should I be the one to back down now?

The disappointment in Grímr's eyes is devastating. He's been by my side so long now. He's one of the few people I'd trust to always have my best in mind, so why is he against me? Why doesn't he understand why I need to do this?

"They . . . they tried to trap me . . . us," I manage. "I just can't let that go anymore. It has happened too many times now. I need to make sure the world knows it can't keep doing what it wants."

He needs to understand why. I don't want him to look at me with those eyes filled with disapproval and sorrow. It hurts too much.

I twist my head toward the three centzon that just moved close enough for me to sense. They must notice my attention as they lower their cloaks, allowing us a clear sight of them. They trudge toward us through the knee-deep water.

"Let me deal with this, all right? You don't have to like them, but please don't attack again."

I want to refuse. To keep the wrath churning my smoldering flames. But I give in. Grímr's disappointment has already put an end to my anger. If they decide to attack again, I won't hold back, even if I have a lot of water to avoid now.

Now that we have a clear look at the centzon, it is clear they relate to the mermineae, if distantly. Their bodies are hardly similar, but their tapered snouts, limb structure, and ears are too close to ignore. In a way, it's like how áed naturally appear similar to the albanic; alike, only with a superficial glance.

Unlike the mermineae, the centzon are stocky, tall, and stand with a slump that leaves their backs raised higher than their heads. In a word, I would describe the mermineae as slender, and these, not.

The trio approaching us each carry a thick pole of stone. I would equate it to a tree log, but the metal braces lining its length surrender its nature as another of their contraptions. Is that their weapon? I'd usually not be concerned about something physical able to hurt me, but they show clear understanding that I can't handle water. Could they have filled each with the horrid liquid?

They are large, though not exactly tall because of their slump. If they were to stand upright, I'd say they'd stand at the midpoint between an adult albanic and ursu.

Grímr stands still, eyeing the approaching centzon with his wings rested by his side. The trio gets closer. Thankfully, even though they take their time, the water doesn't rise higher. The vents still pump an unbelievable quantity out over the plateau, but it continues on behind us rather than flood around us.

Grímr rears his beak. "We would like to talk, not fight," he says with a raised voice.

The centzon stop. Clear surprise crosses their faces as they look between one another. They speak amongst themselves before the center one steps forward.

"If you wanted to talk, then what was that?" he asks in a gruff voice, gesturing to the damaged land and raised walls. "Do your greetings always comprise destruction and fire?"

"You attacked us first!" I accuse. "Nothing would have happened if you hadn't tried to ensnare us."

If they had just listened to us, nothing would have happened.

"Solvei," Grímr chides, giving me a stare.

I just huff and turn away. My body has completed its transformation now, so I could fly off, but I'm still concerned they might attack Grímr while I'm in the sky.

I keep an eye around us in case any other centzon are approaching. There aren't any visible to my heat sense. Either these three are their strongest and they've been sent here to take us out themselves, or they are distractions for another force.

Grímr addresses the three as they come to a stop ten meters from us. "I apologize for the offense. My junior partner is rather sensitive to the idea of being trapped. Please forgive her."

I turn to glare at Grímr. They're the ones that should apologize, not us. And I really dislike the way he phrases my absolute despisement as nothing but a sensitivity.

"I see," the middle centzon says. "What are you? You carry a weapon and cloth that I am unfamiliar with, so I'm inclined to believe you are not uncivilized." He indicates toward the bag and spear that rest in my taloned feet. "But I've never seen your likes before. An alicanto that speaks and . . . a fire? Or are you some vermilion variation?"

"We are from across the Alps."

I watch the centzon's expressions closely. They seem surprised and curious, nothing overly concerning. They don't share glances or murmur amongst each other, which I might have taken as them being greedy to travel there themselves. Well, they might still want to. I'm not about to claim to be a perfect interpreter of their thoughts from body language alone.

"She is an áed. Fire beings from far south. I am . . ." Grímr hesitates, clearly thinking about what to tell this stranger. If he fears or is disgusted by Grímr's race, we probably won't be able to make any agreement with these people. I narrow my eyes at them, asking them to do so. I still want to scorch them to cinders.

Grímr lets out a sigh. "I am not an alicanto. I am what is called a portian. We take over bodies of the beasts we beat."

I drop my eyes to Grímr. It's surprising he's admitting it. He is usually so concerned over what others will think of him that he'll keep it hidden regardless of how important it might have been to say. He kept me in the dark until he literally couldn't hide it any longer, and I was his teammate.

The centzon take this in stride, seeming more interested in Grímr now than anything else, including our origin and my race. It's somewhat amusing not being the target of someone's wonder for once.

"Like the teki?" the centzon on the right asks, leaning forward.

Their interest and lack of reaction to his self-explanation visibly surprises Grímr. "The teki?"

"Yeah, those Anatla that possess revontulet and cause all sorts of problems." Despite his words, he sounds rather excited.

"I'm not sure what an Anatla or revontulet are, either," Grímr says, obviously put off by the direction of conversation.

The center centzon steps forward again. "Not to worry, any creature related to the ones that put the cranky revontulet in their place is welcome here." He glances my way. "Though, please control your áed. I'd rather not have to flood our great regna."

I try to burn a hole in his head with my gaze . . . not actually starting a fire.

The trio turns around and waves to the tower and the torrent of water shuts off in moments. The centzon gestures us to follow them.

What?

Didn't they come out to fight? They've still got their weapons in hand and everything. I glance around us, expecting this to be some ruse. But no, the water level is dropping and with a heavy clank, the walls unlock and lower back into their original position, hidden beneath the ledge.

They flipped from aggression to friendliness because . . . Grímr is similar to another race?

I just can't wrap my head around it.

Didn't I almost kill a bunch of them? And they are fine letting me in the midst of their city? Grímr takes a few moments to follow behind the trio, obviously as flabbergasted as I am.

Wait, what was that about a flooding?

CHAPTER SIXTEEN

Curiosity

I've found that keeping finger-like claws on the end of my wings to be incredibly helpful. Particularly in moments like this. While one of my talons is busy holding my bag and spear, I have both wing-tip digits dug into Grímr's feathers. I might be a bit hot for him too; the metal warps beneath my claws.

I should have killed them all when I had the chance. Why did I have to crumble at the thought of making Grímr disappointed?

We wade through the last of the water before the tower, but much of it flows down into the chasm below now that there are no walls in the way.

The centzon trio lead us to a platform beneath the tower with a worryingly lively gait. Neither the centzon looking down from above nor the ones waiting on the platform seem angered. Curiosity and confusion they have in excess, but not a single one seems even annoyed that their assailant is now being welcomed into their home.

Once we are all positioned on the metal-rimmed stone platform, one of the centzon off to the side turns a valve. Now that I'm looking, there are several valves and levers arrayed along each section of stone within reach . . . and some sections that aren't.

Before I can look further up the interior of the tower, Grímr jerks beneath me. I grasp his feathers tight and look around, ready to strike at these creatures if they lead us into another trap.

None of them act as if anything is wrong. Nor do they look at us with hostility. Instead, I notice the source of Grímr's movement.

Our platform is falling.

Not fast. No, we are being lowered by another of these centzon's contraptions. As our stone ground lowers below the stone floor of the tower, I realize there's nothing underneath. The major pillars of the tower connect to a massive brace that locks into the wall of the canyon.

More of their city—their regna, as they call it—comes into view as we lower. It is unlike anything I've seen. Their metal and stone contraptions cover everything in the canyon. When I say everything, I mean it. All three hundred meters down to the water below, and spreading wide to both sides is their artificial creation.

I don't think there is a single portion of the wall that hasn't been replaced or improved.

The most common structures are enormous, spanning platforms holding entire streets of buildings and homes suspended hundreds of meters in the air. There are regular bridges and the occasional larger building that span the entirety of the canyon cavity.

I nervously tighten my grip at the sight of water dropping along the wall from above. It trickles more than a few meters away, but it's still enough to keep me tense.

"So what brings you to our regna?" the centzon asks as the platform clanks to a stop.

He steps down to the wide bridge and directs us to the far side of the canyon.

"We are mostly here to discuss the mermineae," Grímr says.

I'm surprised we have no issues walking. Grímr isn't exactly small or weightless, yet the bridge doesn't budge under his heft, nor do we face any issues when the centzon lead us into an enclosed area carved in the rock face.

It's concerning to enter, but enough of one wall is exposed to open air that I don't consider it entrapping. I can only thank the changes to the knot for that.

"The yoe? What about them?" The centzon slide their log-like weapons into a slot in the wall and twist them into place. Now that I'm looking, there are a hundred of the things along the wall we just passed. At first glance, they didn't seem any different from the number of other contraptions around.

They lead us across the space to several long tables. The centzon that has led the conversation till now takes the head of the central table. He invites us to sit, which in Grímr's case means sliding a few of the chairs out of the way. I remain on his back for now.

There are a lot of curious gazes following us. As soon as we've settled in, the rest of the tables immediately fill with the other centzon that can't help their wandering eyes.

"First, I'd like to ask your opinion of them."

"What's there to say?" The centzon shrugs. "The animals are good for their fur, something indispensable for us hunters, but I can't say I care for them in one way or the other."

A loud clang echoes through the alcove and the centzon looks up in delight.

"Ah, it looks like the cooks are just as interested as everyone else in our guests. I assume you have the same diet as a normal alicanto?" At Grímr's nod, he turns to me. "And you . . . uh, firewood?" he guesses.

"Anything," I say, trying my hardest not to snarl.

I hate this. They actually seem like nice, welcoming people. I hope they prove otherwise, then I can slaughter them all without issue. Why is it I'm never just given the freedom to punish those who do me wrong?

No. I got my vengeance on Gloria, the general, and the mill owner, so I guess I can't say never. But I hate facing problems I can't just incinerate.

Several centzon enter the large hall. Unlike those I've seen until now, these seem far shorter and less muscled. They are far closer to a merminea in proportions than the rest sitting in this hall.

They bring out platters and place them before each sitting centzon. The one that has been doing most of the talking so far is the first to be served. The massive head of some bird I'm unfamiliar with now taking up a good chunk of the table width. Each of the centzon on our table gets an avian head, but none as large as the head of the table.

On the surrounding tables, there are other cuts of bird meat and some fish heads. Is there some relevance to who gets what? Maybe it's decided by rank. In that case, the one we've been talking to must be their leader. Or at the very least, the highest in this room.

Those serving us can't hide their curious glances our way. I guess they don't get guests here often.

Grímr and I soon get our own plates. My mount getting a pile of that unique metal of theirs and I . . . get a bunch of different things. They've filled my plate with fish, bird, tinder, metal, and a bunch of random stuff that I'd assume they just picked off the ground if not for the ornate presentation. They've somehow even made rock look appetizing.

"Well, I think introductions are in order," the centzon leader announces. "I am Tzilac, Celotl Hunter." He waves a hand over the rest of the centzon. "And these are my hunters."

A short, unified shout from each startles me as they respond to his acknowledgment. I quickly clamp down on the flare I almost snap out at them. Now is not the time.

"I am Grímr, mercenary of the Order guarding the nations of the pact." He motions his beak back at me. "This is Solvei. Though never officially inducted into the Order, she is undeniably an important part of my team."

With that, Tzilac gestures for our plates and moves to start his own. I hop down to my meal, not about to miss a free feast. Before I start though, I realize none of the centzon in the hall have begun eating themselves. They all wait for Tzilac.

Their leader grabs some strange-looking utensil, obviously another of their contraptions. He positions it over the skull before him and, with a clench of his fist, a loud crack rings through the room. A series of similar snaps follow it as the rest of the centzon on our table crack their own birds' heads.

With another utensil that looks like a scoop with a clamp, he picks up a section of the cooked brain within. He raises it in a toast before bringing it to his mouth and swallowing whole.

A cacophony of slurping rings through the hall as everyone digs in.

I pick up the sample of their metal they've given me. I've already melted through and eaten plenty of it back when I destroyed their traps, but eating metal directly is always pleasant. Not exactly necessary, as I get all the taste and nutrition through my inner flame. Maybe it's the extra texture I can feel on my tongue, but it's always nice to eat directly now and then.

I leave the stone and fish untouched. Stone is . . . not disgusting, maybe bland.

I don't really get all that much energy from it either. Fish, I've found, tastes good, but I can never get my mind off the fact they come from water; it's hard to not feel nervous when eating. Doesn't matter how dry it looks.

"So . . ." Tzilac starts, and I take a moment to realize he's addressing me, not Grímr. "That weapon and cloth of yours . . . do you mind if I see them?"

I really don't want to, but as I turn back at Grímr, he's giving me a pleading gaze. Ugh, fine. But it's not because you want me to.

With a physical flame, I send them over to Tzilac, ignoring the fact that I do this entirely because Grímr wants me to.

The centzon inspects my spear first. "Hmm, sloppy metalwork and rough craftsmanship."

I almost lash out at him. How dare he criticize Bunny's work? But it isn't even my self-restraint that holds me back. It's the sudden, unnerving silence around us.

Each centzon has stopped eating. They each look our way with blank, unblinking stares. Without the curious looks they've all had till now, it comes across as incredibly creepy.

"It was all she could make out here without her equipment." I defend Bunny's skill. There is no change in the hundred motionless gazes.

"But this cloth . . ." Tzilac continues. "Is incredible! How are they able to make the threads so tiny? And each is perfectly sewn without flaw." He throws my spear back at me. I catch it with ease, too tense to let something like that surprise me.

"I would love to learn this! The girls on the lower platforms will do amazing work if they could replicate this."

Almost as if it was all my imagination, the centzon around us return to their meals. Those looking our way—which are still most of them—are as curious as they were before.

Did I . . . just miss an opportunity to get them to attack me again?

Wait, no. Stop thinking about that initial trapping. If I hold my frustrations, I'll never be able to move forward. Plus, they've shown they can pump water to the plateau above. It wouldn't be a stretch to assume they can do that anywhere.

I nervously glance around for any vents I might have missed.

"All right then, let's get back on topic. What exactly was it you wanted to say about the yoe?"

"There soon won't be any more in the Euroclydon's Hunting Grounds."

His immediate reaction is surprise, but that quickly morphs into confusion. "What exactly do you mean? The yoe are as numerous as blades of grass. I can't hardly imagine them all disappearing."

"They've discovered the path through the Alps. Right now, they are all trying to make their way across."

Tzilac's eyes flicker between the two of us. "You can't stop them, can you?"

Grímr flinches, and I can't help but sigh at my friend. Did he really have to make the answer so obvious?

"We don't know for sure. The mermineae have control of the tunnel entrance, so we can't return."

Tzilac nods. "All right, we will help you. We hunters have a rather important reason to keep them around ourselves."

My gaze drops to the thick coat hanging over his shoulders. It's strange they are immediately willing to help us. I mean, they are known to skin the mermineae alive, so I wouldn't say they are all too good friends with them. But again, they skin people alive . . . why are they willing to help us when they treat them like that?

"But in return, I want a free trade of technological secrets and research between us and your home."

"I can definitely try to get that, but I'm not an official diplomat, so I can't make any promises," Grímr hedges.

"Hmm . . . in that case, lead a group of centzon observers that I will provide through these nations of yours. We can discuss trade deals with the relevant people then." Tzilac places his hands on the table and rises to his feet before pausing. "Your people honor favors, correct?"

Grímr nods with ease, but I can't help but think back to Imiha breaking the deal with her team. Well, it's not like I'll be telling them about that. But to assume anyone will hold their honor when strained, I can't help but feel is foolish.

"Come, I'll introduce you to Eztli before I organize some things. She'll give you a tour of our regna."

This all went far too well for me to be comfortable with. Grímr seems satisfied and rises to follow the centzon, but I can't help but be suspicious. Maybe I'm paranoid, or maybe it's because I still hate them for trying to trap me.

Regardless of whether my distrust is valid or not, I'm going to keep my guard up and eyes open.

CHAPTER SEVENTEEN

Regna

I follow Eztli into another elevator as I poke at the new patch of my outfit.

The first place they took me was their textile workshop. In return for letting the centzon gush over the alien cloth, they fixed up the holes their traps had torn in my outfit. The quality of their work was far lower than Jav's. I doubt their work would do anything to block the flow of water.

It's not all bad though. They took it upon themselves to sew a layer of merminea fur over the top. I was resistant at first—reminded of the disgusting cloak given by the mermineae—but I'm glad I let them. It doesn't stink or feel rough. Like the centzon hunters, I have camouflage for myself now.

I'll need to fireproof this second layer soon. The metal they have is still strange to me, so without a true understanding of how my fireproofing patterns work, I'd rather not experiment.

Our elevator clanks to the next lowest platform. We're about halfway down the gorge now. There is a lot more housing and structures cramped in the same space down here than the higher levels, but considering the hunters reside up there, I'm not surprised.

I thought the hunters were the standard size, but with each floor we drop, it becomes clear they are the exception, not the norm. The hunters stand a good two or three heads taller than the rest of their kind.

Whether they get more space because of their size difference or their obviously higher social rank, I don't know. It's not like their average citizen is in any sort of the difficulties I'd seen back in the Zadok Kingdom.

Even as far down as we are, the platform is absolutely littered with random contraptions everywhere. Most lay unused, but some see constant use. The trolleys and cargo lifts always have something being transferred from one side of the platform to the other, or even between levels.

Like under the plateau above, there are plenty of massive gears and axles that spin just out of reach on the canyon walls. I'm unsure what their purpose is, but considering the hefty weight I can only assume they hold, they must be important.

"Ahead is what most consider the best view of the waterwheel in the regna."

Our guide, Eztli, is a rather stiff character. She shows the same curiosity as the rest of her kin, but spends most of the time trying to make sure we don't become aware of it. It is unfortunate for her that her eyes betray her. They near constantly stray back toward us any time she thinks we aren't looking.

Grímr and I approach the ledge Eztli motions toward. She's right, it's quite the sight, but I don't think it brings about the same feelings in me as the centzon might experience.

Below is a massive spinning wheel reaching from about a third the way up the canyon down into the depths of the water. It fills the entire width of the canyon and scrapes awfully close to both walls.

The wheel in all its height and complexity might be impressive, but I can't tear my eyes from the water tearing through the gulf. There is so much, moving so fast, that as much as I try to tell myself that I'm safe up here, I can't stop the rising stitch in my throat.

"So," Grímr starts. "Beside the hunters, do any centzon rise to the plateau above?"

I back away from the ledge, not thinking about what is only a hundred meters below.

"We do not. The only time we would is during a relocation after the destruction of our regna. But with the loss of a regna, there are few survivors," Eztli says.

She acts like it's a common occurrence. With this complicated labyrinth of contraptions and constructions they call a regna, I couldn't imagine it taking anything less than entire lives to create.

What could . . . That's a stupid question. I already know there are several incomprehensible beasts in this world. It's not a stretch to assume some creature can break through their immense defenses and destroy the regna. If it wasn't for all the water, *I* might have destroyed them all.

"How does one of your kind become a hunter?" Grímr asks, clearly pushing the conversation away from any mention of death.

"One must contribute to the regna." She turns and leads us to a conveyor. "Many jobs can give opportunities. A miner might conceive a technique for more efficient resource extraction, a cook discover a way to improve energy provided by a meal, or even those on the bottom rung finding a better way to fish."

She invites us on the conveyor that leads up to a section of the regna dug directly out of the wall. I'm surprised it doesn't buckle under Grímr's weight. I'd assume there would be at least some warping in the metal joints considering he is as heavy as thirty of the centzon. Maybe only ten of their hunters, though.

"Well, that's supposed to be the case," she continues as we slowly pass over a thirty-meter drop. The hard stone of the platform below a much more relieving sight than the water. "But you will be hard pressed finding any hunters that didn't originate from an engineer role."

I tune out their conversation as she continues to show us around their home. Grímr is trying his best to keep us on good terms with them, even to go as far as being completely honest with everything we'd originally agreed to be vague about.

I know I'm being unreasonable. Their entire race has shown nothing but curiosity, even though it should be obvious that I'm the one that just attacked their home. I'm incredibly suspicious of their lack of hatred and anger being directed our way, but maybe that's just me projecting.

My flames thrash around me, visible as I think about how we have to rely on the help of these people who trapped us. The writhing fire doesn't even scare the centzon around me. Instead, they watch on in wonder and awe as my inner flame flickers over my body in ways that would be deadly to any of them. I can feel a few children having followed us for a while now.

I left myself visible to scare them . . . not give them a show.

My anger and frustration can't even be blamed on the knots of my psyche. This is all completely natural, unlike the fear I used to feel.

What I want . . . is an excuse to let go. To vent against the world that keeps stoking my flame, but won't let me incinerate the stick that is doing so. As much as I'd initially placed the centzon as my targets to roast, I need to let that go. Knowing how things have gone so far, I'll get a new focus soon. Whether it's the mermineae or some new evil, I'll have to see.

The centzon hunters do not waste time. Before night falls, we are already back on the plains and traveling. Our goal is one of their sibling cities; another regna about a week north.

Unfortunately, that week is at their pace. If Grímr flew a few of us, we'd reach it likely within a day, but they refuse to even consider flying. Well, it's not like the ten we are traveling with are likely to all fit on his back.

Another hunter party is heading west. Their objective much the same as ours; convince the other regnas to join the fight.

"So how likely is it that these other regnas will join us?" Grímr asks as we walk past hunters reconstructing gears and rolling out pre-built traps.

"Oh, there's no doubt that they'll help us. We just need to convince them to invest more of their resources into this venture than they would by default." Tzilac walks beside us with that same contraption weapon slung beneath his arm.

I'm back to riding on Grímr's back. It's the best way I've found to avoid the questions or conversation of the centzon around me. Grímr has been kind enough to take on all communication, so I'm allowed to hide away and soothe the irritation for these people that—probably—don't deserve it.

The camouflage layer to my clothing is admittedly great. It does a great job of keeping me hidden against the green and gold sheen of Grímr's metal feathers. After application of a basic fire resistance on the fur layer, I can simply show my flames when I want to be seen, rather than open it up like the centzon do.

It . . . is somewhat against the teachings of my tribe, but I doubt those teachings could have considered this scenario. It should be fine.

At least the centzon leave me alone while I'm hiding on Grímr.

"Resources?" Grímr asks. "Do you mean more hunters?"

"Well, sure there's that, but we—" Tzilac trails off before a grin plasters over his face. "Actually, I think it would be best to let you wait and see."

"We met some incredibly strong mermineae last time cloaked in dust. Do you think you'd be able to compete?"

"You faced the cult leaders? The cultists are trying to leave too?" Tzilac twists to the centzon by his side, one that was with him when he first came to face us. "Patli, go inform Xipil. We'll need the heavy hitters."

Patli is off running without another word.

"Cult?" Grímr asks simply.

"The direct worshippers of the fake god," he spits. This is the most heated I've seen Tzilac get. It's good to see they aren't as perfectly averse to wrath as they pretend to be. I should push for more.

"What makes you think she's a fake god? What even makes one a god?"

He spins on his feet and points toward the Alps, where the Euroclydon watches over all, peering worryingly close to us. "That is the only thing that could be considered a god. Kalma, the fake, is a being far from comparable to the true gods of this world."

Tzilac lets out a breath to calm himself. "Though her strength is undeniable. Her claims of godhood are as unfounded as they were four hundred years ago, but fighting her is impossible."

"Are the Viisin too much for you, too?" I ask, ignoring Grímr's warning glance.

"We've been fighting them in these plains for hundreds of years. Of course, we've developed ways of dealing with them. Us centzon are intelligent beings and we shall adapt and overcome our tribulations, unlike the savage yoe that leave their bellies in the dirt and subjugate themselves to a creature that does not deserve worship!"

Whelp, I guess they really hate the mermineae. I'd thought they were putting too much effort into assisting us for it to be simply to save the source of fur for their hunter clothing. It's actually quite a relief to know they have a completely justified reason to participate in what is most likely going to be a massacre.

I would trust motivations supported by rage and hatred over logic any day. That's just how people work.

Tzilac hides his anger well, but now that I've seen that insight, I'm sure he's seething, waiting until he can get his hands on those that do him wrong and burn them until they are nothing but ash.

At least he has a target for that anger. I can hardly stay fuming at the centzon for trapping me; they've been far more cooperative than we ever expected. I'm still irritated with them, but I won't lash out.

What type of weapon would the centzon have to deal with the Viisin, I wonder? I'm assuming it's some sort of contraption, considering their obvious focus toward traps and machinery. But then again, I haven't seen them fight. Nor have I seen what their log-like weapons can do.

Do they have mages? Or at least some variant of them? Every race I've come by so far has at least some capability to influence hyle. Whether it be the markings of the eastern races, the natural manipulation of both áed and áinfean, or the weird gifted decay of the mermineae. If they don't, that would only make the structures they've made all the more impressive and daunting.

As I've said, this camouflage is amazing. I don't need to stick to Grímr's side all day now to defend against the dangers of the plains. As long as I keep low to the ground, I'm all but invisible to everyone's eyes. Of course, the moment I use my fire, my camouflage expires. The fur has an odd tendency to want to imitate my flames and I have no idea how to stop it.

Getting some space to myself for the first time in a while is great. The pace set by the centzon isn't anything I can't keep up with. The improvements to my ability to redistribute weight across my body having improved my running speed by quite a lot.

It's also been great to get some actual spear training in. I've spent most of my time in the past few weeks riding Grímr working on my balance. I have absolutely gotten better, but I haven't really been able to apply that to any of my fights recently, considering I've gone back to just trying to burn everything that might be a threat.

I really need to hold back on my flames and just try fighting with my spear. I've already seen that despite the absolutely devastating inferno I can create with all the energy I have, I lack the intensity to kill stronger enemies. Sure, I can char them a bit, but they can just push through until either I'm dead, or they are far enough from me that I can't hurt them.

If I can't even breach the Viisin's cloak of dust, how could I hurt them?

"Revontulet ahead!" Tzilac calls. "Circle to the right."

A revontulet? The beings that unfortunately have the extreme likelihood of being possessed?

I search ahead, and there's no missing the massive white creature tearing its maw into the corpse of something even larger. It has to be at least twice as tall as I am, and far longer from snout to tail.

A pure white fox. A fox that I recognize.

It's the same intelligent creature I'd seen back in the Void Fog.

CHAPTER EIGHTEEN

Recognition

The revontulet is, without a doubt, the same fox I saw back in the Void Fog.

I don't know if this is the exact same one I saw back then. If each revontulet look similar enough, then it probably isn't. Still, it's an incredible surprise to see a creature I'd glimpsed back across the Alps.

If there was any doubt the Fog ignored the logic of distance, it has now departed. There is the possibility one found their way to our side, but I find it unlikely. Somehow, the idea that the Void Fog can surpass any barrier just seems more believable than a revontulet rivaling Hund's strength would go unnoticed. Especially considering their unique body shape compared to the other races across the Alps.

Does this mean there's a way to travel across the Alps through the Fog? That would be so much better than needing to use the tunnels. But . . . how could I find it? The last times were spontaneous, and I'm no longer being changed by it, so it has no reason to appear around me as it did last time.

Would it even welcome me? The Void Fog assisted me last time, but assuming I could even find a way in, would it remain on my side? I can't help but feel the answer is no. The Void Fog did as I wished because its creation in New Vetus was connected to my desires. It was intricately linked to me. If I found my way in, it would no longer follow my will, but that of whatever creature the Fog is changing.

It's disappointing, but I'm not about to get an easy path back.

Now that I think about it, why don't I consider the Void Fog itself a prison? It's like an entirely separate world locking me within. Of course, I know how to escape, but I should still have a similar response to the thought as I would about diving into the tunnels . . . but I don't.

Exactly what are the conditions for something to 'trap' me?

I shake my head. Not the time to be thinking about this. We still have the revontulet ripping flesh from the corpse it stands upon.

It has somehow caught an absolute mammoth of a bird. Easily five times larger than Grímr's body, the bird of prey—or the preyed upon bird—isn't something I've seen before. The centzon lead us far around the revontulet and its catch.

The revontulets are the other race the mermineae are terrified of. But unlike the centzon, I didn't have a method to find them. Now we have. Could we convince them to help us too? The one I'd met in the Void Fog hadn't been hostile. Uncaring, maybe, but not hostile.

"You think we might get a revontulet to help us?"

"If it were a teki, then absolutely, but it's better to leave the revontulet alone," Tzilac says. "They are a grumpy lot, but they won't bite as long as you keep out of their way. Having a revontulet by your side is no better than tying a noose around your own neck. They'll turn on you in a moment of whimsy."

Ah. So they're strong, but unreliable. I wonder if Spenne would get along with them?

I'm self-aware enough to know my growth has been unnaturally fast. Even with a perfect environment for energy consumption, I've probably grown more than normal. The blocks I'm facing with my control and heat, I just somehow know I skipped it for my energy growth.

I'm not totally sure what is the source of my improved growth, but no doubt it is a part of me that was changed by the Void Fog. Considering the only other person I know that survived the Fog with their sapience intact is the strongest ursu—by far—I have to assume the revontulet from the Fog is of comparable strength.

"How strong are they?" I ask, trying to get information about a species that may prove dangerous in the future.

"Hmm . . . you've seen the cult leaders, they're about as strong as them on average."

I can't help but widen my eyes at that. "Their entire race?"

"Well, sort of." Tzilac scratches the side of his head. "Those called revontulet are simply ice foxes of the northern Icebelts that have lived long enough to gain sapience."

That is a surprise to hear. I'd never considered the possibility that a creature not born with intelligence could grow into it. That surely couldn't be the case for all creatures. The arachnids down under the Alps were all dumb as rocks, despite being terrifyingly dangerous and likely old.

I send a glance toward the buzzard. How intelligent are the Titans? Do they realize how many lives they end with a simple movement? Do they have a reason to care?

I doubt I'd be able to remain unmoving for long, even if I knew countless lives depended on it. If they weren't people I knew, would I even care?

We continue with our detour, all except for Grímr remain hidden from view. There's no chance the fox hasn't seen the bird, but our obvious avoidance is apparently enough for the revontulet to continue gorging on its meal and ignore us.

"How long does it take for them to become sapient?" I ask.

"About a hundred years? Give or take," he says. "I don't envy those of them that decide to have children. Who'd want to deal with a feral beast for a century before you can even start to be proud of them?"

"You have kids?" Grímr asks.

"Yep. Five. My oldest is amongst the group headed west. He's been a Palotl hunter for a few years now."

Tzilac talks at length about his children. My attention falls away to the horizon, not caring that his second daughter is at the top of her class, or that his youngest recently made their first gizmo. Besides the revontulet behind us, there is very little of interest to withstand my boredom.

Well, back to training. I have to get past these walls sometime.

* * *

Finally, after much more running, we arrive at the second city. Resting along another gorge—I wonder if it's the same long canyon as the other regna?—sits two towers. This city has a whole extra tower. Separated by a greater distance than the last regna's width.

With the regna still far in the distance, the centzon pull us to a stop. Tzilac waves to one of the hunters by his side and they step forward, unstrapping the large contraption from his back.

The hunter places the flat bottom of the metal cylinder on the ground. With a grunt, he tugs a section from the side, which twists into place with a click.

Now, the log has a crank.

The centzon leaves the handle alone for now and places his hands on both sides of the contraption. With a quick twist, another click is audible, almost satisfying to the ear. The weapon slices into three sections. No, 'slices' is wrong. The parts remain connected, but they slide along one another with ease until the contraption is leaning away from us, while remaining upright.

The hunter kneels low behind the weapon and seems to make tiny adjustments when looking toward the towers. His hand returns to the crank and he winds it until the machine creaks under the pressure. He presses a few odd switches and buttons before reaching into the back pocket of his heavy coat and pulling out a tiny, stone marble, barely the width of my finger, and shoves it in a slot near the top.

He rises back to his full, slouched height and just when I think he's done with whatever he's doing, he kicks the thing. Instead of toppling like it should, a loud crack rings out and the something speeds out the top of the weapon, too fast to see. It reminds me all too much of the whip-like snap of Remus's tentacles.

Seconds pass before a low, droning hum returns from the towers.

The centzon wait, so Grímr and I do the same. The droning noise slowly dies out and after a few minutes a slow, repeated bell's gong replaces it. Everyone finally moves again, so I take a closer look at the contraption that just sent the stone well over a thousand meters.

"Is that what it's for?" I ask as I crouch beside the centzon, who in a few motions, has it looking like it did originally and back in his hands. "Why didn't it topple when you kicked it?"

The hunter looks over my shoulder to where I feel Tzilac nod his head with a shrug. Instead of slinging the contraption over his back, he pulls it up for me to see and tugs out the handle once more.

"Its mortar mode is far from the most impressive thing this beauty can do. Here, try winding this." He gestures for me to the crank while he holds it in one arm.

Doing as invited, I place a hand on the crank and try to spin it. It doesn't budge. I try with both hands. It doesn't budge. Not wanting to fail a third time, I shove as much control and weight into my arms and shoulders as I can, and push. It moves, but hardly anywhere near as much as I wanted.

The centzon laughs. "You got quite the bit of strength for a young elemental."

I stare at him oddly. "A what?"

"You know, the creatures that surpass the binding threshold of their bound element. Quite a few revontulet have reached that point with ice in the past. There are also some unique ones to the east."

Wait, so any of the other races could become like áed if they raised their binding with fire? Huh. Does that mean these other elementals might know how to raise one's binding? The Void Fog was a shortcut for me, but I don't know how Elder Enya raised hers, so I don't think I've been able to raise it since.

Maybe I should try to find them one day. Well, only if I can't get back to the other side of the Alps. If I can get back home, I should try to find the Agglomerate and ask the elders there how I might reach the next threshold.

The hunter places his own hand on the crank and spins it, this time not while grounded. He lifts the base so I can watch as a flat metal ring twists into a drill and rotates a good arm's length out of the contraption.

So it digs into the ground. That's why he was fine with kicking it.

He slaps a switch on the side, and the drill snaps back into the contraption. "How 'bout I show you some of the most useful modes?"

As we walk toward the regna, he does exactly that. He twists what I thought was supposed to be a weapon into a bunch of configurations that I don't think anyone could consider as such. A mode for fishing, digging, and even some weird method of telling the time. He never showed me any weapons, not that I believe for a second it doesn't have any, but I guess the centzon do have some wariness within them.

Honestly, I'm relieved. Until now, they've been far too welcoming. It's kinda creepy, in a way. If I was in their place, I never would have let the possible dangerous people into my home. Nor would I have been so quick to listen.

The slow, rhythmic bell chimes as we approach the closest tower. We would have been well into the field of traps at the last regna by now, so in curiosity, I pass a tongue of flame over the surface. It takes no time to find a crack and my flames soon envelop a contraption right beneath my feet.

I stop in place, but the centzon continue on without care. Despite the hazardous earth, not a single trap triggers. I spread my flame further through the cracks in the ground, careful not to melt away the contraptions this time, and find the heavy stone gears and axles unmoving.

So they've deactivated the entire field for our approach? Is that what this slow alarm is for? To indicate the approach of friendlies rather than enemies.

I hurry to catch up to the others and ask, "Did that stone somehow tell them to deactivate the traps?"

Tzilac glances down at me. "Yes. It's a method we use to communicate. We hit one of the hidden bells that informs of our intentions. We are safe to approach as long as their tower's bell is ringing."

Centzon hunters await our arrival at the base of the tower. One rushes forward once we are close and grabs Tzilac in a headlock. Without breaking free, Tzilac takes the hunter in a headlock of his own.

"Ah, brother, it's good to see you again." The new centzon twists his head within the tight grip, appraising each of us standing behind Tzilac. "You didn't bring Xipil? Shame."

They separate and Tzilac laughs. "No, I've left an important task for him. He can't stay by my side forever. Now, we have some important business of our own to discuss. It's best not to wait around."

"Of course, of course. Come." Tzilac's brother leads us toward the elevator.

The tower appears similar enough to the last. A mix of metal and stone rising high above. Hinges, gears, valves, and levers decorate the walls the entire way up. Like last time, many of the contraptions that I'd assume are there to interact with are far out of reach.

Why would they place them there?

My curiosity must be obvious as Tzilac calls out to a centzon standing by a wall of gauges, "Atl, take the girl for a tour of the tower. She seems interested. Her partner here, Grímr, should be enough for our conversation."

I glance at Grímr, but he just shrugs in return. "You'd rather stay up here, right? Try not to burn anything."

I return a glare at his unfunny attempt at humor.

Before long, I'm left alone with these centzon I don't know. I shouldn't feel like this. I spent weeks on end without Grímr being by my side in the tunnels. But I can do nothing about the bubble of concern as I watch Grímr descend away from me.

"So, you're interested in our tower, right?" the centzon, Atl, says jovially. "I'm sure you'll like it; the view is incredible."

I somehow doubt the sight from this tower could beat that of flying, but I follow him up the stairs anyway.

The slow, repetitive bells finally cut out as we make it up the last flight. Likely giving warning to the field of traps' reactivation.

Atl talks about how each lever has an important purpose, but I lose my focus over the plateau. I was right, it really isn't much of a view. All there is to see is the gorge behind us and the Alps ahead. As with every time I look over the giant mountain range, my eyes eventually fall on the Euroclydon.

The hard gaze of the predator locks far to my north. It is clear as day when it decides its prey. The hunt has begun.

A loud, screeching siren blares from a horn right beside my ear. The ground beneath me jolts as the tower shifts. Centzon rush around, shouting, and I cannot tear my sight from the buzzard.

I belatedly realize just how dangerous this situation is. I'm in a tower, about to be hit by a gust that can tear trees to splinters.

The Euroclydon beats its wings.

CHAPTER NINETEEN

Caavaa

Despondence was the usual state for mermineae.

It was the frustrating, terrible, hopeless state of the world they were forced to live that birthed nothing but cynicism. Mermineae feared each day would be their last. Death was so common amongst the race that by the time one was an adult, they would be numb to the pain of loss.

Caavaa had lost so many close to him, and yet he still felt dismay in his chest at the demise of his two most recent partners. He'd known they would die. He thought he would die.

The infiltration amongst the traitors had gone smoother than they could have hoped, but the successful mass-ambush was still not enough to compete with the sheer numbers. They'd successfully assassinated as many traitorous Forvaal as they could, sacrificing thousands for the effort, but once he'd seen the power of the Viisin, he questioned whether those deaths were even necessary.

He'd stayed close to Aana and Muuro, hoping to protect them once the element of surprise was lost, but they had been unlucky. Their kills had been clean, yet they weren't prepared for the retaliation. Caavaa had arrived only seconds after his own kill. That was still too late.

Everything had devolved to chaos after that. The Viisin joined in a brawl, tearing through more of his kind than the outsiders as they butchered their way forward.

Caavaa had fled. It may not be his proudest moment, but in a battle like that, where even the skies turned against them, nothing short of the Viisin could compete. The Viisin did compete, and now two lay dead. Beaten by the power of an outsider.

It was the first time he'd seen the strength of the Viisin, but it wasn't a surprising sight. They'd been given their power from god herself. What was downright baffling was that the outsider not only stood toe to toe with Kalma's chosen, he actually killed one. It was unthinkable.

With his belly close to the earth, he ran at full pelt until the Temple came into view. It was not a place any merminea liked to be, but there was no choice for many. The slaughter that would follow should Kalma decide the mermineae were lacking in their dedication would take many years to recover. Caavaa lost eight siblings and his mother in the last culling.

Thankfully, she'd remained appeased for the past few years, so no major disaster had occurred since.

Caavaa knew that if she ever found out about the current issues, the punishment would be far worse than they could imagine.

As much as he didn't want to be here, he had a job to do. Taanoraa and Saad had tasked him with bringing information to the Viisin Neero. It was vexing that the two of them weren't doing this themselves. Bad enough that they didn't contribute to the battle at the tunnel, they had to slide this responsibility onto him?

The two of them had lost both their sight and the gift of decay from excessive use, but they still had far greater strength in their bodies than most Forvaal. Lives as long as theirs were a rarity.

As they were his seniors, Caavaa couldn't argue against them, no matter how much he thought they were self-centered pricks.

The Temple was a mighty structure. Built with generations of hard labor by his predecessors. Wide and sloping upward, it was designed to survive the intense winds of the Euroclydon's regular flights.

A flight of stairs rose on both sides of the pyramid, leading to Kalma's throne; a room of comforts, where the god spent most her time.

Mermineae didn't like structures, it went against their very nature. A large blemish on the land like this would leave them exposed for leagues around. But what Kalma orders, she gets.

The most horrible thing about the structure is that if you are on the top half of the pyramid when the Euroclydon spreads its wings, death is assured. Reaching the earth before the blast hits would be impossible, and taking refuge in Kalma's throne would result in a fate worse than death.

Caavaa made his way past the Field of Discipline, where the pained screams and wheezes of gradually decaying mermineae dug into his ear. As with every time he'd been here, he tried his hardest to keep his eyes locked on the dirt below so that the rotting, living bodies of his kin didn't disturb him.

As always, it failed.

He swallowed a nervous knot in his throat as the scent of decomposing flesh burned his snout. He had to hold his breath to push on without retching. It wouldn't be pleasant to attract attention to himself.

Caavaa crawled his way up the stairs, nearly slipping a few times on the smooth stone. Before he crested the final steps, he took a deep breath and suppressed any emotion that might show on his face.

As soon as he took a step over the ledge, a wave of pressure crashed into him. He pressed his body close to the ground on instinct, trying to make himself as small as possible.

The presence of the god was suffocating.

He would prefer to keep his head bowed and crawl back down the Temple, but doing so was more likely to drag Kalma's attention to him. He strained the muscles of his neck against an intense instinctual desire to freeze and hide. Slowly, he brought his head away from the ground, and tried his hardest to glance toward Viisin Neero without observing the god.

He failed.

Kalma lay on a large cushion crafted by an enslaved centzon with a mixture of down and fur, of which he assumed only a small portion was a merminea's, considering the lack of camouflage.

The god was completely hairless. If Caavaa wasn't so terrified, he might have considered it ugly. Her small stature and thin, almost emaciated body belied her overwhelming strength.

Caavaa stifled a sigh of relief at the fact she wasn't looking his way. Her temper was known to explode at the smallest of things. It was best to keep even the smallest of noises stifled.

"Hmm . . . these are delectable. Where did you find them?"

Every fiber of his being froze, screaming at Caavaa not to move. The voice washed over him without intensity, and yet parts of himself melted away, only to be replaced before he could feel pain. Each word brushed through his being and scraped at everything he was.

Kalma took a bite out of a strange white fruit. Her upper fangs protruding outside the lip of her mouth as she swallowed the last bite. She snatched another out of the hands of a young, trembling Forvaal standing by her side.

"Thank you, Goddess Kalma. My two children died to retrieve these from the wall of the great trench." The jill let sadness reach her face as she stood there with the bundle of fruits in her arms. "It's a shame, they—"

"Shut up," Kalma snapped.

Caavaa tensed, knowing the Forvaal likely wouldn't live the next few moments.

Surprisingly, nothing happened. The god continued eating in her laid back posture. Nobody died. No one was screaming.

She must be in a good mood.

Kalma's tails waved gracefully through the air. Both thin limbs just as gray as the rest of her skin. It was the best indicator they had to tell she was exceptionally happy right now. For what reason, Caavaa didn't know. But it meant she still had absolutely no clue about the traitors' escape attempt.

Still prone at the entrance to Kalma's throne, Caavaa finally locked eyes with the Viisin he needed to talk to. In as close proximity as they were to the god, the Viisin appeared rather normal, lacking the cloak of dust that expelled from them everywhere they went. Neero looked like any other merminea, except for the empty eye sockets in his head.

The Viisin bowed their heads toward Kalma, before lowering their chest to the ground and pacing to Caavaa's side. One of the god's large ears resting at the top of her head twitched toward Neero as he brushed by Caavaa and down the Temple's steps. Caavaa moved to follow, wanting to be as far from Kalma as soon as possible. But just as he was about to follow down the steps, he risked a glance back.

Kalma's large eyes dug into his chest. Her curiosity was terrifying, considering the information he hid. Laying further back on her cushion, she hung her head back and flashed him a sinister grin. The fact she was relaxed did nothing to calm the sudden panic that gripped him. He couldn't tear his eyes from hers.

She knew. She knew and was only playing with them.

Caavaa found his breaths coming in shorter and shorter gasps. With each moment her eyes pierced him, his terror rose and hyperventilation intensified. Only when he was tugged out of her sight by a jerk to his tail, was he able to snap out of the onset of panic.

He didn't move, letting himself be dragged down the steps by the Viisin, expecting the god to come and send him off for punishment amongst the others in the Field of Discipline. But Kalma didn't come. Like the jill before, he was let off.

She didn't know.

Relief overwhelmed him so much that it took a moment to realize the Viisin dragged him halfway down the Temple. He scurried out of his grasp and joined Neero in his descent.

"You have news, I take it?" Neero didn't delay.

Caavaa sent a nervous glance back, concerned they were still within hearing range. "Yes."

Without another word, Neero led him past the decaying mermineae. Kalma's power was able to keep them alive for as long as she liked, tormenting those she despised with never-ending pain.

As the two reached a secluded space, the Viisin turned to Caavaa. "Speak."

He struggled to collect his thoughts. Usually Caavaa was better than this, but the few moments he'd been the focus of Kalma's attention had left him unsettled. Neero glared at him expectantly, the lack of eyes doing nothing to diminish the Viisin's scrutiny.

"The mission was a failure; the path remains open," he said. "Two Viisin are dead."

Neero grunted, his voice much harsher than a moment ago. "I know. I killed one of them." The shroud of ash slowly fell off the Viisin, apparently too far from Kalma to suppress it. "Tell me of the outsiders."

Caavaa frowned in consideration. Had his two seniors really sent him only to report that the outsiders could no longer close the tunnel? He'd thought the deaths of the Viisin were the most important detail to deliver. It wouldn't be long before Kalma realized their presence missing.

"They won't be able to reseal the entrance. Most have returned through the Alps."

Neero looked strangely unconcerned. They'd have very little hope of stopping the flood now that the path was not only open, but widened.

"Most?" the Viisin asked.

"We've had reports of three outsiders that have not returned to their lands. Two of which travel together and aren't much worth themselves. The other is the lightning elemental that instigated the mess that battle became. Neither, I believe, is capable of resealing the hole."

Neero hummed. The sound grew coarse as his throat struggled to keep from falling apart under the accelerating decay. "You may leave."

Caavaa didn't need to be told twice. He turned and didn't look back.

Neero waited as the coward left his sense range, ignoring the growing agony assaulting every fiber of his being. Paying it any attention was a mistake only the young made. The squirming, screaming, and whimpering forms of the mermineae in punishment blazed in his inner eye.

They hardly had much decay eating through them, but each pleaded for death. He suppressed a snarl as he walked through the Field of Discipline, uncaring where he placed his foot or how many breaks and cuts he caused. They were weak, unable to handle even the slightest pain, and yet they dared to annoy him with their incessant whining.

He started back up the stairs of the Temple, idly noting that the stairs had worn away in the Titan's winds. He would have to have them replaced. Again.

The only sense he'd kept with the 'gift' Kalma had given him was hearing. All else withered away with the constant deconstruction of his body. Though, he'd long lost his sight, even prior to the 'gift.'

In place of his old senses, he'd gained a new one. One reliant entirely on observing decay. It was not something he'd have originally thought would be a good way to see, but apparently, everything was falling apart on its own ever so slowly. His own body shone in his sight, and while the stone steps beneath him were dull, they were still visible.

Only the god herself, he couldn't see. Kalma was like a void, completely invisible if not for the very air itself being ever so slightly visible. The path left by the Titan as it tore through the Euroclydon's Hunting Grounds was the only thing that came close.

The Viisin returned to Kalma's throne to find she'd already cleared the room of any other mermineae. The god, relaxed on her cushion and facing Neero, exerted pressure through his body. Unlike before, where he returned to the state he'd lived before her 'gift,' he now decayed at an accelerated rate. A mountain of dust flowed down the Temple behind him.

He forced himself not to gasp for air, despite the intense breathlessness that came from his lungs disintegrating in his chest.

"Are you going to tell me? Or do you feel like waiting a bit longer?"

"The outsiders are on their way home," he choked out. "Only the lightning elemental that killed my partner remains a threat."

"Wonderful!" she cheered, not letting up on the deconstruction of his body.

"Go find the three on foreigner hunting duty and make sure the elemental won't be a problem."

He bowed and crawled back the way he came. Now he had to find the other Viisin under her direct orders and go hunting.

The mermineae were fools to think Kalma wouldn't know.

She always knew.

CHAPTER TWENTY

Boxed In

The rapid expansion of distorted air quickly obscures the Euroclydon before the ground lurches out beneath me and I lose my footing. I slam on my back and twist to regain my feet, but find the surface continuing to slide away from me. The tower is tilting. We're falling, but the blast hasn't even hit yet. How?

"Hold on!" Atl shouts as several handholds jut out of the stone floor.

I grasp at the closest protruding rail as the grinding and creaking of the tower mixes with the blaring alarm. The tower jerks once more, and we are falling faster than should be possible. Our floor quickly transitions to a wall before we slam into place. I only barely hold on as the sudden stop almost throws me down into the gorge below.

The tower now rests at a right angle, our viewing box suspended directly over the center of the canyon. Beside me, the many centzon on the tower with me hold their own handrails.

The regna is much like the last one I saw, but now, everything seems alive. Not only are all the gears spinning and pistons thrusting, the structures themselves are moving.

A bridge directly beneath me twists on itself. Rock scraping against rock as the two sections split before rotating toward their respective wall.

The massive building constructed between both sides of the canyon divides into four sections, each blooming away from a central spinning pillar. The four quarters slide along the vertical surface before they slam into place and gradually pull inside the wall. Spinning ever faster, the massive column remains where the building once stood, connecting the canyon walls.

I can hardly understand what I am seeing. Their entire city moves!

Lost in awe at the sight, I almost lose my grip on the handle as the tower yanks back into motion. A hand from Atl holds me steady against the wall, seemingly experienced with this.

My eyes flicker back to the moving regna below. The many platforms where most centzon live are not untouched by this strange occurrence. They were slower to start, but each massive slab of stone rotates into the gorge wall where huge sections of stone have flared out, like fingers ready to grasp and pull.

The second tower lays horizontally over the gorge and slowly pulls into the wall it's attached to. Is that what's happening to us? The tower hasn't fallen, we're just folding away like everything else?

Everything disappears so quick. They all slide into or rest flush against the walls of the canyon. If not for the waterwheel below and the spinning pillar once hidden within a building, I would never have realized this place was inhabited. Maybe a bit of an odd-looking canyon at most.

Even as I think that, the hundred meter tall waterwheel rises from the water and settles within a nook on one side of the gorge. From the opposite wall, a massive slab of metal-framed stone clicks out of place and crosses the open space before locking over the wheel. Pistons decouple from the slab, and slide back into the wall.

Finally, the pillar bridging the walls snaps in half. Locks holding both sides together open, and each side flies into a slot on their respective sides. A tremor runs through my hands as it slams into place.

The regna is a contraption. Every part of it. I'd thought there were just plenty of concerning-but-neat moving parts throughout the city, not that the city itself was a trap.

I realize far too late that I'm being locked in. Trapped. Again. The ceiling of the tower slides into the rock wall and the room goes dark.

There is a moment of complete, absolute silence. The grinding of the gears comes to a halt and not a single centzon breathes.

Of course, the moment does not last long.

The tower slams deeper into its hole and I lose my grip. A maelstrom of noise erupts around us. The grinding and groaning of gears, stone straining under the immense pressure abusing our tiny enclosed room.

I slam into the ground now below me, but I hardly notice. While the Euroclydon's winds pelt the contraption surrounding me, I'm struggling to keep myself still.

Trapped once more by the centzon, the knot within me demands action. I need to free myself from their clutches. Burn a hole through stone and escape. I scream in my mind, my voice leaking out without intent. I'll be exposed to the Titan's winds if I free myself now. Where exactly will I go? The bottom of the gorge is a river. If I melt away the wall protecting me from the deadly gusts, I'm likely to send myself spiraling into the depths below.

Not to mention all the centzon around me. Would they survive if I exposed this little protective hole to the elements? We still need the centzon's help in taking the path. I can't see them remaining friendly if I cause a dozen deaths.

My psyche's knot doesn't care. It wants me to burn my way out, and I can feel the flames flicker around me, illuminating the space and every centzon within view. They grow and spread toward the wall and former ceiling. A couple of hunters step away, startled by the sudden spread of my fire.

It's supposed to be logical, so why doesn't it understand why this is a horrible idea?

Tremors shake my hands pressed against stone. The flames go against my command, scorching the wall that keeps us safe. A few centzon shout in panic.

I am a prisoner of my own mind.

Agony.

I clutch at my head and fall to my side. My flames spasm and curl back around me. It feels like my mind is tearing, straining from the pressure of being tugged separate ways. Fire writhes around me. I'm unsure whether it's trying to protect me, or eat into my head.

I've finally realized.

I'm not free. I haven't been free since the Void Fog changed me.

My desire for freedom may have amplified, but it was twisted. I was gifted everything I needed to avoid any form of entrapment, but in doing so, the Fog chained a part of me I'd never even considered. Something far more important than what a simple cage could contain.

My freedom of thought.

The pain flares again. The rope of my psyche pulls taut by the realization. Each point of resistance, each knot in my rope, strains under the assault, inflicting unmitigated anguish through my being.

If I can never do the things I want to do, because the changes to my mind forcibly prevent me . . . nothing could be a worse prison. I want to lie. I want to enter homes.

I want to return to those I care for.

The idea of being stuck in a box, unable to escape, is the most terrifying thing I could think of . . . but I would take that over these chains on my mind.

Worse than the pain of water sizzling over my body, the knots snap. One by one. The smallest fraying first, then gradually tearing through the larger ones. Most I don't even know what they were a blockage for, constituting too few threads of thought for coherence, but they all snap regardless.

My body feels distant. The centzon surround me. I can see them, feel them, but they don't seem real. My thoughts grow sluggish, like swimming through molten rock. Are they here to hurt me? Kill me? Trap me?

I send a wave of fire at them, but my inner flame only seems to constrict my body. Never have I had this little control. Each second, the world creeps further from my grasp. I'm nothing more than a child again, crying out at the world and incapable of control.

The knot, the largest and most intrusive bundle of conflicting desires, is all that remains fighting against the strain of my rope. It lashes out. It floods my mind with memories, the most horrible feelings I've ever experienced. Grief and loss. Overwhelming terror. Pain.

The knot fights my control, shoving me out of my own body. I can feel its intentions. It is not malicious. It just wants to keep me safe, keep me from losing my freedom as I have so many times now. Virtuous it may be, but shunting me into a corner of my mind is worse than anything I can imagine.

I won't be able to live with this in my head. I can't.

The picture of my rope of desires comes to the forefront of my thoughts. It looks more frayed than it's been since the Fog. Each snapped knot, now a mess of threads poking out of the coherent whole. I reach out and with only a moment to brace myself; I tug.

The pain is excruciating. I scream and the knot screams, but I hear no sound. My mental grip doesn't loosen despite the pain. If I let go now, I'll never be free. I need to do this.

The knot tightens, threads snapping each second. The bundle of conflict screams louder, deafening me despite the distance of my body. My very being is tearing apart, but I continue to pull. With one final agonizing yank, the screaming stops.

I'd hoped for relief, from the pain, from the memories, but it does not come. My mind throbs as the threads of desire try to reorient. The knots try to wind themselves together once more, but the constant pressure keeps the fraying strands from tying.

I don't feel good, but my mind is my own once more.

Gradually, the world comes back into focus. Centzon surround me, peering down from a good meter separation. I turn my head. My body isn't in pain, but the lingering aches of my mind echo across my form. Flames wrap me in their warmth and I notice I'm half-submerged in a shallow pool of glowing rock.

I get a hold of my flames, suppressing them and hiding my form. At least I try to do that. My body is sluggish and my fire is slow to do as I want. I push myself until I'm seated, noticing that the grinding of stone has stopped. The winds have stopped.

Past the centzon obviously concerned for my sake, the wall between us and the canyon is intact. Somewhat molten and definitely thinner than before, but intact. Thankfully, I didn't breach the wall and subject all of us to our deaths.

The enclosed space of the tower still surrounds me. The opening in the wall— where stairs used to be—now opens to the large central columns of the tower. No longer are the stairs visible, having moved out of the way while I was stuck in my mind. Small torches line the walls and light the tower interior. It is enough for me to see there is no path out.

I am trapped, and yet my decisions are my own.

No longer do I need to flail in panic or sacrifice choice to remove myself from this situation. Unfortunately, that doesn't mean I'm fine being stuck like this. I've gotten rid of the knot limiting and controlling my actions, but freedom is my top priority. Only now, I don't need to sacrifice others' lives for my gain. I can stare at this wall as long as I want, and there's no urgent need to burn my way through it.

Slowly, I rise to my feet. My body responds to me better with each second, and my flames finally listen to me. I'd be embarrassed at unwillingly losing my grip if I wasn't so exhausted. The pain and effort taken to snap the knot out of my psyche has left me drained.

I want to do nothing other than pass out and get some rest. But, while my mind is free, my body is not. I don't want to break my way out, but I still don't want to be stuck in this enclosed space.

"All clear!" the shout echoes through the prone tower.

The surrounding group twists their heads as one, all but forgetting about me as they rush off in a burst of activity. Only Atl remains by my side, giving me a moment of much needed space.

"We'll need to get positioned. Are you all right to walk?"

I blink up at him, his words taking longer than usual for my tired mind to parse.

The tower jerks around us, sliding out of its lock with a clank. The proceeding groaning of gears finally makes me aware of my surroundings. They are reopening the tower. I won't be trapped.

I hang my head back in relief. The barrier to the gorge opens up and exposes us to sunlight. The walls around me slide along stone, but the ground underneath me doesn't move. Realizing I'm standing on earth and not the tower, I quickly grab my spear and follow Atl's lead to what was a railing, but now works as a platform.

The centzon rush around me, using the plentiful rails to climb to different gauges, levers and valves. Atl looks down at me with curiosity. I turn away from his gaze. I'm sure I left a shameful display, squirming on the floor like I did, but considering what I'd regained, I could hardly manage a mote of embarrassment.

We slide out into the open and I get a perfect view of the damage, or lack thereof. Each centzon structure is flush inside the wall. Their regna designed perfectly to fold away at a moment's notice. Really, in the panic of the Titan's incoming blast, I hadn't really paid much attention to how fast their mechanisms moved.

An entire city, able to fold away within the six seconds it takes the Titan's blast to hit. And I'd thought the first ursu mining village was impressive.

My legs dangle over the edge as I sit again. Our tower slides into place over the canyon and freezes in place. The first structure to follow is the waterwheel, which quickly slots back into place and spins under the immense strength of the river below.

The river itself has been whipped into a frenzy. Its rapids tearing up the canyon faster than I ever want to see water moving. The wet walls of the gorge tell of a far more dangerous situation than I'd thought. During the blast, not only would I have had to worry about the wind, but also the water flung high.

Soon, the buildings, platforms, and bridges unlock from the wall and reset themselves in their original state. I watch over the massive contraptions as they work. There is no rush this time, so everything moves with an ease ignored while time was of the essence.

The longer I watch, the harder it becomes to focus. My fatigue washes over me as the tower finally starts moving back upward. I try to stop myself, to remain awake, but it's an impossible game.

I fall asleep, feeling truly free.

CHAPTER TWENTY-ONE

An Easy Fight I

A few weeks have passed since I'd regained full autonomy. I don't feel much different. Even as I think about traveling through the Alps again, I can't stop the shudder that runs down my back. The idea of being stuck beneath a mountain of stone I cannot melt through fills me with dread.

If I was given another chance to join my team, would I? Do I have the nerve to put myself through that again?

I can't say for sure. Without the enforced fear and manipulations of the knots, there should be nothing stopping me from jumping at the chance . . . but hesitance and doubt still overwhelm me. I can't even blame it on anything but myself anymore. I'm a coward that would put my freedom before my friends' safety.

The wheels of my ride rattle and clank beneath me. One axle must be slightly out of alignment as it clicks every full rotation. Maybe I should introduce the centzon to Henosis; at least they had a smoother riding experience with their vehicles.

The picture of the inverse occurring and the Empire getting their hands on the mechanical prowess of the centzon immediately makes me fear for the future. The few centzon regnas we've pulled into this attack are heavily interested in a trade of technologies. If they are that interested after simply seeing the sewing talent of Jav's sisters, I'd hate to see what would happen should they shake hands with the Empire.

As I look around at the convoy of multiple hundred siege engines—which is what Grímr called them—I can't help but question if this is the right action. Can we trust them not to take the mermineae's place as our aggressors in their search for new knowledge?

Well, it's too late for these thoughts, regardless. They are helping us for now, and if they turn on us in the future, we'll just have to deal with it then.

Beside me, Grímr absently pumps a lever with his heavy taloned foot. I might have considered our ride to be impressive to not buckle under his weight, if not for how heavy this massive machine was itself. Behind us, clear trails remain of where the wheels dug through the earth to drag us forward.

In any other scenario, I'd be concerned about something finding our trail and following it to us. But out here in these vast plains with so many huge contraptions, I'd be more surprised if something couldn't find us. We've had countless birds fly down and investigate already on our trip.

Grímr keeps his eyes forward, watching for the first sign of resistance that should come any time soon. We've been busy since the Euroclydon's last hunt, so even though we've been beside each other most of the time, I've never had the chance to speak to him about my mental state.

My eyes drop to my hands, fidgeting in my lap. No, there's been plenty of times I could have told him, but I never did. Despite telling myself I would talk to him, I've been too wrapped up in nervousness to speak up. My mind always falls back to the last time I talked about my thoughts and fears. Even though I trust him more than anyone else, it's still hard.

There's probably no true need for me to tell him, but I should and the more I think about the necessity of things, the harder it'll be to just take the step I need to take and actually put my faith in him.

I take in a deep breath. "The Void Fog changed me." I realize how sudden and confusing I might sound, so I quickly say, "I mean, more than my body. For the longest time, my mind was bent in ways I wish it weren't."

Feeling foolish, I look up from my hands to see the alicanto's entire focus on me. He doesn't speak, but his welcoming gaze encourages me to continue.

"I know you already know that the Fog altered my body, increasing my binding to what it is, and gave me unreasonable fear, but that's not everything. I . . . it altered my mind."

My eyes are in my lap again. Heavy scratching makes me raise my head. Grímr scoots closer to me and slowly sweeps a wing over my back. An obvious act to comfort me.

I laugh at his stiff motions, but it comes out choked.

"In those tunnels, I pushed through the fear until the changes gave up and adapted. That's when I learned just how deep its intrusions were. Instead of fear, my very thoughts and actions were taken from me. There were so many times I wanted to stab you in the back, to sacrifice you for a chance at escape."

I am actively sobbing now, leaning into the winged hug. His metal feathers aren't particularly comfortable, but I don't care.

"I'm sorry. I'm sorry those thoughts crossed my mind. I'm sorry I've been so hard to deal with. I'm sorry you haven't been able to go home because of me."

The words, apologies, all my guilt just flows out without restraint. A self-deprecating laugh bubbles up through the sobs. Why am I doing this? We're on our way to start a war, and I'm here crying about an unchangeable past.

"You're free now, right?"

"What?"

"You specified 'were.' The Fog doesn't have its grip on your mind anymore?"

"Uh, yeah," I say. "Back in the regna, I was trapped and fought to regain control."

Grímr nods, as if expecting this. I guess I had passed out for a good few hours. Of course he'd know something happened.

"Don't concern yourself with what happened before then. I am here because I want to be and you never went forward with any of those thoughts, even while your mind wasn't your own."

He looks me in the eye. "Solvei, I don't truly know what you've been through, and you've done incredible to grow as you have, but you can rely on others. After we're done with the mermineae, we'll celebrate you overcoming the Fog. Magnesium is your favorite, right? I've gotten better at telling the difference between metals. We'll go on a search for some, yeah?"

I nod, not lifting my head because of the shame I feel. I'm not a child anymore, so why am I acting like one? Why am I being comforted when Grímr should be angry at me?

I stand and push past Grímr's wing to stare far ahead of us, trying to calm myself down with some distraction. We'll have to fight soon, so I need to get over this. Staying as emotional as I am won't help anyone. It's comforting to know Grímr doesn't blame me, but the knowledge doesn't reduce the guilt I feel.

He's right, I'm free now and I should focus on that.

The hole is visible now, which is concerning. Rather than the thin fissures along the side of the Titan's path, the entrance is now massive. A large section on the border between blackened rock and normal earth has opened. A pit leading to the depths of the mountain.

It is clear now, the battle between the Viisin and Spenne caused more damage than I'd imagined. Strangely, only the ranked stone on the side of the Titan's path is damaged. A near-perfect straight line separates the enhanced stone from the void that drops to the dark cave.

The mermineae aren't visible yet. We already assume the largest congregation of them has already passed into the Alps, so it's not a surprise they aren't populated enough for their camouflage to become ineffective. Hopefully, that means we won't face much opposition.

Without Imiha or Spenne with us, I'm concerned about what will happen if we face a Viisin. Tzilac has assured us they can deal with them, but we've still not really seen them fight. The extent they've shown so far is the harpoons when a bird of prey attacks. The hunters hit them then drag the birds to the earth where they are ended without struggle.

I'd expected to face at least some opposition before we got this close. Unhidden as we are, they would have had days to plan ambushes to slow our approach, but we experienced nothing.

It should be encouraging, as it means there really aren't all that many of them to face, but I feel tense all the same. It might be the concern over the Viisin, or it could be the approach of my dreaded choice.

Finally, at the edge of my range, I feel the heat of a merminea. They scuttle away almost as soon as we reach them, but every few seconds we catch up to them. At the speed we're moving, there's no way we're outpacing a merminea. More likely, they are just watching us from a distance.

A horn blares from off to my left, followed by many more along the line of siege engines. The front of the caravan slows and spreads, allowing the lagging machines to thread between them. In no time, a long line marches toward our target.

"Solvei, Grímr, we'll be starting soon. As we've discussed, please remain with your machine." Tzilac slaps the back of our siege engine in emphasis before moving a row back to his command position.

I've been all but banned from using my fire. Apparently, the heat and visual impairment gets in the way of their machines' effectiveness. For now, I'm stuck using my spear on any mermineae that get close, which is something I've been meaning to do for a while. I need to improve my spearmanship and not rely on my flames for everything. With an army backing me, this is the best possible place to improve.

There are four rows of heavy stone machinery in the centzon's army. The first are the largest contraptions in their arsenal; massive, bulky things that could be mistaken for walls themselves. Egg-shaped machines in the second row cover the gaps between the weapons of the first. The third row—the row we are a part of—contains an array of different sized siege engines.

The final, rear row is a series of towers on wheels. While larger and heavier than the front-line machines, they don't appear anywhere near as dangerous. They are likely only used as command centers for the hunters . . . is what I would think if I hadn't already seen how they their regnas work. I don't believe for a second they are as simple as they seem.

As we reach a league away from the hole, we grind to a halt. Almost as soon as we do, mermineae creep into my range. They are slow, but there are a lot.

"They're sneaking up on us now," I say to Atl, who's our siege engine operator. "About a hundred meters away."

He nods, unsurprised. "We have ways to find them. As much as they think they'll have the jump on us, it has been a very long time since a yoe caught us unprepared." He points to one of the egg-shaped contraptions ahead of us. "Just watch."

Four centzon hunters each pump the crankshaft embedded in the back of the mechanism. Despite their combined strength, they still seem to struggle to spin it. They spin the shaft until it stops moving with a click and slides within. Three of the hunters immediately run back to our row, clambering up both our engine and our neighbors. A similar group does the same further along the line.

The last remaining hunter stands behind the egg contraption holding a lever, but looking ready to bolt at any moment. What are they waiting for? The mermineae are getting closer by the second.

I grip my spear tight as the mermineae prowl within fifty meters of our front line. Even in the small range I can feel, there are already hundreds. It's not nearly the same density as the last time we attacked, but there are still so many.

A siren blares.

The mermineae freeze. The centzon before us pulls the lever and sprints back to the safety of our siege engine.

Nothing happens.

Seconds pass, and I'm ready to turn and question Atl when I hear a heavy clank. Like something falling into place. The egg-shaped contraption springs forward. From stationary, it lurches forward, its uneven form flinging it high into the air as it rolls.

The machine lingers in the air, soaring toward our frozen enemies. As I watch, the skin of the egg twists inside out, leaving the once smooth stone and metal exterior as a disorganized mess of protruding blades and spikes.

A few hundred meters to each side, I catch sight of a couple more of the egg-contraptions flying.

The weapon slams into the ground just outside my sense range, but the bright red blood dyeing the snow leaves no doubt of the deaths inflicted upon its first bounce. On the second impact, the egg hits the tapered end and bounces back our way, tearing through dozens of mermineae as it does.

We made the first attack, but our enemies don't stand and take it. The thousands discard attempts at subtlety and sprint toward us. Forvaal amongst their ranks work to melt away the weapons shredding through them, but the eggs prove to be self-propelled and continue to roll around in completely random directions.

The rest of the centzon army hasn't been stationary in the meantime. The front line of siege engines flare walls of stone wide, clanking as they lock with their neighbors. I knew the centzon liked their walls, but to bring one to the battlefield?

I quickly learn that those leading machines carried not only their walls. As the mermineae throw themselves at the wall, they find themselves limbless. I can't see what cut into them, but what I can is the transformation of vehicles holding the walls.

The wheels twist sideways, and the machine decouples from the wall. Now, each moves along the newly set defensive structure with the smooth effortlessness of a rail. A crew works a series of controls to direct the machine. A piston slides out the back as the centzon pump their cranks and I finally get an answer to their purpose; the piston disappears from my sight, but the congregating mass of mermineae on the other side of the wall are either pulped or sent flying.

"Good, right?" Atl grins down at me. My awe must be showing on my face.

They've barely even dipped into their collection of machinery and yet the mermineae can't do anything. The egg in the distance finally slows to a halt, the Forvaal melting away enough of it to stop it doing anything more than spinning on the spot.

It spins for a few seconds, but when it's clear it isn't moving, the mermineae ignore it . . . which is a mistake. The egg explodes. Hundreds of blades and spikes from the remains of its exterior burst outward, ripping through hundreds of mermineae unlucky enough to be nearby.

Atl laughs at my side. "They never learn."

The gaze Grímr passes over the battlefield is far different. Concern and resignation the most I can pick out from his body language.

Well, at least it'll be an easy fight.

CHAPTER TWENTY-TWO

An Easy Fight II

Despite their losses, the mermineae continue to throw themselves against the centzon's defensive wall. Their efforts often in vain as the wall itself tears them apart and the slingshot ram plows through any that remain.

I'm not sure how that massive piston works, as the wall still appears fully intact whenever it rolls away. Then again, I don't really understand how any of their machinery works.

Several mermineae jump over the wall, bypassing the defense entirely, but are shot out of the sky by the harpoon launchers or descended upon by the hunters with their own weapons.

I finally get my first look at what those logs can do. Some hunters' contraptions become spinning saws that remind me of Grímr's plumage. They cut right through the mermineae with hardly any application of force. Is that what is on the other side of the wall? Do spinning blades bisect our attackers?

The buzzing saw is by far the hunters' favorite weapon against the mermineae, but there are some that use different forms. A piston with a spike or blunt head used with enough force to kill in one strike, regardless of impact point. A shoulder mounted cannon that pelts the mermineae with hundreds of tiny pellets that remind me far too much of those bullets used by the albanics.

I haven't seen a single use of water. It is relieving to find their weapons aren't filled with water ready to attack me. Though, it's still possible they are carrying some with them. Hopefully, without the river to pump water from, they won't be able to hurt me easily.

I shake my head to clear the suspecting thoughts. They've yet to show anything suspicious. I can't keep treating everyone I meet like they're looking for ways to end my life or steal my freedom the moment I turn my back.

I've been in plenty of vulnerable states while with them, and they haven't once tried to end me. After I'd regained the freedom of my mind, I'd spent days in an exhausted haze. If they'd attacked us then, I wouldn't have survived.

They've already proven they are on our side—at least for the time being—so I should try being more trusting.

The machinery from our row finally joins the fight. Our two adjacent siege engines unfold into three large spinning wheels cutting into a wide tube. In moments, the machine flings a boulder half as tall as I am over the wall and into the mass of mermineae.

I can't follow its path after it passed the wall, but I can definitely track the corpses it leaves behind. The stone rolls far further than it should, considering its arc. But that isn't the weirdest thing. It doesn't tear through them in a straight line. It curves far off to the left, even taking some mermineae in their sides.

"You idiot!" I hear the shout from the origin of the boulder. "Match your ammo to the enemy!" The other hunters on the weapon grumble, but got to work.

The next projectile out of the machine appears much the same at first; a stone sphere, but it quickly becomes apparent the difference between this boulder and the last. The ball splits into several flat discs that fan out as they pass the wall. Spinning at an astonishing rate, they hover through the air before the mermineae find themselves once again at the mercy of the hunters' weaponry.

Some discs continue spinning out of the range of my senses, slicing through any not hugging the ground close enough. Others' flights are disturbed, and tumble along the earth like runaway wheels, but still sharp and fast enough to cut.

I glance down at my spear. I'm not going to get the chance to practice, am I?

"Is it usually this easy for you?" I ask.

Grímr's eyes finally snap away from the bloodshed before us. He looks like he wants to say something, his eyes darting between me and Atl, but keeps his silence.

"Against the yoe? Yeah, they never learn. We adapted to their swarm methods centuries ago and they've never thought to try anything different. But what can you expect from animals?" He shakes his head with a sigh. "The cult is a different story. The unnatural power of theirs can be rather frustrating."

As he says that, a portion of the wall before us decays before our eyes. A concentrated effort of the Forvaal must have finally breached our defenses.

"But we've worked on countermeasures."

An egg-shaped contraption launches through the new gap in the wall, obliterating the many trying to rush through. Like the first ones, this egg spins and jumps around amongst the mermineae without resistance.

Each of the rams along the wall stops. They dig into the ground and instead of moving along the fortified walls, they lift the wall and push it inward. The damaged section is ejected, and the wall locks in place, reformed. In only a few seconds, the rams are back to slamming through groups of mermineae and the breach is closed.

"But the cultists are still yoe at their core. They never learn. Never adapt."

We stand there for a minute, just watching the never-ending swarm of mermineae continue to throw themselves to their deaths. Near the edges of our lines, they try to move around us, but what appear to be far more controlled versions of the egg weapon protect our flanks. The large wheels move fast and cut off the enemy's attempts at repositioning.

Another new siren blares from the towers behind us. Immediately, most of the hunters around us abandon the siege engines, leaving only a few to continue their operation.

Atl clambers off the side of our own. "We've spotted a cult leader. It's time to leave if you don't want to get caught in the crossfire."

The hunters trigger the rest of the egg-contraptions which bound over the wall as their operators flee to the rear of our formation. The hunters controlling the moving wall rams jump off and follow.

Grímr and I climb off our siege engine—which has yet to see any use—and join Atl as he flicks a lever and runs for the back towers.

Despite not having any more operators, the pistons along the wall continue to slide along and hammer through the wall.

"If you don't need to be on them to operate, then why have any hunters manning the machines in the first place?" I ask.

"They can only run a short while with no one to operate the cranks," Atl says and points to a ram. "If you pay attention, the piston has a repetitive pattern. Without a hunter to guide it, they need to rely on simple cycles."

He is right. There are only three places where the ram breaks through the wall now, rotating through each in order. The Forvaal decay another hole through the wall, but the machines don't close the gap as they did before. Mermineae flood through, still struggling to break through the barrage of projectiles.

The command towers groan as we pass them. I glance up, unsurprised to see the first stages of a transformation. The walls twist and the upper platform of stone slides outward. Even at my low angle, the long barrel is easily visible as it rises high into the air.

It is entirely made of that strange metal the centzon use. The tower rattles as the barrel stops rising. It spins as it angles down on the front line, exposing an absolutely huge contraption at the barrel's base. Each of the commanders jump off the flat viewing platforms and take a position upon the machine.

We make it to the rear of the towers, each of which now supporting its own long barrel as an explosion erupts from the wall. The wall is well out of my sense range now, so I have to twist on my feet to see the source of the explosion.

A dust cloud billows from a wide missing section in our defense. It's not far from the breach left by the Forvaal, but it is easily on a far greater scale. The Viisin is finally here.

Barely visible through the smoke and ash is a silhouette of our greatest threat. The centzon have shown absolute superiority until now, but I struggle to see how they could beat this being. I saw it shrug off decapitation, after all. It jumps forward, obliterating the first siege engine on touch.

In near-perfect unison, the towers unload on the Viisin. The massive barrels launch another projectile every second, loud clanks and thunks proceeding each blast. The sustained fire from hundreds of rounds does more damage to our defenses than the Viisin has yet managed.

Despite the damage it takes, it stands strong. Legs, arms, its head; it doesn't matter what part of the Viisin's body is annihilated, it heals through it.

It doesn't take any permanent damage, but the continuous fire prevents it from advancing. Instead, it dashes to the side, intent on destroying much of the other defenses and siege engines along our line. Some of the projectile launchers throwing spinning disks hit the Viisin, but they decay on contact with its skin, leaving no damage at all.

This isn't all they have planned, right? It's obviously not effective. Even if the cannons are incredibly powerful, it means nothing if we can't kill the Viisin. I glance to Atl at my side, but he seems completely unfazed by the ineffectiveness of their weapons.

He turns to me and I look away, but I'm too late.

"Don't worry, this is just supposed to stop the cult leader from approaching. Normal projectiles don't work on them. We have these auto-cannons to blast it with special, pressurized capsules that explode upon impact and pelt them with shrapnel designed to decay far slower than normal. It lets us actually hurt them."

Hundreds of mermineae rush through the new breaches made by a combination of Forvaal, Viisin, and auto-cannon efforts. I now realize that many of the machines after the wall are long range, so the swarm of mermineae faces almost no opposition until they reach the siege weapon Grímr and I rode on.

The mermineae must trigger some mechanism as the—until now—unused machines now blast liquid all over the attackers.

I clench my fist. For a moment, anger bubbles in me as I realize they had me riding on the machine they'd filled with water. But that anger quickly fades as I notice the liquid is black. It's not water.

Each of the strange liquid carrying machines starts rolling forward, pushing past the mermineae and coating them all as they pass.

Atl touches my shoulder. "I know we said to hold back, but you can go ahead for now. Try not to damage our machines, please."

I look at him, confused, before sliding my attention to the now visible black mermineae. Unsure, I throw a stream of flame forward, careful to keep my inner flame away from the liquid. As soon as a single spark touches the black substance, everything before me engulfs in fire.

My eyes widen and I quickly shove everything into the fire. The liquid is unlike anything I've felt before. It's like the flammable jelly down in the tunnels, but amplified, compressed, and oh, so much more tasty. My fire spreads over everything in an instant.

My flames are pushed far hotter than they've ever been, glowing bright yellow, then white, then strangely, they disappear. Well, they disappear from my sight, but I know they're still there, burning and incinerating anything they touch. It's a struggle to hold myself back from annihilating those contraptions so inconveniently in my way.

"Don't touch the oil-wagons," Atl says, only barely quick enough for me to stop eating my way up the streams.

Each of the wagons now rolls past the remains of the wall, coating every merminea it passes in my new favorite food . . . or, I guess, drink. That feels strange to think. I've never drunk anything before.

The mermineae and the Forvaal amongst them try their hardest to break the machines, but an extra thick layer of the centzon's strange metal delays their attempts.

"How do you deal with something that can not only brush off most attacks, but will actively recover from the hits that reach them?" Atl asks suddenly.

The Viisin stops plowing through the defenses and throws itself toward the oil-wagons now deep amongst the mermineae.

"You hit them so hard they don't have a chance to recover."

The Viisin lands on the wagon and that's the last thing it does. There's a flash of light and my flame involuntarily rockets through the air, spreading with an intensity I've never felt. Only a moment later does the blast rattle my body.

Atl pulls me out of my stupor. He drags me under the arch of the tower, alongside Grímr and all the other centzon. After a few moments, a rain of metal shards falls from the sky. I listen to the rapid thunks as the shrapnel pelts the tower above us.

I can't feel the Viisin anymore. Either it is dead, or it is now outside the spreading flame.

I shake off Atl's grip and poke my head around the side of the tower. Smoke rises hundreds of meters in the air before curving outward. My flames linger within the rising clouds.

What was that? It felt more intense than being hit by Spenne's lightning. I almost missed it, but in the fraction of a second, I felt heat near incomprehensible. Something I've never felt before. Lightning was similar, but there was some distinction between the feelings.

The mermineae that remain now flee. I really don't understand how they could keep trying to overwhelm us when they saw their kin dying by the hundreds before their eyes, but at least now they give up.

Unfortunately, they flee down into the Alps. Don't they know we are here to cut our way back to the east? They are going to die by going down there. Is their god, Kalma, really more terrifying than facing the centzon?

The memory of Hund tearing through an army is all the answer I need.

At least we know the centzon can fight off the Viisin. Hopefully, we won't have to deal with any others until we reach home.

Huh . . . I guess I've already decided.

We're going home.

CHAPTER TWENTY-THREE

Fortified

The breeze through my feathers is amazing. I've been too hesitant to just spread my wings and fly lately. It's mainly because of the threat of those giant birds that could be anywhere, but I really should have tried flying in proximity to Grímr's huge form earlier.

My friend is keeping his word about finding me a magnesium deposit. I'm not sure exactly how he can tell where to look, but he says it's like having a third eye; there are some colors he can see that his past bodies couldn't.

After the obliteration of the Viisin, we faced no opposition as we moved to the vast hole. The centzon made short work of converting their machines into fortifications. Within a day, they already had their field of traps set up and that moving wall aligned over the ledge.

There were still several oil-wagons that survived the explosion. I'd watched the hunters repurpose the thing into one of their traps.

I'm not sure how I feel about them leaving bombs as strong as those lying around.

. . . I wonder if they'll give me some of that oil if I ask?

The two of us soar along for a few hours until Grímr finds a deposit. I take the time to enjoy myself, knowing that the moment we enter the tunnels, I'll be back to that constant stress.

I still need to tell Grímr that I've decided, but . . . there's a difference between telling myself I'm ready, and actually saying it. Grímr has been kind enough not to push me. Even as much as he wants to go back, he considers my opinion before anything else. I have to tell him, but I want to extend the time I have just a little.

I suppress the pang of guilt that rises from my selfishness.

Grímr slows his descent and touches down with an ease he couldn't have managed a month ago. He takes barely any time to slice his wings into the earth and dig. I could probably just melt my way down, but if I didn't want to leave a pool of molten sludge, I'd have to eat all that rock. Not an appealing prospect.

Grímr tears through the earth. His metal feathers slam into stone and come back unmarred. As thin as they are, I'd assume they'd bend easily, but no, they stay straight and sharp.

A large chunk of our target clunks on the ground before me. It's the good stuff! I quickly engulf the magnesium-filled rock with my flames, enjoying the unique crackling as I peel it away from the stone wrapping it. I leave a small chunk to swallow. As it reaches the inside of my body, I enjoy the burst of heat that ignites once it warms enough.

Grímr chomps through a slab of his own as he climbs out of the deep hole and lays at my side. We stay there for a while, simply relaxing before we have to return to our responsibilities. Grímr is quiet, but his presence is comforting.

"I think I'll be fine now, Grímr. Let's go back. Let's go home."

He turns to me, surprised, but soon it morphs to concern.

"Solvei . . . I appreciate it, but there's no need to force yourself into this."

"No. I can do it," I say before he can continue. If he gives me a reason to back down, it might tempt me. I need to do this. If I don't push myself through this challenge now, then what will happen next time? Will I cower and back away then? I don't want that to be who I am.

Those I trust—those I care for—I don't want to leave them in danger. I want to protect them. Even if that means I have to push myself.

"It will be hard . . . but this is something I need to do. I'll never be able to return if I don't force myself now."

Grímr gives me an encouraging smile . . . or at least his eyes and body give off that impression. His metal beak isn't exactly capable of facial expression.

"I'm proud of you, Solvei."

It had been hardly a week, and yet the centzon's fortress had grown far more than I'd expected. The defensive wall now completely encircles the massive hole in the earth. They'd hidden their trap field now, too.

Between the repurposed siege engines and a convoy of materials from the nearest regna, they'd put together an impressive defense. One that had been tested regularly by the mermineae still down inside the earth. None of their attacks were any more than probing strikes by the mermineae that didn't even have decay eyes, so the centzon had no troubles warding them off.

Now is the time I'd been dreading for days. I'd agreed to challenge the depths again, and I will have Grímr by my side, but it's still nerve-racking as I stare down into the dark cavern that hides those massive arachnids and centipedes.

We'll be making our way back through the Alps, leading the centzon the entire way. Because of Grímr's size, we'll be traveling through the caverns, only digging down into the tunnels when we come across those massive cave walls.

I'll have to go back to keeping my flames hidden, which isn't something I'm looking forward to, but at least I'll have more time to practice my spear.

"Here." Atl hands me a canteen that appears no different from the containers they use to hold water.

I hold the thing far from my body and give him a conflicted glance. Why exactly is he handing me water? Is this a threat? No, I shouldn't assume the worst; they've proven their trustworthiness enough by now.

"Oh, don't give me that look," Atl huffs. "Open it."

My eyes linger on him a moment longer, looking for anything I should be concerned about, but see nothing. With hesitance, I twist the lid as slowly as I can and hold the bottle away from me. Once the cap separates from the container, I swoon at the scent.

He's given me a canteen of that hyperflammable black oil. It smells incredible.

Atl chuckles. "You better portion it out. We won't be able to take our war machines with us, so we can't carry any more."

I take a deep breath of the fumes coming out of the bottle. Yeah, definitely better than the explosive jelly in the glow-bug traps.

"Thank you," I say as I reluctantly replace the lid.

I wish they'd given me a different type of container, though; I'll be nervous about a mix-up every time I open it.

Thunder rumbles in the distance. I look up, expecting to see an approaching storm . . . but there's nothing. Not even a cloud in the sky.

Wait, Spenne?

I'm proven right when, in the distance, a branching flash of light spreads across the horizon. The thunder rolls over us seconds later, but by then I see more lightning bolts fork outward. The áinfean quickly appears, zipping across the earth in jagged motions.

Now able to see Spenne, I realize he's not alone. Explosions of ash blow into the air each time he makes a jagged motion in his sprint. The distance closes incredibly quickly and the sirens of the fort ring out around me. I can see him clearly now. His white wraps are in tatters, exposing his electric body to the world.

He's being chased by Viisin. Not one. There are four of them behind him, and Spenne's leading them right to us.

I immediately rocket toward the nearest tower, burning an immense amount of energy to blast myself forward with a jet of physical flame. The centzon don't know that Spenne is on our side. They're just as likely to hit him with those massive explosions as they are the Viisin.

I slam into the tower and tumble onto the viewing platform. With how urgent this is, I care little for a stable flight.

"The lightning elemental is a friend," I shout to Tzilac over the blaring alarm, using their own term for our races.

The hunter leader barely looks my way before pulling a lever amongst the tens at his side. "The way is open. Make sure he comes to our tower and our tower only," he orders.

I assume he means the only safe path is directly to us, so I spread my flames, not to burn anything, but to show the áinfean that I'm here and guide him. My fire spreads wide so he couldn't possibly miss it, before concentrating it on a thin line between him and myself.

Spenne turns in mid-sprint and flings out a lightning bolt that chains between the four chasing him. Each of them stumbles and collapses, but it isn't enough to kill them, just halt the chase until their legs regrow.

Fortunately, the áinfean understands my signal and stops dodging to the sides. He runs directly for us. The moment he's within a dozen meters of the tower, Tzilac slams the lever back into place. Just in time too; the lead Viisin follows the path Spenne took, but runs right into the field of reactivated traps.

The Viisin has absolutely no time to react once the ground beneath it opens and snaps around it. Like the trap that originally pulled me into the earth, the teeth cut right through the Viisin. But unlike the one I experienced, it doesn't drag the creature underground. It simply holds the Viisin still for a second.

And that is all that's needed.

While the gifted merminea is stuck, the earth opens to its side and a barrel of metal taller than I am flings toward the Viisin. The creature can do nothing but watch its incoming doom.

My body shakes from the explosion. Like the one a week ago, I can feel the tremors through the earth as a blast of air rushes past me. Once again, a shower of shrapnel rains down from above. I belatedly note pieces of metal wedged into the ceiling a short distance above my head. I'd completely missed those over the quaking explosion.

I jump as a hand lands on my shoulder. "Whoa, that's quite the bomb you've got there."

Spenne stands over me, somehow getting here in the few moments since I'd lost track of him.

"Thanks, kid, I owe ya one." He looks up at the centzon still looking out over the trap field. "And to this group too, it looks."

There are barely any white straps around him anymore. The arcing electricity of his body continually flows out of his feet and tail, scorching the stone ground. Is he unable to stop it? Is that why he wore those straps?

It takes a while for the smoke to clear. We wait, ready for the last three Viisin to jump over the trap fields and attack us, but they don't come. Eventually, it clears enough to see, but the trio just stand there, watching us.

"What are they doing?" I ask. I know that one of the other Viisin just died before their eyes, but I've seen them jump far distances before. Why don't they just jump over the field of traps?

"If there's one thing the cultists and yoe have learned, it is to never attack our fortifications," Tzilac says. His hands never leave a set of levers while his eyes stay locked on the Viisin. "They know how futile the attempt would be."

The Viisin pace around the centzon's walls for a while, obviously frustrated. After a tense half hour, they turn on their heel and dash away.

Were these Viisin a part of the fleeing mermineae? Or the ones trying to stop them? If it's the latter, then there shouldn't be an issue with the centzon setting up here. But in that case, why were they chasing Spenne?

"What did you do?" I accuse.

"Hey! Nothing! They just came after me," he says with arms raised in defense. "Unless they somehow realized I found out what they were up to."

"What they were up to?"

"You're not going to like this, but the Viisin have been hunting down other Beiths for months now. I think I'd just become their latest target."

I'm not sure why he'd think I care. It's his and the other Beith's fault we're in this mess. If they hadn't opened the path through the Alps, none of this would have happened.

"We should get going. We were ready to leave before you showed up. Now that you're being targeted, are you joining us?" I ask as I step on the rail of the tower.

Spenne breathes in deep, before letting it all out in a huff. "I hate running, but even I know when I'm outmatched. I could take one, not their whole fucking hit squad. It was fun while it lasted."

"All right, then." I jump off the tower, ready to meet with Grímr, and finally face the Alps again.

Dropping into the enormous cavern again turned out to be easier than I'd anticipated. Sure, I am nervous to be under the earth, but actually being down here, and not experiencing any of those past horrors, is a relief.

I glance around. The glow-bugs are nowhere to be seen. We've traveled quite far now and yet they still don't appear. Back in the cavern we dropped into, with the sunlight shining through the half-circle in the ceiling, it had seemed empty, but I'd assumed that would change as we follow the path of destruction I leftover a month ago.

It hasn't.

No matter how far we lead the centzon through the cavern, the glow-bugs never appear. Unfortunate. I'd been hoping for another snack on our way through.

It's not all bad though, the giant residents of this cavern seem to have left with the glow-bugs. I know this for sure, simply because Spenne seems completely unwilling to control his lightning. We keep him at the front where we won't be hit when the arachnid monstrosities inevitably drop on him.

But miraculously, despite shining like a thousand glow-bugs, he remains unattacked.

The tunnels I exploded through on my way here are still as charred and dug up as I left them. No more of that explosive jelly to play around with.

Well, whatever happened to all the creatures down here, it's given us a clear path to follow and no need to creep around. Unfortunately, it is clear the mermineae use the lack of danger up here to their own advantage. With the centzon and Spenne, we have no trouble fending them off, but that I left them with such a clear path to our home is troubling.

After a while of traveling with the centzon, Tzilac confirms his ability to both follow the damage I left behind and track the passage of the mermineae. We agree to meet them once he and his hundred centzon hunters make their way to the other side of the Alps.

So Grímr, Spenne, and I take advantage of the concerning lack of monstrosities in these caves to cut our expected travel time to a mere fraction. I fly on Grímr's back, while Spenne remains as bait ahead of us. Our áinfean's not too happy about his role, but he did say he owed me one.

Hopefully, the mermineae haven't caused too much damage by the time we return.

CHAPTER TWENTY-FOUR

Doe

Doe opened the set of double doors with a calm poise that poorly reflected her inner turmoil. The commandeered town hall was an old, rickety wooden building that was closer to a cabin than the command post it had become.

She wasn't happy to be this close to the war zone, but she'd been given orders—with no uncertain terms—that she was required to be here. Why? She did not know.

Ever since the team under her management went missing, she'd been stuck in a limbo of paperwork and concern. Most of her time was spent trying to clean up the mess Remus and his new adoptee caused in Joiak. The kingdom had pulled all funding from the Mercenary Order. Of course, the Order wasn't about to take that—regardless of whether the problem was made by one of their own or not—and pulled out the mercenaries in the nation.

Only a few bottom-rung Saille teams had been left to satisfy the terms of the pact signed by each nation.

It was an open secret that a nation only got as much defense as it paid. Originally, the Order was a shared army between the nations of the pact. It would protect the borders of each country as if they were all one collective, and each nation would invest in the cause.

That model had barely lasted a generation. Nations that didn't have contested borders started pulling back on their funding. Disputes between two nations of the pact also couldn't take advantage of their shared army, which led to many relying on their own militaries again.

After many failed reworks of the treaty, the current system of hired military had formed; the birth of a horrid cesspool of corruption and bribery. Its flaws—major as they were—still better than the alternatives.

Doe had to wonder how Joiak was handling the sudden invasion. Not well, she predicted.

These new creatures appeared from nowhere and within a month had already taken South Boreen and cut the Joiak Kingdom off from the rest of the pact.

Doe took some sadistic delight in that. They'd been giving her so much grief recently, considering negotiations with them had been dropped on her shoulders. The Order wanted her to fix the mistakes of the team she was supposed to control, despite knowing just how fickle mercenaries could be.

Joiak had wanted the head of the girl Remus brought back, but there were two problems with that. First, she was Remus's choice for replacement. The old dohrni had become incredibly picky with who he allowed on the team. She'd been trying for months to find a mage he would accept before he found her.

The second problem . . . well, she'd disappeared along with her team. They could hardly have the head of someone who they couldn't find.

"Commander Darton is expecting me. Where can I find him?" Doe asked one of the two dohrni scratching away in their logbooks at the front desk. Dozens of team managers like herself rushed in and out of the surrounding rooms.

"Doe Maral, I presume?" she said, not looking up from her notes. "He's waiting. Furthest room up the stairs."

Doe gave a nod and said her gratitude, hiding her annoyance at the lack of respect shown. She stepped toward the set of stairs at the back of the foyer. She needed to remain civil and not let others' rude, dismissive attitudes impede her work.

She didn't know why she'd been called here. Without her team to direct any orders toward, she could only think of a couple reasons they might ask for her. The knowledge from her talks with Joiak, or her team had come back.

The former was far more likely. Any team missing in action for more than a month—particularly once they'd passed the crevasse to the Lower Elevation—was as good as dead.

It was unfortunate, as it meant she would likely be stuck with a Fearn team for a while before she could find herself in charge of another Luis. Direct management for a Beith seemed impossible now, especially with over half the Beith roster having up and disappeared.

She'd been so close to that promotion.

Only a few weeks before the invasion from the west—by a race never seen before—there had been word spreading that the Beiths were gone. Most of her colleagues had considered this blatant misinformation, with the Henosis Empire as the most likely instigator.

A meeting with her superiors had revealed the truth. The strongest defenders of the Order had up and fancied off to some new land, whisked away by the thought of growth.

The top brass had fired the Beith's managers for failing to control them, but Doe knew that was just them trying to pass the blame and save their own asses.

This was a failure of the system.

For so long, they'd bridled their strongest mercenaries with the temptation of supporting their growth. It was not easy for someone to become as strong as the Beiths, so they usually gave those that found success plenty of support, regardless of their personalities. As long as they had no ties outside the pact nations, the only thing that mattered was the strength they could return to the organization.

Enabling those with dubious loyalty was an obvious mistake in hindsight, but controlling those whose sole desire was strength was simple when you held the only path for them. It was impossible to predict they would abandon their role without the knowledge that there was another path.

At least it made sense why they wanted Doe's team to investigate. Remus was both experienced and trustworthy. They hadn't sent him and his team up the Alps and out of their depth for a simple punishment. They'd sent them there because they'd lost trust in the Beiths.

Well, the brass could have sent their hounds—the Order's loyal Inner Circle that had been given more opportunities for growth than any Beith—but like any nation's elite, they would remain hidden until no other option remained.

Doe arrived before the large wooden door that led to the commander's office. The second floor was near empty, unlike below. Only one of her khirig kin worked away at a desk beside the door, ignoring her as she stepped forward.

Doe made sure her antlers were as clean and sleek as ever and patted down her robe-suit before she rapped her thin bone digits on the wood. The door opened and she was led in before she registered who answered the door.

Remus gave her that idiotic eye-grin of his as she stared.

"You're not dead," she stated after collecting herself. This was good. She wouldn't have to worry about a demotion if he was still around.

"How kind of you to notice." His mouthless grin only seemed to widen. "It's good to see you, too."

"Where's the rest of your team?" Doe asked as he led her to the desk of the commander she was here to meet. She quickly gave a bow to her superior. Low enough to show respect, but not so low that she might come across as lower in standing. While he was technically higher rank than her, she had the greater bureaucratic power. "I am here as ordered, sir. I assume Remus is the reason I'm here?"

"Hmm, yes. We'll catch you up with that in a moment," Commander Darton said from his place behind the large desk.

"I sent Jav back to his family. Despite his wishes, I believed he needed some time to recover."

Sending his partner home at the beginning of a war? Doe worried that the old man might not be taking this seriously, but she also wasn't particularly knowledgeable about the state of the war, so she held her tongue.

"We met Princess Imiha while we were gone. Her and Bunny have gone to convince their homes to take this threat as seriously as possible."

The former Princess of Meja was one of the Beiths that had abandoned the pact nations? That was not something Doe had expected.

"While that sounds great," Darton said. "We shouldn't expect any help from the Vanguard. I received word yesterday that the Theocracy has launched their own war."

"That isn't good. We'll need everything to fight off the mermineae invasion. They aren't something we can ignore," Remus said.

Doe couldn't argue there. These mermineae had wiped South Boreen off the map within a week of their first appearance.

Darton nodded, as if he'd heard this before. "We won't, but this is still not the worst possible circumstance. We've been concerned about the Empire to the east. They've been poking at our defenses for a good month now. If they were to attack, and if these mermineae continue their relentlessness, then I'm afraid there might be nothing we can do."

"Regardless of the action Henosis takes, we cannot hold anything back. That is our only chance," Remus emphasized for the second time. Doe could tell when someone was trying to convince her of something, she just didn't know what these two wanted from her yet.

"What happened to the rest of your team? The portian? The áed?"

Doe hadn't known the kid was an áed when she'd met her. She didn't even know what an áed was at the time. She'd thought the kid was an insane albanic, or at least the child of an insane albanic that forced fire markings on her.

Fire mages had the unfortunate caricature of being completely masochistic or mad. That was the only explanation one could have for setting their own body on fire for the sake of using the element.

When she'd seen the literal fire in the young girl's eyes, Doe could admit to being unnerved. From what little she knew about mage markings, they only went skin deep. To burn one's own eyes and not flinch seemed impossible.

But it turned out her assumptions had been wrong. She was an áed; a race adjacent to the áinfean. In a way, it was like a bucket of cold water over her initial fright.

"Grímr and Solvei are still on the other side of the Alps. There were some circumstances. They're staying over there for the time being."

She'd heard it before, but it still mystified Doe that these invaders came from beyond those titanic mountains. She'd grown up with nothing but fairy tales about what was beyond, but nobody was supposed to have found a way through. Now? An entire alien army had come. It seemed unreal.

"Come here. Let's not waste what time we have," the khirig commander grunted. "This is the land they have taken so far. They cut us off from Joiak, so we have no intelligence in that regard, but we expect them to hold out for a few weeks at the very least. They may lack the Order's support, but they are wealthy enough to have their own elites tucked away, I'm sure."

Doe took the invitation and glanced over the map. As she'd expected, the entirety of South Boreen had been taken, from the Alps all the way to the Vanguard's border. What did surprise her, though, was the line drawn up along the Alps. It rose as far north as Meja.

"Why haven't we stopped them along the Alps?" she wondered aloud.

"Have you forgotten your history lessons?" Darton asked. "Setting up defensive positions along the Alps would be asking for a massacre. The mermineae only seem capable of this due to their race's natural camouflaging and familiarity with such danger." He looked to Remus for confirmation.

The dohrni nodded. "What's even more concerning is that each of them is naturally as strong as the average Fearn, with plenty far greater. The only thing we really have in our favor is the lack of variation in the way they fight. Once you've fought one of their Forvaal, you've fought them all. While I'd like that to sound reassuring, the average Forvaal is about as strong as I am, and there are likely thousands."

"Are there any stronger than the Forvaal?" the commander asked, sounding suspiciously rehearsed.

"I never met one, but what are the odds that there aren't? I'd bet on there being plenty at least equivalent to the Order's Inner Circle," Remus said, looking directly at Doe, despite the question coming from Darton.

Ah. She knew what they wanted from her now.

"So, Doe. Are you willing to do this tiny little thing for us?" Remus pleaded.

"Tiny? I'll be demoted for even bringing it up!"

"But if we fight this war how it would normally play out, everyone will be dead by the time we bring them into play." The commander slammed the flat edge of his arm's antlers on the desk, sending the map and a stack of papers tumbling to the floor. It wasn't particularly intimidating, considering Doe had spent most of her career surrounded by powerful mercenaries.

Remus motioned at Darton to calm down and stepped before Doe. "With all the Beith's managers already demoted, you are one of the highest ranked in the Order that has direct communication with the top brass. If you don't convince them, you won't have a career. The Mercenary Order will be done."

Remus curled a tentacle to one of the subtle pouches beneath each of his six limbs and pulled out a letter. "If nothing else, please deliver this to Ankor. He and the others I know should at least put pressure on the brass from the inside."

Doe ran her digits along her antler cage, creating an irritating scratching noise. It was an old stress habit she'd thought she'd moved on from.

She didn't want to even consider the idea of approaching her superiors about this. Demotion wasn't even the most concerning risk she'd take on. She could be labeled a traitor. Put to death. What if they listened to her and the hounds died? They would lay the blame entirely on her.

Even if Remus's letter would have the Inner Circle act themselves, getting permission to visit any of them was difficult in itself.

"I'll have to think about this," she said, snatched the envelope, and made her way out of the office without waiting for dismissal.

How would she even approach that meeting? She'd have to soften them up first. Maybe she'd take them out to a nice restaurant before having them choke on their food as she made her proposal. At least then she wouldn't have to deal with the fallout; they'd be dead.

Was she really going to go through with this? Could she convince them to unleash the Inner Circle?

CHAPTER TWENTY-FIVE

Return

There was no way for us to remain hidden during our journey, both because of the pace we kept and Spenne's complete disregard for subtlety. While running past thousands of mermineae we pretended not to notice, I'd once asked him why he didn't control his electricity. He'd looked at me like I'd grown a second head. Apparently, áinfean are much like the Agni tribes in that they don't bother controlling their bodies.

Luckily for the mermineae, they freeze whenever they notice us, clearly not knowing how visible they are to my eyes. I've considered burning through them as we travel, but Grímr has been adamantly against it. I'm not sure why. Their race has done nothing but cause problems for us.

It's not like it would have been reasonable for me to go through with it, anyway. Despite only cutting away the tiniest portion of the mermineae's army, I would tire out far too fast spreading my flames like that.

So, we run without acknowledging their presence. For three weeks.

While a far shorter duration than my last trip, the time still feels like centuries. I may have overcome the limitations on my mind, but I don't think I could ever be comfortable underground. It doesn't help that we're on a timer. The longer we take, the more damage the mermineae might do.

The entire path I had originally taken is clear of its usual residents. Fortunately—making our trip easy. And unfortunately—providing the same ease for the mermineae.

It's relieving we don't have to deal with the monstrosities, but those very monstrosities could have wiped out a sizeable chunk of our problem.

Far ahead of us, light finally breaches through the permeating darkness. Three weeks with nothing to look at beside Spenne's backside hasn't been fun.

I perk up on Grímr's back, abandoning my latest attempt at breaching the wall I'd been stuck slamming against for so long. I'm not the only one to notice. Grímr's metal feathers flutter beneath me and Spenne's body involuntarily zaps the ground around him.

The air charges with static, and I don't have to see the number of mermineae that lay ahead to know he's preparing to attack.

I throw myself off Grímr without so much as a thought to the danger. With a risky burst of flame, I slam into the áinfean's back and try to pull him back.

"Don't you dare!"

He jerks his head back at me, confusion marring his face. "Why not?"

As he sprints forward, the density of mermineae grows, confirming the likely scenario of our approach on the exit.

"You think they don't have Viisin at this exit? If you attack, you'll bring them down on us."

"Great! I'm feeling good and ready to take 'em on again."

I groan and try to tug his head back, but he doesn't budge.

"Grímr and I need to get back to the others. Can you at least wait until we are out of the way before you try to kill yourself?"

Spenne hums in consideration. The thunder rumbles through my chest from the contact.

"All right. But I want you to join me for another battle in the coming war."

"Fine!" I throw myself off his back as he veers off to the side.

Grímr slows his flight and I jump on his back. With how long I've spent riding the large alicanto recently, I've had plenty of time to practice my balance. My balance isn't the only thing I've been trying to improve, but it is by far the only focus that has led to growth.

The heat of my flame, my control, focus, and binding are all aspects that just don't seem to want to improve, no matter how hard I try. Well, I don't even know how to improve my binding in the first place, but I'm sure it's possible.

So when I wasn't banging my head against one of those walls, I was staving off boredom by practicing my balance and spear-work. The same way Bunny first trained me. Even if it had been at my request, Spenne had been a bit too happy to throw rocks and electric arcs my way.

As we move a few leagues off the side of my path of destruction, the glow-bugs become apparent once more. There aren't many, and they concentrate far off in the distant dark, but it is a sign that they are specifically avoiding the area where there are no more bug-traps.

If there had ever been any doubt of me being the root cause of the missing ecosystem, it is clear now. It is entirely because of my greed and hunger that an uncontested path is available to the mermineae. I'm not sure what to think about this. If I hadn't done what I did, I wouldn't have had the power to free my team. But having done so might have doomed our home.

No. It's stupid to think that; they could already make it across the Alps even with all the dangers of the caverns. At worst, I just cut the time it took them to pass.

"You think the rest of the team got through okay?" I ask Grímr. The thought has bothered me for a while now. Imiha is strong and can probably fight off however many Forvaal they face, but she can't compete with a Viisin. Do they even know about the Viisin?

"I trust Remus enough to believe they'll get through fine. He's not the strongest, but he's got more experience in situations like this than anyone else."

"He's got experience escaping an unthinkably massive cave system through a hundred thousand creatures that would kill on sight?" I ask with slight amusement.

Grímr chuckles, his chest vibrating beneath me. "Nothing that specific, but he has a long history of getting his teams out of dangerous situations. Also, remember that Imiha is with them. She should be able to cut her own hole to the surface."

As we close in on the light, skirting the border of the lifeless cavern, it becomes clear the entrance is far wider than it had been when we first passed through. In retrospect, it should have been clear from the light itself. There are still many tunnels above one would need to pass through to reach the surface. The light shouldn't reach this cavern.

Had the Viisin torn open the path on this side as well?

A thick section of the ceiling exposes the sky above. It is wider than the other side. Did the Viisin get caught in a fight here too? Is that why so much of the ceiling is simply gone? Or did they just widen it to allow the mermineae a less congested path?

Now that I think about it, if Viisin can tear through the ranked stone like this, then why did the clergy even bother to have us try to close it in the first place? As long as the traitors have even one hidden away, they can just reopen it in a moment.

Before the Viisin began chasing him, Spenne found evidence that they had been going around killing all the Beiths even while we were working with the clergy.

Which side are they on?

If the ones hunting down all the Beith mercs are a part of the traitors, then why? It is because of the Beiths that they even have a path to follow. They've been hunting them too long for it to be revenge for our attack.

Maybe they were trying to kill all the ones that had the capability of closing the path in the first place . . . but again, that makes little sense, considering the Viisin can reopen it with ease.

The clergy have proven themselves to have a decent knowledge of what is going on in the plains. They directed us to Imiha and Spenne, after all. So I find it difficult to believe that they didn't know the traitors had their own Viisin wandering around.

Then, are they a part of the clergy? Their knowledge of each Beith's location can be explained if they had been actively hunting them down.

But why? What reason do the clergy have to go after us? Sure, if they'd started doing so after that battle, I'd pin it on them being angry at Spenne. But again, they'd been doing this since far before that battle.

Their focus is to stop the mermineae from leaving the plains, right? Then why had their strongest been wasting their time hunting down outsiders? It was as if they didn't care for the reasons they told me.

Does Kalma even exist?

Of course she does. The centzon spoke of her themselves, and the mermineae have shown genuine fear at her mention.

Were the strongest perhaps not as terrified of the god as the rest of their kin? But that Viisin during our first attack on the tunnel seemed intent on freeing the mermineae from her grasp. He'd been clearly hateful of the clergy Viisin trying to stop him.

The whole thing was a confusing mess. What is true? How much of what the mermineae have said is fabrication?

Well, nothing changes. The mermineae remain our enemies, regardless of the details. Whether it's the traitors or the clergy killing the Beiths, it doesn't matter. Until we're given a reason to think otherwise, we'll fight both.

A deep growl rumbles through the cavern before I hear a heavy thunk. I freeze as the arachnid monstrosity's presence washes over me. Without time to even process, the large silhouette scuttles out of the darkness and chases the light ahead of us.

"Shit! Go!" Spenne shouts as he bursts out of the monstrosity's path with a crack of thunder. "I'll be back to take you up on your word. Prepare for a good fight." He laughs as he leads the giant toward the crowd of mermineae.

Grímr and I just watch as the terrifying creature chases the áinfean. A mindless animal chasing bait laid before its eyes.

"Well, I guess it's just the two of us again," I say. "Let's get moving in case there are more around."

Grímr grunts his approval and directs his flight toward the massive hole in the ceiling. Hopefully, the Viisin and Forvaal will be too busy with the monstrosity Spenne is leading through their numbers to notice our escape.

I crouch, hands gripping feathers on Grímr's neck as we fly over thousands of mermineae. Ropes made of sap and fur dangle from the ceiling, but most of them scale the ceiling ahead of us. There must be a wall further down the cavern.

There are so many of them. Even more than there were when we attacked the other entrance as a team. How exactly are we going to fight off this many? I'm certain the average strength of these mermineae is far above that of the people on our side of the Alps. Do we have enough at the strength of my team to hold them off?

I hold tight, expecting a Forvaal to burn us out of the sky, a Viisin to jump at us, or any form of opposition.

But it doesn't come.

We fly out into open, chilly, thin air without so much as a breeze to block our way. The mountainous landscape falling away to the lands that are home to my friends. The ones I left behind so long ago.

Grímr sticks low to the earth, flying above crowds of mermineae in a dash to get as far in as short a time as possible.

I peer to the south, hoping to glance the home I've not been to in years. Not since my tribe died. Unfortunately, the Alps block the wasteland from sight. If I want to see it again, I'll have to return.

But not now.

Now, I need to ensure the home of my friends remains safe. I'd been too young, too powerless to stop the Henosis Empire's invasion of New Vetus. I am neither anymore, and I will do everything I can to stop it this time.

I've been front and center to what can happen to good people when strained by war. Gloria had always been a cruel manipulator, but the rest of her race had been nice to me, until war made their lives hard.

Ash, Leslie, Kerry, and the twins are immigrants to Meja. Will they face the same disdain I did back in the ursu's country at the height of war?

I don't want that.

Grímr and I are finally back, but we have a lot of work to do. First, though, I want to head to Meja and make sure they are safe. If I meet my team on the way, then that would be perfect.

CHAPTER TWENTY-SIX

War

Grímr and I fly north, descending the Alps as we go. Well, we intend to. That is, after we backtrack south to cross the crevasse over the bridge left in the Titan's wake. Grímr adamantly refuses to fly over the chasm.

I know the wind is strong, but he's a big bird; more relevantly, he's a heavy bird. He will plummet as long as he closes his wings; it's not the Euroclydon's gust, after all. But he is determined to take the safe path.

I wonder if the mermineae attempted to cross the crevasse before they found this bridge, or did they simply follow the Titan's path down? There's no reason they would have known about the chasm until they came across it themselves. On the other side of the Alps, there is no crevasse. Is that a result of the Titan's winds too?

Once clear of the bridge—and the mermineae swarming it—we agree to head back to Meja. That's the most likely place we'll find our team, assuming the pact nations aren't completely overwhelmed yet.

The invasion has long since begun. We knew that coming in, but to see the defensive structures along the Alps destroyed is troubling. Nothing remains of the garrison where I'd learned to play Bleed. Hopefully, the mercenaries fled and held the mermineae away from people's homes.

We won't know until we leave the Steppes if they succeeded or not. Are they holding the mermineae at bay, or have they been overwhelmed? It is unfortunately clear they have not pushed them back, but one can hope that all is not yet lost.

"When Spenne comes to have you join him in battle," Grímr says. "I would prefer if you don't enable him."

I look down at him, confused. Grímr keeps his eyes locked ahead, refusing to look back at me. "What do you mean?"

"It's hypocritical of me to say, considering I have no intention of backing down in this war, but I don't want you to kill unless necessary."

"Why not? They're our enemies, and I've killed hundreds already."

Grímr twists his beak back to me. "That is exactly the problem." He pauses, his eye flicking over my body before he turns ahead again. "I'm afraid for the day you learn exactly what that means."

I scowl. Of course I know what it means. They're dead. There's not much more to learn. And good riddance. Gloria, the general, the mermineae; they all deserve death. What does he think he knows that I don't? Why doesn't he just say it if it is so important?

I don't respond, and we descend into silence.

I force my eyes to the horizon. It's strange not to see a perfectly flat line anymore. The hills and mountains paint the landscape with definition that the plains lacked.

Doesn't Grímr realize I've killed because I couldn't have survived otherwise?

The moon still hides behind the Alps above, so I can't check if the scar beneath it is still there. What could it mean if it really is only visible on the other side?

Does Grímr really think killing is bad? What about hunting? Or survival? Is killing to live wrong in his eyes?

I wish I could see the wasteland again.

Is Grímr disappointed by the actions I've taken?

No matter what I try to think about, my mind always drifts back to Grímr's words, the tension of this silence doing me no favors. I want to be mad. I want to shout why he's wrong, but the words get stuck in my throat.

I've done nothing wrong.

It was too much to hope that they held the mermineae at the nations' borders.

Hundreds of meters in the air, I stand upon Grímr's back as he flies over the ruins of what was once a city. Portions of the defensive walls are simply gone, as if removed from existence.

I'd been told that the Forvaal go slightly blind each time they used their decay eyes. Was that a lie? They've been incredibly quick to burn their own eyes if that's the case.

The city is silent, so we move on.

I would like to imagine the residents evacuating and the mercenaries deciding to hold defenses further back to wait for reinforcements. While everyone's homes are destroyed, they are still alive in the safety of some other city further ahead. They have trains here after all, they can still move faster than the mermineae can run.

I would like to, but the red-soaked streets dispel any illusion.

This isn't the first settlement the two of us have come across. Neither is it unique in its residents' misfortune.

The bodies do not remain, and I can only assume what the mermineae have done with them. Despite the murder, I see no problem with the mermineae returning their bodies to the cycle, but I can tell Grímr is struggling with the thought.

I pat him slightly on the back, but I'm not sure if it's helpful at all. It might be easier to console him if I were to share his beliefs, but I try not to be annoyed for now, not about his strange counterintuitive traditions nor his words from days ago that never seem to leave my mind.

The mermineae could have approached our nations with diplomacy, but no; they chose to invade. Each meter we fly is another ripped from the dead hands of those who once called this place home. When will we find the border? How far have the mermineae already pushed?

Even with the Henosis Empire's clear military advantage over the ursu—ignoring Hund—they'd taken over six months to push to the heart of New Vetus. The more land we find overrun, the worse the situation appears.

Grímr changes course, angling a touch further east. I soon hear why. Slight popping and crackling prelude the tiny bursts of light on the horizon. Explosions. But none so big as what the centzon are capable of.

Finally, we've found the war.

I rise to a crouch, ready to jump into the fray with my spear in hand.

Rather than rushing in, Grímr slows down.

I tilt my head at the giant bird, but he gathers his thoughts and speaks. "Solvei, I . . ."

His eyes roll over my form. Something makes him pause.

"Please be careful." He turns toward the approaching battle.

I don't know if battles are supposed to be like this, but it is pure chaos. Thousands of mermineae wail on a defense of pact nation races numbering only in the hundreds. With coordination, the mages unleash varied elemental attacks while the more physically attuned try to hold the swarm off.

Their attempts, while somewhat effective, are pointless against the continual onslaught of mermineae. Some particularly powerful warriors amongst the defenders hold off good portions of the mermineae advance by themselves, but even they can't stop each bounding over their line.

A continual rain of metal is the source of the explosions. Each missile of iron drops from the sky and explodes on impact. Unfortunately, they only seem to kill upon a direct hit. Shrapnel tears into those close by, but they survive. I follow the trajectory back to their source and spot hundreds of cannons similar, but far smaller than the ones centzon use. Each supported by large wheels.

Many volans fly above the battle, some dropping to the cannons and their crew every few moments. Unlike how I'm used to seeing Jav fight, none of these seem to actively participate in the battle.

A few meters behind the front line, which I assume are the mercenaries, is a mess of disorganized soldiers holding guns like I'd seen from the Henosis. The mermineae that have already bypassed the mercenaries' defense tear into these soldiers. The gun-wielding races panic and fire blindly. Just as many shots hit the backs of a friendly soldier as they do mermineae.

The bullets do nothing more than slow the beasts down, while each bullet into a soldier almost guarantees death. The mercenaries hit by the panic fire appear to come off less injured, but the mages are vulnerable. Several collapse from rather unfortunate shots.

I haven't even seen a Forvaal use their eyes yet, and the defense is already crumbling.

Some mercenaries riding beasts chase mermineae going for the line of cannons, but their rides cannot keep up, and soon the rear weapons are being torn apart.

Grímr and I finally reach the battle. The portian comes in at full speed, tearing through the dozens that don't dive out of the way in time. I throw myself off Grímr and ram my spear into the back of a rather unfortunate merminea that just survived my friend's devastating swoop.

Heavy scraping and a cloud of dirt tells me they pulled him to the earth, but even without the ease of flight to cut through mermineae, Grímr has enough weight that he just slides along, crushing those still in his path. I look back to my own fight once Grímr rises to his feet.

I plan to steer clear of the mercenaries' defense. There's no chance I want to be anywhere near the water mages as they fight. I'd wanted to practice only my spear-manship, but they look like they're struggling, so I have no choice but to unleash my fire while running around with my spear. I shouldn't go so far as to create a firestorm; its uncontrollable nature is a bit much to let loose so close to friendly fighters.

As I dash around, shrouding my spear in physical flame to boost the strength of my thrusts with a momentary blast, I keep an eye on the mercenaries. There is one particularly tall albanic that tears through mermineae like they are nothing but rodents. In his hands is a longsword with a ripple-like blade. A flamberge . . . which is strange that I actually know that. I guess Bunny's been rubbing off on me.

I wonder where she is right now?

An explosion from my side peppers me with hundreds of tiny bits of shrapnel. I should focus. Stop letting my thoughts wander. My eyes drop and I find my outfit in shreds. Really?

I'm ready to turn up the heat and burn these mermineae where they stand despite the source of my irritation being from my side, but my eyes land on the albanic again. In moments, an arm and a leg disappear, leaving him to crumple to the ground in agony.

I dash toward him, intending to help, but a wall of water rises before him, startling me. With as much physical flame as I can handle in the moment, I blast myself backward, hoping the water won't chase me. It remains still.

Through the distortion of the liquid, another mercenary drags the albanic flamberge wielder to the rear of their line.

I jerk my head to the side, looking for the gray-eyed Forvaal hidden amongst the swarm. Are they waiting for the stronger mercenaries to show before burning them? My flames spread to cover as much ground as I can reasonably control and I push the heat to my max. Bright yellow flame burns through hundreds of mermineae. Their screams bring up Grímr's words to the forefront of my mind, but I quickly shove them out.

The mermineae that aren't dying in my fires are the ones I need to target.

I dash to the first, spear raised at its chest. The Forvaal notices me coming and leaps back, eyes already flicking my way. I'd seen this coming though, and add mass to the flames surrounding us. It stings a bit as the Forvaal decays through my physical flame, but it is manageable compared to the pain a direct sight line would bring. With all the clear open ground around us, I can keep the physical flame fed without digging too deep into my reserves.

I run at him again. This time, he stands still for me, absolutely trusting in his ability to kill me before my spear can touch him. To his credit, he eats away at quite a lot of the flame coating my weapon before I pierce him between the eyes. No need for anything fancy, if he's going to just stand and take it.

Not that I'd trust myself with anything fancy, yet.

I don't wait and move toward the next, trying my hardest to hide within my flames so this one doesn't notice my approach. I almost succeed too, but the creature's round ears twitch and it leaps out of the way at the last moment. Still not enough to avoid the spear running them through, but it saves the creature's life.

It hisses at me, but once again, the flames block its eyes from turning me to dust. This Forvaal is quick to realize, and it backs away, limping as it does. I press my advantage, raising my spear for another lunge, but there is no need.

In the chaos I've brought, the mercenaries finally push back. A volley of stone projectiles clatter against the Forvaal as it backs away from me. The rock knives barely pierce its fur, scratching or bouncing off without so much as a flinch from the creature.

Now realizing it's stuck between me and the mercenary army, it turns to attack the easier targets. Well, I won't miss the opportunity if it wants to show its back. With a jet of flame, I burst forward, my spear ready to thrust.

I'm knocked away before I can reach it. Another Forvaal collides with me and sends us tumbling to the ground.

Damn! I haven't been paying attention to my surroundings. The Forvaal doesn't even try to use its eyes, instead it scratches at me and tears my outfit apart even more.

Seriously, I need to find clothes that won't be destroyed in a single fight. This is getting frustrating.

As the Forvaal wails into my chest and throat without result, the concern and fear become palpable in its eyes. They glow a deep gray, but I've already got my physical flame burning into them, both blocking its decay ability and boiling its eyes in its head.

It shrieks a high-pitched wail and doubles its efforts into my chest and head, which simply flicker around its claws. It may not have the strength to hurt me, but I'm mad about my outfit.

My spear slams into the side of the Forvaal's head. It jolts to a stop for a second, but quickly resumes its assault. I'm sure I hit its brain, but the damn thing still moves. Well, whatever, it isn't much of a problem. I move my flames along the length of my spear and in through the wound in its head. With easy access to the brain inside its head, it quickly burns away. Inner organs tend to be much less resistant to my flames than fur and skin.

I scorch the blood off my clothes and spear and rise to my feet. The mercenaries are as far as a few meters from my fire now, hesitant to move inside. Do they think I will burn them too?

The defensive wall of water before many of them is a bit too close for comfort, so I back off my flames, exposing the few Forvaal that have yet to flee. They don't last long. Even if the mercenaries were having trouble till now, they are quick to push their advantage and flank the mermineae my flames could not reach.

The battle is soon won. Too bad thousands of soldiers from the rear now lay dead. The unenhanced truly have little hope against the mermineae. Considering the lack of strength even their weapons could provide, I struggle to understand why they are even here.

Is there a reason they all had to lose their lives?

CHAPTER TWENTY-SEVEN

Fire Mage

It felt good to use my spear. It might have been possible to wipe the Forvaal if I'd let loose a firestorm, but with so many allies nearby, it would have been too dangerous.

I'm really glad the mermineae are so easy for me to deal with. Some mercenaries are strong, almost to my team's level, but still struggle when fighting too many of the standard mermineae. I'm fortunate in the sense that no matter how many come at me, as long as they burn, they cannot touch me.

Grímr is helping carry our dead to the far rear of the line, where they have pitched temporary structures: tents. The sight of them dredges up old memories and I have to tear my eyes away. They are far too similar to ger for my liking.

Most of the soldiers and mercenaries focus on the strange metal bird helping them work, so I get to walk around undisturbed. They keep their distance, but never take their eyes off him.

I pass another row of piled bodies as I make my way to the cordoned off section of the former battlefield for the injured. The dead are taken away, but those needing treatment stay. I'm slightly tempted to burn the bodies and reuse their energy myself, but the vast majority are unenhanced, which would be worthless for me now. Best leave them for others to make use of.

Wait, Grímr's around. Are they going to bury them?

For now, I put it out of mind. We're already at war with the mermineae, I don't want to start any dumb internal conflicts that would be better avoided.

I finally find the flamberge albanic, still without his arm and leg. I find it strange that he hadn't been healed immediately. He's obviously one of their stronger warriors, so I'm surprised they didn't have him rush right out to the battlefield again. Even more surprised he's still in this state.

He sits in the back of the carriage, staring up into the sky. The pholos strapped to the wagon lay asleep. It is strange to see the creatures again. I'd thought only Zadok had the animals because they don't have the trains every other country seems to. Then again, there aren't exactly any rails out here. Do the pact nations not have those cars? Or is that something only the Henosis Empire has?

I climb up and sit across from him. I'm not all too sure why, maybe curiosity? Thick, crimson-stained bandages cover the stubs of missing limbs: his arm at the shoulder and leg just above where his knee should be.

When he doesn't lower his head after a minute, I ask the question on my mind. "Why haven't you been healed?"

"Are you mocking me?" The albanic drops his gaze to mine, scowl on his face. It slackens when he sees me, but confusion takes its place.

"No," I say. "I just thought it strange they didn't want one of their strongest continuing to fight."

"That's not possible, you know." His eyebrows furrow as he looks over the tattered remains of my outfit. "Why are you even here? Did you not evacuate before those beasts attacked? Wait, are you even albanic?" His eyes widen as they rise to mine.

"How can you tell?" I ask, surprised. While my flames are hidden, most just assume I'm an albanic too. Even the albanic themselves. I flicker my body to flame and back to confirm his guess.

"No reason," he says while locking eyes.

Huh, maybe the blue of my hair and its dark shade were enough for him. I had covered it in dirt and grease when I was intentionally trying to hide, after all.

"That was you before? The fire that helped us?"

"Yep."

He bows his head, the action somewhat stiff in his seated position. "Then, thank you. It is likely because of you that my team and many others are alive." His gaze drops to his missing leg as he speaks.

"Your team? Where are they now?" I glance around as if they'll pop out of nowhere. "Also, what did you mean it's not possible? My teammate had his tentacle regrown in a fight." Remus said he would have to wait until we got back across the Alps to restore his limb, but then we'd come across Imiha. There have to be more amongst the nations that can heal, right?

"My team is debriefing with the commander now. And your team must be incredibly lucky to get one of the Lu-lum to support you in battle. They typically refuse to be anywhere near conflict zones. I'll be enjoying a nice, day-long train ride north just to be put on a waiting list." He clenches his only remaining hand. "Who knows what might happen out here by the time I'm back?"

I don't respond. I don't know how. This battle was a victory, but it was tiny in the scheme of things. There are still hundreds of thousands of mermineae. What's to say these few hundred mercenaries won't face overwhelming numbers next time? Grímr and I can't stay forever. We need to get back to Meja.

Grímr is still helping them carry bodies, so I settle to wait until he's ready to leave. I want to head back as soon as possible, but I'm sure he feels the same way, so I'll be patient.

My eyes wander over the encampment. The area for injured people I'm currently sitting in is the only place where both the soldiers and mercenaries intermingle. Outside, they steer clear of the other. Despite the number of casualties amongst the soldiers, there are still far more of them than the mercenaries.

A flock of people leave the largest of the ger . . . tents. They spread out amongst the mercenary teams resting after their fight. Each wear clean, formal clothing that is out of place amongst both mercenaries and soldiers.

A group of three albanics and a pair of khirig walk our way. I assume this is my limbless friend's team. They seem more interested in me as they approach.

"Yo, Mors. Who's this?" An albanic woman jumps on the wagon and sits shoulder to shoulder with the flamberge wielder—Mors.

"She's the cause of all that fire."

"Really? But she's so young." I twist my head back to the khirig standing behind me. Her antlers giving her an impressive height over me.

"Is that really so strange? Is there no one my age as strong?"

"Incredibly," Mors says.

"The only ones that even have the possibility are mages, but kids talented and driven enough are incredibly rare. Plus, there aren't many that would risk letting their kids experience the world before they've taught them everything they need." The woman across from me leans further into Mors's side.

Another albanic man leans over, inspecting me. "And yet I can't see a single marking on your body." His eyes widen and I have to groan. I know what's coming. "You wouldn't happen to be an áed would you?"

Typical mages.

Thankfully, the khirig behind me speaks up, so I don't have to respond. "Oh! The commander is looking for you." She steps back and waves her long antler arm to someone off in the distance.

The rest of the team winces at the khirig's action. Another khirig steps forward to pull down her arm.

"The commander isn't too happy with you, so prepare yourself," the woman beside Mors says.

"Huh? Why? Didn't I help?" I'm aware of my strength enough to know that there would have been many more dead if I hadn't joined the fight. Why would their leader be mad at me?

"You did, and we are all thankful, but—"

"You!"

The shout makes me turn. A short female albanic with a uniform adorned with many medals stomps her way toward us. A bored-looking man follows on her heels. Despite his slouched posture and baggy clothing, I can tell he's the most dangerous person here.

I can't feel it. Not in the way you could immediately tell when someone was strong. No, he doesn't show his presence. Instead, I can feel the energy moving along and around his skin, just beneath the clothes that cover every millimeter of his body beside his face.

He's a fire mage.

He notices my gaze on him rather than the commander currently asking the khirig behind me whether she's certain I'm actually the one she's looking for. An amused smirk spreads across his face as we stare at each other, but he says nothing, and does nothing as the albanic woman pushes between us again.

"Present yourself!"

"What?" I stumble to my feet on the wagon as she puts her face far too close to mine for comfort.

"Your name and team." She crosses her arms and glares.

I look around, hoping for any of these mercenaries to either explain why she's mad or calm her down. When neither comes, I return my attention to this rude woman before me.

"I'm Solvei, with Luis-Eight."

That turns some heads. As with back at the garrison, the name of Remus's team is enough to attract attention. Even the commander's eyes widen slightly before she narrows them at me.

"Why did you not announce your presence to me when you arrived?"

"I arrived in the middle of battle. Why would I do that? So many more would have died if I hadn't." My eyes flicker to the mage standing behind the commander and I realize something I should have when I first saw him. "Why didn't you help?"

I jump off the wagon and push past the commander, who lets out a gasp of indignation as she stumbles out of my way. She's clearly unenhanced. The fire mage keeps his calm attitude while I close the distance. He's a full head taller than me and I don't enjoy having to look up to him, so I engulf myself in physical flame and lift myself to his height. I lift myself a little higher, so now I'm the one looking down on him.

"You were here. Why did you leave these people to die?" I can feel the well of flames hidden within the markings beneath his coat. "You are strong enough to kill all the mermineae yourself, so why did you not help?"

Still unmoving, he grins at me. "I would have loved to join." He directs his gaze to the uniformed woman. "But Commander Irena here wouldn't have it. Maybe you should ask her for details."

I return my focus to the fat lady once more, the deep scowl doing nothing to hide her anger. "It appears you are still a child, despite your strength. You cannot win a war by saving everyone. Some sacrifices are necessary."

"What?" I'm more shocked than angry. They intentionally let those soldiers and mercenaries die? I'd assumed it was negligence, not intent. "What do you mean 'sacrifices'?"

"Beiths must remain out of battle until we can force the enemy to show their elite." Her eyes flicker to the fire mage before returning to me. "Not only did you give yourself away, which might have been fine if it were you alone, but we have no hope of hiding our Beith now." She calms herself before she continues. "They have all the cards they need to deal with us in the next battle."

That is absolute foolishness. Keeping your best mercenaries from fighting for only a slight advantage in information? Sacrificing thousands for that information? It just seems wrong.

I feel the thread of fire as it approaches from behind me. I've felt it ever since the fire mage created it. Right before it connects with my flame, I send a curious glance the mage's way. I've never met a fire mage before now, but I really feel like he has absolutely no idea what he's doing. He's guiding the fire with horrid inefficiency. It's like he's trying to strangle it in the direction he wants it to go. Even when I struggled with my control as a child, I was never this bad.

His fire links with mine, and I feel him try to gain control. His grasp moves over the flame carrying me and to my very body. I can feel him trying to influence my fire. He doesn't even come close to being successful, but the attempt itself is invasive. Infuriating.

I crush his attempt in an instant and amplify the heat of the tether between our bodies. My fire rushes into his body. The markings resist me in the same way I might have trouble stepping over a stone in my path. I burn the fire in him until the clothes he wears ignite, scorching away to reveal markings glowing bright yellow with my flame.

He screams. His bored, uncaring attitude melting away along with the skin beside his markings.

I really shouldn't kill him; he's probably needed for the defense of the pact nations, but I can't calm down. Did he really think he could snatch control away from me that easily?

I absently note my inner flame is twisting around me. The carriage is on its side as my flames have incinerated its wheel. One of Mors's team has picked up the commander and taken her away. Everyone keeps their distance.

The fire mage before me collapses to his knees and I lower myself to the earth. His body is resistant to my flames, but I'm scorching the muscles inside him just as much as my flames run over his skin. The markings give me free access to his entire body.

"Did you really just try to use fire against an áed?"

There's no need for me to make myself taller when he's kneeling before me. His head bowed low to the earth. His ragged breaths wheeze with effort.

"I thought mages were supposed to be smart, so why is it they tend to make the dumbest mistakes?"

I lift his head, wanting to see the fear, the acknowledgment of his mistake. Attempting to violate my fire, no matter how poor the attempt, is unforgivable. When his eyes reach mine, it is not fear or regret I see, but mad joy. He laughs as he tries to amplify the fire within him, which does nothing but make me press harder.

He winces before hiding it with another grin as his body melts and burns. He tries again, but I don't give him the satisfaction.

I step away, only to find Grímr standing behind me. I clutch onto his plumage as I rip my flames out of the insane mage, who gasps and collapses face-first into the dirt.

"Let's go. I don't want to stay." Not with a commander willing to sacrifice her people for the slightest advantage, and not with the mage who thinks he can control me. I just escaped that which bent my mind against my will, and now someone attempts to take my very being away from me?

Grímr, ever on my side, takes off without a word.

CHAPTER TWENTY-EIGHT

Letty

Should we have left like that?" I ask, laying my head into the sharp feathers of his neck.

"Probably not." His chest rumbles beneath me as he speaks.

Even if we should have stayed, I'm glad Grímr listened to me. I'm glad I don't have to be near that mage again. If I had to be around him anymore, I would have burned him to a crisp, even if the insane bastard enjoyed it.

Sharing our flame, or Kindling, is a private thing. Intimate even. It is done between family. But to not only have someone attempt it forcefully, but for a non-áed to try, with the artificial control of those markings, is insulting. He attempted to join a song when he could not sing, so he squeezed his hands around my throat to pull me to his level.

I should have killed him.

Just the thought of his action is enough to infuriate me once more. I will never experience Kindling with my family again, but this deranged mage thinks he can come in and force it upon me? To take it further and try to control me?

"Why did he enjoy it? I felt his body melting under my touch, but he didn't care."

"Well . . . fire mages have a reputation for not being completely sane," Grímr says. "I'm sure you've a better idea than most about how fire doesn't mix with people's bodies. Common perception is they burn away part of their minds to wield fire as they do."

"Common perception?" I ask.

"Well, I prefer not to listen to general opinions like that. Most consider my kind as dangerous monsters, after all."

Now that I think about it, Grímr is the only portian I've met. Do the rest stick to themselves, or do they just hide in bodies without anyone knowing? If the rest of Grímr's race share his views on sapient bodies, the latter probably isn't likely.

"What about what she said? Do they really keep the strongest fighters from fighting?"

"Is that what angered you? It only applies to the Bei—"

"No, no. Well, it did annoy me, but I attacked because the mage tried to put his influence over my flames." I push myself off his back and rest on my knees. "But then, why was the commander so furious? I'm no Beith, so there should have been no issue with me eradicating the mermineae."

Grímr sighs. "You revealed our elite is a fire mage, even if unintentionally. If our foes were any but the mermineae, they'd be bringing water mages to the next battle. Also, you should be aware by now, you are easily within the range of a Beith. You overpowered the commander's allocated elite, after all."

I had thought he was incredibly strong at the start, hadn't I? "But his control was horrible. There's no way he could have beaten me."

Grímr snorts. "You sound just like my old friends talking about lightning mages. But that's exactly my point; even if his control was lacking, you took him out without resistance. This is someone who's considered an elite for his fire-wielding capabilities, losing to his own element."

I smirk a bit at that. They must see the mage as completely worthless now. Really, why would they even bother trying to control fire when such a thing is so completely beyond them? But regardless of the control he lacks, he is strong enough for the Mercenary Order to keep him in reserve.

I can kinda understand the logic; lose the first battle so you can win the ones that count. But what is the point of having the gun-wielding soldiers around? Their weapons were almost completely ineffective against the mermineae. Only incredibly lucky shots could down one of their opponents before they were on top of them. Were they bait? Living targets? Is that all they're good for in war?

It just seems so inefficient.

"Then why not move the Beiths around after each battle?" I ask. "Have the fire mage here one fight, and have them switch with the nearest Beith. Maybe bring in a physical fighter as a replacement."

"Too much of a risk." Grímr shakes his head. "If the enemy ever found out, we'd face their full offense without the support of our hidden elite."

"But these are the mermineae we're talking about. The only ones amongst them that don't hide are the Viisin, their elite. Should they really hold back when they all have the same abilities?"

"How certain are you that what we have seen is the extent of their abilities?"

"Huh?" Wouldn't they have shown more against the centzon if they had anything more to give? The centzon seemed pretty sure they had nothing more than their Viisin.

"It's never good to confuse your assumptions with fact. We have a good reason to believe they have nothing more, but we should always consider the possibilities. The Forvaal's power comes with the cost of their sight, so why is it not possible the Viisin or some other type of mermineae have an ability that requires a much greater sacrifice?"

I peer past Grímr's head over the land ahead.

"Besides," Grímr continues, "it will take a lot of convincing to change the methods of the Mercenary Order, even if it is the right way to fight the mermineae."

I look behind me, at the Alps, and finally realize something's wrong.

"Where are we going? Why aren't we going to Meja?"

"The major forward operating base. I was chatting with some of the other mercenaries and got a rough idea of what's going on. There's a good chance we'll meet Remus there."

I swallow my impulse to insist on continuing toward Meja. I need to check up on my friends, make sure they're safe, but I know it's probably better to meet with our team first.

This time, we follow the appropriate procedures when arriving at the military outpost. After we land—Grímr terrifying a bunch of soldiers and lower ranked mercenaries as we do—we move toward the largest building in the repurposed town.

There are a whole lot more people around here than back at the first battle-site. The flight wasn't long, but there were soldiers almost everywhere along the border and we could only thank the extensive fortifications put in place and the mercenaries mixed amongst them that the mermineae haven't pushed past them completely.

Those guns and field cannons might not be much on their own, but with enough to rain iron on the mermineae if they got too close, it is enough to make them hesitate in their attack. None of those defenses would mean much if the Forvaal join the battle, but the soldiers and their weapons are just barely enough to hold the normal mermineae at bay.

Though, I do wonder how they deal with the mermineae's camouflage.

Grímr attracts eyes as we walk through the wide street, his massive golden-green body shining in the early evening moonlight. It is only when we reach the large double doors to the command building that we realize he couldn't possibly fit inside. Well, he could, but I don't know how we'll get him out without breaking through the wall.

"I'll see if I can get them to come out and see you," I say.

Grímr is a lot stronger than he was in that panther body, especially now with how well he can control his body. Could he be considered at the level of a Beith now, too?

I push through the doors and approach the two dohrni women at the front desk, their membrane a deep purple compared to the blue of their male counterparts. They don't notice me until I speak, too busy with their work.

"Excuse me, could you ask the commander to come down to meet with us?"

"Name and reason? Wait, you want the commander to come down for you?" The dohrni on the left finally raises her eyes to me, her partner following suit a moment after.

"Solvei, and yes," I say. "I was told I had to present myself to the commander when I showed up, but Grímr can't come inside." I gesture over my shoulder where the alicanto pokes his head through the door.

"Gosh, girl. What happened to you?" She jumps to her tentacles and circles the table, eyes glued to the remains of my outfit that barely cover me.

"Uh, we got into a fight earlier today, and I wasn't as careful as I should've been."

I look down at Jav's gift. It is going to be much harder for him to fix this up than it was before.

"I can't let you walk around like this. You're coming with me right now." One of her limbs grasps me by the hand as she leads back toward the double doors. "Tell Darton he's got a visitor," she calls back to the other dohrni. "I'll be back in five."

I send a baffled glance toward Grímr as he moves out of our way. The bird finds this amusing? He doesn't even hide the amusement in his eyes as he watches me being carted off down the street.

I peer down at my hand, knowing I could burn her grip off at any moment I want . . . but I don't. This is the first time in a long while someone has grabbed me and I don't have the immediate urge to tear out of their grip.

She leads me toward a building with wide glass windows. Behind the panes, three wooden life-size replicas of an albanic, khirig, and dohrni lay collapsed to the side. Heavy wooden crates take the space I assume the fake people might have stood.

I'm led past a couple of soldiers standing guard and through the front door into what I'm sure was a clothing store at one point, but is more of a storage room now. Some clothes hang on the wall, but large wooden crates fill most of the space.

"So, Solvei—ah, call me Letty—how'd your clothes get all torn up? You didn't get hurt, did you?" Letty says as she tears open a crate, revealing piles of folded cloth.

She grabs one and holds it up over my chest. It hangs low to my knees. There are a bunch of soldier uniforms in the box. Apparently unsatisfied, Letty tosses the shirt to the edge of the crate, but misses and it falls to the floor. She doesn't seem to notice and grabs another.

"A Forvaal got a bit angry at me. Tore me open before I could do the same," I say.

"What?" Her tentacle freezes as she grabs another shirt.

"What do you think you're doing?" a gruff old voice grouches from the back of the store. "Letty? Those are military fatigues. You know you shouldn't be going through them."

Her eyes linger on me for a moment longer before they spin to the old albanic walking toward us. "Come on, Nomar, the kid needs *something* to wear."

"Not the army equipment, she doesn't. Check what we threw out the back; there might be something there."

"You didn't toss them?" She discards the second brown cloth back into the box and drags me toward the back door, leaving the old albanic to grumble about tidiness.

It's much darker in the back room, so I ignite my hair for some light. Just as many crates in here leave little space to walk around. Most of these are open, though. The first we pass is a box stacked upon others with several identical guns.

I'm curious to how they work, so I reach out for one, but notice Letty's attention before I can touch them.

"Can you, uh . . . stop your fire? There are a bit too many explosives in here for you to be doing that." Her eyes flick to the door we just came through. "You'd better stop before Nomar comes back. He's not exactly polite in the best of times." She laughs, but it is strained.

I don't delay and do as she asks. She pulls me further into the dim room, taking me away from the crate of guns. I'll have to see if I can grab one for myself. They aren't exactly the best weapon, but they can do a lot of damage to those who cannot resist the impact. The speed they hold would be great if I can figure out how to launch my spear like it does the bullets.

"Right, Solvei," Letty says, but I get the feeling she's not actually addressing me.

While I'm led to the side wall, where a pile of cloth lays discarded behind a row of crates, she rolls her eyes back in her head toward me. "You're the áed on Remus's team, right? He'd said you were young, but I didn't expect you to be this young."

"Remus is here?" I ask. It has only been a few months, but it feels like so much longer since they made it through the tunnel. Does he know about the Viisin? Probably not. I should hurry to meet him and tell him about the threat beyond the Forvaal, but . . . the sooner I meet him, the sooner I'll have to tell him about my mind. Even if Grímr has been nothing but understanding, I still want to put it off.

"Yep, he's been meeting with the commander almost every day since he arrived." Letty lets go of my hand and climbs over the crates, grabbing an array of colored clothing from the pile.

"So, skirt or pants?"

I look at the two pieces of clothing she holds up. Somehow, in only a few moments, she's found garments that appear close to my size.

"It doesn't matter. Either way, they'll just get damaged the next time I try to use my spear." Getting in close enough to use my weapon always ends up with my enemy able to strike back, so no matter what I go for, it'll be destroyed before long, just like the snowsuit I'm wearing.

"Oh, don't be so boring. That's it, the skirt for you." She pushes the clothes into my hands and pushes me into a corner, obscured from sight. I'm not really sure why she's adamant about keeping me out of view, but I do as she says.

While I put on the new outfit, lamenting the lack of boots to go with it, Letty continues. "I don't know about getting clothing that's indestructible, but I've heard some luxurious garments imported from Riparia have self-mending qualities. Maybe you can look into something from there? They are exorbitantly expensive, but if you're a part of Remus's team, you should have enough cash in no time."

"How do you know of albanic clothing?" I ask. As a dohrni, Letty's six tentacles and bulbous body don't exactly accommodate similar clothes. In fact, many don't bother with clothing at all. Letty herself only has some ribbon sleeves along the thicker part of her limbs.

"Of course I know about them," she says. "I've grown up with albanics and khirig. Everyone has. I know just as much about their fashion as I do our own."

Huh. I guess that makes sense.

I walk back into view with new clothes on my back and Jav's gift in hand. The number of tears through the outfit really interfered with the fur's camouflage, so I never had the chance to try sneaking around with it. Maybe I can keep it and have it remade when I meet Jav next.

I will absolutely look into the Riparian clothing once I'm able, but that will have to wait until this war is over.

Letty stares down at me, unsatisfied. Does she not like the outfit she chose herself?

"Solvei," she starts. "Remus welcomed you onto his team despite your age, so I know you are strong . . . but that makes me concerned. The Mercenary Order will do everything they can to slap a leash on you, especially now that most Beiths have run off. Please know that you do not have to do everything they say. Take care of yourself first."

CHAPTER TWENTY-NINE

Commitment

Letty's words remain on my mind as we walk back to the town hall turned command center. If the Mercenary Order wants to chain me down, it would be just another on a now rather long list. Of course, I'll never let them, but it is concerning that I can't seem to go anywhere without something or someone trying to control me.

They've done nothing so far, so I don't intend to take any drastic actions. Though I acknowledge Letty's warning with my full being, I cannot fight the mermineae if I'm always expecting betrayal by those on my side. I'll be careful and aware, but that is all I can do for now.

Grímr is right where I left him. By his side is an albanic wearing a similar formal uniform to the female commander I pissed off earlier today. Remus is there too, his cheerful tone cutting through the gloomy air of the rest of the people rushing through the street.

"Solvei! It's great to see you!" His eyes remain as joyous as ever. "I hope your trip back wasn't difficult?" While still cheerful, I can hear the concern in his tone.

"It was . . . fine." I look around, expecting the rest of the team to show themselves. "Where's everyone else?"

"Off on their own tasks for now, unfortunately."

"As much as I'm sure you lot want to enjoy your reunion, we are at war. I don't have time for idle chatter." The albanic I assume is the commander pushes in front of Remus. "What can you tell me? Has anything changed since your separation? What are the mermineae's positions, numbers, anything? Tell me all that can help." He turns between Grímr and me as he speaks. I guess they haven't talked yet.

Letty waves to me as she passes back through the double doors. I give her a small nod in thanks before turning to the commander.

"I don't know about exact numbers, but there are a lot still moving through the Alps. They aren't our biggest concern. The mermineae have Viisin, which are strong enough to tear holes through ranked stone."

"Wait, they have that capability? Then why have us close the tunnel in the first place?" Remus asks.

"I've been thinking about it, and the best answer I've come up with is they were trying to flush their traitor's Viisin out," Grímr says. "Unfortunately, Spenne joined their fight and put a target on himself. They were hunting him down when we next met."

"So, strong enough to have that áinfean running, huh?" the commander considers. "Not good."

"They're a bit like the Forvaal; there's no variation in how they fight," Grímr says. "Their power likely all comes from Kalma."

The commander turns to Remus. "You've mentioned this Kalma, their so-called god. Is there any chance she might show up on the battlefield?"

"I hope not. Both merminea factions are entirely against letting her find out. If they fail, it's hard to say how she'll act. She might cripple their army, or she might massacre all, our side included. She's an unknown, but considering the depth of the mermineae's fear, we can assume her reaction will be vicious."

"Shit. I guess sending a team to probe her is off the table." The commander bites the knuckle of his finger as he paces.

We are attracting attention now. These two had to come downstairs to meet with Grímr, but that does nothing to keep the conversation private. The old albanic isn't oblivious of the ears either. He turns in his stride and opens the door.

"We'll be in the shed round back, send them my way should any managers come looking," the commander calls to the two dohrni in the foyer before walking past us and around the side of the building. "Come, I'd rather keep some of these details from spreading."

The 'shed,' as he called it, turns out to be closer to a guest house linked to the town hall by a brick path. While smaller than the main building, the doorway is just as large.

"Is that the outfit Jav gave you?" Remus asks as he falls into stride by my side, his eyes falling on the merminea fur sewn to the outside.

"Yeah. I . . . haven't been able to keep it in the best condition."

"No worries." He takes the outfit from my hands. "I'll send it to Jav and his sisters. I'm sure you'll have it back in only a couple weeks. Plus, Jav would be happy to hear you're safe."

"What about Bunny?"

"Ah, she was pulled into another war. We probably won't hear from her for a while."

"Another war? Not with the mermineae?" Is the Henosis Empire trying to invade other countries again?

"Unfortunately. The Theocracy—as opportunistic as they are—sent an invasion force into the Vanguard the moment they saw weakness."

So neither Jav nor Bunny is around? That's disappointing. As much as I'm hesitant to tell them of my regained freedom, I'd wanted to do it all at once. Now, I guess I'll have to figure out how to say what I want to say to Remus alone.

"Don't worry about damaging the building. Break down the walls if you have to; the owners are no longer with us," the old albanic says as he opens the double doors.

I follow Remus through the door. Grímr hesitates, eyeing the building as if he doesn't want to touch it. His eyes fall on me and his wings droop in defeat. Gingerly, he presses himself through the doorway, his large wings gouge divots into the wooden frame, even resting against his chest as they are. He ducks, but still tears off the head jamb.

Remus closes the doors once Grímr's entire body is inside—not easily, but they do close when he puts in some force.

There is some space for the large bird to move around now, but I can imagine getting out again will be a challenge. At least there isn't anyone here.

"Now that we don't have any sticky ears, I'm going to go into some sensitive information. You have Remus's trust and praise, and for my purposes, that is enough."

"Hold on, Darton," Remus says. "I'd like to hear their good news first."

"Good news?" the commander—Darton—repeats. "Well, that would be a pleasant surprise, but are you certain they have any?"

Remus, instead of responding, casts a curious gaze our way.

"We found a . . . like-minded group that helped us take the western tunnel entrance," Grímr says.

"Take? You mean to say you seized the entrance rather than simply passing through?"

Grímr nods. "The centzon are a particularly capable race. There are nearly a hundred coming to support us from the rear of the merminea invasive force."

"Oh? Only a hundred? How do they compare to our elite? Are they equivalent to our average Beith, or better?" Darton asks, his hand scratching at his white, short-trimmed beard.

"Well, I can't say. We never saw them fight. Not the strongest of them." Grímr shrugs, accidentally slicing a hole through the wall. He drops his wings and pretends it never happened, but his eyes continue to flick back to the large new opening to a side room.

"You never saw them fight, yet you managed to take one of the two major choke points between our nations and theirs?" Commander Darton is disbelieving and I don't blame him considering Grímr's vague answer.

"They build weapons," I say. "Weapons strong enough to kill a Beith in a matter of moments."

I consider the weapon the Henosis Empire tried to have me power. They put a lot of effort and resources into making that operational, do the centzon have to put a similar amount of effort into creating each of those Viisin-killing bombs?

"Manufactured weapons powerful enough to take out an elite? That is a concerning thought." Darton furrows his brow. "What is their reason to ally with us?"

While Grímr details what they want to the commander, I'm too busy focusing on how this is news to him. Does he not know that the Henosis Empire is working on something similar? I'm not sure I want to tell Darton how I know, so I approach Remus while Grímr explains the centzon's objectives.

"Henosis has something similar," I say. "They're working on a bomb that can kill elite. They tried it during their war with New Vetus, but the Void Fog got in the way."

Remus stares at me for a long moment. Maybe he doesn't believe me. I've told him about the Void Fog, but never my time being held captive. I never so much as want to think of it again, but if he needs me to, I'll tell him.

"All right, thank you." Remus turns his eyes back to the others, his tone flat. "Keep this to yourself for now. I'll talk to some . . . people who will need to know, but for now, it's best this doesn't spread."

I guess it's good I didn't tell Commander Darton, then? I hadn't really thought about it until now, but if war is determined solely by the battle between those at the top strength, and those of lesser strength are only used to bait out information, then being able to make a weapon to remove one of those elite would change everything.

"All right, I think it's about time I told you why I brought you here," Darton says. "This morning, we got word that the Joiak Kingdom is still holding on. This came as a surprise as we wrote them off as dead, along with the Zadok Kingdom, which has been silent since the war started."

The commander walks up to the fireplace. "The mermineae have been nipping at the Vanguard's ass since their initial unhindered advance, and now that we know Joiak isn't done for, we have the opportunity to cut them off and surround them. It is clear these creatures have no history of warfare strategy. They simply attack where they find weakness."

He grasps an old fire poker and lifts it before his eyes. "Battle after battle now, we've been on the back foot. It is time we fought back."

Commander Darton turns to me and Grímr. "Under regulation, I should assign you as Beith rank and have you wait in the back line until the entire operation is a bust, but this needs to work. I am going to have you both on the front."

"What? No! I thought you wanted her as a messenger." Remus stomps in front of the commander and flicks the fire poker out of his hand. "I'm not leaving her to the battlefield."

Commander Darton remains still as his eyes follow the poker as it lodges into the brickwork wall beside the fireplace. He has no enhancement of his own, so I'm sure Remus's anger must be terrifying, but he remains steadfast.

Calmly, his eyes turn back to the dohrni standing tall over him. "We're stretched thin here, Remus. Every day we lose more ground and the mobile mercs we have to patch our defenses are growing weary." Darton turns my way. "I need everything I can get my hands on if this attack is going to be successful."

"I won't let you. She's too—"

"Remus," I interrupt, before addressing the commander. "I will help. The way the Order keeps their strongest on the sidelines is not something I agree with."

"Solvei." Still looming over Darton, Remus's eyes watch me. "Getting you involved in that mission up the Alps was a mistake. I don't plan to continue that mistake. I'm not letting you be pulled into this war."

"Let me? I'm sorry, Remus, but I'm not about to back out now." I have my own reasons to fight, limited as they are.

Grímr is as frustrated as Remus, but at least he doesn't voice it. I appreciate both their concerns, but I've been fighting for my survival for years now. It's about time I fought for something more.

I want to protect the home of my people.

I can't say if I will ever call the pact nations my home, but I want to protect the families of those I care for. For a long while now, I've been selfish. Only prioritizing myself. While I could blame the Void Fog's manipulations, that would be nothing more than a lie. My team, the former homeless kids from Zadok, and even Leal; I want to make sure they do not experience the grief of losing family.

"You don't want this, Solvei. Trust me," Remus pleads, but I ignore it. What's different now than back in the Euroclydon's Hunting Grounds? It was merminea slaughter then, and it'll be merminea slaughter now.

"When do we start?" I ask Commander Darton.

He eyes Remus for a moment before clearing his throat. "You'll have a week to prepare. If all goes well? We'll cut the mermineae off in another."

Remus walks to the fireplace and crouches without a word.

Darton reads the room well enough to make his hasty exit, brushing past Grímr and out into the warm night air. The door buckles and doesn't latch, leaving it to hang ajar.

Grímr's eyes follow the fleeing albanic, and I can tell he feels uncomfortable. His eyes flick to me, a curious yet hesitant quirk to them. I shake my head. I need to talk to Remus, but I'd much rather Grímr stay with us, even if he doesn't speak.

A few steps and my hands tug the fire poker from the wall. My feet place me at the dohrni's side, and my hands restore the iron stick onto its rack. Delaying the inevitable, that's all I'm doing.

"I know you only have the best intentions." The fireplace ignites before us; I need something to fiddle with while I speak. "But I need you to stop treating me like a child. You didn't when we first met."

Remus's eyes follow my flames as they burn yellow and the surrounding bricks glow. I lower the heat, not wanting to damage the fireplace.

"I brought you onto the team because it had been a relatively controlled environment. Originally, you were only meant to support us where I could always be around to watch over you. A few years would pass like that. You would fight only when I thought it was safe. Eventually, you would have enough experience to join us properly."

His eyes turn to me. "Everything has gone completely out of control since. If you are sure you want to do this, I won't force you. I won't make the same mistake again. Just as long as you're willing to run if it is ever too much."

He looks away before he can see me nod. I'm willing to go to battle, but survival is still a priority. I wouldn't sacrifice myself for another. Though, I would try my utmost to save them if I cared for them.

"One last thing," Remus raises his voice so we know he's talking to Grímr as well. "I won't be able to join you both. I'm stuck heading north for the next while and likely won't return before the battle starts, so Grímr, I'm entrusting you."

Grímr nods seriously, and I can't help but roll my eyes. At least now Remus isn't completely opposed, but I still have one more thing to talk about. He shouldn't take my admission badly, but there is always the lingering chance that will bother me until I actually go through with it.

CHAPTER THIRTY

Cutting Off

Marching along with thousands of soldiers is a rather unique experience. Despite my short stature, I keep up rather well with the many far exceeding my height. It shows how far I've come since the little girl who had to ride on the back of her uncle's wagon for half the day.

Our first battle will begin the moment all the troops are in position amongst the dug-in line. Grímr and I are to meet with the Luis teams for this dedicated section of the front before working with them to take down any priority targets that arise.

I had my little talk with Remus, admitting to wanting to leave him to the mermineae and save myself. How I had considered their treatment by the mermineae a proper retribution, despite the horror they'd endured. He just laughed it off, saying it was a fair judgment in a stressful environment after what they'd done.

He appeared happy to hear I'd overcome the Fog's influence over my mind.

We approach the temporary quarters of the teams we will be working with. There are four teams waiting for us. Mostly comprising albanic and khirig, they chat amongst their own as we stop before them.

Their eyes linger on us before casting over the remaining soldiers marching into position. Their murmurs grow louder as they don't spot what they expect to.

"Where are our reinforcements?" A khirig mage steps forward, her markings weaving through her antler chest cage.

"We are it," I say.

"Don't joke, kid. Why are you even here? Sure, your bird looks tough, but we expected to at least double our strength."

Grímr sighs. "Yes, you can expect us to at the very least double your fighting potential."

The khirig frowns, but an albanic amongst the other team speaks up. "So we have an arrogant portian and a child in unsuitable clothes as backup? And they expect us to push back those creatures? The brass surely love us."

Grímr flinches at the mention of his race, and I look down at the clothes I'm wearing. They do seem a bit too colorful compared to what everyone else is wearing, but with my snowsuit back in Jav's hands, I'm left with whatever spares I can get my hands on. Letty scrounged up a selection for me, which is good because I don't believe the ones I'm wearing will survive a single battle.

"What I wear matters little." I walk past them, toward the front line with Grímr close behind. It would have been more beneficial to work with them to form some strategy. Well, I was mostly hoping the mercenary here would direct me. Despite being in a team for a long time now, I've barely relied on teamwork or cooperation for any of it.

The khirig mage grabs at my arm. "It's unsafe. You ca—"

My arm slides from her grasp as it devolves into flames. I snap my head back at her. "Do not grab at me," I snarl, intentionally letting the flames of my body grow visible. I'm annoyed, not truly angry, but I need to give them a reason to respect me, at least somewhat. They cannot be getting in my way.

"Obstruct me again and I'll burn you to charcoal. I'm only here for personal reasons. Don't think I won't just because we're on the same side."

I may have laid it on thick. Grímr's eyes stab into the back of my head, but I ignore it. It might have been rude, but it isn't particularly untrue. I really don't care for them, but if they fall in my firestorm, there will be less to protect the home of my friends. Well, that and Grímr would be unhappy with me.

The Luis teams leave us to walk toward the front line, either aptly intimidated, or simply intelligent enough to let us pass in silence. Soldiers rush around, lugging ammunition and other equipment into position before the innumerable field guns roll. Grímr and I will take the leading point of this offensive, with the mercenaries backing us up and the unenhanced soldiers behind them.

The fields before us are silent. Not a merminea in sight. They should be out there somewhere, waiting for a weakness in our defense before they rush us down. We expect to face resistance as soon as we push the line forward, but until they attack, I don't have a target. None are within the range of my sense.

I'm strangely nervous coming into this fight. Not sure why? It's not like this is my first battle. Maybe it's the immense number of people we have on our side. As much as I'd like to trust those on my side, I still struggle with applying that willing- ness to trust. I've simply been hurt too many times by those that should have been on my side.

"Solvei, after this is done—once we no longer have to deal with war—I want you to meet more people. I'll introduce you to the áinfean and my kind," Grímr says as we walk past the last defensive line onto the crater riddled battlefield.

Is this really the time? "Sure, Grímr. Once this war is over." I ignore the fact that he brought this up after my not-so-civil interaction with the other mercenaries.

A deep, chorused bellow heralds the unified movement of the army. The line of riflemen and artillery move as one. Compared to the individualistic actions of the mercenaries following a suitable distance behind the two of us, the unenhanced soldiers show immense coordination.

What might an army of Luis level enhanced soldiers look like? Or even Beith? If the strong were a part of the disciplined military rather than a separate organization, what would that look like?

The encroachment of our army isn't fast in any sense of the word. The combined march limited by the slow field guns ready to fire at a moment's notice. I'd asked Commander Darton why he didn't just send us in with a team of the stronger mercenaries at his disposal. He'd shown willingness to use what he had, and a concentrated attack would be best to wipe as many of the mermineae out as possible and cross the distance between us and Joiak in the shortest time.

Turns out, there is more work for the military than simply being bait for information. They are required to seize and hold vast stretches of land. An attack by any reasonably enhanced enemy could cut through them, but they couldn't take the land away without a numerous force of their own. Well, unless they went around killing every soldier. Not even most Beiths had the energy to do that.

No surprise that Hund is stronger than most Beiths.

Decapitation strikes are so common simply because the line of defense can often be meaningless against those of greater strength. The pact nations have experienced this enough times that their commanders have become near immediately replaceable. I felt a bit bad for Commander Darton when I heard that. Not so much for Commander Irena.

We've been walking for a good few dozen minutes now, and we still haven't faced any opposition. It's strange; I'd expected to face opposition immediately. I guess this area is less of a focus for the mermineae? If so, then our job will be easy.

I unbuckle the flask from my hip and twist off the cap. With a deep breath, I bask in the fumes rising from the oil. So many times in the past weeks I've been tempted to delight in its taste, but the thought that I might never get to experience such nectar again stays my tongue. Experiencing the delicious aroma is enough.

Volans fly overhead, returning from far downfield. They land amongst the army, which comes to a unified halt with little delay. That's all I need to know the mermineae are coming.

"Give me a signal if you need help. I'll keep an eye out," Grímr says and takes to the air without delay.

"Same to you!"

I run toward our enemies, controlling and shifting my weight for extra speed. I'm already far from our line, but the further I can hold the mermineae, the better. Cannon fire booms and explosions pelt the land ahead of me. Through the smoke and rubble, it is hard to tell if they are even hitting anything, but I can't imagine the mermineae able to pass through the onslaught of iron without taking some casualties.

Finally, as I approach the metal downpour, the mermineae enter my range. They run at full pelt through the artillery bombardment. The soldiers' aim is spot-on despite no clear sight line. Even without the ability to fight like Jav, the volans of the army are still incredible scouts.

Fire swirls around me as I push it to grow and consume. In minutes, a firestorm brews further than I can normally control. The smoke from the initial artillery salvo giving me a perfect environment for the rapid spread of self-fueled flame.

In the intense heat of the blaze, even the Forvaal struggle to push through. They avoid my fire, trying to skirt its sides. But the heat spreads fast, sparks ignite already roasting debris from the deluge of iron. Soon, my fire spreads half a league across. I can barely even feel the edges of the flame as it spreads without control.

Thousands of mermineae die. I feel their coats vaporize before their flesh incinerates. Some survive long enough to flee back out the rear of my flame, but most collapse, burned alive before they can escape.

I peer back at the Luis teams amongst the hundreds more mercenaries staring upon my world of flame with shock. It's delightful to see. No longer am I the one watching on as others with far greater power do as they like. Now, it's me being looked on with awe and fear. There's no chance they'll interrupt me now.

The mermineae are too scared to approach my flames. Time to push on them, then.

Honestly, I probably should have foreseen this.

Our operation to cut through merminea-controlled land and reconnect with the Joiak Kingdom had gone near perfectly. It only took two weeks, but I'm more exhausted than I think I've ever been. Fueling such large fires drained me of so much of my energy. After the first battle, I had to pull back a bit on how much influence I had on my firestorms, leaving their spread to rely entirely on natural growth.

We are lucky the mermineae hadn't destroyed the rail tracks—likely out of a lack of understanding—so travel and logistics between the nations is rapid. But when Commander Darton and some other important people traveled to Joiak to coordinate the next phase, things became messy. There would usually be no issue and they'd want all the help they could get in such a situation, except for one small thing.

They still want me dead.

Turns out, a young girl able to wield as much fire as I do is rather rare. Who knew?

Really, I don't know why they care so much about me. I was doing them a favor by cleaning out that textile mill. Well, unless they are all scum like the mill owner . . . If that's the case, maybe it would be better to leave them to the mermineae.

The point is, Joiak refuses to work alongside the Mercenary Order while I'm still alive, and Commander Darton refuses to kill me while I'm as valuable as I am. It is no exaggeration to say I'm one of the core reasons the operation went as smoothly as it did.

So now, while the stalemate in discussion goes on, we are stuck defending the land taken instead of jumping on the opportunity to push forward. To pressure them while they're surrounded.

I start up another inferno, letting it spread amongst the ranks of mermineae before pulling my inner flame from it. The firestorm blazes nowhere near as intense as it might with my influence, but it is enough to scare off many of the mermineae.

Grímr and I have been stuck flying along the defensive line for weeks now, joining the fight whenever the troops down below appear to have trouble. The past few days, the mermineae have grown desperate. They attack our defenses almost without care for my fires.

Between the borders of the pact nations and Joiak, the only place these cut-off mermineae have to go is south into Zadok. As far as I'm aware, they don't have a military even comparable to that of the pact nations. So why are they rushing for our defenses with so much fervor? They couldn't have taken the entire country already, could they?

The mermineae below are far greater than what we've yet had to deal with. Are they finally deciding to deal with us seriously? The fighting has been tough, but nowhere near the challenge they showed over in the plains. Will the Viisin show themselves?

Once they do, it shouldn't be long before they finally bring the Beiths out to play.

I take my time to change back into my normal form. Flying is fine for speed, but it prevents me the use of my spear. I don my replaceable clothes, keeping the repaired snowsuit in my bag. It's kind of annoying to have more than one set of clothes, but when I'm fighting as close as I do with my spear, damage is bound to happen. I want to make sure the outfit is intact when it rains.

As Remus had said, Jav got it to me in only a few weeks. Neither of my teammates returned alongside it, unfortunately. No word why.

I leap off Grímr's back, his eyes following me as I fall amidst my firestorm. Through the regular recent battles, Grímr and I know what to expect from the other without even talking.

I land amongst the remaining mermineae. Well, I say land, but it's more of a crash. My flames disperse on impact. It takes a moment for me to pull myself back together and leap toward the nearest mermineae engulfed in flames.

Dropping like this is pointless—I could slow my descent with my physical flames or use jets—but it's fun.

Grímr soars above with a lingering shroud of my fire to block a Forvaal's sight. He no longer bothers swooping for the general mermineae. Any time he does, he gets held up fighting on the ground, which is just not that effective compared to swooping on priority targets.

It'd probably be more efficient for him to fight further away from me, but he refuses to leave my side, which I can appreciate. I can look after him at the same time.

My spear pierces through the neck of my first Forvaal. The creature is completely oblivious to my presence until its blood splatters along the ground.

Its choked gasps warn the others, but instead of trying to turn their gaze on me or throwing themselves on me, they raise their heads to the sky and screech. Loud, high-pitched shrieks dig into my ears.

I slice through two of them before they cut their yowls and scatter, not even attempting to fight. They flee back amongst their ranks. Do I scare them so much that they won't even fight? Heh. I guess the centzon were wrong about the mermineae being unable to learn.

While they run to the edge of my flames, I debate chasing them, but I'm distracted by an odd lack of feeling in my spreading flames. Something is moving toward me far too quickly. I whip my head to the oddity as it enters my thermal sense range.

A Viisin. Coming for me.

CHAPTER THIRTY-ONE

Cornered Animals

Barely. I only barely move out of the way before the Viisin tears through the space I stood hardly a moment ago. The little flame that breaches its coating of dust disappears. Painfully. It's like the gaze of the Forvaal, only at a far greater intensity. I can't let it touch me.

It throws itself toward me, and I don't even attempt to compete. A jet of flame rockets me out of reach. The Viisin doesn't let me open the distance though, springing after me as soon as its claws find nothing but empty air.

I jerk to the side, barely dodging the decaying creature. It is too fast for me, there's no escape. I'll have to fight it. My flames do nothing to it though, and it hurts every time the Viisin removes them from existence. The only chance is to kill it with my spear. There's no other way to deal with it.

It leaps for me again, but instead of running away, I stop. With a tight grip, I thrust into the creature's trajectory. My aim is perfect. The sharp blade thrusting directly into the featureless head of dust.

For a brief moment, I think I've won. It hurts a bit, but I cover the blade in physical flame to stop the decay. Half my spear's length lodges within the head of the Viisin.

Then, my arm disappears.

Agony hits as the Viisin brushes past me. I push away before it can do any more damage. I've lost limbs before, but it is always so horribly painful. My remaining arm lifts my spear in some form of self-defense, but my eyes fall on the missing blade, along with most of the shaft.

Did I even hit the creature? Or did my weapon melt away before it could touch it?

The remaining pole clatters along the ground, discarded in frustration. It will do me no good now. The only thing I have is my flame. I pull it in on myself, concentrating the swirl of fire entirely on my immediate surroundings. My fire can't breach its decay, but maybe the heat alone will be enough.

As soon as I do so, swarms of mermineae rush our defensive lines. I follow the countless creatures as they cross the burnt landscape. They were waiting for me to stop. I want to spread the flames once more, but I can't afford to lose focus.

With no way to defend myself against this nightmare of a creature, I'm back to sinking all my energy into each dodge. It's exhausting to move around like this. Barely am I keeping out of its claws, but this can't keep up.

The Viisin takes on a more controlled offense. No longer launching itself through the air toward me, instead keeping its feet. I don't have to deal with the explosive movement, but it is far harder to dodge now that it can switch directions in an instant.

Grímr's large form enters my range, and I do my utmost not to look toward him. The Viisin dashes for me, but its head inclines upward. I panic. It knows Grímr is coming.

I direct the swirling twister of fire down on the Viisin, compressing the flame and increasing the heat as far as they'll go. Frustratingly, my inner wall blocks the flame growing any more intense. It isn't enough to even hurt the creature.

Grímr's talons lash out as he swoops past, but so too does the Viisin. His metal claws disintegrate on touch and the Viisin swings an arm, obliterating a wing and leaving deep gouges in the alicanto's chest. Grímr gasps, his voice reverting to a metallic grating.

Momentum carries Grímr away from us. He slams into the earth, and dirt explodes into the air as he rolls dozens of meters.

I can't tear my eyes away as the alicanto skids to a stop. He doesn't move. I want to do nothing more than rush over to Grímr and check on him, but I can't. Even if the Viisin goes after Grímr right now, there's nothing I can do. I hate abandoning him here, but I need to give the Viisin a reason to keep chasing me and leave its already downed opponent.

I flare my flames, not toward the Viisin, but the mermineae rushing our defenses. The best I can do is to burn through as many of them as I keep out of range of the Viisin's touch.

My chest aches. Why is it only after I've escaped the knot that told me to abandon him, I actually do so? The world is cruel.

Without my spear, I have to rely on my body to deal with the Forvaal. Claws grow on my one remaining hand while the other regrows. I tear forward, burning each merminea and clawing at any that doesn't incinerate. It's not all that effective, but I can feel the Viisin chasing me, so I can hope Grímr is fine.

I last a long time doing this. So long, that my arm almost fully regrows . . . though I'm not sure how long that actually is. It feels like hours, but probably no more than minutes.

Of course, my luck doesn't last.

The Viisin tears forward once more, and I'm simply not fast enough to dodge completely. A scratch to my chest is all it takes to put an end to my run. I stumble and collapse. I hit the earth and what little remains of my clothing tears. The canteen of oil clatters beside me.

I'm exhausted. I don't think I have the energy to run, even if I'm not missing a chunk of my chest. The Viisin is annoyed. Not that I can see its face through the mask of dust, but it stomps toward me with clear agitation. I take some pleasure in knowing I've upset it, even if it's only a small feeling amongst the anger and frustration of my own.

What can I even do? Nothing I throw at the Viisin hurts it, nor can I run. I don't want to give up, and I won't, but no ideas come to mind. My flames curl up around me, as hot and dense as they will reach. I don't have the energy for physical flames anymore, having used it almost nonstop since the fight with the Viisin started.

I reach for the bottle of oil, hoping the temporary boost in energy will be enough to recover. Maybe let me run for another few seconds.

My clawed fingers wrap around the neck of the canteen, the long-since-peeled paint lumpy in my hand. I reach my other hand to take off the cap, before I realize I don't have it. Instead, I melt the cap off and immediately bring the sweet juice to my mouth before it can explode.

I'd rather drink this nectar directly if it's going to be the last thing I drink.

The taste is amazing. Better than I remember. The pain of my missing arm and leg disappears to the heat that floods my body. My flames press on me, hiding the intensity within me where I don't have to share. My entirety feels hot, excruciatingly so, but it also feels wonderful.

I forget about the world outside myself. I do, until the Viisin is above me, reaching down to end me. My arm lashes out, striking through the dust ridden limb before it can touch me. Pain flares through me, but not nearly as bad as before.

The Viisin still stands above me, but its arm is gone.

The creature seems as shocked as me. It looks down at its arm as it regrows before my eyes. My own arm is quite the sight; bright, pure white flame takes the place of my normal flame.

I strike out again before the Viisin can, taking its head and scrambling backward.

My fingers are now gone, but my hand remains despite going through the Viisin's head. I shakily rise to my feet. While the pain in my arm and chest are gone, they haven't regrown. Neither has my energy increased after drinking the oil.

I finally realize what's happened; the heat of the oil pushed me past my barriers. The flame of my body compresses far greater than before, as does my heat.

I'm still exhausted and temporarily crippled, but I now have a fighting chance.

My flames rush toward the Viisin, but they immediately revert to yellow and fail to even singe the Viisin as its head regrows. Why? Don't tell me it's not permanent. The heat rushing through my chest tells otherwise, as does the steady white the flames making my body. Why can't I apply this to my inner flame?

A guttural growl escapes the Viisin as it takes a step toward me, its head regrowing with frightening speed. The dust billowing off the creature clouds my vision, but I can still see the thousands of mermineae falling as they rush toward our defenses without hesitation.

Our line is holding up far better than I expected considering the number and desperation of the mermineae. With the Viisin held here with me, we're actually holding them off.

The smirk rises to my lips before I even realize, gloating to the Viisin. This battle isn't over. I'm at the end of my rope, but I can hurt it now. There is a way and I'm not about to roll over until I've burned this creature with all I have.

The Viisin hisses at me, the gravelly voice hiding none of its fury.

My flames can burn away its body before the decay can melt away my fire, but I have nowhere near the recovery speed it has. So if I'm to do this, I need to get all of it in one go. If I leave any of its body to recover from, I can't imagine success being possible.

As the Viisin prepares to throw itself at me again, a tremor shakes the earth beneath our feet. Amongst the constant peppering of artillery shells exploding, a louder blast booms over the battlefield.

The Viisin stops, along with every other creature on the battlefield, and turns toward the origin of the heavy quake. I can't stop myself from doing the same. The presence that floods over the battle is impossible to ignore. The claws of a monster dig into my chest and prevent movement.

The presence exceeds anything I've felt before. Stronger than even Spenne's. Like what I would imagine a Titan's presence would feel like.

It is familiar.

It is hostile.

Beyond the furthest merminea is a being I would recognize anywhere. It rises to its full height, towering over everything on the battlefield, easily visible despite the distance.

The Viisin snaps out of its daze and gives me a single glance before it throws itself into the army behind me, cutting through rather than fighting. The rest of the mermineae follow suit a moment later, rushing toward our defenses in a hysterical panic. They are not fortunate enough to escape the giant ursu.

Hund.

The massive warrior lifts his towering blade and bounds forward. Between his massive heft and the extended blade, hundreds of mermineae vaporize in an instant. In the wake of his movement, a shockwave rocks thousands of others, followed by a barrage of shrapnel.

Hund only takes a few moments to crush the swarm of mermineae. Even the Forvaal fall like children to the incomprehensibly strong ursu. He doesn't waste time, nor does he enjoy the battle, simply cleaning up the battlefield as if it were a chore.

I'd seen it before. Felt his presence before. But I never truly understood the depth of his strength. I'm not sure if I do even now.

Soon, he is done. No mermineae remain. His gaze falls on me and I feel just as much a child as I first did under his attention. He takes a step toward me before halting, a perplexed expression crossing his face.

He recognizes me. I don't know if that's a good thing or not.

I suppress the instinctual fear that overcomes me in his presence. Choke it down. I promised myself I would thank him the next time we met. Considering he's saved me again just increases the need to do so.

Gathering my courage, I take a step toward the giant four times my height. Hund remains still, but his eyes narrow. Instead of letting me approach, his face becomes resolute and . . . wistful. Hund turns away from me and walks back the way he came.

I stop my approach. Does he not want to talk to me? Was I wrong that he'd helped me out of kindness back then?

Far beyond him, I notice movement. At first I think there must still be mermineae not yet dealt with, but as I focus, I see an army of ursu push across the land, trailing in Hund's wake.

They've come to help? Did the mermineae already try to push into New Vetus? What has happened to the Zadok Kingdom?

Well, that's all irrelevant. With Hund on our side, there's no chance we could lose.

CHAPTER THIRTY-TWO

Victory Celebration

I gorge on the artillery reserves. Technically, I'm not supposed to help myself, but they have so many to spare and considering how much I've assisted in this war, they can hardly complain about a few missing explosive projectiles.

After Hund left without a word, the first thing I did was check on Grímr. Thankfully, he was up and moving when I reached him. The damage to his body is extensive though, and it will take him a while to regrow the wing he lost, even consuming as much metal as he's been given.

I burn through the casing of another shell, devouring the explosive powder within before it can blow the roof off this storage building.

Everyone along the front is in a celebratory mood. Unsurprising, considering we had expected to hold down for the next month while the Order and Joiak figured out their differences. To have such an easy win so soon is enough for every soldier and mercenary to cheer.

Of course I'll sneak some free food out of the military's reserves while most guards are off drinking. Even if I am supplied with metals, there are simply not enough to recover my energy.

Hund and the ursu army running up the mermineae's back explain their desperate attacks in the past week. Stuck between us and the encroaching New Vetus troops, they had no other option. Hund himself would likely terrify them enough to send them running rather than take him on. The Viisin clearly didn't want to fight the massive ursu.

I create a ball of fire in my hand. If anyone else were here, they might fall into hysterics. Most aren't exactly fond of the idea of me starting fires around so much explosives. But there's nobody here to stop me.

The flame starts as a familiar yellow. Slowly, I add to it, increasing the density as the heat rises, my past barrier no longer stopping the flame from reaching that pure, untainted white. Even to me, it feels intense. Just to make this small, palm sized ball, I need to use the equivalent energy of twenty meters of yellow flame.

There is some level of that for the lower temperatures, but the jump has never been this extreme. No wonder I struggled to pass that wall; I never pushed hard enough.

Back with the centzon, I hadn't been trying to compress the flames. No, I'd been enjoying the taste and spreading the invisible flames as far as they would. My body hadn't experienced the heat directly. Whether that is a factor or not, I'm unsure.

I stare in awe at the small flame. It is far brighter than the flames I could make before. Despite the tiny size, it illuminates every corner of this storage warehouse. It's so intense that I find it hard to understand how the next stage is invisible to sight.

It's really annoying to know I could have reached this heat months ago if I used the oil as a catalyst from the start. Now that I know it's about sheer scale to pass the barrier, I'm sure I would have succeeded, eventually. Sooner rather than later.

But something bothers me. If white flame is this intense—hot enough to melt rock and stone at a touch—then just how hot is blue fire?

I assume blue flame is the step further than clear, so that would place blue fire at an unthinkable heat. It wouldn't be a leap to say an áed with blue flame would be far stronger than me, right?

So then, did Elder Cyrus actually die?

I know I could survive the earth crumbling on top of me if it were to happen now. Maybe it wouldn't be clean; I'd have to wade through a lot of molten earth to escape, but I could escape.

. . . Unless he was crushed before the stone could melt. He didn't have my binding, after all.

I . . . I shouldn't think about this now. Maybe there's a chance he is still alive, but there's no use lamenting the past. Whether he's alive or dead doesn't help me now.

After cracking open the last of my shells and burning both the explosive inside and its casing, I leave the munitions storage. I wave to the guards as I walk past them. They do a double-take before paling considerably, but they don't chase me down. Perks of being well known.

The merminea fur of my outfit can be rather useful. Jav's sisters outdid themselves with this one. It is clear they'd taken the fur from my old snowsuit and reintegrated it into this one, but they hadn't simply used it as a fur coating. No, they somehow combined it with their own thread and made it as waterproof as it was before. Only now, they'd integrated the camouflage so that I could use it only when I wanted to, with the pull of a string conveniently placed on the inside of my collar.

Now I don't even have to show my flames when I want to be seen through the camouflage. Not that it had been an issue before; the outfit having been torn up far too much to ever go unnoticed.

The tarp door of Grímr's tent makes way for my hand and the wide space holding nothing but the alicanto's form and a pile of scrap metal welcomes me. It's great to have people delivering us food at all times like this, but I wish they'd give us something other than iron for a change.

I have my own tent, with my own delivery of iron scrap, but my size seems to have influenced the thoughts of whoever is in charge of both. My tent is tiny and the platter of metal I'm given is nowhere near enough to recover from that last battle.

Doesn't matter much. I spend all my time in Grímr's tent, anyway.

These tents are sparser than the ger I'm used to. They feel simple and less homely. I'm rather prideful about my race's obviously superior mobile living quarters. This thing doesn't even have a proper door.

"How's the recovery?" I ask as I drop by his side, leaning against him like a backrest.

"Slow." He angles his metal beak toward me. "The talons might take a day, but the chest and wing will be a week."

I'm unsure why, but an intense sense of guilt hits me as I gaze over his crippled body. Despite being the target of the Viisin, I recovered from my injuries in only a few minutes, while Grímr is stuck with his for an extended period. Doesn't make much sense, it's nothing either of us can change, but I feel guilty about it all the same.

"That . . . was too close, Solvei. It was foolish not to realize you were painting a target on your back." Grímr stares at the plain canvas wall, peering at nothing. "I'm not strong enough to protect you. I know you don't agree, but I don't want you entering battle unless you have a Beith ready to take the Viisin's aggression."

"No," I deny. "You're right." It's not only myself I've put in danger here. Grímr's current state is enough proof of that.

Once the Viisin had me in its sight, I couldn't escape. I think it's wrong that the commanders allow the weakest to die for the sake of hiding their elite, but I don't care about those soldiers enough to put my life in such a dangerous position. Maybe that's cruel of me, but I'm not suicidal.

I especially don't like that Grímr threw himself into that fight.

I'm able to actually hurt the Viisin now, but only by trading my body for theirs. Considering their rapid regrowth, I would still need to get lucky. Better to leave them to the people able to fight them effectively like Spenne or Hund.

At least, until I can apply my white fire to more than a hand sized amount of my inner flame.

The mermineae between Joiak and Vanguard are dealt with now, so we'll soon be traveling to the main merminea invasive force. Other than retaking a massive amount of land, we've also removed an entire front from the Vanguard, so hopefully Bunny will have an easier time fighting off the Theocracy.

A rapid clanging of bells rings through the encampment. Grímr and I share a glance before rising to our feet. An attack? But the mermineae should already be dealt with.

Gunfire rings out, but the bangs of artillery do not accompany them as usual. Soldiers scramble for their weapons, many stumbling from intoxication after the celebration.

I whip the tarp out of my way, striding outside with Grímr hobbling close behind.

I twist to the south, toward the heaviest commotion of shouts and gunfire. The ursu army is already in full formation. Our own, not so much. In the dim moonlight, my eyes scan over the landscape, but I can't find a single merminea. Did they sneak up on us? How did the volans miss them?

A squad of large ursu men charge the line of riflemen, shrugging off gunfire and swinging their blades through the varied races.

The . . . the ursu are attacking? Why? Weren't they helping us deal with the mermineae? They even set up camp right beside us. We all thought they were allies. Why are they attacking?

The ursu army continues forward, cutting through any that stand in their way. Their imposing figures send many fleeing. Gunfire hails down on them, but they shrug it off. Thick armor and helmets taking the impact of the projectiles.

Flames churn within me. They would dare betray us? Me?

I'm rushing down the hill before Grímr's protests can stop me. As I pass the barracks of our soldiers, I feel the tall, heavily muscled creatures within. Amongst cooling bodies.

They're already in the camp? But they haven't yet passed our defenses? How could the ursu of all creatures sneak in without being noticed?

Not the time. I need to get down there and stop them now.

My flames spread around me, but an errant thought has me stumbling to a stop. Where is Hund? It doesn't matter how angry I am at this betrayal, I don't dare go against him. There is no possibility of winning against that monster.

Fire returns to me, and I backtrack to Grímr. I shouldn't have left him alone. Not in his current condition. Not while there are enemies within the camp.

As I run up the slope, I feel one of the hidden ursu turn their attention toward me. I dig my heels in and slam myself to a stop with a blazing jet, avoiding the stream of water passing before my face. The flow slices through tents and gouges the earth a dozen meters up the hill.

I stumble backward, only for another stream to blast through the air, blocking my retreat. Both streams come from the same ursu, so I jump in the air with a blast of fire and rocket toward them. They need to burn before they can get another spurt out.

I keep my senses peeled as my body soars toward the ursu, and I'm glad for it; from both sides, a pair of water pillars rush to cover my target. Sacrificing my offense, I fall back. The intersecting flows collide and splatter mist through the air.

I tug the hood over my head, snapping the mask and goggles into place. How lucky I am to have not removed my outfit for this battle.

Water mages? Seriously, what are the odds that I'm the one unlucky enough to be ambushed by them? Low. Likely impossible . . . unless I was targeted.

There are three ursu water mages. One ahead of me and one on each side. There are plenty of other ursu still amongst the surrounding barracks, but I have no way of knowing which are mages and which aren't.

My outfit should be waterproof, but I really don't want to risk it against these pressurized streams. Just looking at the tattered tents says enough about their power. My outfit is waterproof, not tearproof.

The trio of water mages close in on me, so I take a risk and rocket out the rear left, toward the smallest of the hidden ursu. One less likely to be a risk compared to any other.

The massive wall of water rushing at my face immediately informs me of my folly. There is no dodging this time. I brace, burning as hot as I can and hoping my outfit can handle the impact.

I don't hear tearing, but the pain of water eating away at my chest is enough to know the cloth didn't completely survive the impact. It stings, but nowhere near how much it should to get hit with that much water. Steam surges off me as I lay in a puddle.

I scramble to my feet, not trusting the already torn outfit to hold out the water. My legs shiver at the unnatural slosh of stepping through water, even as it vaporizes on contact.

Of all people, I should know not to underestimate someone for their size.

This can't go on. I need to get out now if I have any chance of survival. A moment before I throw myself skyward, a wave of water curves over me, connecting with the puddle on the other side and hovers over my head. The sides curve in on themselves, making a sphere of curving water streams around me.

I'm trapped again. Seriously?

The water droops. A cage like this is obviously against the nature of water, but the mage keeps it flowing rapidly, curving the roof well above my head.

A few drops of water fall, but curiously, they vaporize before even touching me. I create a tiny ball of white flame—only as much as I'm willing to suffer the pain of losing—and hold it near the wall. The water boils around it.

I brace myself and push the tiny white fire into the water. It is painful, extremely so, but a good section of the cage vaporizes the instant my fire touches it. Unfortunately, the wall recovers, replaced by the surrounding water. My fire doesn't survive the contact.

"Please, leave her to me," a young voice says, coming from the short ursu mage.

"What? We can't do that. You know how dangerous she'll be if left alive," one of the ambushing mages says.

I can't make much of that white fire outside of my body. And I'm especially not sure I'd be able to handle the pain of walking through water, even if I can burn away a good portion of it now. As much as I absolutely despise it, I'm stuck. Trapped. At the whim of these mages. No longer am I beholden to the knot's manipulations, but I still prioritize freedom and detest entrapment.

Whatever their plans are, I'll make them burn.

"Remember that favor I asked?"

The other mage takes a moment to reply. "If you are certain. Make sure she's dead after you are done." The ursu mage says hesitantly before taking the other ursu around us and rushing down the hill to join the battle against the losing pact nation's army.

With the others gone, the young ursu steps forward, her voice strained. "It has been a while, Solvei."

Even through the white heat, my chest runs cold.

"Leal?"

CHAPTER THIRTY-THREE

Leal I

Two Years Earlier: Morne

Leal ran through the empty streets as she hurried home. At this time of night, Solvei should have been safe to stay hidden away in that nook of the library until the caretaker arrived late the next morning. For now, Leal just needed to get home before the reksha arrived.

If they had no reason to believe she hadn't gone out tonight, it would make it far easier to brush off whatever accusation Gloria made. Leal could still hardly imagine the woman having done such a thing. Gloria was like an aunt to Leal. She'd been her mom's friend for as long as she could remember.

How could someone they thought they knew so well be so evil? Leal had always been uncomfortable around Gloria, but that was a feeling she'd always felt around other ursu besides her parents.

Finding her friend trapped within that furnace had felt like a knife twisting in her chest. It had hurt when she was told Solvei had returned to her homeland after they snuck into the library. So caught up in her self-conscious thoughts about whether she'd made a mistake and it was her fault her friend didn't want to stay with her, that Leal didn't consider how unlikely Gloria's story was until far too late.

When Leal could get Solvei to open up about her old tribe and the homeland she once traversed, the áed had revealed finding her people would be no simple task. Solvei didn't like to be alone. And yet Leal was supposed to believe that girl was willing to travel a year or more in complete solitude?

Leal's thought transitioned from self-conscious to self-loathing when she realized how long Gloria had fooled her. Looking into the older ursu's activities quickly amplified Leal's suspicions. Only when she found the small form of her first friend down in that dark oven did Leal truly learn what it was like to hate someone.

Leal rounded the final corner to her home and almost tripped over her feet. There, in front of her house, was a squad of reksha. What were they doing here already? She tried to stop, to turn around and leave, but they'd already spotted her; doing so was only going to raise suspicions. Swallowing what felt like a stone in her throat, she forced herself forward.

The front door of their building opened, and out walked one of the reksha, leading Leal's mom with a hand on her back. She could only be thankful that they hadn't tied her hands and dragged her out, but it was clear she didn't have a choice.

Leal tried to follow, but another reksha intercepted her path. "They'll only be a short while. Why don't we go inside and have a little chat?"

Her voice sounded friendly, but the nervous jitters clamped down on Leal's throat too tight to speak. Leal cast a glance after her mother, who caught her eye just before being taken around the corner, likely being taken to the continae.

"Don't worry so much." The reksha pushed open the front door, inviting Leal to follow. "As long as you don't hide anything, you'll both be fine."

Leal failed to respond through the choking anxiety, but followed.

"So, your explanation for being out so late is because you were experimenting?" the reksha asked with obvious doubt. "Exactly what sort of experimentation is one as young as you performing?"

It was the best explanation Leal could come up with for why she was out. She would often do exactly that, so she hoped her mother would use the same excuse when they talked with her. The reksha had yet to ask whether they were housing a fugitive or whatever other such accusation Gloria threw their way, but Leal knew they were fishing for contradictions between her story and her mother's.

Well, despite knowing what their goal was, it didn't make the conversation any less daunting for Leal. Even trying to get out the simplest explanation for where she'd been had her freezing up in constricting anxiety as the what-ifs bound her mind. It took her almost ten minutes just to get her fake story across.

She didn't want to get caught in a nervous, stuttering wreck again by explaining, so instead she just showed what she'd spent the last few weeks practicing. If Leal weren't as young as she was, the reksha would never have let her activate her markings, but thankfully she simply narrowed her eyes and allowed Leal to proceed.

In her outstretched hand, Leal allowed a sphere of water to form in her palm. Her new markings lit with the activation and remained glowing while the ball sat in her hand, sagging slightly from gravity. She twisted her hand so that her palm faced downward, yet the water clung to her fur, refusing to fall.

Leal knew doing such a thing would be easy if she had a more advanced marking. Her basic one was designed to teach form manipulation, and only that. Applying the more practical aspects of higher grade markings on one not designed to allow that was difficult, though not impossible, assuming the mage knew what to do.

Slowly, she let the sphere droop. An increasingly smaller surface connected the water to her hand until all that remained was a thin strand of water connecting her marking to the orb. From her glowing fingertips, the sphere hung like a ball on a string. It was one of the things she'd been trying to accomplish ever since she'd seen Solvei control her fire remotely; holding her influence over water with lesser strands to connect her hyle.

Doing all this was a feat none of the other students could achieve. Most were determined to put in the least amount of effort before they could jump on the chance to rise to higher grade markings. Leal would be the same, if it meant giving her access to markings with far greater allowance for manual control, but the academy hadn't gone unchanged by the war. Now, there was a greater focus on markings that operated near automatically.

The markings she could take if she asked for advancement were far stronger than what she had, but gave almost no room for experimentation. No chance for her to improve upon what she knew. Worst of all, they were attack markings. Methods of twisting water with the intent to harm. It was not something she wished to know.

Leal looked up at the reksha, who looked wholly unimpressed despite her clearly impressive feat. Once again, Leal was reminded just how nonplussed most of her kind were to the wonders markings allowed . . . and their dangers. Even with a supposedly weak race like the albanic descending their nation into such a war-weary state unseen since the revolution, Leal's kind still believed physical strength would surpass everything.

The pride Leal had in what she'd learned would always be overshadowed by her diminutive size and lack of muscle.

A slam came from the front door. In came another reksha, looking harried. "Leave the girl for later. We've got bigger problems." He was gone again the next moment.

"Stay here, kid. I'll be back to talk later." With her piece said, the reksha rushed after their colleague.

Leal sat, unmoving and alone in her home. She feared disobeying the reksha, but she was simply too curious why they ran so quick. Leal rose to her feet and crept toward the window. Outside, the sky glowed like a second sunset had arrived, but no, the smoke was all too clear; there was a fire.

Against her better judgment, Leal fled her home. She'd be in a lot of trouble if the reksha found her, but she needed to find Solvei. Make sure the áed had done nothing to reveal herself.

Leal knew it was too late before she even began running; the glow around the buildings was clearly coming from the academy. She ran for the academy, anyway. When the burning building came into sight, Leal winced. Her home away from home wouldn't survive such an intense blaze. Thankfully, the water mages that remained in the city had all congregated to save what remained.

Did Solvei do this? Leal should've known leaving the girl made of fire in a library was a stupid idea, especially with how emotionally disturbed she must be. Where is she now? She's not still inside, right? If the reksha found her now, Leal didn't even want to think about what would happen to her friend.

Shouts grabbed Leal's attention. Amongst the mages and ursu surrounding the collapsing building, many were pointing off to the center of the city. Turning, Leal was shocked by the sight before her.

The city was on fire.

Not only one or two buildings, but an entire swathe burned within a growing inferno. There weren't many tall structures around the academy, so it was easy to see how fast the blaze was spreading.

Solvei, what have you done?

There's no chance it wasn't the áed, Gloria's home was right in the center of the flames. Leal could understand the anger Solvei must have felt, but Gloria wasn't the only one who would be hurt by such a massive blaze.

Realization hit her all too suddenly. The continae her mother was taken to was within the fire. Her mom was in danger. Leal's feet carried her forward without thought, sprinting toward the inferno that leapt between buildings with ease. It was spreading too fast. Far too fast for a captive of the reksha to be prioritized in the evacuation. Was she trapped?

Leal ran through the streets, brushing by ursu watching the blaze with not nearly enough fear. Didn't they realize how fast it was spreading? Didn't they realize they needed to run?

Pounding forward, Leal never realized the contradiction between her words and actions. Reaching her mother was the only thing on her mind, not that she'd have absolutely no chance to survive should the fire overcome her.

Nearer the blaze, the reaction of the city's residents was far more urgent. Many ran in opposition to Leal, getting in her way and slowing her down. She tried to push past them, but one man picked her up, rushing away from the roaring blaze that cooked the air.

Leal slammed her hands into her captor, screaming for this stranger to let her go. The world blurred around her. Whether by the growing heat or the jostling endured, Leal was left disoriented. She couldn't break free, not when she needed to most.

Clarity shone through the fog of delirium as Leal watched the tower taller than any other collapse within the spiraling flames. She stopped resisting her captor, enraptured by the collapse of the continae. It was horrific. The explosion of dust from the toppling tower only fueled the spread of flames.

Something clutched at her heart. Claws raked within her chest, cutting away her insides before inviting the blaze inside to scorch her just as much as it burned the buildings around her.

Leal watched on as the flames crashed forward. A tsunami of fire smashing glass and sizzling air as it tore toward them. Her eyes stung, but they were far too dry to shed tears.

It had been so long since she'd heard from her dad. She didn't want to lose her mom, too. Leal loved her. The thought of losing her had never even crossed her mind. She didn't need to go out into the dangerous wasteland like her father. She didn't need to go to war. So why was it Leal's mom stuck within the flames, burning alive?

It wasn't fair.

Leal's captor dropped her unceremoniously to the earth. The ground wasn't paved. A mix of soil, grass, and weeds softened Leal's fall, but she wouldn't have cared if she fell on razors. She spun to watch Morne as it continued to burn. The fire had spread to engulf most of the city now. There would be no stopping the spread. Morne was as good as gone.

Leal's home, her school, her clothes and books and teddies. Nothing remained. Leal didn't care about any of that. She only wanted to hold on to hope that her mom survived, so she rose to her feet and began walking through the survivors. The man who saved her life, forgotten.

She circled the blaze, searching until the farmland on the edge of the city caught fire and blocked her way. Leal turned around and continued her search. She walked for hours, until the inferno was nothing but cinders, but she still found nothing.

Leal had to face it; her mother wasn't coming back. She was dead.

And it was Solvei who killed her.

Her friend shouldn't have let it grow this strong. Sure, if she wanted to get back at Gloria after what she'd done, Leal could understand, but this is so much worse than what Gloria did. How many died tonight? Solvei never should have let the blaze spread. That it had showed how little she cared for the damage her flames could unleash.

It hurt. To know her only friend killed her mom—whether it was intentional or negligence didn't matter—it burned greater than the heat that clung to the air and pinched through her fur.

Leal looked around her, finding many in a state no better than her; kneeling over the earth and bawling over their losses. She choked as the sound of other's cries broke her last hope. Tears flowed without restraint as she curled up on the ground.

Alone.

CHAPTER THIRTY-FOUR

Leal II

Prior to New Vetus's Surprise Attack

Leal longed to return to the times before her life collapsed. Back to when her mother had been there to hug her, and her father to play and joke. She'd welcome the isolation she'd felt if it meant she could go back before the war.

Life had been nothing but misery since Solvei killed her mother.

Leal flinched as the needle pricked her skin. The first was always the worst. Collecting herself, she pressed into her arm again, watching as her own variation on a water hyle medium bled into her skin. The removal of her previous markings had been a painful experience, but she now had a clean canvas to paint her own designs into her arm. She'd already had the head mage mark along her back.

Along with thousands of others left homeless and isolated, Leal had struggled to emigrate into a city that could not support them. She'd thought she knew what loneliness was, but that hadn't been true. Only when she had nobody but herself to rely on for survival did Leal realize how harsh the world was. How utterly suffocating true loneliness was.

Leal grabbed a wet cloth and wiped off the excess medium from her trimmed fur. Any mistake now could undo hours of effort. She'd been working on this marking for months now, one that would allow almost free control over the shape of water while retaining enough speed for it to be useful in battle.

The hyle consumption would be exponential rather than linear, as per most markings, but for her purposes, it would be fine. By the time she would be tasked with anything beyond its capabilities, she expected to have replaced it once more.

She, along with many other ursu, had been left with no other option but to join the military. They'd begun identification checks at the Bratchinas. Things had gotten desperate; you couldn't eat if you were unaccounted for.

But before they could send her to battle, her luck seemed to flip. The war ended. They'd won! She'd considered the likelihood of her father remaining alive to be almost nil, but her superiors sent her to an infirmary camp where he was being taken care of.

That's when she realized her misfortune hadn't disappeared. It simply took a new face.

Her father wasn't uninjured, but a missing eye and bandaged leg was better than death. He was sickly, and needed to remain for treatment. Their reunion was joined by a looming pair of guards that refused to give them space even as she squeezed into her dad's chest. He held her tight, and yet his eyes revealed neither relief or happiness with her presence. Leal ignored it the best she could, but he had looked at her with a sadness and fear she couldn't understand. Whatever concerned him, he did not say.

She didn't comprehend at the time, but as the nation changed around her, it became clear. He was a hostage. If she didn't do her best to support their reforming army, they would have him killed within the day.

Leal wasn't the only victim to this extortion. Every mage she knew spoke in hushed discontent. They were each leashed by their relatives trapped within the gulags.

With the collapse of the previous council and the chairman, Military Commissar Oso acted immediately. He placed himself in position as chairman, and supplanted all other commissars with trusted members from his military.

The catastrophic invasion had opened the nation's eyes to their inadequacies. Within weeks, New Vetus's doctrine shifted, both political and military. No longer were they content with how things stood. Mages, along with many other disciplines, were no longer given the freedom of academic advancement. Now, they were integrated within the military. Any and all creations had to support the rapid advancement of New Vetus's military growth.

Leal switched out her needle for a razor-sharp scalpel. The last part of her markings required immense precision that just couldn't be achieved without cutting into the thick skin of her hand.

She was proud of this marking. Even the mages of her unit couldn't make heads or tails of it, despite some being decades older. Leal couldn't understand their lack of enthusiasm for creation. They settled for the standardized markings taught to all, but those were so limiting.

No matter how many times Leal tried to show them that the alternatives were so much better as long as you put in the tiniest of effort to understand, they never listened.

When the only escape Leal had from this horrid world was the creations she made, it was disheartening to have nobody to share that enthusiasm.

She made the last few cuts on her thick fingers before submerging her hand in the hyle medium. Hopefully this time, it wouldn't become infected. Sometimes, no matter how careful you were, material other than the pure mixture would get inside your body. By wiping at the wounds with a cloth soaked in a special substance, the risk could be mitigated, but the chance was still there.

Leal would have to wait a few hours before she could fill her reserves with hyle and try the markings. She was both excited to try them out, and concerned for the circumstances she would be required to use them.

Two months ago, the newly totalitarian council considered the buildup of forces enough to begin their conquest. The Zadok Kingdom had fallen almost without a fight. Despite the ease, it still took time for the land to be ripped from the hands of the albanics. Rebellion forces were aplenty. They made unfortunately good targets, and her superiors jumped at the chance to give both her and the other mages battle experience.

Leal hated fighting. Hated her creation being used to spread death. She'd seen other water mages with a focus on crafting blades or pressurized streams. The sheer efficiency with which they cut through people horrified her. It directed her marking design in the completely opposite direction, much to the irritation of her superiors.

She'd be concerned about them threatening her father again if she weren't one of the few actually creating new tools for their arsenal. Instead, they'd thrown her into almost every battle they could. Obviously, they wanted to desensitize her to murder, but all it achieved was to amplify the hatred for her country.

"Leal," a voice called after she'd finished cleaning her arms.

She turned to Hefkos—one of her unit members—as he dropped something heavy on her workbench.

"Here," he says. "Weapons of the northern states are a step up from Zadok's, so new armor is being distributed."

Leal eyed the slab of leather and steel. The one she already had was heavy enough, she wasn't looking forward to lugging around something even heavier. She would have to focus her next marking on a dedicated water barrier. Something that she could keep up for an extended time that didn't weigh her down like these suits of armor.

Most of her kind didn't have an issue with the weight, but Leal wasn't exactly built as heavily as the rest of the ursu. Each ursu warrior had taken on the protective gear with enthusiasm. After the war with Henosis, the pride of the ursu in their bare-knuckled strength had been crushed. When one could fall from such measly little pebbles, arrogance quickly dissipated.

The body armor couldn't block a direct shot, but it would slow the projectile enough for an ursu's thick skin to take the blow.

"Should you be doing that now?" Hefkos pointed to Leal's freshly cut markings. "We'll be moving out tonight while they are celebrating, and I don't want you having issues with an untested marking mid-battle."

Leal didn't know what to say. Her markings would work, she was certain, but they didn't seem to trust her ability regardless of the times she'd proven them wrong.

Before she could express her confidence in words, the older mage continued. "Word of warning: refrain from applying your markings yourself. The reksha were a suspicious bunch even before being given oversight of the military. If they find you applying unapproved markings without direct observation, who knows what they might think?"

"But the division's head mage already gave me the go ahead."

"Doesn't matter. At the very least, make sure you have a partner to watch over you when you next apply them."

Leal wanted to argue further, but she knew it would be a wasted effort.

Heavy thuds had both mages turn to the giant ursu walking away from reksha command. The warrior left the encampment and sprinted south, his looming form snatching fearful gazes until it was gone beyond the horizon.

"Where do you think he's off to?" Hefkos asked, leaning against Leal's workbench. She wondered if he had nothing better to do than bother her.

Leal's eyes lingered on the horizon. Tore Hund had always been a legend. More of a fairy tale than a real person, until she'd laid eyes on him herself. The hero of New Vetus. The reason they'd broken free from slavery almost two centuries ago. It was unbelievable that he was still alive, and yet he looked no older than her father.

"Looks like we'll be moving on without him for now," he said. "Eh, we don't need him. Our enemy's strongest soldier is a fire mage."

That caught Leal's attention. "Fire mage?"

"Yeah, Armelle's unit is tasked with taking them down. Even with the elemental advantage, it will not be easy for them. The mage apparently has enough hyle to set the entire battlefield alight."

"A fire mage," Leal mumbled under her breath. The image of a blazing city flashed across her mind. "This mage, are they an áed?"

"Uh, maybe?" her senior mage said. "I only know what the brief said." His eyes narrowed. "You didn't read it, did you?"

She didn't answer. Instead, she was up and striding toward the reksha. The ursu that enforce the will of the council.

Only an áed would have enough hyle to ignite a battlefield. Even as suicidal as fire mages tended to be, it was far harder for them to grow their capacity when their element naturally worked against their body. Either it was an áed, or an ancient fire mage. And if it were an old fire mage of that caliber, only Tore Hund could beat them.

Was it possible? Was Solvei so close after so long?

Leal hated her for the death of her mother. Everything had gone wrong since she'd shown up. If the girl had just stayed still in the library back then, like Leal told her, then everything would have turned out fine. She would have figured out a way to get her out of the city, and thousands wouldn't be dead.

She didn't realize what she'd done until it was too late. Leal had stormed in on a meeting amongst the reksha and officers. They all stared at her with either amused curiosity or blatant annoyance, but nobody had yet reprimanded her.

Well, she was already here. Might as well go through with it.

She snapped into a salute and made her request. "Please let me fight the fire mage, sirs." The words struggled on her tongue, but she forced them out.

The reksha in charge of her mage division appeared surprised and pleased, which was far better than the wrath and irritation of the many others she'd interrupted.

"Junior Lieutenant Leal, you are willing to rush into battle?" the reksha asked.

She nodded, unwilling to risk speaking once more.

"Granted," he said, as a few protests rose from his side. "Expect a court-martial for your actions today. Prove your worth and your punishment might be lighter. You are dismissed."

She hurried away, berating herself for her impatience.

She imagined he'd only been lenient as he had been trying to force her enthusiasm for war. But if this really was Solvei, then she finally could avenge her mother's death. Leal had been practicing what she would say to the áed if she were to meet her again.

First, she would trap the girl. Then she would tell her how much she'd been waiting for this and maybe gloat a little.

She couldn't fight against New Vetus, but a girl younger than herself? The frustration, hate, and despair that had built up in the past years could finally have a target.

She approached the mages' supplies. Hyle storage devices were exorbitantly expensive, but the military had confiscated all within the mage academies for their own purposes. It also made transporting water easy.

Leal placed her freshly marked hands on the large barrel-shaped hunk of metal, and filled her reserves with water hyle. Her well was smaller than most of the other mages in the army, but she still surpassed many in terms of capabilities.

There were three things that mattered to a mage. Their hyle reserves, the markings they hold, and the understanding they had of those markings.

The first was how much hyle the mage could contain. A special array of markings held hyle, but the total maximum they could handle was determined mostly by how much exposure they'd had to the element. One could become a strong mage with minimal understanding, simply by continually flowing the hyle through their bodies for decades.

Markings were the most important aspect. They were the technology that guided the hyle to do what the mage wanted. The simplest markings had no variables and could be used even by those with a lacking understanding, but they would be limited in every aspect.

The more one understood the working of a mage's markings, the more complicated ones they could apply. The more complex the marking, the more work the mage would have to do while operating to keep it functioning, but the effects that could be created were well worth it.

Leal grabbed one of the small backup hyle packs they had for 'novice' mages like herself. A heavy metal disc wider than her hand with a strap to bind it to her chest. These would be almost useless to any of the older mages, but it would double her capacity. It was just unfortunate it had to be so heavy. She was already going to struggle with the new armor.

Leal lifted her head to the half-moon of early evening. Not long now. Not long until she'll be able to get some closure on one part of her life. Once she'd gotten back at Solvei, everything would feel better.

Her first friend had died that night. It was time to murder the one that took her place.

CHAPTER THIRTY-FIVE

Leal III

During New Vetus's Surprise Attack

Sneaking within the camp of the mixed races was surprisingly easy. The few volans on lookout were cut out of the sky with the silent pressurized stream of a fellow mage. Not even the bodies crashing into the ground made a sound. It was Leal's job to make sure of that, and she was glad for it. Better to catch the dead volans than be the one to kill them.

On top of the heavy armor, they all wore thick, tightly bound clothing to cover the glow of their markings. Their large bodies were hard enough to hide while sneaking into the enemy's camp, doing so while shining like light bulbs would be asking to be discovered.

They made it to their first assigned tent and the others in her unit immediately moved to assassinate the sleeping soldiers. Leal looked away. If this was her own squad, she would be forced to participate, but Armelle owed her for the efficiency upgrade Leal had designed for her.

It was late into the night, and those that weren't sleeping were intoxicated and celebrating around campfires. There were guards watching the perimeter of their camp, but not even they expected an attack from the ursu. Leal despised this war. There was no reason to attack and push forward. At least against the Henosis, they'd been defending their homes. Now? They'd only become like their enemies.

Leal forced herself to shake the thoughts. The whole reason she'd forced herself into this unit was so that she could kill. She needed to focus on her opportunity to make things right; to avenge her mother. Ruminating in the wrongness of murder wouldn't help her achieve what she was determined to.

They had a pretty good idea of where the áed was, and her path once the battle begun. The brief they'd been given left little doubt in Leal's mind that the fire mage was, in fact, Solvei. The reksha were able to amass quite a detailed account of her suspected abilities and habits from the battle they'd watched not even a day prior.

Leal could never forgive Solvei for what she did. And she would make sure her former friend was punished for the horror and pain she caused. Leal hated killing, but she hated Solvei more.

If it hadn't been for the áed, things would still all be all right. Her mom would be alive. They would still be living in Morne together, and her dad would have returned to them, rather than being stuck in the gulag. Everything went wrong with that fire. Leal just knew if it hadn't happened, then everything would all be all right.

The first barrage of artillery snapped Leal back to reality. The rest of the unit dashed out of the tent, off to cut down as many waking soldiers as they could while remaining stealthy. They were already in position to ambush the áed, they just needed to wait until she arrived.

A small form barreled down the hill, her short stature looking incredibly out of place for a battlefield. Leal had no doubt it was Solvei even before the flames wrapped around her form, snapping out at the air as if ready to ignite their surroundings. The heat radiating off the áed was far greater than anything Leal could recall. Whatever happened, she would be careful not to let them get close.

Leal thought she was prepared to see the girl again. She wasn't. Solvei had grown, but the sight of her brought back memories she'd rather forget. Horrific moments where she and countless others suffered after the fall of Morne. Sad memories of her mother's passing. Worst of all, Leal remembered the joy she once had alongside Solvei.

She didn't want to remember those times. Solvei was evil. She was the cause of everything going bad, so Leal refused the good memories she once shared with the áed.

Solvei stopped as she passed Leal's hidden position. Fire swirling around the girl revealed her inner turmoil. She hadn't detected the ambush, had she? The áed spun on her feet and began running back up the way she came. She must have.

One mage in Leal's unit shot a stream of pressurized water to cut off her path of retreat. Solvei reacted with unreal timing, blasting herself backward as large swathes of flame spread out ahead of her in her stead. The same mage tried to hit her with a second stream, but the áed was already aware. Throwing herself skyward, Solvei launched herself at the mage with clear murderous intent.

If not for Armelle, the first mage would have been dead. It was only for a moment, but bright, white flames coated the áed's hands. Hot enough to sting just looking at.

The mages quickly surrounded her, and Leal realized she would need to act soon. Leal wanted . . . no, needed to be the one to end her. She needed some form of retribution against the one who'd made her life a nightmare. Preparing herself to do what she had to do, Leal readied her marking. She would spear the girl through with too many water spikes to dodge. As long as she got some water under that snowsuit she wore, Leal would succeed.

Leal didn't expect Solvei to dash her way before she was ready. Reflexively, she sprung her marking, exploding forth a wave of water from her hands. The water collided with the áed, sending her to the earth as water crashed around her.

Leal stared in confusion. Hadn't she meant to spear her through with that attack? It was impossible for a marking to enact any effect not directly intended by the user. What happened?

Steam billows off the girl as she scrambles to her feet. Before she could leap away, Leal curled the water around her, entrapping the girl within a sphere. As usual, she had to keep the water moving constantly to stop it from sagging under gravity.

Finally, the opportunity was before her. She could relish in defeating the one who killed her mom, making sure she understood exactly how her actions would be her undoing before Leal killed her. It's better that Solvei hadn't died immediately. That would've been too quick, too easy.

As Solvei flared out at the trapping sphere only to hurt herself, Leal spoke up to Armelle. "Please." Unhappy with how hesitant her voice sounded, she gathered her resolve. This was what she wanted. "Leave her to me."

"What? We can't do that. You know how dangerous she'll be if left alive."

Leal knew all too well what Solvei could do, but if she was going to talk to her former friend before killing her, she wanted to do it alone.

"Remember that favor I asked?" Leal hoped Armelle could overlook her actions just this once.

Armelle's eyes waver between Leal and her captor. "If you are certain. Make sure she's dead after you are done."

She signals to the rest of her unit before they all rush down the hill to join the one-sided slaughter.

Leal gathers herself. She'd practiced what she would say if she ever saw Solvei again. Clamping down on the nervousness, she stepped forward, out of the tattered remains of the tent.

"It has been a while, Solvei."

"Leal?"

The absolute shock and befuddlement in Solvei's tone both delighted her, and sent her heart racing. It was clear the girl could never imagine someone surviving the inferno she wrought, nor it being her former friend to be the one to deliver retribution.

"Solvei . . . You appear to be doing well." While Leal had been suffering alone with her mother's death, her father's imprisonment, and the upheaval of her life, Solvei had been off massacring thousands on the battlefield. She was probably enjoying life right up until Leal got the upper hand on her.

"I . . ." Within her cage, Solvei turned away. Clearly, she knew exactly what she'd done.

"I've missed you."

Leal burst out in laughter, but she wasn't amused. No, Leal was pissed. How dare she pretend like nothing had happened. What? Did she think Leal would forget about the horror of that night? In what world could she ever overlook the crime the áed committed?

"You missed me, did you? Well, I've missed my mother, but you wouldn't care about that? Would you?"

Solvei flinched, as if struck. Leal assumed she would feel satisfaction from such a sight, but all she felt was emptiness.

"What happened to Calysta?"

Leal's jaw dropped. Solvei had the gall to act like she didn't know. Did she think playing ignorant would save her from Leal's encasing water? She knew very well how dangerous water was to the áed. No matter how strong the girl before her might have grown, she would always remain susceptible to Leal.

"You happened," Leal growled. "You killed her, along with a thousand others in that fire."

"What?" The flames circling Solvei's body extinguished with a puff. "No, I—"

The girl before her failed to form words. Her knees quaked, but she remained standing. Leal waited for the excuse she knew would come. Solvei would claim innocence. Claim it wasn't her, or it wasn't her fault. Leal waited for Solvei to give her excuse and flimsy explanation so that she could tear her down and make her face the repercussions with her full fury.

"I'm sorry." Solvei's head dropped. Her eyes broke from Leal's and rested on the ground, unseeing.

Solvei acted like the world was crashing around her, but Leal knew better. It was all an act. How could she not have known the damage she caused?

"Deivos shit. Lies." Leal disliked using the lord of spirit's name, but if he existed, she was sure he would understand. "Why did you do it? Why burn everything?"

"I—" The áed's mouth opened to deny what Leal knew to be truth, but struggled to find the words. Any moment now, she'd gather her thoughts and come up with some fabrication so Leal would drop her cage of water. Solvei might well burn her too, given the opportunity.

Leal had her right where she wanted her. She knew that once Solvei realized she couldn't convince her, the áed would try to burn her way out. Leal had seen those white flames; she could get through the barrier if she tried. But Leal was ready for it.

"Punishing Gloria was all I wanted. I let it get out of control." Solvei stumbled through her words, but managed to gather herself for an apology that almost sounded sincere to Leal's ears. "I'm sorry."

This wasn't the order it was meant to go.

She was supposed to plead innocence, or claim ignorance until Leal begun her punishment. She was only supposed to apologize and beg for her life after Leal made her feel the same pain her mother must have felt trapped within the continae, burning alive.

"No." Leal's fists clenched hard enough to hide from the pain swelling in her chest. "You don't get to be sorry." She altered her marking, shrinking the sphere of water and crushing Solvei between walls of water. Steam rose from within, but Solvei just looked Leal in the eye with pain that mirrored Leal's.

She pressed the cage down further, to end her most hated person's life right here and now. The áed flinched away from the enclosing wall, falling to her knees and ducking her head as the water flowed over her head. This wasn't going how she imagined. Solvei wasn't fighting back. Even if it would be a meaningless resistance, she should be fighting with everything she could to survive. But instead, she simply let Leal do as she pleased.

Despite Leal's wishes, the cage didn't crush Solvei. It let up, giving the áed room. Why was her own spell disobeying her? That should be impossible. She stared down at the áed before her, who returned the gaze not with resentment or hatred, but with guilt and sorrow.

Tears ran down Leal's face. She was crying. Why was she crying? She was angry, not sad. This was her opportunity to finally achieve vengeance for her mother's death, so why were her markings refusing her?

Why was her friend letting it happen?

Former friend, Leal berated herself for even thinking of her that way. Even now, Solvei was tearing things apart. She wasn't acting her role. She was the root cause of all Leal's problems, so why was she resisting? Why wasn't she selfish, like she'd always pictured her mother's murderer acting?

Why did Solvei still care about Leal, when Leal had given up on her years ago?

"This is unfair." Leal stepped forward. If her markings wouldn't listen to her, then she would do it with her own hands. The cage disappeared, crashing along the earth in a large puddle as Leal wrapped her hands around the áed.

But, no matter how hard she pressed, her hands refused to squeeze. She couldn't hurt her.

Then she noticed; wisps of fire flickered out from the áed's eyes. It was so unlike normal tears, and yet it was fundamentally the same.

"You're supposed to be evil," Leal sobbed, realizing her voice was wavering. "So why are you the one crying?"

As Leal continued her vain attempt to crush Solvei, she felt the heat the girl exuded reducing. An áed that should have felt at the very least like she just put her hands in an oven was no more warm to the touch than cloth on a hot day.

Even without the water to stop her fighting back, or running away, Solvei remained within Leal's grasp. She hated it. She hated everything about how things turned out. Solvei wasn't the evil murderer Leal had convinced herself she was. Even if she'd started the fire, it was clear it was hardly intentional. But then, if not Solvei, who could she blame for what her life had become?

She needed to be real with herself. No matter how much she told herself she hated Solvei, she just couldn't do it. Now that she was in the position to actually hurt her old friend, it became impossible to follow through. Only now, with Solvei right beneath her hands, did she even consider that the girl couldn't have wanted things to go the way they did.

"I had so much I was going to say when I saw you again. I wanted to enjoy my retribution." The words escaped her in a waver as she crashed to her knees before her first friend, embracing her. "I missed you, too, Solvei."

She didn't intend to say that, but as much as she tried to deny it, it was true. She'd missed the casual, daily joy she'd had when she could drag Solvei around the city, getting up to all sorts of nonsense that she wouldn't have been brave enough to do before meeting her, nor had the luxury to do after.

Leal longed to return to the time when she didn't have to worry about anything. Before they moved to Morne, before she lost her mother. And before her father was held hostage at the gulag.

Dread washed through Leal. She was already facing a court-martial for her actions, but if she returned to her superiors with Solvei still alive, it would be her father who would face the punishment. She needed to kill Solvei to keep her father safe, but doing so was impossible; Leal simply couldn't do it.

Her only hope now was the friend she just tried to kill.

She arched her head over the smaller girl's shoulder, to hide from her gaze. "Solvei, I need your help."

"Anything." No hesitance. Leal appreciated that, but what she was about to ask would likely get them both killed. Even if she knew how suicidal it was, Leal had no other option.

CHAPTER THIRTY-SIX

Repentant

Leal?"

I can't believe it. I'd planned to eventually go looking for her, but I'd never expected her to be here. On the other side of war.

I'm so happy to see her alive and healthy, but . . . why is she trapping me?

She's older, taller than I remember. Her body now covered in the familiar glowing markings of a mage. Two distinct lines curve around her eyes, illuminating where it hadn't nearly two years ago.

"Solvei . . . You appear to be doing well." Between the gaps in the swirling water she traps me within, Leal walks before me.

"I . . ." How can I respond to that? Tell her things have been horrible? She's still one of my closest friends. My first. I don't want her to worry. "I've missed you."

She laughs derisively before sneering down at me. Her near full-meter height advantage makes me tilt my head back. "You missed me, did you? Well, I've missed my mother, but you wouldn't care about that? Would you?"

I'm not sure why she's acting like this, but her hostility stabs my chest worse than the spray of water. "What happened to Calysta?" I spent enough time around Leal to know how nice a person her mother was.

"You happened," Leal growls. "You killed her, along with a thousand others in that fire."

"What?"

No, that can't be right. Only Gloria was supposed to die back then. I didn't have control. The fire . . . my fire shouldn't have spread so fast they couldn't escape.

"No, I—"

I what? The possibility that the fire I started killed anyone hadn't even crossed my mind. I hadn't even considered it when I discovered how flammable people outside the wasteland were. Thinking back, it's impossible to deny. Thousands likely died because I wasn't careful.

I killed my friend's mom. Put Leal in the position I'd declared I never would; I took away her family.

My ignorance isn't an excuse. In my carelessness, I'd done the same as the Titan did to my family. Instead of protecting her from a situation like mine, I replicated it.

"I'm sorry." The words feel empty even as they leave my lips. She has a reason to hate me, and words won't bring her mom back to life.

"Deivos shit. Lies." The hatred in her voice stings more than the water that pulses with her words. "Why did you do it? Why burn everything?"

"I—" What can I even say? My actions have already killed more than I ever intended. Regardless of whether I intended those deaths or not, those lost lives are entirely my fault. "Punishing Gloria was all I wanted. I let it get out of control. I'm sorry."

"No." Leal clenches her fists and scowls. "You don't get to be sorry."

The cage around me suddenly compresses. I'm forced to my knees as the water presses down on me. Pain wracks my chest and face as water splashes over my fire.

The water hurts, the knowledge I killed my friend's mom is agony, but it's the hateful glare of Leal as she compresses me further within the cage that rips through my chest worse than anything. She was my first friend. My best friend. To know I betrayed her trust to such an extreme degree is crushing.

Maybe she's right. Maybe I deserve this.

"This is unfair. You're supposed to be evil." She steps forward, dispelling the water cage and gripping her large hands around my shoulders. "So why are you the one crying?"

I collapse the heat of my body to not burn her, letting the water sting worse than ever. Leal's hands grip me tight, but I don't run. Tears pour from her eyes. She tries to growl, but it only comes out choked. Her head drops.

"I had so much I was going to say when I saw you again. I wanted to enjoy my retribution." Leal drops to her knees and I'm engulfed in a crushing embrace. "I missed you, too, Solvei."

What can I say? What can I do to make it up to her? I killed her mom. There is no way I can make up for that. Nothing I can think of will return things to the way they were, so I just lean in and return the hug, wallowing in guilt.

We kneel there, embracing on a battlefield.

"Solvei, I need your help," Leal mumbles in my ear as gunfire diminishes. The pact nations' army is losing, but I don't care. My friend needs me more.

"Anything."

She breathes a sigh and leans back. Even on her knees, she's taller than me. She has bulked up since I last saw her, but still not to the same degree as the rest of her kind. Though thin for an ursu, she has more muscle than Bunny.

"They have my dad," she says, looking into the dirt.

He's alive? I'd thought for sure there would be no chance, considering how the war progressed before Hund's intervention. If Gerben, the ursu that originally found me collapsed in the wasteland, is alive, then Leal still has family to stay by her side.

Did the Henosis Empire take him as prisoner?

"Who does? Where is he?" I ask, ignoring the water pooling around my boots.

Leal hesitates, her eyes trailing down the hill where her kind are cleaning up the remaining stragglers from the pact nations' army. "The reksha are holding him at a gulag back in New Vetus."

She lets me go and rises to her full height. I thought I'd grown a lot in the past couple of years, but it's nothing on her growth. She scans my body and her jaw clenches. "Solvei, I can't forgive you. Not for what happened to mom."

My arms fall to my side and I turn my gaze away. I give her a nod of understanding. I wouldn't forgive myself either. For me to hope things return to the way we left them would be far too greedy.

"They'll consider me a traitor for not killing you here, so I need to get my dad out before they send the order to kill him," Leal says. "I can't get him out alone. I'm not strong enough."

"I told you I'll help. If we need to leave right now, I'm with you."

"Thank you."

"First, I need to meet with a friend." I grab her hand and run back up the hill.

The encampment is in chaos. The ursu's surprise attack is nothing if not effective. Only the mercenaries appear to put up a proper defense. All others are left to fall under the coordinated offense. Besides a few odd pops, the sound of gunfire has ceased.

We find Grímr struggling against a trio of ursu. His damaged chest and missing wing giving him far more issues fighting them than it usually would, but he holds his own. An ursu lays dead beneath his talons.

My flames surge forward, ready to burn those attacking Grímr. A squeeze to my hand makes me hesitate. The golden flames instead encircle Grímr, forcing the flammable ursu to back off.

I lead Leal into my blaze. She tugs against my grip, but I don't give her the chance to pull away. Her reluctance disappears as soon as we are within the blaze. Tongues of flame roll off her fur without burning.

"Solvei, you're okay!" Grímr relaxes as I walk into sight. "We need to leave, now. We can't . . . Uh, who's this?" he asks as his eyes fall on the ursu I'm pulling along. He doesn't act immediately hostile, thankfully, despite the rest of her race attacking us.

"This is Leal. She's a friend." I create a path of flame to the north. "Let's get moving."

With Grímr's current inability to fly, we have no choice but to walk our way out of the battlefield. My flames should scare off most of the ursu army, but I'm certain they'll also attract the water mages.

"Leal, do you think you'd be able to stop any water mages as we escape?" The only solutions I have for the mages are both painful for me and deadly for them. After discovering the death I've already caused around Leal, I'd rather avoid what I can.

"I'll be able to tear away control from a few of them easily, but there's nothing I can do about the more experienced mages." She shakes off my grip, keeping her hands free. A dim glow flashes along the thin lines winding her fingers. "I won't be able to do so for long."

"That's fine. Just long enough for us to get out of the encampment." I twist to

Grímr, who's hobbling alongside us. His injuries mean we're limited by the speed at which we can run. "Grímr, once we're out, will you be fine returning?"

As I keep my senses strained, picking through the ursu I can feel and looking for those heading toward my flames, Grímr narrows an eye at me. "I'm not about to leave you here to fight a war alone."

"No. I'm leaving the battlefields," I say. "Leal needs my help, and we need to move quick if we want to save her father."

Grímr watches me in contemplation, likely determining if I'm being truthful. He turns to inspect Leal, who is running in silence but obviously listening.

Unlike the last ambush, I feel the waiting ursu long before they can douse me.

"Leal, two ahead of us. On our right." As soon as I give her the warning, I pull back on my flames, extinguishing them before any water can come near them.

In the same moment, the two mages ahead of us blast identical streams of compressed water toward us, Leal shoots out a pair of thin streams of her own. Leal's are far thinner and have nowhere near the power that the opposing mages have. Why isn't she using that wave of water she used on me? What can those two tiny things do?

Leal's and the enemy mages' streams collide into one another, and, as expected, Leal's flow is overpowered with ease. She still managed to capture me, so I have to assume she has more planned.

Thankfully, she does. The enemy ursu's streams curve down into the earth within a couple meters of the point Leal's water makes contact. Each stream soon cuts off, and Leal's hands glow once more. The new pool of water explodes into a thick mist that blocks sight to the mages.

We rush out of range before they can find us again. I don't reignite the path ahead. We've come far enough that there aren't many people around. Ursu nor the other races.

We face no more opposition as we flee alongside a dozen soldiers escaping the losing battle. The New Vetus army is settling to solidify their hold on the area rather than chase stragglers.

"Are you sure you trust her? She is a water mage. I don't need to tell you how dangerous she is to you." Grímr looms over me, glaring at Leal, who can't keep his gaze.

"Yes," I say. "She had the chance. Plus, I owe her."

Apparently satisfied, Grímr relents. "All right. Don't worry about me and make sure not to take on anything you can't handle. I don't want another Viisin situation." Grímr pulls me into a hug with his sole wing. "Come back safe, okay?"

I lean into his side before breaking away. "You better have that body in perfect condition by the time I'm back. Also, save me some magnesium if you find some."

Grímr huffs in amusement before nodding and turning. We go our separate ways.

It's sudden and saddening. Grímr has been by my side for so long, and we hardly have any time to enjoy our goodbye. I shake my head to focus on the task at hand and turn to Leal.

She looks conflicted. An expression that seems to have made a permanent home on her features since I've met her again.

"All right," I start. "Where exactly is Gerben?"

"Across the isthmus, in the east of New Vetus," Leal says. "We can't use the new military rail. It's too well guarded. But if we hurry through Zadok, we can sneak onto a civilian train."

She plans to run through the Zadok Kingdom? "Won't that take weeks?"

"Yes, but what choice do I have?" Leal kneads her hands before her chest. "I can only hope they don't send the order back immediately."

So she needs to get back faster than a train, but doesn't have the benefit of flight? "Hmm. Give me a minute. I want to try something."

She gives me an anxious look before turning over the sparse earth, her hands fidgeting all the while. We'll need to cross the new front line her own kind have instated if we want to travel to New Vetus. That, on top of our uncertain deadline, must be at the forefront of her mind.

Well, if my plan works, then neither will be a problem.

I morph into a bird. Unlike usual, I don't limit my size. My body grows double my natural height, wings spreading five meters from tip to tip. As I enlarge, I can tell I won't be able to use my white fire anymore, my size too large to allow the density of that intense heat.

Before, I'd been limited in how far I could expand or shrink my form. That is another restriction surpassed by knocking down my wall and achieving the next stage of my flame. When I get time, I'll have to test exactly how large or small I can force my form.

What I never expected is for the transformation to only take a minute. Despite adding far more fire to my form than I'd ever tried before, the flames settled into my pictured form quickly.

Out of the corner of my eye, I spot Leal gawking at my transformation. Right, the Void Fog was after I last saw her.

My form is just a sized up version of the same falcon body I'm comfortable with. I'd considered imitating Grímr's alicanto body, but I figure familiarity will be important as time is of the essence.

"Well—" I cut off before I can even start after hearing my voice. Creepily low pitch, though still my voice. A quick change to my throat returns my voice to normal before the size up. "Climb up. I'll get you to your dad before the first train even leaves the station."

She stands there staring for a long minute before I step forward and crouch, nudging her with my wing. When she finally shakes her head and climbs on my back, gripping at my flaming plumage, I have to hide the sudden doubt I feel that this will work.

Leal is heavy.

Subtly, I increase my size. It's a strain, but I manage another two meters to my wingspan. It's not even close to Grímr's fifteen meters, but even this makes me feel like I'm stretching too far.

I guess passing that barrier isn't enough for me to become a Titan. Unfortunate.

I take a step, trying to get accustomed to the girl on my back that must be at least five times my weight, even with my new size. My talons scrape against the dirt and I stumble forward, not having lifted my leg high enough for the added weight. With spread wings holding me upright, I hope I'm able to hide the stumble.

If I can't even walk, then how am I going to fly like this?

My neck twists and I watch Leal inspecting my long, burning wings with that same interest she'd had when watching my pillars of flame in our secluded space years ago. At least her mage curiosity distracts her from my embarrassing mistake.

This might take more effort than expected.

CHAPTER THIRTY-SEVEN

Overburdened

Taking off should be no problem. I'll just blast us into the air with a jet of fire. The problem will come once I'm at speed. I can hardly keep shooting myself forward with physical flames. Doing so will exhaust me in minutes. Especially up in the air where I don't have earth to burn and mitigate the energy I expend.

No, I'll need to apply what I've learned of airflow from my firestorms to my wings. I have ideas, but I've yet to try them. I'm unable to do so until I'm already in the air.

It'll be a trial by fire.

Some of the other races use that saying. I find it amusing. For them it means to learn by doing, in a dangerous situation. My first assumption had been the complete opposite.

I stretch my wings and lean forward, straining not to tip under Leal's weight. My wings slam downward as a plume of flame rockets behind me. Despite the extra heft, we thrust into the air without issue. Leal clenches her arms tight around my neck. If I were one of the fleshy races, I'd probably suffocate from her strength.

With widespread wings, I accelerate through the air. It's rather pointless to flap while I've got the thrust of physical flame pushing me through the sky. Probably didn't even need to do so when I took off.

A squeak reaches my ears, so I turn my head. Leal presses into me, not daring to look anywhere except the flickering depths of my plumage. As I look over her, I remember another failure of mine. The guilt layers on top of everything I already feel.

"Leal, I'm sorry." I turn back ahead as my acceleration slows. "The jacket you lent me, it was destroyed."

"What?" she mumbles.

"I wanted to return it when I finally met you again, but—"

I'm cut off by her laugh. Her breath brushing my feathers tells me she still isn't looking up. "Why are you worrying about some old bit of cloth? I can't even remember the thing." I can feel her shaking her head without raising it. "Honestly, how could I have ever thought you could do that intentionally?"

I don't know how to respond to that, so I just focus on my flight. Since I left Morne in a fiery blaze, I've killed many more. How many times might I have caused innocents to die without me knowing it? I've been indiscriminate for a long time now. I've burned through any in my way.

Is . . . is it possible that amongst the thousands of normal mermineae, there are those like Leal's mom: innocent, but only there due to circumstance?

No. They're here to invade. That is clear by the actions they've already taken. They could have simply stayed back in their own lands and not caused us problems.

I'm losing speed. Fast. Without the boost that comes with jettisoning physical flame out the back of my wings, I won't be able to keep us airborne for long. Maybe I should have had her toss the armor. It would have lightened the load at least a touch.

As I'd learned to do with Grímr's wings, I heat the air beneath my feathers without consuming it. My flames encourage the air to rise into my stretched wings. The lift is considerable, but not enough.

I expected I'd need this to fly, but it doesn't even let me glide. Not indefinitely. Hopefully, the other applications I've been planning will work.

The first change is to have the feathers on the top half of my body eat the air. If air can push my solid wings upward, then it's reasonable to think that the air above might block my rise, right? Having my flames do so isn't even hard. Slightly disorienting, forcing two opposite effects so close together, but not difficult.

Surprisingly, it works on the first attempt. The strain on my wings increases and I level out. I flap my wings with the joy of success, and immediately destabilize my flight.

The difference in air doesn't play nice as I beat my wings in habitual motions. With Leal strapped to my back, our combined weight is incredibly off center. My momentary loss of control has us rolling in the air.

Leal shrieks and her fingers dig ever deeper into my neck while her legs clamp around my side. I struggle to twist us the right way up and soon regain level flight.

Okay. Nothing more than basic movements until I know how all this works. Especially while I'm holding a passenger.

"Sorry," I call back, but she doesn't respond nor loosen her grip. I'm pretty sure she hasn't opened her eyes since we started flying. What ever happened to the curiosity of a mage?

I spread my inner flame through the air above my wings, and increase the amount of air consumed. While that improves my lift, it's hardly worth the effort with how minuscule the rise is from simply burning the air touching my wings.

It is great that removing the air above my wings pushes me past the point of a stable flight, but I want to move faster. We'd likely outpace the ursu's trains at this speed, but it would still take well over a week. After enjoying the intense pace set by Grímr's massive metal wings, this feels like crawling.

This next change is the one I have the most hope for.

I've noticed, after creating many firestorms, that air will rush into flames. It doesn't even matter all that much whether I eat the air, or heat it enough to make it rise, the air will rush in as if to fill the space left empty. The air I heat myself will almost always rise, but it will only rise. The air in the surroundings, not directly affected by my fire, can rush in from the sides or even from above.

If I could force a breeze to rush in from my rear, I could have the wind not only lift me, but push me forward as well.

Well, that's easy to say, but I'm not really sure how I can do it. My goal is to somehow modify my flames so that the air coming in from the front is minimal, but the air coming in from my back is as strong as possible. If I create a fire behind me that eats the air, none of the air will actually reach me to push me forward, but if the fire behind me heats the air, it'll fling upward. Though, maybe the answer lies in how hot I make the air?

Thinking by itself isn't about to give me any answers, so while the flames above and below keep me gliding through the air, I spread my inner flame to cover the area behind me.

Only heating the air a little allows the wind to blow into me, but the breeze isn't all that strong. I'll take it—every little thing will add up—but I was hoping for something with a lot more oomph. Changing the temperature doesn't make much difference. Hotter air moves faster, but also rises instead of pushing me from the rear as intended.

Covering my front in air-eating fire solves my issue of the air whipping into my face, but when I spread it too far, I find myself falling rather than gliding. Right, can't fly if there isn't any air.

Also, I have to pull back when Leal gasps for breath.

I think back to the self-fueling firestorms. They are at their strongest when air and fire twist in a spiral, flinging flames dozens or hundreds of meters ahead. An attempt at creating the swirling flame in midair only results in the air dispersing with each turn.

If I had to take a guess, I'd say the surface underneath is how it remains formed normally. The air pushes down from above, which keeps the twister's shape. Unfortunately, that simply doesn't work in the sky.

Unless . . .

On a whim, I create two tubes of physical flames around both sides of my body. Not eating the air, nor allowing it to pass through. At the front end of each cylinder I burn away air, but at the rear, I leave the only entry point. Inside each tube, I spin my fire, superheating the air all the while.

This . . . is effective. There are a few problems, like my wings interrupting the cycle of air, but I can work on the efficiency later. The physical cylinders will tire me out eventually, but they're far more efficient than jets of fire; I'm not actually throwing away the physical flame.

Wait, couldn't I make these tubes a part of my body instead? I'd have to sacrifice my wings and a bit of my chest mass, but this might just be too good to pass up for long-distance flights.

With my flight settled and speed assured, I turn my attention to my passenger. She still won't look up.

"Leal, you should have a look. The world looks amazing from this high up."

She doesn't speak, just shakes her head into my neck and refuses to open her eyes.

"We're going to get to your dad far before they ever get any message," I try to reassure her, but still get nowhere.

This is getting concerning. I feel horrible for what I did in Morne, but it has been so long since I've seen her. I want to talk to her. Find out what she's been doing all this time. Not that I deserve it, but I want to be close to her again.

"Leal," I start softly. "We'll be flying for a few days. The sooner you look, the quicker you'll get over it."

She lets out a quiet groan, but lifts her head. Her hands clench my feathers as she finally opens an eye. As she gets a glance over the horizon, I can tell we won't be having any problem with a fear of heights. She can't tear away from the horizon, where the starry night sky meets the dimly lit earth of the post Ember Moon evening.

A breath of relief passes my beak. It is important for us to move fast, but I refuse to fly if she had stayed terrified. If I were to force her through her fear, I would be nothing but a hypocrite. It's a struggle I would rather avoid putting on her shoulders.

Leal tenses as her eyes finally fall below. We are flying at an incredible height, almost a thousand meters up. I consider flying lower, but Leal is unenhanced; there's no chance she'd survive a fall regardless of altitude. At least with this height, I can catch her if the worst were to happen.

I may also just prefer the view up higher and want to show off.

We fly for a few hours in silence. I experiment with changing my body and eventually settle on a form best for reserving my energy while also keeping us speeding along. Unfortunately, with how heavy Leal is, I'm still tiring rather quickly.

I've wanted nothing more than to just talk with her, but I don't feel comfortable being the one to speak first. Leal has every right to not talk to me.

The first stray twinges of light peek over the horizon when my hunger and exhaustion reach their peak. Below, the odd towns mark the land. Buildings litter the roads between each.

What might have happened to the albanics after the ursu took their land? It's hard to tell from this high, but most buildings we've passed are intact, so I'd have to imagine Hund hadn't just gone on an indiscriminate killing spree through the kingdom.

I land within a section of forest far from any settlements. Whether it's ursu or albanic living here now, it's better to avoid any contact for now.

"I need to rest for a bit, then we can get moving again," I say.

Leal jumps off my back, and I can't resist the urge to let out a sigh of relief when she does. She looks up at me. This form is taller than her when I'm not bending down under her weight, which means I'm looking down to an ursu. Huh.

Her eyes drop to inspect herself and I realize my relief might be too obvious.

I turn away and engulf a few trees in fire. Wood isn't anywhere near as filling as metal, but they are in excess and I'd rather not waste time melting through rock in a blind search.

A clatter brings my attention back to Leal. Her armor now lies in the dirt by her feet. Strapped to her chest is a thick plate with an incomprehensible array of inscriptions along its surface.

"You should have just told me earlier," Leal says.

I collapse to the earth, not bothering to change to normal. I'd had to revert my wings back from the vortexes to properly land, but I want to get back in the air as soon as I can.

"There's no problem."

It may be hard to carry her around, but I can hardly complain. What right do I have?

Leal sits before me, her eyes in her lap and her fingers tracing the lines along her palms. "Solvei . . . thank you, for dropping everything for me. I hadn't really been thinking when I asked you. The possibility we might move faster than his execution letter seemed impossible." She lets out a shaky breath and looks me in the eye. "I'm not about to reject your help, but the gulags are well-guarded prisons. It will not be easy to get him out."

I lift my head and try to appear as confident as I can for her. "You don't need to worry. I'm a lot stronger than I was two years ago. As long as you keep any water mages away from me, there won't be anything that can stop me."

Leal is obviously doubtful. Maybe I should give her a proper display of what I can do?

"New Vetus military adopted many of Henosis's methods after the war. All the corpses of the last war went to enhancing a few amongst our highest ranks. One of these few is the warden for the gulag where my father is held. No matter how strong you are, we still need to be careful."

I give her an earnest nod. It's her father in danger here; no matter how sure I am that this elite ursu won't come near Hund's strength, I'll give him the same apprehension as a Viisin.

The Viisin just so happen to be burnable.

CHAPTER THIRTY-EIGHT

Gulf

While I rest my wings, the two of us talk about our lives since that fateful day. I spoke of my actions that night, and the permeating hatred toward Gloria that pushed me until I'd lost control. The Void Fog, crossing the Alps, the wars. Everything I'd been through, I told her.

Leal had to go through hardships of her own. Many of which were kick-started by Morne burning to the ground. Barbs of guilt prick me whenever I think about what my mistake has caused.

New Vetus has changed since I was last there. Molded into something barely resembling the nation it was before. The war against Henosis scarring them for the worse.

Gone is the place that originally welcomed me without restraint. Gone is the community focused society Leal grew up. Now, it is nothing but a machine to fuel their newly minted war efforts.

I remember only months' worth of the country it was before that welcoming atmosphere twisted to hostility, but Leal knew far more of its good side, so the brutal state it's fallen into clearly hurts her.

Once I feel rested enough—and burn down a small section of the forest—I rise to my taloned feet, ready to fly once more. Leal, thankfully, leaves the armor on the ground. She's still heavy, but it should make flying easier.

My wings spread wide for takeoff before I notice the sky far to the south.

"Hey, Leal. You wouldn't happen to be able to stop rain, would you?"

"Sorry, no. I could make a barrier, but I would struggle to hold it up long."

"Well, we're going to have to go around, then." I take off to the west, wanting to get as far from the thick mass of gray rolling toward us.

After a while of flying, Leal breaks the silence. "Solvei, are you not worried?"

"About what?"

"About declaring yourself an enemy of New Vetus. About me. You're letting a water mage so close to you without hesitation. I didn't care when my anger and frustration were the only things on my mind, but you've let me close from the start."

"I'm already the national enemy of Joiak. What's another country to that?" I joke, but she doesn't laugh. "You're one of the few people I care for."

"I haven't forgotten how dangerous water is to you, so how could you not feel worried being near me? Especially after I tried to hurt you?"

"Leal." I don't want her to feel bad for her anger. The hatred she must have felt after experiencing her mother's death. "Beyond freedom and survival, there's not much I truly desire. The one thing that can compete is my intention to prevent those I like from losing their families. Not only did I fail that with you, I was the cause." I turn my head back to Leal. "I don't want to hurt or die, and probably wouldn't stay still and take it, but I would understand if you were to attack me."

Leal groans and drops her head into my plumage. "This would be so much easier if I had a target."

I say nothing. My hatred had been fortunate enough to have two. Killing Gloria and the general didn't undo the things they did, but it had been incredibly satisfying to watch them burn.

A few hours flying southeast around the brewing storm lands us on the coast. The unimaginable expanse of water stretches far beyond the horizon, and now I'm stuck with a dilemma; do I wait out the storm, then head south? Or do I brave the sea and fly southeast to the eastern landmass? Both will take us into New Vetus, but the one that puts me over the ocean will get us to Gerben faster.

This is the same place the Henosis loaded me onto the ship. The trip across the water had taken weeks, but I have no idea how fast that ship had been moving. It might take me minutes to cross the water, or it might take days. No matter how much I want to help Leal, putting myself in such danger for so long is unreasonable.

Down in the docks below, ships and jetties crawl with ursu soldiers. The men and women rush around, transferring cargo before the rain can hit. None need to worry about falling water as I do, but they still move to finish their jobs before the downpour.

Do we have the time to wait out this storm? That is the question.

It might take a week at earliest for the message to reach the gulag via rail, and at our current pace, we'll be there far earlier. But it wouldn't be the first time I've been stuck for days on end because of unending rainfall.

Can we risk it?

No.

Just looking out over all that water terrifies me, but if I can push past this, it'll be just a small thing to make it up to Leal. First, I'll have to make sure I'm absolutely ready for this.

"Hey, do you mind if I drop down and eat some of the metal down there?" I incline my head down to a large, trussed metal structure lifting a wagon sized crate off a ship. These are Leal's people, so I don't just want to damage their equipment without her permission.

"The crane? Sure. As long as we don't stay long, burn whatever you need. Just . . . only as long as you can stop the spread."

The crane is a bit too close to the water for my taste, but it's the largest quantity of metal I can see in the area. Slowly, I lower myself to a landing. The workers below me rush out of the way, appropriately fearful of the large flaming bird before them. I ignore them and twist my flames around the beams of the crane.

Iron. It's somewhat disappointing, but I shouldn't have expected anything else. Better to fill my reserves than the wood and stone buildings around us, but why not use any of the other metals? Whoever decided iron would be the primary metal clearly hadn't tasted the others.

Leal climbs down my back and approaches the dock ledge. Her markings glow as she submerges her arm in water.

A groan snaps my attention to the crane above me right before it collapses sideways. The support beam snaps after my flames make it glow, and the entire structure topples over the large box it was lifting. The crate smashes, scattering a hundred books and scrolls amongst the dried meats along the dock.

Kinda strange to transport books along with food, but I could hardly care and just finish my way through the remains of the crane.

Ursu rush in toward the fire with large buckets of water only to stop at the sight of me. Thankfully, they are smart enough not to throw the contents of their containers toward me, but I take a couple steps back anyway. Amongst them there are a couple of excessively terrified ursu, but neither is looking at me. Their eyes flick between the books and their partner.

Is there some other big flaming bird around that lets them consider me less threatening than their own comrades?

"Hey, Solvei?"

I turn to Leal, who's reading one of the fallen books.

"Yeah?"

"Could you separate the nervous ones from the rest? I want to talk to them."

I nod and send a blast of flame toward the ursu with buckets, making sure no inner flame remains when the fire brushes past them. They react as I'd hoped, tossing the water in their buckets and running for safety.

Without the water to worry about, I weave a wall between the ursu, cutting off the two clearly suspicious workers. With their escape route cut off, they have no choice but to turn to us. Is it weird that I take a bit of pleasure in their fear? Most don't see me as intimidating until I'm already burning through their body. Maybe I should keep the taller stature.

And give up my white flame? Never.

"Hurry and clean this up," I hear Leal tell the two. "We'll only be here for a short time, but it should be long enough for you to hide your collection."

I give her an odd look, but she moves to help the two by piling the books and scrolls together. The crane is already long since consumed, so I'm just waiting for Leal to tell me she's done. Every few seconds I have to scare off some hero trying to throw water on my wall, but otherwise I have no issue waiting.

The two toss out a couple barrels of fish and fill them with the paper before locking the lids again. They wave to Leal before jumping into the water. I just stare after them, feeling left out of the loop. They became quick friends with Leal, didn't they? You'd think they'd be mad that we got in their way.

Leal climbs up my back once more, ready to go. "Sorry about that. It must be tiring to keep your fire up for so long."

I give her an insulted look, but I can't stop the laugh from slipping out. "This? Tiring? You've seen nothing yet."

Sure, this was beyond me a few years ago, but it is hardly anything now. Even though Leal has grown herself—the way she submerged me in that fight says enough—she still doesn't comprehend the extent I've improved.

As I take off, I distract myself from the vast body of water by questioning Leal. "So, what was that with the books?"

"Banned documents," she says. "Philosophic or political books are now illegal under the new council. I'm pretty sure those two were archivists."

I can't really say I know much about either topic but a blanket ban on all? "Why?"

"I wish I knew. They've been heavily banning, blocking, or murdering anything against the council's ideals. They have Hund at their command, so it's not like anyone can fight back."

She fiddles with a satchel I don't remember her having earlier. Did she snatch it from the docks? My guess is proven true as she pulls out a cut of salted meat like the ones I'd seen scattered amongst the books. Well, at least she planned ahead.

"Um, do you mind?" Leal lifts the cut of preserved meat in question.

With no further explanation, I curl my flames around the salted flesh, careful to cook but not burn. My flames dig through the meat and distribute the low heat equally through. It takes a minute, but Leal soon has her meal.

"Well, that's convenient," she says with a slight smirk before digging in.

I suppress the happy trill that threatens to run up my throat. As much as I deserve her hate, she is my friend and I want to get along. Once we have freed her father, I don't want her to avoid me.

Happiness freezes as my eyes fall to the surface below. The sea is far too close, and despite my attempts, I can't keep the fears from circling my mind. What if we don't find land by the time I'm too exhausted to turn back? What if my wings stop working for whatever reason and I plummet into the water?

I want to raise my altitude more than I already have, but I don't. My team has given me plenty of warning about flying too high. Originally, I'd thought they'd only meant on top of the Titan Alps, but Grímr never let us fly higher than a thousand meters out on the other side.

They told stories of volans, or even portians able to fly, rising higher than a league and never coming down.

I seriously consider the risk, just to move the tiniest bit away from the high likelihood of death below. If I do, I could even fly higher than the storm and not need to risk crossing the sea.

But, no matter how much the water terrifies me, it would be foolish to add another risk. If something cut off my wing, could I regrow it by the time I crash into the water? I doubt it.

Only positive way I could spin the worst-case scenario would be that the water below is all liquid, so Leal shouldn't be hurt by the fall. I hope.

Thinking about this isn't helpful. I'll just keep my course straight and make sure nothing sends us plummeting to the dark depths. If my eyes stick to the horizon, I'm sure land will appear at any moment. That is all I need to focus on.

My determination to not look down is immediately defeated as a shadow moves in the corner of my eye. Down within the water, something massive just moved. My eyes dart along the dark greenish gray sea, but I can't find the shadow again.

I've been so worried about the water itself that I never considered what monstrosities might live within. Only the most horrifying existences could ever consider the ocean their home.

"Hey, Leal. You wouldn't know anything about massive creatures beneath the water, would you?"

"Hmm?" She looks up after chewing through the last of her meal. "Oh! Yeah, they're called gyian. Huge creatures, but they're not aggressive until you reach the ocean. Some believe there is a massive tunnel underneath the isthmus that lets the gyian travel between oceans."

"This isn't the ocean?" I ask, bewildered. I can't see land in any direction anymore. How could this be anything but the ocean?

"No, it's a gulf, a sea at most. The ocean is larger and far more dangerous."

"Dangerous? Even to you?" She's a water mage. Shouldn't the ocean be the best place for her?

The answer comes to me even as I ask. Of course, if the ocean contains the worst of the worst monsters, then not even the benefit of an environmental advantage could help her.

"The heqets own the ocean. Their raiders pillage our coast and their battleships sink all outsider vessels," she says. "They're the reason Henosis didn't invade from the south."

Her answer is not what I expected. Am I mistaken for assuming there would be monstrosities within the ocean? Or do ursu just not see enough of the vast waters because of these heqet?

Well, whether sea or ocean, it doesn't matter. I'd die falling into either. Best to just keep my head straight and fly until land.

CHAPTER THIRTY-NINE

The Gulag I

Despite my fears, land finally graces us after a day of flight. We land on the ledge of a tall cliff overlooking the gulf. Without wasting time, my flames burn through the surrounding flora, regaining my energy. The journey was long, but nowhere near what I'd been dreading, so I could still keep going for a while longer, but there's no reason to refuse food when it's available.

The landscape isn't anything like what I remember when Henosis dragged me to this side of New Vetus. Fewer beaches and more rocky overlooks. The isthmus should be south from here . . . somewhere, but I couldn't say how far.

"Do you know where to go from here?" I ask Leal.

Her arms raise above her head as she stretches. "Depending on where we are, it shouldn't actually be that far from here. Maybe a couple hours with how fast you move."

"Huh." I'd half expected to need to cross to the far south. Well, I'm not complaining. "Then we best get moving."

"Huh? Aren't you tired?"

"A little, but I got enough energy to keep going."

"Oh . . . well, I'm exhausted. Let's keep moving in the morning."

I nod in agreement. So long have I spent around my team and others with greater enhancement that I forgot how little sleep they need compared to most people. Even I have slept nowhere near as much as I used to. Though, that's not just because of the energy I've taken on, but the excessive fuel available to me away from the wasteland.

Back with my tribe, even the strongest of elders slept to conserve energy. With enough food to burn through, any áed can stay awake indefinitely. Mental strain might grow the longer the mind goes without rest, but it is possible.

My body returns to its default form, and I relish in the heat that comes with it. It's only been a day or so, but I missed this feeling. The slight temptation I had to keep my body larger than an ursu is immediately wiped away by the comfort of my white flames.

"You know, I don't know if I'll ever get used to you doing that."

Leal is already laying on the one unblemished patch of grass surrounded by a ring of burned earth.

"What? My transformation?" I have nothing better to do, so I lay beside her.

"It goes against what I thought I understood about áed. Your bodies are distinctly solid. Touchable, unlike the fire you wield. They exhibit attributes of fire, but are separate from the element. More lifelike and defined." Her eyes inspect my body, now controlled and not giving off light. "But it's like you've lost that definition. From the perspective of the senses I've trained in the past years, it is far more difficult to tell you apart from your inner flame."

I'm surprised she can notice the connection. My binding has already far surpassed Elder Enya. The intimacy at which fire moves with me is not something I could have imagined back with my tribe. It has always felt like fire is my very being, but it wasn't until my binding skyrocketed to its current level that I realized how shallow that feeling had been.

I want to learn how I can keep pushing that connection. How close can I truly become to my fire?

"Solvei, your loss of definition scares me." Leal chews on her lip with concern before continuing. "As you become closer to your fire, your connection to the form consistent with all life disappears. What if you do not keep your mind? As you become less áed and more fire, will you retain who you are? If you push past the point of retaining your definition of life, will you cease to be?"

I simply stare at the ursu for a long moment, trying to process her words. "I think . . . you *are* tired. There's no way I could lose who I am by becoming *more*," I say. "I've felt no less myself after the Void Fog, so there's no reason to believe I will by going forward."

"If you're sure," Leal says. "Night." She turns away from me and leans her head down on her bundled coat.

I follow suit and drop my head, trying to sleep despite the lack of genuine need.

A minute passes. Two. Five. Soon, an hour is gone and I still can't nod off.

Damn. Her words got to me.

I know it's a completely nonsensical theory of a tired mage, but that tiny, lingering 'what if' is enough to worry me. It hardly even makes sense. I am fire. I can't lose myself by becoming closer with what I am.

Eh, whatever. It's probably better I stay up and watch over things. Don't want some random stranger to sneak up on us while we sleep, or a sudden shower to drown us, or Hund to crush us. That's honestly my biggest concern. Not whoever they tasked as a warden amid war.

If Hund were to be sent after us once we break Leal's dad out, I'm sure there's nothing we could do. I'll sit on the logic that it would never make sense for the ursu to send Hund after us while they are trying to push into the pact nations. What is a single mage and her father in the grand scheme of things?

The warden might be hard to deal with, but for the same reason New Vetus wouldn't keep Hund away from the war, they wouldn't keep one of their more skilled elite this far back home. Sure, he might reach the lowest equivalent of a Beith, but any more doesn't seem reasonable.

Tomorrow morning, we are going to get there and save Gerben before they have the chance to even realize something is wrong.

The gulag is a dreadfully gloomy looking place. The ursu's incredible stone masonry is wasted on this place. A massive complex with towering walls of unmarred gray stone sits alone on a lifeless plateau. The lone steel gate is the only visible entrance to the compound, neighbored by a small administration building at its side.

Watchtowers nestled on the ramparts hold ursu guards. Most watch over the inner grounds, but there are a few peering over the sparse land around the prison. I could approach with my merminea fur outfit, but there is no way for Leal to come with me and remain unseen.

Leal and I hide behind an outcrop overlooking the plateau. There is no cover between us and the gulag we could use to hide our approach. Once we move, we'll be in clear sight of those watchtowers.

"Do you know where they are keeping your dad?" I ask.

"No. They brought him to the visitor rooms when I was allowed in," Leal says, poking her head over a rock to inspect our target.

It really would have been better if we'd had the time to have a merminea coat made for Leal as well, but for now it looks like I should move ahead myself.

"All right, I'll go sneak in. See if I can find Gerben." I pull the cord within the neck of my outfit and the merminea fur pulls into place, camouflaging all but the few tears on my torso. "You should stay here for now."

"No, I need to get in there. It's my father. I can't stay while you risk yourself." Her eyes finally fall on my concealed form. "Ah. Now that's unfair."

"You don't need to worry about me," I say. "I'll find your dad and get him out. If I can't do it myself, I'll come back and we can figure out another plan."

Leal is clearly not happy about my proposition. "How will you even get in? You can't fly over the walls, they'll see you."

"Simple. I'll melt a hole through the stone."

Leal just stares at me, or at least what she can see of me. "Right," she drawls. "Of course you can." She sighs before locking eyes. "Solvei, if you get into any trouble, signal for me and I'll be over the wall in a second."

I nod, pull up my hood, and scamper out onto the plateau. The fur works much better when the body is closer to the ground, so I stay crouched as I run toward the wall on the opposite side of the entrance gate. I could probably mimic a merminea's body and allow myself to rush along with my belly against the ground, but then my body wouldn't fit my outfit all too well. Not to mention I'd give off light by changing my body from its default.

I still haven't hidden my flames on anything but my normal form, even after passing the barrier that had been holding me back. I've been working on my control almost nonstop, but it's just not as easy to improve the manipulation of my form in a short time compared to compressing my fire or taking on energy from my fallen foes.

A guard in the closest tower turns my way and my body freezes. The ursu haven't fought against the mermineae long, so I can only hope any method they might have devised to find the creatures hasn't passed this far back within their country.

His eyes linger on my area for far too long for comfort before sliding further along the landscape behind me. I don't move yet, in case he sees any movement. The ursu holds a gun slung over his shoulder. The weapon is fatter than any other I've seen, looking more like a miniaturized cannon than a normal rifle.

I've never seen the ursu using this sort of weapon. Even on the battlefield I just came from, they only used swords. I guess after the war with Henosis, the effectiveness of the weapon was pounded into the ursu. Are those not trained with the sword given guns now instead? How much more damage could that mini-cannon do compared to the rifles used by other armies?

The guard's gaze turns away enough that I can continue my approach without obstacle. Upon reaching the wall, I move along it, trying to find a place that a casual inspection won't notice.

After a few minutes of search, I have to settle with a fairly visible part of the wall. There is no secluded space. The best place I figure to melt through the wall would be right below a watchtower. It's out of sight of the other towers, and the ursu above will have to look directly down to see it. Only issue is if any guards patrol the exterior, there's no chance they will miss it.

My white flame burns into the wall and in no time at all, it melts into a viscous puddle at my feet. I climb through and find myself in a storage room of tables, chairs and other rather unimportant goods. Of course, most are made of wood, so I need to put out the fire that started from the molten stone dripping into the room. Thankfully, this seems to be the basement level, so the lava doesn't drip into some lower room.

Dust swathes all. Likely, nobody has been through here in years. Good, it means I'll have nobody noticing the hole through the thick wall of stone from the inside.

It might have been a risk to just rush in like this without knowing what was on the other side, but I had no other plan. If I set off the alarm immediately, it would make my job much harder, but I still believe I can get Gerben out regardless of the attention on my head. As long as I can find him first.

That's really where this might become difficult. This compound is huge. How will I find a single prisoner amongst thousands? As much as I know Leal wanted to come as well, she wouldn't be able to wander around freely, anyway.

I make sure my outfit still hides me well enough and push against the typical heavy door. Locked. Fortunately, a tiny lick of flame into the keyhole destroys the lock, and I push into a wide, deserted hallway. Echoes of conversation come from my right, so I move in the opposite direction.

Soon, my path is blocked by another large door. Like the last, the mechanism inside the lock melts away and I squeeze through without opening it too far. I'm back outside, this time within the large walls.

An extensive structure sits in the central point between the stone walls. The dull, gray building lacks the usual features of normal ursu construction. No architectural uniqueness. No decorations. Just a simple—yet large—stone building with thin slit windows.

A wire fence circles the inside of the compound, separating the structure in the center from the tall walls to the outside. I've seen an ursu's strength. There's no way the guards expect that small fence to hold them in, so what's the point? There's already a major wall to lock them in.

I go to move toward the obvious place where I'll find a prisoner, but press myself against the wall beside the door as a pair of footsteps come my way. A duo of ursu guards, each holding one of those enlarged guns, turn the corner and walk directly for the door I just came from.

I don't dare to move as they walk within a few meters of me. Neither have noticed yet, but it will only take them observing the slight distortion on the stone to realize I'm here.

Wait . . . why do I feel anxious? Even if they find out I'm here, I could kill these two before they have the time to tell anyone else. Their weapons would do nothing to me. Well, except damage my outfit, which would be incredibly annoying more than anything.

One of them grabs at the handle and it immediately snaps off. Whoops, probably burned a bit too much of the lock.

"The fuck?" the first stares down at the handle in his hand.

His partner groans. "Just put it back on and let the next person deal with it. My tongue is dry and I'm not wasting my time here."

The first wedges the handle back in place—though at an odd angle—and follows his partner into the building protruding from the outer wall.

Huh, that is convenient. They don't even question when a door is broken. Could I break my way inside the main prison and have the guards think they broke each door along the way? Doubtful. It's clear no prisoners come near the wall.

There are too many eyes watching the wire fence, so I lower to the ground and crawl forward. If it works for the mermineae, it can work for me. Only it cuts my speed instead of increasing it as it does for them.

By the time I reach the wire fence, I can finally get a look at the treatment of the prisoners here. The first thing I notice is the absolute emaciation of the ursu here. They don't have anywhere near the normal muscle mass. I can even see the necks of some instead of the usual mass of flesh and fur which make their shoulders.

Many have old, torn, and blood-soaked clothes with accompanying wounds. The crack of a whip, not unlike that of Remus's dangerous attacks, resounds through the muted compound followed only by pained shrieks. The silence itself is strange considering the number of ursu around.

I trace the source of the whip and find a row of ursu kneeling with bowed heads as a guard lashes them one at a time. A crowd stands uniformly, watching as the guard walks up and back, striking at each of the bleeding people cowering in the dirt.

The temptation to just burn everything to the ground grabs hold of me and won't let go. Some things just deserve to be incinerated. But I have to hold myself back, for now. My priority is Gerben. Once I get him and Leal safe, I'll come back.

I'm glad Leal can't see this.

CHAPTER FORTY

The Gulag II

There are many more captive ursu than I could have expected.

I burn a tiny section of the wire fence away to give me just enough space to crawl through. As I slowly make my way forward, doing my best to ignore the crack of the whip and the wails of its victims, I get close enough to feel the heat of the people inside the prison building.

There are thousands. All cramped within what I can only imagine is a tight space considering how close they sit or lay. The prisoners far outnumber the guards, but each guard is fed, has a weapon of their own, and doesn't look like they're about to pass out at any second.

If the prisoners are to rebel, I can't see it going well. Amongst them are children not even half my age. Considering how some kids sit near the guards, I can only imagine they are being used as hostages to dissuade rebellion. Hardly any different to how Gerben is being held hostage for Leal.

How many of these ursu are here to tie a leash to someone outside? How many on the battlefield are only there because they fear for their families?

I drag myself along the ground. The dirt is soon replaced by stone paving as I crawl into the shade of the structure. Nobody has noticed me yet. Now, how do I find Gerben amongst the thousands of bodies? It is too hard to tell the difference between individuals from their thermal signature alone, so I can't just pick him out from the crowd.

Maybe I could ask a prisoner? That could be risky. What if they demand me to free them as well or they'll call the guards? With the sheer number of ursu held here, there is a good possibility whoever I ask won't even know who Gerben is.

Leal might have to wait a while, but for now the best course of action is to be patient and look for him myself. Hopefully, he hasn't changed much since he first found me out in the wasteland. Considering the gaunt bodies and defeated expressions around, I have little hope.

I need to get inside the building, but I can't simply take the main entrance and the guards will immediately notice any hole I create. My eyes follow the building's exterior up past the slit windows to the edge of its roof. If I can get up there, I should be able to keep my entrance out of sight.

With a quick glance over my shoulder, making sure no one has seen me through the camouflage, I dig my fingers into the gaps of stonework. My fingers melt deep grooves to hold my weight. It would be easier to burn the grips directly in the face of the masonry, but that might be too visible. By digging only into the gaps, I can keep my passage at least somewhat hidden for now.

The stone melts beneath my fingers. Liquid rock trickles from the hole as my fingers push deeper, before solidifying as I pull back the heat. I do this repeatedly to climb the wall. Any close inspection will reveal the damage, but like the hole through the outer wall, it should be a while before anyone notices.

It's not hard to scale the building, but I keep my movements slow. I'm in the open. If I'm not careful, an ursu might notice me even through the stolen camouflage.

I pull myself up over the ledge and tumble onto the flat roof. My body freezes as an ursu guard glares my way. Damn. I thought he was looking away when I threw myself over. The giant man readies his mini-cannon and walks my way.

Thankfully, he hasn't called any of his friends, so I doubt he saw anything other than a disturbance. Regardless of what he thinks he saw, he's coming my way. There's no chance he will miss me if he's right on top of me.

The other guards I can feel on the roof aren't in direct sight, so when he gets close, I can probably burn a hole through his head without any noticing. It's the safest method; I'll incinerate his body and leave not a trace of his death. They might notice him missing, but it isn't likely to happen before the hole in the outer wall is discovered.

Flames churn within my chest, but I don't dare move until he's close. White fire ready to extinguish his life. I'm prepared to strike. The moment he looks down at me, I'll jump forward. But as he steps within a couple meters of my prone form, I hesitate.

This isn't something Leal would want, is it? What's to say this guard doesn't have family of his own held hostage somewhere? Leal would definitely want me to spare him, but how could I do that without raising the alarm? I still haven't even started looking for her dad.

Leal doesn't have to know.

As long as Gerben gets out safely, does it really matter if I kill someone willing to assist with imprisoning his own kind?

My mind bounces between jumping him while I still have the element of surprise, or refraining. I can't decide, and soon it's too late to act. He walks right past me without even realizing I'm only a step away.

The ursu's eyes don't stray from the point I climbed over. He leans against the stone border of the roof and peers over the side. Apparently satisfied there isn't anyone hanging off the side of the prison, he slings his gun over his shoulder. He doesn't turn away, though, instead he leans over, inspecting something.

He's found my fingerholds, hasn't he? The tall ursu leaning over the side of the building like that makes me consider if he would die from a fall this height. Would the other guards assume he just tripped? Or would they assume he was pushed?

The ursu takes a step back, nearly stepping on my head. He still doesn't notice me. Twisting on his feet, the guard—instead of returning to the place he'd been standing before—walks down a few steps to a lower section of the roof. He walks casually, without rushing, so even if he saw the holes in the wall, he mustn't think much of them.

"Oi, one of you, take my post. I need to get the supervisor."

So he's leaving? Perfect. I scuttle along out of sight before another ursu can take the first guard's place. I squeeze myself between the outer wall and the clearly new wooden frame of the water tower. Not a place I would like to sit under, but it keeps me out of sight of each ursu.

I don't think I could have ever asked for such good luck. Did the guard not think to look down from his massive heights, or was the camouflage that good? With things going this smoothly, I should be able to find Gerben in no time.

Of course, it's the moment I have that thought that the alarms ring.

First, it's a quiet jingle coming from the wall back where I broke through. Then the loud clanging of bells rise from all around. They must have found the breach I left in the outer wall.

Immediately, all the heat signatures around move in a frenzy. Guards round up the prisoners and direct them inside the building. Those struggling to walk after their lashings get shoved into the stone ground for their sluggishness. The bang of a single cannon fire is enough to settle most of the prisoners into a reluctant stagger to their cells.

Below me, it is harder to distinguish the shape of each heat source I feel, but I can tell they are being crowded into tight spaces. Ten ursu within a space no larger than the oven I once spent so much time inside. With some ursu over three meters tall, it is far more cramped than it ever was for me.

As the guards force everyone into their cells, it gives me a decent layout of the building. The building is three floors of rooms circling a central staircase and an area with no activity, which I imagine is the guards' quarters.

Now that I see the order each of the ursu have been stored away with, I have to believe that luck is still on my side. This will make it much easier to find Gerben.

I wait until there's less movement beneath me and melt my way down. Now, my priority is speed, so while the camouflage stays up, I don't bother crouching or crawling around. At the first cell, it is clear I'm noticeable; many of those within the cell look my way with confusion. They have trouble focusing on me, but they definitely know I'm here.

I don't see Gerben amongst them. This is the first time I've had a close look at the prisoners. The scars, injuries, and starvation they each suffer is appalling. I want to burn the bars of their cage off and free them. Doesn't matter who it is, I hate the idea of leaving people trapped.

Until I find my target, I can't. I need this order to find Leal's dad and I don't like the odds of trying to keep everybody safe while also achieving my main purpose.

Four cells I pass before the first guard raises his cannon toward me and shouts. He doesn't see perfectly well, but he has noticed me. Before he can fire his weapon, a white flame melts the gun in his hands. Liquid metal dribbles over his palm before he can even toss the weapon. The guard shrieks in pain and rushes toward the stairs.

I check a few more cells without luck before I'm attacked by a few more guards in the corridor. Each of their weapons melt the same as the first, some misfiring because of my fire. The guards flee in pain. A stubborn ursu leaves only when every hair of his hide is ash.

This isn't working. The guards will rush up the stairs in no time, and I've only searched through ten of the hundred cells on this floor alone. I need to change my approach.

I pull down the hood of my outfit and coat my body in flames. Should I need it, my camouflage remains ready. For now, the prisoners need to see me.

I step before the next cell on my list to check, and mentally note Gerben isn't here either. Each of the ursu stare through the bars, dumbfounded. "Does anyone here know which cell Gerben is?"

None of them answer. More interested in gaping than helping.

"Now!" I demand, my impatience leaking.

Guards flood out of the central stairs and move to surround me. I can feel them moving before they even come around the corners. This would be so easy if I could just melt them all. Burn them alive and walk out without opposition. Leal doesn't want to kill, so I won't.

So, how do I keep these unenhanced ursu out of my way without giving them an early cremation service?

Fear.

My inner flames spread through the wide hall, not spreading and burning as I usually would, but instead taking the form of eight-legged beasts hissing down at both guard squads.

They are a pale imitation of the arachnid monstrosities from beneath the Titan Alps. Only large enough to fit in the corridor and the hiss is a replica created with burning air, but it does the job. Half the guards run terrified at the sight of the flaming beast as strikes from the white tips of its spindly legs leave molten scars in the stone. The others fire their weapons, then follow their comrades when they realize it does nothing.

I turn back to the group that still hasn't answered my question. "Well?" I ask with crossed arms. "Gerben?"

Most have backed away from the bars, but an elderly ursu remains. "I know three men named Gerben. How old is yours?" The old man appears strangely calm amongst group looking out at me in fear.

"Old enough to be a father," I say. "He was a soldier from the start of the Henosis war."

"Then check the northern cells of the floor below and the east of the ground floor." The old ursu gulps almost imperceptibly and hardens his gaze. "If you are freeing him and not here to kill him, then please take what children you can with you."

"No!" a woman gasps from behind him. "Don't you touch them!"

Despite the middle-aged ursu's protests, she doesn't stop cowering near the back of the room.

"Koda," the elderly says. "This is the only—"

"I'll come back," I interrupt, not having time for their debate. "Thanks."

I take a step away from their cell and melt through the floor. It's far faster than going for the stairs, especially considering all the guards huddle around that area. The pair of flaming arachnid beasts unleash upon the guards of this floor and I once more have space to move.

I ask around for the Gerben who's supposed to be in this area, only to find this Gerben isn't the one I'm looking for.

Another floor melts away, and I scare off more squads. Finally, I arrive at the cell of the first non-áed sapient I'd met. Despite the immense loss of weight, I recognize the ursu immediately.

The bars separating us liquefy in a wave of flame and I step into the cell. As the ursu within watch, their fright heightens and Gerben and another stand before the others as they huddle in the corner.

Gerben is missing an eye and all the fingers on his left hand, but he still stands protectively before the others. It's kind of insulting that he doesn't recognize me immediately.

The ursu standing by Gerben's side is an insane three and a half meters. The tallest ursu I've seen. Well, except Hund. Hund is still nearly double this ursu's height. As I move toward Gerben, the tall ursu steps forward and swings his fist at my head.

He hits nothing. His knuckles pass right through without effect. Though I leave the fur of his hand charred for the attempt. I'd thought he might be enhanced considering his size, but he isn't. Or at least, his punch didn't feel like that, nor did his fur have all that much resistance to my flames.

I can see the moment Gerben realizes who I am, and my grin is involuntary. His eyes widen and he clasps the hand that actually has fingers over the shoulder of the tall ursu.

"Solvei? What are you doing here?"

"Nice to see you too."

CHAPTER FORTY-ONE

The Gulag III

It's great to see Gerben alive, but I shouldn't stand around talking. Leal is waiting.

I step toward the rest of the cell's residents and the tall ursu moves to stop me. Gerben pulls him back, his eyes not leaving me.

"Move," I demand.

The group's eyes flick between the massive arachnid looming in the corridor behind me and the flames around my form. When they don't move as asked, I step forward again, forcing them to scramble to the corners. That's good enough for me. Fire blasts into the cell's rear wall.

The tall ursu tries to break from Gerben's grip, only to find his head locked under Gerben's fingerless arm.

"Calm down. I know her." He looks up from the struggling ursu in his grip. "Solvei, this is not a place you should have come."

"Oh? I'm sure your daughter would love to know that you don't want us here," I say, trying to suppress a smirk as I pull my fire back into myself. All that remains of the back cell wall is a puddle of molten rock dribbling onto the paving outside.

"Leal is here?" He doesn't sound happy. His voice wavers at the knowledge she is here.

"Yes, now come. Don't make me drag you to her," I say and push through the new opening.

Hesitantly, he follows . . . as do the other dozen ursu in his cell. I want them to stay where they are until I make sure of Gerben's safety at Leal's side. Can I tell them to stay while I help another right in front of them, though? If it were possible to take them all out together, I would, but I cannot protect them from those mini-cannons the guards wield.

A round of gunfire crackles from the north. Where I originally broke through the wall, a sphere of water rolls toward the wire fence.

Damn it, Leal. You were supposed to wait outside.

I spin around Gerben, his height making my plan rather daunting.

"All of you hide in your cell for now. I'll come back," I try to reassure the others before throwing myself into Gerben's chest and rocketing us into the air. It takes an immense jet of flames just to push us off the ground.

And I thought Leal was heavy.

In moments, the two of us are speeding over the wire fence. It's a struggle to slow us to land without splatting Leal's dad across the ground, but I bring us down safely. Flying off with him will be impossible.

My flames spread out over the mesh fence and consume every section that falls within my range. I expended a lot of physical flame to thrust Gerben a few hundred meters, but at least I'm close enough to Leal to keep her safe.

I look up, ready to take out the guards attacking my friend, only to find long tendrils of water striking out of her protective shell and easily disarming each guard as if they were only an annoyance.

Suspended inside the ball only slightly bigger than herself, she rolls along the earth toward us. Leal doesn't slow, and I have to jump away as she crashes into Gerben. Her sphere melts away as she envelops him in an embrace.

I feel sympathy for Gerben, first being tossed around by me, then taking his daughter's charge. Despite looking like he's about to collapse at any second, he does well to hold Leal upright as she loses all focus on where we are.

"Leal," I say to get her attention. She lifts her head to lock eyes with me but doesn't let go of her dad. "Take him and leave."

She nods her head but freezes in mid-motion. "You are coming with us."

"No, I'm going to free the others." I step in close and ignite an inferno around us, scaring off the guards trying to approach and obscuring their sight. "I don't want to make the same mistake with you again. If I kill the guards, I can be sure to get the prisoners out safe. It is up to you."

Maybe it's cruel to pin the choice on Leal, but I care more about her choice than the lives of those stuck here. That is probably cruel of me, but I can't lie about how I feel.

"No. We need to go now!" she ignores my question. "We can't compete when the warden shows up."

Too late for that. I feel an ursu with a thick longsword moving within my range even as she says that. He doesn't come right for my fire right away. Instead, he's conversing with the guards standing near the now cleared fence.

"He's already here, Leal. Can I kill them or not?" I don't mean for my tone to be as harsh as it is, but we won't have long before he comes.

"But, can't you . . . I can't . . ."

She can't respond, and just before I settle on her answer being no, Gerben pats her head and addresses me. "Yes, do what you need to. I will take responsibility."

I nod and angle my head to the wall she came from. "Leal, take your dad and get out."

"I will not let you fight alone."

Despite her desperate declaration, I have to smirk back. I can see the ursu through my flames now. He doesn't have mage markings. He doesn't have the terrifying inscriptions on his blade that the Henosis general had. The only thing he has is his blade and a hell of a lot of strength. I'm sure he would be a challenge to my team, but this matchup is terribly out of his favor as a purely physical fighter.

Hund is the only physical fighter I could imagine killing me.

"I told you before, but you really shouldn't worry about me." I turn and clear my flame, giving the enhanced ursu clear sight of me.

His eyes narrow as I stare him down. I'm giddy for this fight. Not long ago, I would have been terrified, but I'm confident in my strength. It would be nice to have a spear with me, but I'll have to do without. Today, I have an audience to show off to.

The warden doesn't hesitate. He dashes toward me, affronted that I could dare to think myself his equal. At least, I assume so from his indignant scowl.

He moves fast, and I can immediately tell my outfit is going to end up as rags if I keep it. Instead, I allow my body to become incorporeal and abandon the snow-suit where I shouldn't have to worry about it. My body, burning with intense white flame, bursts forward, ready to meet the ursu half way.

Fire twists through the air ahead of me, but the warden takes my golden flames head-on. I'd expected it, but the flames barely burn his fur. This fight will be white flames only, then. I won't be able to just submerge my surroundings in fire, as I usually do.

His sword arcs toward my chest, which is around knee level for him, considering he is more than double my height. The advantage of being so small lets me duck beneath his swing with ease.

The claws I formed on my hands slice at his leg, but I don't have the strength to penetrate. I grasp at his ankle instead and his flesh bubbles. A grunt is the only sign he even feels it before his blade drops on me. A burst of physical flame throws me back, but not quick enough to dodge the longsword.

Both my arms are dismembered, only to lose their definition and reconnect to my body within moments.

I grin up at the warrior, waving both unharmed arms at him. He dashes forward and severs my head with a clean cut before I can react. I simply laugh, inciting an enraged growl from the large ursu.

This is great! He moves just like the general, but I don't need the Fog's assistance anymore. He can't touch me, nor can he defend against my flames. I could stand here and take attacks from his blade all day . . . but I probably shouldn't in case the ursu has some hidden card like the general did.

I dodge beneath a swing and dart forward. My hand slaps the back of his knee and sizzles away some of the flesh there. My white flames stay behind, but a swipe of the ursu's free hand clears it off. Shame. He strikes again, an overhead arc this time. With the faintest touch of physical flame, I dodge out of his sword's path before I dash in again for another strike.

The fight turns into a game. For me, at least. The warden grows increasingly agitated.

"What. The fuck. Are you?" he asks between swings.

Maybe it's the exhilaration of the fight, or the audience watching on, or even just a whim of the moment, but his question goads me. My firestorm builds around me once more, swallowing the area as far as my flames can reach. I don't let them burn, though. No, I form my flames into the most terrifying existence I've ever seen.

The Titan.

A conflagration of a crocodile stands over a hundred meters tall. An instinctual feeling rises within me, and I let it guide me. The mimicry of a Titan rears its head, jaws opening wide, and a roar of wind deafens the world. At the same moment, the feeling within me unleashes, applying pressure on everything and everyone around.

The warden's body goes rigid, freezing up under the concentrated pressure clamping down on him.

I make the Titan crash its maw down on the ursu, compressing the entire being into its teeth as they clamp around him. I replace the crocodile with white flame and rush in before he can brush them off again. His blade swings wide while he tries to step back, fear in his eyes.

He bats at me with the flat edge, which I have to admit is more effective against me than simply slicing through me. As it comes, I have an idea. Instead of letting myself be bisected again, I harden my body and catch the blade. At least that is the intent. I'm scooped up by the sword and carried along.

I hang in the air off the ursu's sword as he takes a moment to realize where I've gone. Not exactly what I planned, but this works.

The blade glows beneath my touch. It is clearly not normal steel, as it isn't melting immediately, but it is only a matter of time until his weapon is no more.

The warden clearly understands what I'm doing as he attempts to crush me between the blade and the ground. Unfortunately for him, I simply reform on the other side of the blade. No worse for wear.

It takes a dozen seconds for his sword to become nothing more than a handle. His body doesn't look in much better shape, either. My flames leave his body a patchy mess of burnt flesh. He staggers back, fear and pain predominant on his features. This is already over, and he knows it.

Thermal signatures enter my range at the same time the warden spots them. His demeanor flips. Instead of the fear at his defeat, he grins victoriously. I can feel what's coming, but I turn regardless.

A squad of guards herds children toward our battlefield, holding their guns toward kids as young as five.

"Give up now, or I'll give the order," the ursu I'd been playing with not a moment ago jeers at me, assured of his victory.

I sneer in return, but more angry at myself. I'd seen how they kept the kids as hostages with the adult ursu around. Why did I think they wouldn't try the same with me? Honestly, I'm confused about why the warden is so sure this would work. I'm not an ursu, so why would he think this would stop me?

I still plan to keep them safe, but from everything I've seen, people of different races care very little about those other than their own. The pact nations being the only exception. Even there, some races' differences cannot be overcome.

The warden thinks this is enough to beat me. He thinks threats will cow me. Just the thought of him getting his way irritates me more than a bunch of kids being threatened.

My eyes flicker to Leal, standing beside her father. I'm not sure whether I look her way in apology for the risk I'm about to take, to assure her I know what I'm doing, or simply to make sure she's still okay.

I stare down the guards with their mini-cannons held dangerously close to the heads of the defenseless kids. What I did before is not something that makes a lot of sense, but I intuitively know that was my presence. It showed itself before, and I know I can unleash it any time I want. It's instinctual. A part of me has broken free and can never be locked away again.

So I let my presence be known. It feels a bit like shining the light of my fire over an area, telling everyone I'm here and forcing them to pay attention. I focus the pressure on the guards and they feel my anger. I'm glaring at them with the world itself assisting me.

Their fingers go stiff, bodies freezing under the pressure of a being far greater than them. Something *more*. The guards cannot move, and I make good use of that opportunity. Tiny balls of white flame appear over each of their hands, burning through the fingers holding each gun. It is immensely difficult. Both remotely creating and controlling seven individual intense flames at very precise points strains my control far more than creating a firestorm ever could.

But it works. Each of the weapons falls out of their hands. Pained shrieks resound and snap each out of the stupor my presence locked them in. The mini-cannons clatter against the ground. One misfires on impact, and we're lucky it shoots its projectile into the sky without victim.

I move each of the small balls of fire up the guard's bodies and quickly end their lives by burning through their heads. The flesh hardly even burns. It simply vaporizes on contact with the intense heat.

I'm back in front of the warden before he can even comprehend the loss of his winning card. Flames gouge through his chest, bubbling away at his flesh with greater ease the deeper I get within his dense muscle. He lets out a desperate roar, glaring at me with hatred I've only seen in a few. The ursu dashes toward the group of children, but considering it's his only option, I've already positioned myself in his way.

He tries to brush past me, but this isn't a game anymore. The ursu isn't content to leave this just between the two of us, so I make sure he cannot reach them. I swing my clawed hands at the deep burns on his legs, cutting through the tender muscle with an ease that wasn't possible while his hide still protected him.

The towering creature loses motion to his foot and falls to the earth. But that doesn't stop him. His fingers dig into the earth and he throws himself forward. I cling to his back and blast a jet upward, slamming the ursu into the ground once more and grinding his face along the dirt.

I don't care for a clean and fun fight anymore. My flames dig into his eyes, burn through his nostrils and ears. Anything that gives me an easier path to burn through this monster, I take it.

He tries to scrape away my flames, tries to dig his eyes out to stop the spread of fire as it reduces his flesh to a blackened char. The ursu struggles along the ground, forgetting his goal as he grunts and digs his fingers into his own body, desperate to stop the flames now buried within.

I watch on as the flames reach his brain, and he lets out a scream to announce his death throes. His thick chest and strong lungs blast his pain across the entire gulag for every prisoner to relish, and every guard to dread.

The warden's body twitches and jerks as he eventually loses control of his motor functions. Soon, his body stills, and I'm treated to an immensely enhanced feast.

CHAPTER FORTY-TWO

Leal IV

Solvei had not been exaggerating.

Leal could hardly believe it. She'd assumed the moment the warden appeared, they would not be getting away alive. Solvei had simply taken his advance as if it were a game. She played with a man Leal would consider unreachable. The man had been a major pillar of the military long before Henosis invaded. One of the few that actually practiced the art of war during times of peace.

He couldn't touch her.

When Solvei spoke with confidence and assurance that she would get Leal's dad out without problem, she'd assumed the áed was arrogant after fighting the mermineae so long. No, in only two years, she attained more power than Leal could comprehend. The intensity of her fire unheard of.

That monster the áed had created; the unnatural fear that froze Leal where she stood as its deafening roar thrummed in the air; her old friend's sheer, overwhelming presence. It was too much for Leal to believe. How could that otherworldly white flame that burned everything in its way be the same tiny fire that once suffered at Gloria's hands?

Even when the guards pulled that disgusting move of using hostages, Solvei had hardly hesitated. She disarmed and killed each within a moment. What Leal couldn't get out of her mind was the ease with which her old friend had killed them. She did so without a second breath. The act of parting her enemies from their life had become second nature to Solvei.

The way she methodically cut down the warden and burned him alive in such a horrific fashion only reinforced the image of her own mother's final moments.

Leal had already established that it was a mistake. That Solvei hadn't meant for the fire to grow the way it had, but deciding on something, and actually removing the thought from her mind were entirely different.

But . . . even if Leal hated that some had to die, they were horrible people. They'd treated not only her father, but who knows how many more, like dirt.

She couldn't even blame Solvei for the murders. The áed had given Leal the opportunity to stop her, but Leal knew it was unreasonable to expect someone to fight without killing. She had tried herself many times in the past, but sometimes it was impossible to prevent the blood spilling on her own hands.

Her father had given Solvei the go ahead, and while Leal was thankful for him taking that responsibility from her, she felt guilty that she was incapable of bringing herself to take the burden.

She knew, logically, that some people were just better off dead, but whenever she thought about the fact that would be their end, she hated it. Someone might seem cruel from her perspective, but what if they were simply being extorted as well? Maybe they could turn their lives around and become better people. She wanted to believe that was possible.

Everyone should have an opportunity to better themselves before they entered Rod's domain.

"I'm going to free the rest. Leal, take your dad and find somewhere safe."

Solvei was done. She'd burned away the last of the old warden and now picked up her snowsuit . . . which was a rather odd thing to wear in this climate.

Before Leal even had a moment to respond, the áed was off toward the compound again, leaving her father and a bunch of kids to gawk after her. She looked up at her father, and any complaints she might have had for Solvei melted on her tongue. Leal spun a ball of water around her and her father, ready to take them over the wall again, away from what remains of the guards.

Her father placed his large, nostalgic hands on her shoulders. They felt much smaller than the last time she felt their reassuring touch. "Leal, you are coming back after taking me out, aren't you?" he asks.

She nods. Solvei had already dealt with the major barrier to saving everyone, so she can now help more than just her father. She wasn't about to leave them to fend for themselves, but her dad took priority.

"Then I'm staying," he said, only for Leal to give him an unconvinced look. "You think I'm about to leave my daughter's side after finally seeing her again?"

Leal was ready to refuse, when her dad wrapped her in a hug again. She didn't want to leave him in danger after finally getting him back. He'd been the only reason she had to push forward, and now that he was finally in front of her, she wanted to hide him away. Prevent anything like this threatening them again.

Where could they go now? Where could any of the people Solvei freed go once this prison was destroyed? It was a question she didn't know how to answer. She never planned for more than her father's freedom. Never considered even that reasonably possible. She'd come here expecting to join her father in a cell, at best.

"Come on, let's round up those your friend has freed." Leal's dad patted her back with his fingerless hand.

As he led her toward the stunned kids, her eyes passed over his body. Her father hadn't come out uninjured. Not only was he missing an eye and most of his left hand, he limped along at a pained gait. Despite looking like he should collapse at any moment, he trudged forward. His arm around Leal's shoulders was comforting, rather than using her for support.

She was still far shorter than her father, but she was tall enough to help him walk. Leal put her arm around him and joined the kids as they watched the bright light that shone through many of the second floor slit windows. Solvei had already made quick progress of the compound. Many confused or doubtful people hesitantly spread out from the main building.

A tall man directed the many disbelieving captives. It was hardly believable to Leal that there were no guards halting their escape, even after what she'd seen Solvei do to the warden. These people who lived at the guard's discretion must have found their sudden freedom jarring, even if it should be a time to celebrate.

There were far more congregating than she thought could possibly fit in the building. Murmured discussion grew as they found no resistance to their escape. Reluctantly hopeful or cynical voices combined in a babble that gradually grew with each member stepping outside the large cubic compound.

Leal's dad, with her at his side, approached the tall man commanding many of the freed members into sorted groups. Some rounded up kids, reuniting them with their parents while giving them protection. Another group helped those who struggled to walk on their own. Leal noted there were many in that category.

"Adalbern, any issues?"

The tall man turned toward them. He carried a gun, likely pilfered from the guards. Whether those guards were dead or not, Leal chose not to think about.

"Ah, Gerben, good to see you're fine. I worried when that kid flew off with you."

Leal's dad let out a strained laugh. "Yeah, not about to say that was the most pleasant experience ever, but she brought me to my daughter, so it's hardly anything to complain about."

"Oh? This is the kid you always talk about?" Adalbern's gaze dropped to Leal and he bowed his head. "I appreciate you doing this."

"What? No! It was all Solvei," Leal said. "I couldn't have done anything without her."

A sudden explosion stopped Adalbern before he could say anything. Everyone turned as a massive fireball blew out the top corner of the complex many were still fleeing from.

"Talking about the áed." Adalbern turned to Leal's dad. "Can you stop her from destroying this facility?"

"You don't want it destroyed?" Leal asked.

"No. We will need it for now," the tall man said. "Too many are in a state that they wouldn't be able to take care of themselves should we all leave, and there aren't enough hands to care for all. It will be impossible for us to hide in the cities. Our only option is to hold this fort until we have enough hale bodies to field a resistance."

"A resistance? Like the revolution?" Leal wondered. The revolution was a major point in their history. Every ursu knew about how they overcame their oppressors and took the land which became New Vetus. Could it really be a resistance if it was against their own kind?

"Yes, but we can worry about that later. Now, can we stop the young áed before she reaches the food storage?"

"Uh, sure. I'll go get her," Leal said, but she needn't have worried. Solvei had already finished.

The áed jumped off the tall roof and splattered against the ground. Her form momentarily lost its structure and flames spread out before pulling back into herself. Leal knew it didn't hurt Solvei, but the visual of her body splitting and morphing like that made Leal squirm.

She directed her hyle through the markings around her neck and up her cheek. The thinnest layer of water coated her eyes, giving her an enhanced look at her friend. This marking array was something she'd always considered her favorite. It wasn't all that impressive by itself, only giving a mage a slight improvement to how far one could see, but that wasn't why Leal found it so interesting.

The marking proved that there was so much more that could be achieved than simply manipulate an element. She would have spent all her time researching the possibilities, if it weren't for the military's refusal. The lack of applicable uses for their purpose prevented her research of what might be an unexplored field.

Most thought an element only had two states: Hyle, where it could flow freely through a medium; and the natural state, which would interact with the world. A mage's markings could still control an element after it had transitioned from hyle to its natural state as long as they remained connected.

Leal might have thought the same if she hadn't seen Solvei's fire for herself.

The áed's hyle had changed since the first they'd met. Leal was sure some of that was influenced by her improved understanding of her secondary senses marking, but the girl had become innately different.

Solvei's fire had once been very similar to elements that a mage could produce. Now, Leal couldn't even tell whether it was hyle or natural fire. The pattern of influence was imprinted upon all elements touched by life. The pattern even Solvei once had was now near indistinguishable. To Leal's senses, it seemed like she was losing her distinction from the world around her.

While that sight concerned Leal about the safety of her friend, it also raised some very interesting questions. Her fire clearly contradicted the dual state model, so were there other variables which could determine how an element might act? Could she, with her markings, induce a state between hyle and natural? Could the hyle state be manipulated to suppress even more of itself from the medium in which it carries?

There were so many possibilities if any of this proved true. What effects could she create without relying only on element control? Could the impossibly dangerous elements be made safe?

Leal shook her head as she realized Solvei was already standing right before her. It was a bad habit to get lost in her thoughts like that.

"Are you ready, Leal?"

"Ready? For what?" she asked.

Solvei pointed over her shoulder. Leal turned to watch hundreds of able-bodied prisoners marching toward the large steel gates. Gates which held the last bastion of the guards' defense.

Leal mentally berated herself again for not paying attention to the movement of people around her. It wasn't the first time, but she really hoped it would be the last.

"Could you keep the wall and gate intact?" Leal asked. "They want to use this place as a fortress, so it would be helpful if we still had the walls."

Solvei's eyes widened slightly. "You are fine with that? I can kill them?"

Leal clenched her jaw and turned her head, but she nodded anyway. She wished Solvei hadn't been so direct with her question.

"Yes." The single word was difficult to say. "I don't want any of these people to be hurt anymore. If you can deal with the guards before they can do anything, I would appreciate it. Even if they need to lose their lives."

Leal hated the words coming from her mouth. No, she knew it was the only thing that could be done. If only it wasn't necessary. She knew it was the only way, but she couldn't do it herself. She had to rely on Solvei.

The áed took no time to rush ahead of the congregating prisoners, all readying themselves. Whether they were prepared for an attack from the guards, or were ready to attack themselves, Leal didn't know.

Cannon fire rattled the air as the guards both on the walls and behind the gate fired on the áed with their newly adapted technology. Dozens of projectiles ripped through her body without effect. She ran on, hardly even slowed by each impact. Guards hurried to reload their weapons before firing once more through the gaps of the portcullis, but again, Solvei paid the tiny projectiles no mind.

Solvei ran full tilt toward the gate and threw herself at the steel grille. Her body passed through the metal bars without issue, to the terror of each guard. None survived the ensuing inferno that engulfed them.

Leal couldn't understand how Solvei could murder without hesitation. Had she always been this way? Or was it the world that had forced her to be like this? Watching on was too much for Leal to bear.

In no time at all, the gate was clear, and the ramparts left without a soul. The sheer efficiency Solvei had when killing was terrifying. No matter how she tried to think back to the girl Solvei had once been, the picture of an overwhelming fire consuming uncountable lives continued to eat at Leal's thoughts.

She felt horrible for thinking that about her friend, especially after she'd come all this way to save not only Leal's dad, but so many others. Solvei had dropped a war she clearly hadn't been forced into for Leal's sake, and Leal couldn't even think nice things about her.

Leal hoped she'd be able to repay Solvei one day, but right now, she needed time alone with her father.

CHAPTER FORTY-THREE

Bratchina

I clean the last ursu guards from the top of the wall. There isn't any challenge to it. Nothing they do can slow me, let alone hurt me. A few ursu amongst the guards had swords of their own and far more enhancement than their comrades. Even these warriors might as well be tinder after my fight with the warden.

Thankfully, Leal gave me the go ahead to remove these ursu. After the treatment directed toward the prisoners, they deserve no mercy. On top of the abuse, entrapment is still one of the worst things you could do.

I'm glad Leal agreed. If she hadn't wanted me to kill them, I could have probably subdued most of them alive. Without the warden, they are weak. Some people simply don't deserve to continue living.

The guards got to be test subjects for my presence experimentation. The ability doesn't make much sense. What made it show itself? How does it differ for others? Maybe there is just some unrecorded threshold of strength one needs to reach before it becomes available.

Its operation is completely natural. No different from influencing a flame or moving a finger. I can turn it on or off whenever I'd like and even focus the pressure it exudes upon a single target.

What is this pressure? The first time someone feels it, they most often freeze in place, but that paralyzation wears off after a time, even with the presence still bearing down on them. It seems to inflict an instinctual fear within the target.

I jump off the side of the wall and arrive in front of Gerben and that tall ursu from before. Leal is off to the side, clearly lost in thought as she watches the gate.

"There shouldn't be any left," I say to the two. The tall ursu has taken command of the rest, so I should be able to inform him and get back to Leal.

"I appreciate what you have done for us." The tall ursu steps forward and clasps my hand in his grip. His hand dwarfs mine, but he shakes anyway. "Will you be staying?"

"Uh, no. There's still a war I need to get to. Well, more than one now."

The tall ursu nods his head, but is clearly disappointed. "Please, come back whenever you wish. We could use the help." He finally lets go of my hand and walks back amongst the ursu stunned at the rapid change in their circumstances.

Leal joined her dad's side while I was distracted. Now that everything is done here, I really need to be getting back to the pact nations. My eyes fall on Gerben's missing fingers and eye.

"Hey, I know someone who could heal you," I say. With both Leal and Gerben, it'll be impossible to fly, but as long as we're careful not to attract too much attention, I'm sure we could rush back to the pact nations over land.

"Solvei, thank you, but I'm needed here." Gerben laughs. "Half blind and fingerless as I am, my experience could really help this resistance."

My gaze strays to Leal, and I know what she's going to say before the words touch her tongue.

"I'm going to stay with Dad," she says. "This could never have happened without you. Thank you."

So, that's it? Time to say goodbye and see each other . . . whenever we see each other? Maybe it's my fault for thinking that we would stick together. I can understand why; she's got her dad back. If I had my mom or uncle or aunt back, I'd spend every second I could with them.

No matter how much I understand it, the disappointment still hits me.

For a moment, I seriously consider staying. I could abandon the pact nations and stay here to make sure Leal and her dad—and by extension, all the people I freed—remain safe. But doing so would abandon the others I care for to whatever fate may befall them.

My friends back in the pact nations won't be able to defend themselves should the merminea invasion continue, but Leal will be in just as much danger once New Vetus realize they have a rebellion festering. What could any of these ursu do if they send an army here? What could they do if they send Hund?

The void-touched ursu hasn't overcome his desire. The giant is still tied to the whims of the New Vetus Council. It would be nice if I could talk to him and somehow help him through the chains of his own mind. That will be hard for a multitude of reasons, primarily because I don't actually know what his desire is, and by following the council's orders, he's just as likely to kill me as he is to listen.

"Ah, all right then," I say. "I'd better get back, then."

"Come now, you can't leave like that." Gerben stops me with a light smile. "At least stay for the celebratory Bratchina."

The feast was every part a celebration as it was a horde of ravenous beasts stuffing their bellies. The now freed ursu raided the kitchens and storage areas to put on the largest feast I've seen. Larger even than the Bratchinas held in city centers.

I am surprised there was so much food stored away within the compound, considering how thin everyone is. The guards hadn't even been starving them because of a lack of supplies.

"Thank you so much," another mother says as she bows her head, her young child clutching at the fur of her leg.

I just nod. "It was no problem."

If I'd known I would have this much attention on me, I might've left before this celebration. Sure, I know they're thankful, but I really don't know how to respond to their gratitude. They also keep getting in the way of the remaining time I have with Leal.

I don't want to leave, but the longer I stay, the more stressed I feel. Am I putting my friends in danger by relaxing right now?

My sight passes over Leal and I chuckle at how even through everything, she still hasn't changed. Despite most of the attention coming my way, Leal looks more uncomfortable than I do. She's still no good with crowds.

Before another excessively thankful ursu can approach me, the tall ursu—Adalbern—clears his throat loud enough to cut conversations amongst the gathering.

"Today, we celebrate our freedom, thanks entirely to the áed Solvei and Gerben's daughter, Leal." I watch in amusement as Leal ducks her head from the praise. "This moment reflects a turning point for us. No longer will we allow the council to descend us into oppression. We shall tear them down and rebuild New Vetus the way it always should have been."

Adalbern pauses for a moment as murmurs resound. "Our future will not be easy. We face the entire army, and I don't need to mention Tore Hund. The council has twisted our hero around their fingers, so we cannot hope to face them outright. It will be hard—damn near impossible—but we have an opportunity. If we play things right, not only can we save ourselves, but we can be the saviors of the hero of New Vetus."

"We will stay here until everyone is healthy, then we will spread and build our numbers. Our success will rely on every person's contributions. Convince who you can. Sabotage those you can't. In time, we will tear the chairman's seat from its pedestal, along with the rest of the council. This is our path."

The crowd doesn't cheer. Some applaud, but most simply hold determined, yet resigned faces.

This isn't something they wanted. I realize now that while many of the ursu here were used as hostages for those outside, once the army discovers what happened, their roles will be reversed. Everyone here knows just how bleak their prospects truly are. Even if they want to hold a resistance force, they cannot face the council's forces head-on.

Most of these former prisoners don't have any enhancement to speak of. If it ever reaches the point where a battle is unavoidable, they have already lost. I now realize why Adalbern was so disappointed to see me go. I could single-handedly give them far greater odds of success.

As much as it pains me to do so, I have to leave. Who knows how long it might take for them to overcome the council? If they had a plan to take out the council now, I would help them immediately. But they don't, and I need to help push back the mermineae and the New Vetus army attacking the nations protecting my friends.

Maybe staying and applying pressure on the ursu army from here would be effective, but I'm afraid the same thing will happen as last time. The New Vetus army will quickly send a team of water mages to deal with me, and the resistance will be without strength.

Also, I'll be dead.

The mermineae don't have command over water through the use of mages as most other races do, so I needn't worry when fighting them as much, but that assault where I met Leal taught me a valuable lesson. The nations keep their elite out of the fights for a reason. If that hadn't been Leal to find me that night, I likely wouldn't be here.

Creating hit squads to counter detailed abilities and weaknesses is a very real thing armies do to beat the strongest of their foes. I'm unfortunate enough to have my enemies know how horrifying water is to me. Can I even attempt to fight against the ursu anymore now that I know a group of water mages will hunt me down on sight?

It's probably best not to think about it now. If the time comes where I have nowhere to escape from a mage ambush, my white flame should give me at least some opportunity to flee, or if I'm lucky enough, get a killing blow on those mages.

"Hey, Solvei. I've been thinking." Leal pulls my attention from the many ursu somehow filling their gullets with an amount of food equivalent to their weight. How they can fit so much food in, I don't know.

"Hmm?"

"About Tore. I've been thinking about your explanation as to how he is controlled. I'm wondering if there's a way to free him as you did for yourself. How is his mind twisted so that the council can manipulate him so thoroughly?"

"Well, I know it is linked to whatever his desire is, but I don't know enough about him to know what that might be."

"They always told us Tore did everything out of a selfless desire to do what he could for our nation, but who can say whether that is true or something of a children's tale to encourage good behavior?"

I hum in consideration as I think back on the advice he'd given within the Fog so long ago. He was immensely regretful about his own desire, so it might not be completely alike with mine. If it's his desire that is causing him to be controlled, and not an element of its implementation, freeing him from that control will be far more difficult than it was for me.

"If that's the case, it might be possible to convince him that the council is the problem."

Leal winces. "Ah, that won't work. There have been plenty of occasions in the past where people have tried to convince him to their goals. I've not thought of it till now, but the council made public laughingstocks of those that tried. Tore would always punish traitorous attempts to sway him."

So, convincing him is off the table. Can't say I'm surprised. One would have to have all the luck in the world for the Fog's manipulations to be so easily thwarted. But maybe Hund needs a big enough push. Even if someone had told me the knot itself was limiting my thoughts, I doubt my awareness of the contradiction would have been enough to snap the rope. I'd only broken free after months of tension wore down my conflicting desires to the snapping point.

Well, Hund has been around for over a century. I can't even comprehend that length of time. If Hund hasn't found a way to escape his desire, then maybe there truly isn't one. He is trapped, so his desire clearly doesn't align with mine.

The tables are empty, each ursu long having had their fill. Hopefully, they won't need to eat near as much any time soon. There couldn't possibly be that much food just waiting around for them.

Plenty have collapsed on the earth a short distance away, whether by alcohol or exhaustion, I do not know. The larger ursu not suffering from excessive malnutrition surround Adalbern and Gerben as they discuss their future.

I've enjoyed being beside Leal again, but I continue to grow stressed the longer I wait around. It is time I should leave.

"If you ever need help, please don't hesitate to find me," I say as I turn to Leal. "Again, I'm sorry for what happened because of me."

Leal doesn't say it's all right, nor does she forgive me, but I don't expect her to. She nods, her eyes not meeting mine. "Stay safe, Solvei."

I smile at that. Things aren't perfect, but at least she doesn't hate me. "After everything is over, and our lives go back to normal, would you like to travel with me? I plan to look for my mom's spear once I get time."

She doesn't answer immediately. She looks up from her hands, her fingers tracing the markings over the back of her palm. "Ask me again the next time you are here."

That's better than a rejection. Thinking about what I'm going to do after the war might be premature, but I need something to think about that isn't the bleakness and danger that has overcome the world. When the world is ready to go easy on me, I'll finally be able to do the things I've wanted.

Now that I have strength of my own, there's nothing to fear going back into the wasteland. My family is gone, and I have accepted that. I should at least carry on our tribe's heirloom spear and return the other relic weapons to our Agglomerate.

CHAPTER FORTY-FOUR

Mistake

The travel back to the pact nations has been far more pleasant an experience than it was on the way to New Vetus. I opted to pass over the isthmus, so there was no concern about the sea looming below. While I would have preferred having Leal by my side, I didn't miss having to carry her.

Without needing to struggle against the ursu's weight, I could settle with my usual falcon form. It is so much more comfortable flying at this size simply because my white flame, while immensely more visible in the sky, is unbeatable. It's really too bad I can't keep up the intensity at larger sizes. Being an intimidating creature can be rather satisfying.

I'm sure the ursu below watch me as I pass overhead, but even if they want to stop me, there's no way for them to reach me. I can fly over their lands, cities, borders, and armies without so much as a squeak of resistance.

A part of me is tempted to drop and ignite some fires amongst them, simply to slow down their invasion. But my thoughts go back to what Leal would want. There are likely many amongst them who are only fighting to protect those they care for. Identical to my own reasons to fight.

Is it right to take others' chance just for the possibility it will benefit me?

No. That answer is obvious. But does what is right truly matter when it comes to keeping my friends safe? I have killed people from many races now, but I have massacred thousands of mermineae on the belief that it was to keep my friends safe. Can I do the same to the New Vetus soldiers after I've discovered that many fight because their family is held hostage?

I already know the mermineae are fleeing in fear from Kalma, so is it wrong of me to have incinerated as many as I have? The strength of the average merminea is magnitudes greater than the unenhanced of the pact nations' races, so I have to assume what I've done is necessary. If they aren't stopped, they will cut through the pact nations, killing everyone they can in their attempts to take over. To take the land and carve a home for themselves.

It is an unfortunate situation, but until another reasonable alternative shows itself, killing is the only option. I can't hold off an entire race spread across hundreds of thousands of meters by scaring them with my flame alone. If I simply run them off from an attack, those mermineae will just join the offensive at another location. A location without me to defend.

I shake my head. No use concerning myself over problems without solutions. I know what I have to do, and as grim as it may be, I'm not about to cower from that if it will keep my friends safe.

Below, the land transitions into what was once Joiak. The desolate winding roads weaving between the two kingdoms are now overlaid by a stone path and bridges supporting rail tracks. How the ursu built this infrastructure so quickly is a mystery, but it doesn't bode well for the Joiak Kingdom if the ursu have already built paths into their land.

I don't care all that much for what happens to the kingdom that would endorse the horrid treatment of its people like it did with Mr. Marshall's mill, but the more land the New Vetus army controls near the pact nations, the worse our situation.

Not only are the pact nations fighting both the mermineae and the Theocracy, they have New Vetus now coming from the south as well as the constant threat that the Empire could invade at any moment from the northeast.

Why do all the factions have to decide now is a good time for war? Should I even trust the pact nations to get through this? Maybe I should just grab my friends and take them somewhere safe. But where is safe? I can't bring them to New Vetus for obvious reasons; the Theocracy is more likely to execute them than shelter them, and I don't think I could ever trust my friends to be safe in Henosis after what they did to so many of my kind.

There are countries further away, but I know very little about many of them. It would be especially difficult to get my friends there. I cannot carry all of them at once, so it would take months to move them regardless if we tried to travel by land or I made multiple trips.

That doesn't even consider the possibility that those states might be just as bad as any other.

I'm stuck protecting the pact nations, so that they can protect my friends. And as long as my team doesn't encounter a Viisin, I trust them to survive without trouble. Well, assuming they don't have a hit squad sent to hunt them down.

I fly far past the point where our battle previously took place. Unfortunately, the land is no longer contested. It is entirely within ursu control. Far beneath me, they lay the foundations for their rail network to connect with the one laid by the pact nations after we retook the land from the mermineae.

It isn't a pleasant sight to see all the ground we put weeks of effort into retaking, simply snapped away by a third party we never expected to be against us.

A whole day passes before I finally see where the front line has settled. The ursu have pushed the pact nations further back than even the mermineae had when I'd returned to this side of the Alps. The town commandeered as a command post now lay deserted hours behind me.

The majority of ursu along the line neither have swords nor armor like those that attacked our camp, but they do have the miniature cannons those guarding the gulag used. Most of the land was expansive stretches of trenches, both sides filled with the unenhanced. All simply numbers to fill the space and worth no more.

I fly along the line for a while, simply watching over the fighting. In places, the battlefield favors a particular side and the line bends to account. After a few hours of this, it becomes rather clear that nothing really happens when the unenhanced fight. Both sides hide in their cover and fire, hoping for some lucky shots when artillery doesn't rain from above.

Only when the stronger warriors—the ursu's armored soldiers and the pact nation's mercenaries—enter the battle, does any shift truly occur. If a side is unlucky enough to face them without support of their own, their defeat and death is guaranteed. Those on the ground know it too. When the stronger warriors appear, there are many that try to flee, only to be shot for desertion.

It's horrible, but making an example of deserters is common on both sides of the conflict, and for good reason. Often, the appearance of the stronger warriors is a hoax. Simple soldiers dressing themselves as those stronger in a bid to terrify the enemy. And when the overseeing officer refuses to shoot his soldiers in the back, it works.

Eventually the defensive lines separate, spreading into the distance, but not thinning. Soldiers face desolate land. I've fought alongside the pact nations long enough to know this is merminea-controlled area. It's curious to see the ursu taking a similar defense as the pact nations, despite their lesser numbers.

It is incredibly relieving to witness the ursu trying to push against the mermineae in addition to the pact forces. If they had allied with the mermineae, or attempted to take the pact nations out before moving on to fight the slender race, then we would have no chance.

At least now we have the opportunity to incite the two factions to slaughter the other instead of us. Whether those in charge of the pact nations can achieve that, however, is another story.

As I fly over the border between the pact nations and mermineae, I observe many battles between the two. The Order has finally got itself sorted. Beiths now push against the offenses of the mermineae. The sole fighters are sparse and only show up on the rare battlefield, but they show up none the less.

Having a single warrior or mage wiping out swarms of mermineae is so much more efficient than relying on thousands for a less than equal trade. It might have taken months, but the Mercenary Order has finally adapted.

Still, with the added war, it doesn't make much difference.

Finally, after a long trip—and a volan mage trying to knock me out of the sky—I finally reach the command post. This time, it's in a major city. Most citizens have been evacuated, and it leaves the place eerily quiet in the areas not occupied by the military and mercenaries.

Sorting things out with the pressure mage volan had been an ordeal—apparently calling her an air mage was insulting . . . for some reason—but now I have to present myself to the commander. As before, I expected to find Remus and Commander Darton with him, but that isn't what awaits me as I enter the room.

A trio wearing business suits stand behind a large conference desk. As I step into the room, the two khirig I felt in the corners of the room rush forward. One slams the door, while the other does something strange with its hands. Turning, I notice too late the strand of water connecting the khirig to something above me.

Bars of water drop in a circle around me.

What is this? Why are they attacking me?

I fight the urge to lash out to escape by any means. Maybe this is some mistake. I glance down to see if I could melt my way down and out of the cage of water. But no, the water mage has surrounded my feet in a puddle. Thankfully, he's kind enough to keep the water away from my feet, which is about the limit of the good things I can currently think about any of the people in this room letting this happen.

Remain calm. I still have my outfit, which should keep the water off me. Plus, I'm not entirely defenseless to water anymore. Assuming the other khirig is a water mage as well, I'll only need to kill the two before they can focus their water on me after I break free. Assuming they aren't at the Beith level, it should be easy.

Still, the water around me does nothing to ease my nerves.

"What is this?" I ask, struggling to keep myself calm.

"You are being detained for desertion," the only dohrni in the room says. She wears clean, black sleeves over each of her tentacles, which is strange to see as almost every other dohrni I've met hasn't bothered with clothing.

"Desertion?" I repeat. "What are you talking about?"

One of the well-dressed trio, another khirig, straightens on his slender antlers and lifts a bundle of papers before his face. He recites words from the page. "Infraction: abandoned the battlefield without sufficient reason or consent from a superior. Infraction: failed to report actions at a hearing within the allocated time."

"What? A friend needed my help. I didn't have time to tell anyone."

The khirig continues without acknowledging me. "Infraction: failed to report crucial mission intelligence to command. Infraction: unauthorized dialogue with enemy combatants; treason. Judgment: Confiscation of all personal rights, allocation of handler, and suspension of movement unless given authorization by said handler."

I can hardly believe they are doing this. It all seems like a stupid joke until the khirig behind me that closed the door approaches with arm cuffs dense with glowing inscriptions. The thing looks just as advanced, if not more so than the intricate lines within the Empire's weapon. I don't know what it does, but there's no chance I'm risking that touching me.

I'm done with this shit.

Thin rings of white flame encircle the necks of the two mages behind me while balls of that same fire materialize before the three standing ahead of me. The air shimmers from the unrestrained heat. The room temperature skyrockets. I make sure each of these people knows just how hot those tiny flames are. On top of that, I flood the room with my presence, freezing each in place.

"If any of you makes another move, I'll be the only one leaving this room as anything other than a mote of ash."

The water mage holding my cage twitches, so I burn away all of his antlers to show I'm not messing around. The markings disappear along with the khirig's branch-like external bones, leaving the water to drop around me. My outfit blocks most of it, but some does make it inside the tears of my torso, only to burst into steam on contact.

It hurts, a lot, but I don't lose focus on the four who might still try something. The water mage now lies on the ground, flesh exposed and unable to stand up, but alive. He's not screaming either, so I assume it mustn't be too painful to lose those antlers.

"You realize what you are doing, right?" the third of the trio—an albanic this time—asks with a tone that implies a calmness that is betrayed by the sweat running down the side of his face and his eyes not leaving the tiny orb hovering before his chest. "You are making yourself the enemy of the Mercenary Order. Do you not understand the severity of this mistake?"

"When the alternative is to become a prisoner, I'd rather take my chances," I say. I can't believe they would do this after how much I've helped them. Considering they are so desperate to keep their Beiths hidden, they would never have reconnected with Joiak if not for me. This is exactly what Letty—that dohrni that helped find me some clothes—warned me about. The Order would do anything in its power to put a leash around me.

"What about Grímr? Where is he? Did you charge him with desertion too?"

The albanic raises an eyebrow in question, but answers anyway. "No, he was pardoned under the severe injuries clause during his trial."

Well, that is a relief to hear, assuming he is truthful. Whether they didn't do so because they believe they already control him, or for some other reason, I don't know. All I know is that these charges they are trying to hit me with are nonsense.

"I am leaving. If I find anyone coming after me, I will immolate each of you."

The door burns off its hinges and I walk over the smoldering remains, through the building, and out into the uninhabited part of the city to wait. I gave them an option, and I am ready to follow through with my threat if anyone comes after me.

It was immensely difficult to not just burn each of them where they stood. We are already struggling against the mermineae, ursu, and the Theocracy and they decide they have to ruin what cooperation we could have had?

On the way here, I'd decided the best course of action is to leave my friends here and protect the pact nations alongside the Order. Now? I'm not so sure. Will they use them as hostages like New Vetus did with Gerben to keep Leal in line? If so, I really need to get back to Meja and find the five. They won't be able to defend themselves if it is the Order coming for them.

But first, I need to see if a particular trio of Order executives will leave this city alive.

CHAPTER FORTY-FIVE

Absolution Opportunity

The evacuated city is about as close to ursu construction as I've yet seen outside New Vetus. The buildings are tall and the streets cramped. There is clearly more understanding in the art of construction by those in the pact nations than that of Joiak or Zadok, but they still don't come close to the scale the ursu build.

To be fair, none of the races other than the ursu really need all the extra room. Dohrni are tall at their full height, but still only a portion of an ursu. Plus, they rarely stand tall, usually relaxed at about the average height of the other races. Ignoring volans, of course. A single floor in an ursu building would support two for any other race.

This immense difference is most apparent in the thickness of the alleys between buildings. In the dead of night, and the silence that only comes from an abandoned city, those looming structures are restrictively close together.

As I walk through the dark streets, letting my footsteps be heard and offering any would-be attacker an ideal, unsuspecting target, the towering brick walls feel more akin to underground tunnels than somewhere in open air. It's frustrating that even without the knot layering fears in my psyche, I still find enclosed spaces unnerving.

An hour has passed since I left the three executives in their office. It's surprising. I really thought they'd send a hit squad after me the moment I left. Maybe they are smarter than I thought. Could the Order bureaucrats actually be reasonable?

The repeating slap of a dohrni's steps echo off the buildings. I guess it was too much to hope. Footsteps resound around me. With the tall walls around me, it is impossible to determine the number of attackers, nor where they are coming from. A heat signature behind me is barely noticeable through the buildings, but who knows if there are more hiding?

I can feel heat through one or two walls, but they become less distinct the more that gets in my way. The city, as quiet as it is, is far from empty. Residents that have refused to leave. Soldiers on patrol. It is hard to tell which body of heat is coming for me, and which are simply doing their own thing.

The first door I see, I enter. If they are after me, there is no doubt in my mind there will be water mages amongst them, so an enclosed space will be best to give me an opportunity to incinerate them before they get any opportunity to attack. Worst-case scenario, it's a Beith ranked water mage. If so, I'll collapse the building on top of us and run off.

In a corner, wedged between a staircase and the doorway to an adjacent room, I hide. The merminea fur and lack of light keep me invisible, while giving full sight of the doorway.

The door handle rattles before a dohrni pushes its way into the building. They throw the door closed behind them, no one following. Are they alone? Or are there more outside? Is this dohrni a Beith? Or simply bait?

"Solvei?"

Oh. It's Remus.

I tug the string at the neck of my outfit and step out of my nook. "What are you doing here?"

"It is you." He lets out a relieved sigh. "What are you doing wandering around like that at night? It's almost like you are asking for trouble."

"I am."

Remus stares at me for a moment, before dumbly asking, "What?"

"A few people from the Mercenary Order tried to capture me, because they think I deserted. I told them they would die if they came after me."

A tentacle slaps Remus in the face as he gives off a groan of frustration. "I'm sorry for that, Solvei, it's why I'm here, but killing those that come will only make things worse."

"It's why you are here?" He won't make me fight him, will he?

"Yes." He nods. "I came to find you so they couldn't make some dumb attempt, but I see I was too late." Remus turns back to the door, gesturing me to follow. "They have no grounds to call for your arrest. You never officially signed on, nor did you swear the Order's oath, so they do not have the authority."

"What about Grímr?" I ask as I follow him back out into the street. "They didn't punish him, did they?"

"Well, they did. But it isn't anything to worry about. A fine is all they gave him before reallocating him to Meja. It is different for you, because you are unknown. You haven't proven where your loyalty lies, so some at the top of the organization are determined to lock you down and control you. It's bad at the moment. Considering the typical incentives to keep the stronger mercenaries around have shown to no longer be as effective as they thought, upper management is desperate for alternative methods of control."

The glow of the Ember Moon illuminates the brickwork walls around us in a deep crimson. Oddly, the light makes the streets more comforting. Like a pseudo flame engulfing everything without leaving a physical trace.

"It is, thankfully, only a few that are behind the attempt at your capture, so while it will take some time, I can argue your case." Remus leads me away from the makeshift military district, and I have to wonder if the people from this city actually found a place to stay in wherever they were evacuated to. There are so many buildings that I can't imagine the number of residents being small.

Amongst the infrequent heat signatures, behind me, a region above average suddenly becomes five distinct shapes. Looks like a group just turned a corner. Considering they are heading toward us, it looks like the executives aren't all that smart.

"Until then, you'll need to stay out of their sight."

Ah. He hasn't noticed them yet. "It's a bit too late for that, Remus."

He turns to me in question at the same moment the group stumbles into our alley. The dohrni stops and sighs as I turn to deal with those running at us. They give away any subtlety and rush at us with bright markings painting their bodies. The stone paved road curves up behind us, closing us in the alley with them as a pair pool their strength into a wave of water that floods the space between buildings.

"Solvei, get out of here. Let me calm these fools down."

"No, I can take them."

"They are working for the Order. Killing them will only make things worse for yourself."

I stare back at Remus, before launching myself up the tall walls to avoid the wave as it crashes over Remus. The remaining water encompasses my teammate and traps him in its embrace. A whip of the dohrni's arms scatters the liquid and he jumps to the wall opposite me. The five mages below continue toward us with a smaller wave carrying them. Like that khirig mage that once attacked me, they have spinning blades of water cutting through the pavement on their path toward us.

"Fine, I won't kill them," I say.

Remus nods in thanks and turns his attention to the group as I rocket up to the rooftops. I keep an eye down below, making sure he can take care of himself and doesn't actually need my help. The duo with amber markings get in his way and try to hold him up. They intend to give the water mages time to chase me, but they can't get past Remus that easily.

He shatters the walls of stone they build around him and cuts off the other three from continuing. As easily as he could attack and crush them where they stand, he simply blocks their way and throws them back when they try to come after me.

"Sorry, guys, but I can't let you go further. Your superiors are in breach of protocol. Go back. Wait for a proper trial to be held."

The mages stop and exchange glances. "Remus?" I hear them ask. He really is well known, I guess. I don't stand around. He has everything under control. Even if they decide to attack, Remus clearly outmatches the lot of them. After what happened in that office, I'm insulted they sent nothing better.

I told Remus I wouldn't kill those five, but the Order executives still tried to have me killed or captured. It doesn't matter which. They went forward with it despite my warning. The mages will leave alive, but their bosses won't.

In a matter of minutes, I'm flying toward the command building. I need to be careful to enter without hurting anyone else. It would be easy to simply burn down the building, but I will hurt others in the attempt. They won't be able to escape a spreading fire, as I'd once foolishly assumed. No, normal people aren't that hardy.

Thankfully, I shouldn't have to worry about any Beith mercenary stationed here. If there is, I'm almost certain they would have set them on me with that group of mages. It would be so easy to dive into the building and take the trio out. But do I want everyone to know it was me?

Volan sentinels watch every approach to the building. Even with my camouflage outfit, they would have a good chance of spotting me. Their eyes are just better than most other races. Heck, I'm sure they're watching me right now, flying above and just waiting for me to make some move. Though that isn't exactly all that impressive. I shine like a miniature inferno in the darkness of night.

I should really work on my control. Despite having far more strength than what I assume my tribe ever did, the command I have over my fire is still lacking in comparison. With how much every other part of me has grown, I really should focus more on bettering that which was drilled into me ever since I was a child.

Also, being able to fly and not be spotted immediately would have been really nice right now.

So, how do I get into the building without being seen by the unrivaled sight of the volan guards? Well, I do have an idea.

So it turns out melting my way through the earth beneath buildings has the unintended side effect of destabilizing the supports for the structure I'm crawling under. Fortunately, there was nobody around when the wall of a double-story building collapsed under its own weight. Fortunate, because I wasn't discovered . . . and nobody was hurt.

Now I need to figure if it's even possible to break into the command post with this method, or I'll need to scrap the plan entirely. I can hardly leave a path of destruction on my way in and call it stealthy, can I?

Wait, why am I doing this in my default body? I chide myself while my body shrinks, taking on the form and size of a jerboa. I've never been able to push myself this small before, and it soon becomes clear why; the ground melts under my tiny feet without intention.

I can no longer hold back the heat of my white flames. Any attempt at reverting my body to the cooler golden fire fails. I let my body grow a touch, taking on the form of a fennec fox. The larger size gives me much more freedom and control over how my heat affects the surroundings.

For crawling through the earth, the form of a worm might be the most efficient, but . . . I really don't want to be a worm.

I try to dig once more, beginning at another uninhabited building a good distance from the first. When I melt everything in my way, the rock tends to cave in behind me, so I have to attempt something with more control. The smaller size will help, but I should be more careful this time. Instead of leaving the rock molten as I crawl through the ground, I focus on the heat, pulling it out of the stone the moment I've squeezed past it.

The magma pooling around me hardens but only fills the bottom half of the tunnel I've dug. For now, the rock walls hold. I push forward, doing my utmost to suppress the anxious twisting in my chest.

I chose to tunnel my way in not only because it would avoid the eyes of the volans, but because I despise the fear I feel. It should be all but impossible to be trapped underground anymore, and yet the idea of being buried alive still terrifies me. The knot no longer limits my movements, so I need to prove that I can do this. I need to show the world that a simple fear won't stop me.

The tunnel expands a few streets with no buildings falling on me when I realize I don't actually know how far I need to go before I reach the building used as a command post. I'd chosen a starting point a fair way off from the militarized area, to prevent being noticed, but I now discover that it is far harder to tell how far I've come than expected.

After sitting in indecision for a moment about whether I should go back, I settle on rising from where I am. As my tunnel inclines to the surface, ever so slightly, I feel a heat signature above.

Barely a moment after I feel it, the ground above me melts away, exposing the interior of some building's basement. The body heat I felt is outside, down the street. I climb to the ground floor and get my bearings through the windows. I still have quite a distance to go, but the number of patrolling guards increases from here.

It should be pretty easy to make that distance now. I'll just check every few hundred meters. The massive congregation of people at the command post will be more than obvious, even with rock over my head. I'll need to be careful not to rise too quickly when checking, otherwise I might break through the surface and give myself away.

An hour of crawling through magma later, I finally arrive below my objective. The mass of heat above can be nothing other than the many people concentrated within the command center. The only issue I have now is how do I get in without being noticed?

I could simply dig up and hope there isn't anyone where I breach, maybe choosing a place where the heat feels less dense. If the building has a basement, there shouldn't be too many waiting around, but being careful can't hurt.

I burn a path toward the less dense heat section, hoping to rise with no eyes around, and stumble into a tunnel system already dug beneath the building. The rock melts away before me and dribbles down into this new chamber. Without heat sources in the tunnel, I couldn't notice it until it was too late.

Barely in time, I suck the heat out of the molten rock before it burns through the pipe taking up most of the tunnel. The tube gives off a constant groan as I climb into the space. Even with the pair of pipes running along the wall, there is plenty of space for me to walk, and I take my time to change back to my default form.

I'm not really sure where this tunnel leads, but it is clearly a part of the building

I wanted to get into. Well, this is probably a better entry than what I had planned, but I really wish I didn't have to walk so close to what I am pretty sure is a tube of rushing water. I've been around the other races long enough to know that they find this important, but I don't have to like it.

I eye it carefully as I don my outfit again. Knowing my luck, the pipes will burst before I can even make it up to the basement. Well, no point waiting here.

CHAPTER FORTY-SIX

Unexpected Attack

I may have worried for nothing over the threat of piping.

I don't even have to travel far before a way up shows itself. A hatch above a ladder gives me an entrance to the basement within only a few meters from where I fell into the tunnel.

As well as my body is hidden, if there's anyone watching the hatch, they'll notice me immediately. I don't waste time, though. If I'm seen, I'm seen. It would be preferable to staying in the tunnel with water flowing by my side. Plus, they'll see the hatch moving, not who is lifting it.

With the amount of heat I feel above the hatch, I expect at least someone to spot the movement, but as the metal door swings open, the source of the heat becomes far more clear to my senses. I feel foolish. There is barely anyone down in the basement, and those that are tend to a large furnace not unlike the ovens I once spent so much time within.

Bad memories.

I silently climb into the dimly lit room with a pair of khirig chatting beside sacks of coal. The furnace on the opposite side of the basement from me is nowhere near the size of an ursu oven, and the fire only burns at a fraction of capacity.

The major difference between this and ursu ovens—besides the size—is the thick red lines of inscription glowing across the metal box and spreading over the walls. I finally get to see one of those sources that power inscriptions.

I can use this. The inscription network would spread through the entire building and if I put my influence over the system, I can probably burn the trio from here. It is almost too tempting to try, but it is too risky. Because of Leal, I now know that mages can tell the difference between my fire and that currently spreading through the building. There is also the issue that I have no way of being certain I'm burning the right people until I've wrapped them in flames.

Fortunately, I don't need to rely on such alternative methods right now. I can feel each volan. Finding a path around them should be easy.

The stairs are out of the duo's line of sight, so I have no issue making my way up. The stairs wind upward, with doors to each floor. I won't be able to climb to higher than the second floor using these; a volan and dohrni block my way, watching over the handrail from the third floor. Another pair watches the entrance to the stairs from the foyer, but they aren't watching my way, so I'll have no issue getting past.

I creep up each step, hugging the wall. My outfit hides me from sight, and my reduced physical form carries so little weight, my steps barely make a noise.

Some khirig treks down the stairs, but I'm safely through the opening of the second floor before they pass me.

I have to get to the sixth and top floor to find the trio of executives. Or at least that's where we met the last time I was here. Their clothes and the way they hold themselves are a step up from most of the office workers flooding the building. Very few of them appear to be much in the way of fighters, but the few that are hold themselves with such confidence that it is clear which are the guards.

Still holding myself against the wall, I creep past many mercenary team managers and other workers rushing back and forth between offices. In the center hall, a bunch of bulky metal machines clack with the motions of dozens of people. Paper is spat out and folded into envelopes before being tossed into bins which are rushed down the hall.

The space reminds me much of the mill where I found my friends, and while it doesn't look anywhere near as dangerous for the workers, I find the monotony the operation forces upon each to be too similar to be favorable. Well, it's probably not the worst thing in the world, but it looks so boring.

I crack open the door to one of the few rooms that I haven't seen any worker clambering through, and slide myself inside. It is a tight space that reeks of chemicals, with walls lined with tools, but it is perfect. I take no time to climb the shelves lining the back walls and melt a hole into the roof before pulling myself up.

There's a tiny crawlspace between floors, barely tall enough for a volan to fit, but no one is above, so I melt another hold and crawl into an almost identical room on the next floor.

The climb to the sixth floor is not difficult per se, but definitely time consuming. It would be nice if I could have simply taken the stairs after the third floor, but the guards seem to concentrate there, not to mention the number of people simply walking up and down makes it a hassle.

It took time, but I've made it. The top floor isn't much different from the other levels, though it is clearly not frequented near as much as the other floors. Through a few walls, I can feel those I assume are my targets, sitting behind the same desk as before.

Thankfully, nobody has noticed the holes I've melted just yet, but that won't last forever. I put in some effort to hide my path, but my solutions are makeshift and any curious person will uncover the holes in dark corners, or lazily hidden with potted plants or chairs.

As I'm about to charge down the empty hallway and end their lives before their guards can react, several familiar heat signatures walk their way up the stairs.

Remus leads the five mages who attacked me up to this floor and into the executives' office.

I guess he really talked them down. Well, now I'll have to wait until Remus leaves before I make my move. As much as he hasn't explicitly told me not to kill the three executives, I know he doesn't approve. But I can't let people get away with attempting to trap me, especially after I gave them the opportunity to back down.

As the six of them push into the office, closing the door behind them, I feel one executive—the dohrni—rise to full height and his muffled shouts ring through the hall. A subtle sense of satisfaction bleeds through my chest, knowing how irritated the mages' failure has made them.

Remus stands undaunted at his screaming kin. The mages all stand behind him, almost cowering at their superior's anger, despite the fact each probably has the strength to fight off all three without issue. I consider creeping forward to overhear, but I know Remus is here to tell these higher ups of the Mercenary Order to back down, while also protecting the mages who failed their mission.

The dohrni's partners are far more collected than he, gesturing him to calm down before they move into a conversation with Remus. The talks go on for a few minutes, and I really wish I could see their faces right now. Heat sense simply is not detailed enough to tell much of a person's finer body language, especially through walls. I'm sure each is fuming, though, as Remus walks out into the hall—and into my sight—happy and pleased, almost skipping as he takes the mages back downstairs.

I wait until they're into the stairway before I move toward the executive's office. Before I reach the door, it opens and the two guards that stood in the corner of their office the entire time walk out. I freeze, thinking they have found me out, but both walk right past me and stand on the opposite wall.

Neither are the water mages that tried to trap me the last time I was here. Even if things don't go well, there's not much I have to fear from these two. I wonder what happened to the khirig after I burned off all their antlers?

Not one to ignore such an opportunity, I slide into the room as the door closes, only for the three to explode at each other. Each apparently just as wound up as the dohrni, but unwilling to show as such in front of even their guards.

The executives sent their guards out so that they can argue amongst themselves. I guess things really can go in my favor sometimes.

"I told you this was a stupid idea. You said Remus was busy up north, so why the fuck is he here?"

"He's not supposed to be back for another few weeks. I don't know why he's here and not guarding the commander I paid out. This would have all been fine if you'd brought capable mages. Seriously, are low-Luis ranked the best you could do?"

"This is both of your faults. All you had to do was catch a child and keep away some old laggard. How could you fuck that up?"

"Don't you talk. We wouldn't be in this mess if you hadn't hidden the fact our Beiths ran off."

"It is only because of me we have yet to be demoted to scum cleaners like the other Beith managers. We need to get that áed under our command soon. If we can't, there's no future for us."

"But how? We've lost all the influence over any higher ranked teams and my wallet is running dry. You saw what she did to that water mage, her supposed counter. Anyone we throw her way will only find their deaths."

As enjoyable as it is to stand in the doorway and listen to their squabbling, I need to get this over with. Flames wrap around me, covering my body and alerting each of the executives to my presence. They try to yell for the guards, but their previous shouting has the guards staying where they are.

I consider gloating, showing off and telling them they messed with the wrong áed, but it feels wasteful. None of them means much to me. They tried their utmost to force me into their control and even though I gave them the opportunity to learn from their mistake and yet, they still repeated it. From their argument now, it appears they would have made the same mistake a third time if given the chance.

The white flames remove their bodies from existence within moments. Not even a drop of blood remains to indicate this is the location of their death. My control isn't so bad that I would leave scorch marks anymore.

I stand alone in the empty office.

Maybe I should have gloated, at least somewhat. Offing them like pests, while appropriate, makes the whole action feel too deontic. I could have made the entire interaction at least somewhat entertaining. I was always going to kill them, but doing it without gaining any sort of catharsis just doesn't feel right.

Well, those that attempted to trap me are now dead. It's unfortunate I can't use their lives as an example for others not to try, but I still think it's better nobody knows I was here.

The guards still stand outside the door to this office, so I find a dark spot beneath the heavy wooden desk and burn my way down to the floor below and make my way out, just as stealthily as I made my way in.

At least now I know this attempt on my freedom was an isolated attempt by these three and not the entire organization trying to control me. I don't have to worry about them using my friends as hostages . . . probably.

I think I'm going to go check up on them anyway, just to be sure.

An hour later, I've made it out of the command post, through the tunnel, and back out on the streets. The entire mission went as well as I could have hoped. My three targets are dead, and nobody knows it is me who did it.

Now, I should find Remus. I doubt he's run far considering he knows I'm around, but we set no place to meet, so I'm not too sure how we could find each other without me sending up a pillar of fire to tell every being within a league where I am.

I settle to just go back to the last building we met, but before I can, an odd feeling of wrongness settles within my chest. My eyes turn to the command center

I'd just escaped from, where a mass of intermingled heat signatures suddenly goes cold.

At the end of the street, where the building once stood, is nothing but a dust cloud that quickly settles along the earth. Everything within a hundred meters of the building disappears. An entire section of the city is simply gone.

There is no explosion, no screams, nothing that would typically suggest a tragedy, but that's exactly what this is. Everything and everyone in the area is as gone as the executives after I was done with them. The dust settles as I run toward the site of devastation. A crater now sits in place of the command post. Nothing outside the crater is damaged, but there isn't a soul in sight. I know there should be people in the untouched streets, but it's like they no longer exist.

My first thought is a Viisin, but even they can't do this much damage this quick, especially not without a noise. Has the Void Fog made another appearance? That doesn't explain the missing people in the surroundings.

As I stand at the edge of the crater, a single creature walks out from the last of the settling dust. Some short species I've never seen before with taut, furless skin and two long tails walks toward me. Its large eyes dig into mine and I feel instinctual fear. Its presence, barely a sliver, petrifies me.

The creature gives me just enough pressure to know I couldn't possibly hope to face it. I have no doubt in my mind, this monster is stronger than Hund. I could run, but it would be pointless.

"So." Her voice is laced with power. Unlike Hund's booming voice that shakes the air, hers stings just to listen to. It's like my body is falling apart at the sound. My flames lose their energy and I have to focus to not fall apart in her proximity. "You must be the áed that brought that lot of centzon to block my way."

She stands before me, only her large ears resting on the top of her head reach my height, and yet she exudes such an intimidating presence she might as well tower over me.

"Oh, where are my manners?" She backs up and gives a low, excessively showy bow that only makes it feel patronizing before grinning viciously. "I'm Kalma. You might have heard of me."

CHAPTER FORTY-SEVEN

Kalma's Karma

Kalma? Here? What is she doing on this side of the Alps? Isn't she supposed to be oblivious to the mermineae escape?

Did she find out? Is that why she's here now? But that can't be right. She would be cutting her way through the mermineae rather than wiping out our command post if that were the case.

Nobody here had a chance, did they? Fuck. Did Remus at least get out before she arrived? Plenty of time should have passed while I was crawling through the earth, so he must have, right?

Kalma takes a step forward, and as much as I scream at my body to run, it won't move. An unyielding physical fear stops me from what would be senseless resistance. If she wanted me dead, I'd be dead. If there's something she wants from me, she'll get it. I've never been so sure of something in my life.

The gray-skinned monster tilts her head back, closes her eyes and breathes deep. "Ah. That explains it; you reek of Anatla. The Void truly had its way with you, huh?"

Thankfully, she gives me my space again, and I clench my jaw to stop myself crying out in relief.

How did I ever think Hund was bad? The mere slither of her presence is enough to have my flames break down, losing the energy that holds them together. No matter how hard I try to control myself, my flames burn bright into the surroundings. Like a child once more, I cannot keep myself contained.

Kalma's eyes sting like humid air as they watch me. I'm too slow to hold back my relieved breath when she finally turns away. She pays me no mind. With tails swaying lazily behind her, she looks over the city . . . or at least what's left of it. I feel a heat signature growing from off to our side, but as I turn to look, it disappears. Kalma doesn't react at all.

"You know, it's nice to be back in a proper civilization again," she says. "No matter how much benevolent guidance I give them, the mermineae simply never change their ways. I do so much for them, and they want to run away from me. Like children that don't realize how good they have it."

Another approaching heat source vanishes.

"I'm so good to them. How could they?"

Kalma lets out a snicker before it morphs into loud cackles. She turns back to me with a grin full of sharp teeth. Her long protruding fangs are knives amongst rows of razors. "Nah, that's Titan-shit. I'm an absolute bitch to them." She chuckles again.

Yet another approaching person loses their heat signature. She stands here, having just wiped out an entire block with hundreds inside, killing any who come close, and now admitting to her cruelty toward the mermineae. Why am I not dead yet?

"Don't worry kid, I won't kill you. You're touched by Anatla; the curse you've got coming your way is so much worse than anything I can do to you." She smirks, only her four fangs peeking through her lips this time. "Enjoyed your quick rise to power, did you? Kept that mind of yours intact? Well, enjoy the time you have before the Void regains sentience."

What does that mean? What does she mean? I thought I beat the Fog's curse when I broke free of the knot. It isn't going to come back now, is it?

"What will happen?" I muster up the courage to speak through her presence.

She ignores my question. "You know, I was really pissed when I found out the outsiders I'd let into my lands interfered with my plan and put the centzon in the mermineae's path. I'd put a lot of effort into balancing things and that threw it all off. But the nations over here aren't nearly as unified as I'd assumed, so even without every merminea, it still worked out."

"You wanted them to invade?" I ask, stunned at the implications. "Then why not just order them? They'd be terrified to oppose you."

Kalma melts into dust before my eyes, only to reform behind me. She wraps an arm over my shoulder and a tail around my torso, pulling me in close. "Now where's the fun in that?" she snickers in my ear.

I jolt, but her grip is tight. Even as my flames drop into intangibility, I can't escape Kalma's grasp.

"Sending the mermineae across would be too easy. The battle would end with a simple fight between my Viisin and the elite over here. Now that isn't a war. A war should be fought by everyone. Every single being that makes up the whole, not simply those with the most strength. It's boring and quick otherwise. It wouldn't truly bring out the sheer desperation of those involved."

Uncomfortable in her claws, I struggle to free myself, but she clamps down on me, making each point of contact sting in agony. As if she coated her body in water before touching me.

"So, I sent an invitation to those Beiths. Took many out of the picture while I enjoyed the vain squabbling of the mermineae. I don't think I could state how amusing it is to watch a collective splinter over two impossible goals. My only regret is I didn't get to watch the same happen over here."

I don't understand. She has the power to simply walk through any of the nations and take what she wants. It is unlikely the pact nations have any warriors or mages greater than Hund, and definitely none that could come close to stopping her.

I calm the churning flames within my chest. She's already said she won't kill me and I might as well take advantage of her suspicious willingness to talk. "But what do you hope to achieve?"

Kalma's face goes blank, devoid of emotion for the first time since I've met her. "World domination." Her eyes lock on mine for a long moment before her facade cracks. She snorts, then breaks out in laughter.

Kalma grins, the expression still unsettling no matter how many times it rests on her face. "No, no. I'm messing with ya. It's simply for my amusement. There's nothing quite like an all-out, multi-faction war. What better way to spend the last days before the end of our world?"

"The end of the world?" I ask, doubtful. Considering she's started wars and killed thousands apparently because she considers it amusing means she's either insane or a liar. A claim like that is ludicrous.

"Yeah," she says with a sigh, no longer joking. "The barrier will not last much longer."

Finally, Kalma lets me go, her attention somewhere else. What does she mean? What barrier? Why won't it last? I want to believe she's delusional, but should I assume that?

"Why are you telling me all this?"

Kalma ignores my question and asks her own. "Are you familiar with a certain dohrni that holds gauntlets beneath each of his tentacles?"

Even after having adjusted to her constant pressure, my body goes stiff. "What?"

"I'm sure you've noticed. I've been killing anyone that gets close to us. You've ignored their deaths easily, which is rather cold for an áed." She chuckles before continuing. "But I wonder how you'll react to the same happening to someone you are actually close to?"

My eyes widen and I turn to the growing heat signature rushing toward us. Quickly, Remus enters my range. It can be no one else. Unless there's some Beith that was hiding in the area, Remus is the only dohrni that can run that fast.

Kalma raises her hand, and before she has the chance to hurt him, I engulf her in as much white hot fire as I can manipulate. I'm not sure what I plan to do, but I need to stop her from hurting him.

"Huh, that was easier than expected," Kalma says before an orb the size of my head appears in her hand.

The sphere has an incredibly dense array of inscriptions lining it, and I feel them trying to exert control over my flames. I ignore its attempts and incinerate both the orb along with its holder.

An intense, overwhelming agony washes through my inner flames, and I tug them back, pulling myself back into safety. My inner flame recedes back into me, but I watch as white fire circles the orb. It spins around the metal sphere in Kalma's hand.

They are my flames, but I no longer control them. I don't want to feel that pain again, and I'm sure Kalma will have no qualms about repeating the decay she inflicted upon me if I tried to reinsert my flames.

"You asked why I told you everything?" Kalma, holding the orb and flames surrounding it, smirks at me. "It doesn't matter what you know; nobody will believe a word."

She raises the orb above her head, and the flames spread out. A white inferno covers the buildings bordering the crater Kalma left. I feel Remus stop, thankfully unharmed by Kalma, but he backs away from the heat.

"I said this before: I'm a bitch. When someone gets in my way, I pay them back. While things turned out even better than I'd expected, you still put the centzon in my way. Normally, I'd settle for extended torture, but you already have a cursed future ahead of you, and I wouldn't want to impede that."

The orb disintegrates within her hands as it pushes the fire to spread through the rest of the city.

"So, good luck convincing your allies. You'll need it. You did burn down their command center, after all." With one last toothy grin, she vanishes into dust.

I can do nothing but stand there watching the inferno greater than I'd be able to create myself burn across the city. Remus has moved well out of the range of my senses again, but I'm hesitant to push my control into the fire. I don't want to feel that pain again. Kalma could be around, just waiting for me to try.

The flames don't die out, though; they continue to grow and if I don't do something, they are bound to burn further than I can stop. Just like what happened in Morne.

Hesitantly, I spread my inner flame into the surrounding fire, prepared to pull back at a moment of pain, but it doesn't come, so I force my influence through every part of the inferno. Buildings collapse around me, their supports no obstacle to the unbelievable heat of my hottest fire. I can feel the melting bones of those who couldn't escape in time. Anything the flames touch does not exist for long.

It takes a full minute to bring the blaze under control. Even as I do, I can feel the eyes on me. The heat signatures approaching and watching on as the flames pull into myself. The amount of energy in the fire is insane. An order of magnitude greater than I can put out. I'm momentarily awed by the sheer energy Kalma must have to achieve this until I truly realize the situation she's thrown me in.

I'm the only one to see Kalma here. Anyone who even knows her name thinks she's a thousand leagues across the Titan Alps.

How much of what she said was true? Did she truly orchestrate this all from the start, or was that a bluff? Is the world truly ending? Has the Void Fog affected me more than I thought? Kalma knows so much about me. She knows I am close to Remus. How? It's not like we've met before. How long has she known about the nations on this side of the Alps?

As I extinguish the last of the fire, a familiar thermal presence approaches from behind, and I struggle to think of a way to explain. I'm not stupid enough to not realize how bad this looks. Maybe I could have feigned ignorance if I pretended I wasn't here, but I couldn't let my fire go out of control like that again. Not after Morne.

"Solvei . . . what . . ."

I turn to Remus. The dohrni looks pained. Worse even than when I found him in the hands of the mermineae. It hurts to see him jumping to the obvious conclusion, but I can't blame him for it. My chest aches at the betrayal his eyes express.

More people close in around us. Mercenaries, most likely. Those willing to approach the source of disaster after it has happened, and likely only the strongest around. Remus straightens himself, standing tall above me as he wipes the emotion from his eyes.

"Solvei, tell me, did you do it? Was this intentional?"

What else can I do but say the truth? "No."

"Then leave. We'll meet at the team's cabin and you can explain yourself there. Until then, stay out of sight and don't bring attention to yourself." His voice is quiet, only loud enough for me to hear, and not the counting observers.

He believes me? No, he might not know what to think, but he wants to give me the benefit of the doubt. A mix of gratitude and guilt engulfs me. He is willing to believe me and I'd assumed he wouldn't even give me a chance.

"Leave. Now." Remus's tone is uncharacteristically curt. His eyes twirl to the growing number of mercenaries closing in.

I understand it won't be long until there's a mercenary group either capable or willing to fight me, and there's already been too much death today. With the excess energy from Kalma's fueled flames, I rocket into the air, putting as much space as I can between myself and the mercenaries before my form fully changes.

No longer can I fight on the battlefield alongside the Mercenary Order. With Kalma watching over this war so it will end in the worst possible way for all parties involved, I have no clue what I'm supposed to do. Is there even a chance things won't end horribly?

CHAPTER FORTY-EIGHT

Impatient

Helplessness is a feeling I'm all too familiar with. The overwhelming difficulty of simply trying to live is something that never seems to ease.

Maybe I've become arrogant in my strength. I mean, I can even compete with Viisin now, so I thought it would be no issue to just burn my way to my goals. Burn the mermineae. Incinerate any who threaten me. Violence and murder have become such an easy solution to my problems, but no matter how much power I gather, the world is determined to make me struggle.

Kalma isn't someone I can fight.

Not only would I have no chance against her in a fight, she has gone and severed my ties to the nations that protect my friends. The centzon weren't even an obstacle for her, so I don't understand why she felt it so important to punish me personally.

Does she know Grímr was with me? Has she taken her anger out on him too? If I knew where he was, I would be on my way to find him immediately. Unfortunately, I don't. I can only hope that wherever he was sent for his recovery is out of her reach.

Not that anything could stop her.

Is there anything I can actually do now? Kalma has such a stranglehold on this war that every side will wipe themselves out unless something changes. Drastically. Without being part of the Mercenary Order, I can't try to convince them to switch their priorities. I'm sure nothing could change, even if they know of Kalma's true influence. They still need to fight off each of their invaders.

Can we convince any of the invaders to back down? Both New Vetus and the Theocracy are opportunistic, so it will be difficult. It's the mermineae that have the most chance to back down, but for that to happen, I would have to reveal Kalma's plot to both their clergy and the traitors. That will be incredibly hard considering the immense number of their kind I've personally ended.

Even if I can convince them that Kalma has not only known of their plans to escape from the start, but actually incited that idea within their numbers, would they stop invading? They are terrified of her, and rightfully so. I can't imagine they would go against her wishes for fear of the consequences. Not while they know she's aware of their actions.

It is hopeless.

I have no better idea, so I fly to Meja. I want to see my friends again and make sure they're safe before I meet with Remus at the team's cabin. Hopefully, we'll be able to think of some way out of this together.

My last option is to take those I care for and run. I would lead them to the wasteland and eventually the Agglomerate, if I didn't know for sure that some would refuse to leave.

My flight through the pact nations is not undisturbed, but I shake off each of the volans that try to intercept me. Only the mages amongst them can reach the same pace Jav could after being flung by Remus, and therefore are able to keep up with me. Those that command me, I ignore. The ones that attack, I threaten with flames of my own.

It's not an optimal solution. It will hardly make me look any less guilty in the eyes of the pact nations, but I can't stop. Not now.

When the volan interceptions stop, I know I've entered the merminea-controlled land. Unfortunately, that happens far earlier than I expected.

Half of Meja has already been overtaken. I don't know why I thought the city where I'd left my friends would have remained untouched, but I had. Assuming they've been evacuated, how will I find them? There's so many places they could have gone.

It also means the meeting point Remus set for us is far behind merminea lines. Far from where the Mercenary Order can reach me.

I'm not worried about what the Order might send after me. With how hesitant they've been to utilize their Beiths, I can't imagine they would have one chase me down unless I'm actively attacking them. What I am worried about is that they might punish my friends because of what they think I've done.

Many mermineae pass below. I could spend some time clearing through them to make it easier on the pact nations' defense, but I don't see the point anymore. No matter how many I clear out, it won't make a difference. They aren't the true threat. They never were.

I arrive at Baansguard. I'd been far too petrified of the city's enclosed nature the last time I was here to truly appreciate its scale. Unfortunately, the large carved living platforms have seen better days. Many have crumbled. There are clear signs that Viisin went unopposed within the city's confines.

The sight of dried blood leaves a sick feeling in my chest. My friends were evacuated, right? They couldn't have just left all the citizens to die here. They pulled the citizens away from the cities bordering the conflict zone down south, so it's only reasonable that they did the same here, right?

I have no way to find them, either. The pact nations are likely going to treat me as an enemy of the state like Joiak did before the ursu destroyed it, so it isn't like I can just go searching for them.

All I can do now is hope they are safe. Wherever they might have gone.

With how much land the pact nations have lost, I can't imagine the safer cities doing well with the massive influx of refugees. Even if they got away from the battles without issue, what kind of life are they now living?

There is nothing left for me in Baansguard, so I leave for my team's cabin. Technically, as a part of the team, it is mine too, but I only spent a single night, so it hardly feels like a home. I barely recognize the building when I arrived in the clearing. Like the city, it too is empty. The scratched up wooden deck and door show the mermineae have been here, likely ransacking for anything worthwhile.

I approach the couch I'd slept on when I was last here. A few meters behind it, I dig through the earth and pull up the pouch with my mom's marble. I'd left it here for safekeeping when we first left on our hunt. At the time, it had seemed safer to hide it rather than keep it on me, and I'm glad I did. If I hadn't, I probably would have lost it somewhere along the way.

There's nothing for me to do except wait for Remus, so I jump onto the couch and bring out the small glass orb. The unmoving pink flame still shines with intensity through its black encasing despite all the time that has passed. Like it's frozen in time.

What would my tribe have done if they were here? Would Mom or Auntie or Uncle find a solution that I'm simply unable to see?

With as much time as I have with my own thoughts, my mind falls back on Kalma's words. She mentioned some unbelievable things, like the world is ending and the Void is regaining sentience. I shouldn't believe her, but she made her comments with such conviction that I have to at least consider their possibility.

How might the world be ending? Does it relate to the Void Fog gaining awareness? Is the Void Fog going to kill everyone? No, that's probably jumping to conclusions. She said I smelled of Anatla. What is Anatla? Did she mean the Void Fog when she said that?

Haven't I heard the term Anatla before? They have something to do with the revontulet, according to the centzon. How is the revontulet related to the Void Fog? I saw one of those foxes within the Fog. Is that important?

If the world truly is going to end, why does Kalma not try to stop it? She has enough power to do anything, so why is it only being used to spread chaos?

Wait, if the world is really ending, then why does she think the curse I'll experience because of the Void is worse than any torture she can inflict? Could it be that she won't hurt me directly because I'm void-touched?

It's an incredibly flawed train of logic that I'm sure isn't even close to the truth, but if there's the smallest chance that she can't attack a void-touched because she fears the Fog, or Anatla, then I know what I have to do.

I've felt both their presences, so I know Hund couldn't beat Kalma, but if she can't attack him, then he might just be able to scare her off. He is void-touched as well.

The only problem is that he is still bound by his own version of the knot. If I can disentangle him from the control of New Vetus, we might all have a chance.

I'm on my feet and ready to take to the skies in seconds. This can't wait. The longer I delay, the worse things will get. If Remus gets here within a day, I'd stay, but there is no guarantee he can get here that fast. Every day I wait, the closer the battles get to the heart of the pact nations.

There will be a point that the Mercenary Order is backed into a corner and will unleash every elite they have. If things go how Kalma wants, that will be the day millions will die.

I feel bad for leaving Remus, but this is too important. I burn a message into the outer wall of the cabin, where he couldn't possibly miss it, and blast south. Time to go to the ursu's capital.

"Damn it, Solvei."

Remus stared at the char-black message strewn across the front wall of his team's home. He was glad Ossian wasn't here to see this. The caretaker would grouch when someone dragged dirt inside; the khirig would faint when he saw this.

Despite his original thoughts upon seeing the city in flames, there had been far too many questionable facts for him to believe it could have been the young áed. Not only was that far too much white flame for him to reasonably assume the girl could have supplied it, but the central crater did not match the damage to the rest of the city. Though, that would be impossible to prove because of the black glass coating that had once been molten rock.

Remus had seen the energy cost between different flames during his time with an áed tribe, so he knew Solvei couldn't have created that blaze, even with the capacity she'd accumulated for herself.

Once more in his life, guilt riddled him. He'd assumed the girl had gone for retribution, and paid little attention to the innocents in her way. It was only when he locked eyes with her he knew she hadn't done it. At least not intentionally.

Though none of the other mercenaries would believe him. This was as open and shut as it could get to their eyes. It didn't help that Remus couldn't answer how this actually happened. Especially considering all the mages pointed out the flames had the same signature of influence as the girl herself.

So, to hear Kalma, the feared god from across the Titan Alps, caused the disaster was concerning.

Remus ran to the abandoned cabin as soon as he could, but he was sure he'd been days late to meet her. She'd run off again without waiting, to convince them of the greatest threat to New Vetus. Her goal was foolish and unlikely to achieve anything but her death, but he was already too late to stop her.

All he could do was gather everyone and be ready to help her when she returned, whether that was with Hund by her side, or chasing her with his blade raised.

Fortunately, Remus had some favors to call in.

CHAPTER FORTY-NINE

Those With the Leash

Hund is the only solution to Kalma. He has to be.

Even after the rest of his kind became hateful to nonursu, he had been willing to guide me on how to safely deal with the Void Fog. If not for his Void enforced desire, I'm certain he will help us. As terrifying as he is, he helped me, expecting nothing in return.

I know he cares for his people, but I'm not exactly sure what his desire truly is. What is it that allows the New Vetus Council to control his actions?

Right now, there are two paths I can take: make an assumption on what his desire is and act upon it, or ask those who know.

Hund follows the commands of the council, so if I kill them all, I might be able to convince him without his Void-affected mind being manipulated. The big problem with that solution is it relies on my assumption that he won't follow their commands if he were to regain free will. If he does what he does because he truly believes it best, then I'll be killing his people. It will do nothing but label me a target for that monster of an ursu.

The alternative, and by far my preferred option, is to simply ask someone on the ursu council. All the better if I can talk to the chairman.

Of course, I'm not stupid enough to think they'll willingly give away information like that. But that doesn't matter, because I don't intend to be civil when asking. As long as I don't leave a massacre in my trail, I can hopefully avoid Hund's wrath.

Flehullen, the capital of New Vetus, won't be easy to infiltrate. I don't plan to go through all the effort of digging through the ground again. I just need to get into the offices of the council and threaten the information out of them before their defensive force can react.

As I fly over the city, I don't need to worry about interception as I would in the pact nations. I wonder if the Mercenary Order could take advantage of their lack of air defense and have a swarm of volans attack from above. I shake my head. It isn't the time, nor my place, to give those who might very well consider me an enemy any ideas for war.

I've passed over this city once before. After I'd killed the general of the Henosis army, I had seen this city in a horrible state. The main continae had all but collapsed under artillery fire. The streets had been littered with corpses and rubble.

Now, the city stands shiny and new, as if they hadn't been at the edge of their demise only a few years ago. Despite the changes not being favorable, I can't deny the impressive successes those changes have brought. Particularly the changes to their army. They've gone from a completely ravished military to something that can compete with the northern nations and still have troops to spare for a defense force in their home city.

I'm sure Hund's unbeatable strength has been indispensable for their rapid rearmament and expansion, but that means this new council has actually been willing to use him as opposed to the previous one which kept him in hiding until their nation was already at the brink of disaster.

Much like the current pact nations.

As easy as it would be to crash into the central continae and take the nation's leaders hostage, I'd rather not have the entire city rushing to crush me, especially not the mages I'm sure are somewhere amongst the soldiers.

I'm high enough to be barely a spot to their eyes, but should I drop lower, I've no doubt alarms will wail. My flames are still far too visible in this form.

Now that I think about it, I haven't often tried to push my control much further than necessary. At least not in regards to its physicality. Well, it won't take long to try.

I pull on my body's flames and find it takes form easily. My flickers lose their illumination quickly, but I soon find they refuse to settle into a proper shape. I no longer give off light, but on close inspection, one could still tell I'm made of swaying flames rather than the feathers of a true bird.

How had this not worked earlier? I swear I tried to control myself while I took on the form of a fox while crawling through stone. Is this more about my familiarity with a form rather than my control? That would explain why it's taken so long, despite the improvement of my control.

Now I should look like a normal bird to the casual observer. Good, this will make getting in far easier, but I still feel like I should create a distraction before I throw myself into the ursu's den.

The ursu have adopted guns from Henosis, so they must have an ammunition storage somewhere just waiting to be blown up. My flight drops low enough that I'm easily visible to any who look up. Two loops around the city proves they can't distinguish me from any normal falcon and provides the location of their armory.

There's no use waiting around, so I torch the building before flying off to the continae. When the explosion doesn't go off as I expect, I halt in midair and turn back. The building still burns, and much of those within rush out, desperate to get away, but there is no eruption.

I'm not complaining that the ursu get to safety, as it will make my conversation with Hund all the easier if I have been careful in my destruction, but it should have gone off by now. Don't tell me the ursu have a fake armory.

As I'm ready to fly back and check, the explosion finally happens. It is weak and barely even blows the roof off the building, but it should be enough to grab the attention of their defense force.

I rush to the continae and crash through the large pointy spherical roof, instantly incinerating everything in my way until I land within an incredibly well-furnished office. There is only one man in the room and he stands by the window, looking out over the smoke in the distance.

Between his embellished military uniform and the desk littered with maps and papers, I have very little doubt he is one of the council. Even if he isn't, he's going to tell me soon.

I don't have the time to change back into my normal body, so I just wrap my bird form in flames to give the picture of my default shape.

The ursu reacts, pulling his sword from his waist and crossing the room in an instant. I can tell he has similar strength to the warden of the gulag, but I'm not here to enjoy a fight today. I need information, so I need him to understand that he has no chance against me.

His blade passes through my white flames, which follow along with it. The sword melts away while I spread my fire to eat away his hand and hover around his face and throat.

"Stop or I won't hesitate to end you."

To his credit, he doesn't let go of his weapon even as his fingers blister and the metal dribbles over his fingers. He eyes the flames floating before his face. His body is tensed, ready to move at a moment's notice, but he remains still.

"Now, why don't we get this started with some easy questions. Who are you?" I am pretty sure I have the ursu leader, but better to make sure. "Do note, I'll be burning off fingers if you lie."

His sword is nothing more than a hilt now, so the ursu discards it as he glares at me. "I am Chairman Oso." He relaxes as if he knows everything will go his way. "You understand you won't be getting out of here alive, correct? Tore Hund will return soon. Especially after that explosion you set off outside."

His lax attitude annoys me, but not enough for me to go through with my threat of removing his fingers. I'm luckier than I expected to find the chairman by crashing through the top floor.

"I look forward to it." The slight twinge of his eye is extremely satisfying. He's not happy his threat doesn't have the effect he hoped for. "I came to talk about him, actually. How do you control him? What makes him listen to your council's orders?"

His eyes narrow, barely perceptively. "He follows our will because he believes wholeheartedly in our cause."

I incinerate a finger.

The only sound he makes is a grunt, but I can tell it's still painful.

"You think I don't know about the Void Fog's influence? I guess even the easy questions are too hard for you." My flames spread to engulf the room. They aren't white flames, but the effect is what I'm after. "Looks like I'll have to ask the next council member. Once I've dealt with you, of course."

Chairman Oso glares daggers my way, but it looks like his determination is cracking. Good to see the man has some level of self-preservation. Just as it seems he's about to give something, the wall explodes behind me.

I turn to find three ursu soldiers wielding swords, ready to pierce me from three sides. All three die before they can reach me, reduced to nothing but ash.

I return my attention to the chairman, only to find he's jumped out the window while I was distracted.

Groaning to myself at my lack of awareness, I take off after the ursu. I'd felt the ursu climbing the stairs and was ready to use them as a show of force for the chairman, but I didn't expect him to run like that.

Good thing I didn't bother to change my form; I can catch up before he escapes. I'm outside the building and chasing after the ursu before he even hits the ground below. When he does, the stone paving shatters, and he immediately dashes off at a sprint.

He is fast, but my wings are still faster. Chairman Oso clearly has a plan though, and I can only hope he isn't leading me to an ambush of water mages. I forgo all intent at stealth and blast a jet behind me. Barreling through the air at immense speeds, I crash into the back of his leg. It's enough to send him to the ground, but not to break his leg.

I land before him and spread my flames as he rises to his knees, preventing any further attempts at escape. "Tell me how you control him." I don't give him any more leniency. My flames engulf his feet, moving further up his thick legs as he takes his time to answer.

The chairman lifts his head within my flames and shouts at the top of his lungs. "Hund, get here now!" He stares down at me in triumph, as if he has won.

My white flames burn past his knees and he collapses to his back, and I finally hear proper gasps of pain coming from him. After a few seconds of watching him squirm in pain with no answer, the inevitable happens.

I barely have time to register Hund's thermal presence before he lands before us. The displaced air nearly blows me away as his feet pulverize the pavement. I knew this was coming. I prepared myself for this, but it's still hard to stand before him without cowering.

My flames retract from the chairman, but I leave a flame below him, ready to act if needed. Hund should be willing to talk as long as I'm not actively killing the chairman. If he's not, well, I have a hostage. It's really not an optimal situation, but I'll have to settle for now.

"Hund," I say, before he can get his bearings on the situation. "Thank you for your advice. Without you, I wouldn't be alive." It's a long time coming, but I'm glad I finally get to show my gratitude.

"Chairman Torben?" Hund's eyes linger on the downed ursu before turning to me with a frown. "Why have you done this?" His voice thrums through my body with the same intensity as last time.

"Torben? Who?" I thought the chairman's name was Oso. "I'm sorry, but I wanted to return the favor you gave me. I wanted to free you from their control."

Hund is silent, and his gaze shows no sign of the thoughts within as he glances between the two of us. My flames wring with turmoil as I wait for his response. Once again, I see Hund look down at Oso with the concern one would direct to a friend. Have I made a mistake? Does Hund truly support this council?

"Hund. Kill the fucking áed already."

Hund sighs and turns to me, his hand already on his massive blade. I don't have time to think, I just react. The chairman's body burns at the same moment Hund's blade tears through my fake flame body. The shockwave that follows his blow is enough to send my small bird form crashing into the nearest wall.

I only realized it the moment before he attacked, but Hund isn't seeing the same person I am. He believes Oso is someone completely different. Someone he would do anything for. Someone he has unquestionable loyalty toward.

In a way, his mental limitation is worse than mine. While it is twisting his thoughts, he has no way of realizing they have been morphed.

I have no way of knowing the details of how it works, but I can't use the chairman as a hostage. I have to kill the man if I have any hope of bringing Hund to my side. Even if it is only for a moment before whatever terms that bind him snap back into place.

Chairman Oso struggles as my flames incinerate his fur and burn into the flesh across his body. He doesn't have the strength to resist, and I push the fire to consume his head. Through eyes, mouth, and ears, I force the blaze to dig toward his brain. I need him to die. Now.

I can't move. Hund's blade didn't even hit me and I've already been rendered immobile. The sheer pressure his blade created tore half my falcon body from existence. There's no way I can regrow before he reaches me. All I can do is float my body upon physical flames and watch as he casually lumbers his way toward me.

Finally, I feel the chairman die.

But Hund still approaches.

CHAPTER FIFTY

Grasping One's Own Leash

Even amongst the massive, musclebound ursu, Hund is a giant. Standing above five meters tall, he is impossible to miss. Impossible to keep your eyes off. He is a terrifying existence when his attention is elsewhere. So, to have his gaze squarely on me, hand on blade, and stepping forward with such menacing intent, is nothing short of soul-shaking.

He doesn't even need his presence to drive a chill through my body.

That's the strangest thing about all this; despite his aggressive actions, he keeps his presence in a tight grip. I'm not sure what his reasoning, but if he'd frozen me with his presence from the start, I never would have been able to kill the chairman.

Despite my success, Hund still comes for me. The way he treated the chairman, I was sure I was right. I was sure he was seeing someone else when he looked at the former military commissar. The mental chains should have loosened when I killed him . . . unless I was mistaken.

Wait, does he not know the man is dead?

I shout, to make Hund turn to the burning corpse behind him, but no sound escapes me. Much of my throat was torn out with Hund's attack, and I can no longer speak.

My flames point to the unmoving corpse, only for Hund to ignore them. In desperation, I push my flames over him while I carry myself away. I hardly expect to burn him, but to see my white flames slide off his fur without effect is demoralizing. Even after all this time, I'm nothing before him.

My physical flame carries my crippled form away. But not fast enough. Hund's casual steps close the distance. Each breath he takes shakes the surrounding air. I shiver as he sheathes his sword, obviously knowing he won't need it to beat me after the damage I've already taken.

I knew the risks coming into this. There was always the chance I wouldn't be able to change his mind and he would be aggressive. I only took the risk because it was the only feasible option I had. What else could I have done? Should I have prioritized my safety and never come, at the expense of my friends' lives?

Hund crouches over me, reaching both hands down to crush me. Now more than ever, I realize just how massive he is. His hands alone are as large as my bird body.

This isn't how I'm going to go out. I refuse!

With no strength to fight back and my flames already swirling around him to no effect, I do the only thing I can. I let free my presence, instinctively intensifying the pressure over Hund as far as I can push it.

Hund doesn't even react.

I flinch as his hands wrap around me, gripping me close and ready to crush me. Only . . . the pain doesn't come. He doesn't collapse his massive hands around me. In fact, his hands lift me with remarkable gentleness, considering his strength.

I look up at the giant as he lifts me to chest height.

"How long must you recover?" he asks, his voice quaking through my body.

I collapse in his grip. All the tension leaves my body at once. Was it really so hard for him to give me an indication he wasn't trying to murder me?

His face remains impassive, and I can't help but want to burn his fur off . . . if that were even possible. "A . . ." I clear my throat as it reconstructs itself. "A few minutes."

He nods, looking toward the continae rising high over the other buildings in the city. "Good. Help me, once more." Hund doesn't even send a glance back toward the burning corpse of the former chairman.

"Sure," I say. "That's why I'm here, Hund."

His eyes fall back on me as my wings finally start regrowing. The massive ursu doesn't speak for a moment, just stares with that emotionless gaze. "Call me Tore."

"What? Tore?"

He walks toward the towering building and I belatedly notice the many eyes watching us, awed. "I dislike the name."

"Oh, sure. Tore." I'm stuck in his hands for now, literally, at least until I regrow my wings. Why doesn't Hund like his name? There must be a reason. As I peer up to ask, I think better of it.

Tore walks in silence, and I get the impression he doesn't take part in casual conversation often.

"So, what is it you need help with?"

His eyes drop to mine as he walks, each ursu in the street stopping to stare as he passes. "You have overcome your desire."

I can't tell if it's a question or a statement, but I nod regardless. "Again, thank you. I couldn't have done it without your help back then."

He shakes his head slowly, as if careful not to make any rapid motions. "No. It is your achievement. One to elude me for a century."

It is a horrid thought that he's been trapped for such an incomprehensible length of time as a slave to his desire. "What is yours, anyway?"

"I'm loyal to the chairman. The original was a great man."

"So, you're free now?" I ask. He's not attacking anymore so he must be, but what is it he needs help with?

"No. With the chairman dead, a commissar only need claim the position for themselves." He stops in the open space before the continae. "I need you to kill them."

"And that will free you?" My wings have grown back, so I don't need to be held anymore. I jump from his hands and hover before his head.

Tore drops his arms as he eyes me again. "No, but it will give me time." He points a finger to the curved top of the continae. "Top three floors. The commissars are there."

Well, my body is back in perfect shape, so there's no need to wait around here. I take to the air, blasting toward the highest floors of the building. With Hund's . . . no, Tore's permission, I don't have to hold back.

The upper half of the continae is engulfed in an inferno before I even crash inside. Everything burns, but these commissars are all military men; they have greater enhancement than the rest of their kind. I wonder if they were this strong before they had all those resources fall into their laps at the end of the war with Henosis?

Regardless of how they gained their enhancement, it is no obstacle to my new flame. A swirling inferno encases the building so they cannot escape while I chase down each and burn through them directly. None have the same defense as either the chairman or the warden, so their bodies immolate and add to my strength one after the other.

The strength I gain from them is minimal, but I'm not about to deny what resources I can take from them. These men and women have all been a massive pain in the pact nations' side, but I can't say I truly hate any of them. If not for them, I wouldn't have met Leal and helped her dad.

Actually, these ursu are the ones that started those camps and put Leal in such a situation that she was desperate enough to plead my help. Yeah, fuck them.

A few throw themselves out the side of the building, trying to escape, but my flames cling to them and I simply chase them down, ending their existence before they can hit the ground.

Tore watches on, along with hundreds of ursu. Many show confusion at the central pillar of their city burning and their strongest doing nothing to stop it.

It is almost too easy to clear out the rest of the council. Once the last of them are gone, I extinguish the flame swirling through the air. The entire dome is gone. I won't admit it when they ask, but I could have easily avoided burning the building. The heavy concentration of rare metals that decorated the exterior of the dome is just too good to pass up such an opportunity. Gold and silver truly have an unbeatable taste. Too bad there wasn't any platinum in there too.

As I fly to Tore's side, I consider changing back to my normal form. Tore is with me; I hardly have to worry about being attacked by the congregating ursu. But even then, I'd rather not rely entirely on the old ursu.

Without a word, Tore passes me, approaching the continae as the ursu continue to evacuate. He walks through the open front. The ceiling is surprisingly high enough that he doesn't even need to bend over. The fur of his ears scrape against the ceiling as if designed with his height in mind.

After a minute, where the last of the ursu escape the building, Tore finally acts. He balls a fist and punches the central support pillar. In an instant, the air fills with dust and debris. The tower falls slower than I would expect. Another explosive impact quakes from within the dust cloud. Tore, with unimaginable control, directs the collapse of the continae, tearing it down floor by floor.

I hover amongst the thousands of ursu, watching the destruction of the symbol of their nation by their greatest hero. The intent behind his actions eludes me, but I'm certain it is important to him.

The pounding of levels being demolished stops. Through the cloud of dust, Tore makes his way out of the remains of the continae. He stops before the many ursu and casts his gaze over them. The giant lets out a breath and closes his eyes, tilting his head to the sky.

He stands there before his people, and in return, they wait in silence. Through the entire city, the only sound to be heard is the wind whistling between buildings.

"The council is finished!" Tore thunders, his voice impossible to miss anywhere in the city. "My friend's memory, desecrated for the last time. His corrupted governance shall never see our people mistreated again."

Tore lowers his gaze to the enraptured ursu, his eyes almost glowing with the dense energy held within. "I am your new leader."

It is clear his words leave the ursu stunned. They treat him as a hero of legend, so when the first cheers start coming in, I'm not surprised it becomes contagious. Soon, everyone is celebrating. They laugh or cry at this mighty warrior taking the reins of their nation after suffering at the hands of negligent or totalitarian leaders.

But even as they all celebrate this obviously incredible change, none dare approach Tore.

His powerful, looming figure a daunting prospect for any of the unenhanced to dare come near. Tore's eyes linger on all those before him. Face as emotionless as ever, but it is clear he cares for them. It only makes the separation between them sad.

I really hope I'm not pushing boundaries here. I fly over to him and land on his shoulder, trying to give him some comfort. A brief glance my way is the only reaction I get before he returns to watching his people. I do not know if I've actually helped at all, but he hasn't told me to leave, so I get comfortable.

Tore may not have paid me much attention, but the ursu around us certainly do. As I'm in my burning falcon form, it's hard to say if they even recognize me as an áed. They're probably just jealous that I actually have the confidence to approach this horrifyingly strong ursu.

I'm glad things have worked out here, but I still need to get Tore to help defend us all from Kalma. Whether he can compete, we'll have to see.

CHAPTER FIFTY-ONE

Unconvincing

Wind whips across my body so fast it almost tears me apart. The feeling of simple air trying its hardest to smother my flames is only beaten by the intense jerk as we tear through the skies.

It's insane how fast Tore can take us with a simple jump. Each time the earth rushes to meet us, I'm tossed around in his grip as he taps his foot against the earth and has us hurtling through the air.

Despite each motion being the slightest skip for the giant ursu, I'm sure he leaves craters in our wake.

I appreciate Tore's willingness to assist me once I told him I needed his help, but this method of transport will rip me apart if it continues for long. It's simply incomprehensible that there are people like Tore and Kalma out there with so much skin-deep power that they could destroy their surroundings with a stray thought.

Back when I was with my tribe, I don't even think I would have pictured Eldest Ember with as much power as Tore. But now, as I look up to her crimson moon, I have to imagine she might be beyond even those two. How else could she ignite the moon each night?

After Tore's declaration, placing himself as their new leader, he chose some ursu he must have the barest of trust in, and had him enact his new orders. They had been brief. Essentially halt the war, bring back the ursu, and prevent the council from being re-implemented.

Tore, having brushed the responsibility of his nation onto someone else, did not hesitate to join me back to the pact nations. Rather, he hurried me along faster than I could handle. If I didn't know for certain that he cared for the ursu, I would have said he wanted to be out of the nation as soon as possible.

Finally, Tore lands with a crash, tearing a gash through the earth as we slow to a stop. I tumble out of his hands and sprawl across the ground. I've been flying for years now, and yet I can't help but feel dizzy from his form of transport.

When I regain my senses and look around, I find we are already at the border between the ursu and the pact nations. Nearly a week of flying, cut down to a few hours.

Tore towers over the misshapen dead earth of the former battlefield as he watches the tail of his soldiers pushing forward into abandoned land. Is he going to send them all back himself? As much as I would love for him to do that, I'm uncertain whether we have the time to travel along the entire front.

That the pact nations have abandoned these borders is not a good sign. The Mercenary Order is about as cornered as they've ever been. If they don't throw out their heavy hitters now, then I doubt they have any at all.

If we waste time along the front, sending the ursu away, we are likely to miss our final opportunity to talk. To give the mermineae a reason to stop fighting. I know how incredibly slim the chance of us successfully convincing them, if not because of their hatred toward me, then the sheer terror they have of Kalma.

The ursu can wait. I doubt they'll attack if they see Tore standing with the pact nations.

I pick myself up and rejoin Tore's side. If it weren't for his hard stare over his soldiers in the distance, I would have urged him to continue onward.

"I never wanted this." Tore's gruff voice is quiet, but impossible to miss. "This wasn't my first opportunity to reclaim my will. I had been a coward then. Even now, I regret destroying Torben's creation."

I understand now that Torben was likely the first chairman of New Vetus, and it was that ursu's efforts that created the nation it now is. Torben created the council and by placing himself as the ursu's leader, Tore did away with the council entirely.

To be free of the chairman and council's hold, Tore needed to destroy the governing system his friend created and take control himself.

"I am a warrior, not a leader. I am not worthy to take his place, but neither is any other." He holds a hand out to me, ready to continue on, but his eyes linger on his soldiers.

His soldiers. They aren't only of his kind now; they are his warriors. His people. His to be responsible for. If he has refused to take this position for over a hundred years, I can only imagine the burden it places on him. But compared to the last council, who engaged in unnecessary war while mistreating their own kind, and the one prior, which encouraged discrimination against nonursu, I believe Tore surpasses them by far.

Though it might be hard for him to lead, if he's always on the front line. Hopefully, New Vetus isn't in too much chaos from his disappearance.

I climb into his hand once more, not exactly looking forward to this ride, but knowing it is our fastest option. "Tore, let's find the Viisin amongst the mermineae. If we have any hope of stopping their invasion, we'll need to find them."

I walk by Tore's side through the expansive, merminea-controlled area. We are using ourselves as bait to reel in a Viisin. All we want is to talk, so the two of us have done our utmost to show absolutely no hostility. Though, even without intending to, Tore's sheer size, and the way each of his footfalls can be felt through the earth, are likely terrifying signals to any onlookers.

And there have been onlookers. Some mermineae come close enough for my thermal sense to pick them up, even though they could have easily seen Tore from thousands of meters away. All we can do is hope they run off and tell the Viisin, or whoever commands them, that we are wandering through their land.

They cannot ignore us forever. Not if they plan to keep up the invasion. We are occupying a major chokepoint between Meja and the southern half of the pact nations. Or former pact nations.

Many states have already crumbled to the ursu or mermineae. I can only hope Vanguard is still safe. It is doubtful, as they are likely now facing the full brunt of the ursu offense in addition to the Theocracy. I hope Bunny is safe.

It is difficult to wait around like this when I know how tight things are getting, but if we can get the mermineae to back off before the Mercenary Order unleashes their elite, then we might stop the coming slaughter.

I know it's hypocritical of me considering I've already inflicted countless deaths upon the mermineae, but I don't want them to die in droves once the strongest of the Beiths are unleashed. Unless those of lesser enhancement flee from the battlefields, I can't imagine any of them surviving the devastation that will no doubt occur.

I've seen how Spenne fights. I know how I fight. In a battle between elite greater than that, unintended casualties will be massive. Not only on the mermineae's side, either. The pact nations still defend their borders en masse with unenhanced soldiers that will pose no obstacle for the fights that are sure to break out.

The best we can hope for is that the Viisin all run away from our strongest, rather than try to take them on, but that is wishful thinking. Unless we can give them a firm reason to back down now, they won't when we need them to.

Finally, after a full day of blocking their major route, we have a Viisin grace us with their appearance.

Unlike their kin, the thick plumes of dust falling off their decaying bodies prevent them from any form of subtlety. They run across the earth on all fours until it stops thirty meters from us.

Now that I think about it, both the Viisin and Forvaal take on differing levels of decay to their bodies. The Forvaal experience it in their eyes, but only as a cost to their power's use. The Viisin are unfortunate enough to experience the decay near eternally in exchange for the power it brings.

What about Kalma?

Does the decay affect her in a way worse than these mermineae? Could there be some downside to her power we can capitalize on? Well, if there is, it isn't obvious to the naked eye.

The Viisin growls at us, his voice ragged and throaty. "Leave if you do not want death."

Despite his threat, the very fact he's giving it rather than attacking us on the spot means he's worried about facing Tore. The Viisin looks small, but I can't tell if that's just because Tore stands so many times taller at my side, or if he's actually smaller than his brethren.

I remain quiet, expecting the older and more experienced of us to take over negotiations.

Nobody speaks.

I look up at Tore, but all he does is raise an eyebrow at me, almost quizzically. Really? You're going to leave the important, war-defining communication up to a girl that's spent the better half of the last year incinerating her way through so many of the other side's race?

As if reading my thoughts, Tore nods and gestures toward the Viisin.

I sigh in frustration before walking toward the dusty merminea. He seems relieved my partner hasn't joined my side, but he lowers himself, clearly ready for a fight.

Maybe he doesn't know I'm the one that incinerated his brethren? Maybe he just thinks I'm some albanic. I find the idea annoys me, but it is still better than letting him know who I am.

"We aren't here for a fight. We came to tell you to give up on these lands."

I can't see their face through the dust, but I can definitely hear their sneer. "You think we'll back down because you ask, do you? This is not something we have a choice in. We cannot give up now."

"No, I'm telling you to give up now, because this is Kalma's plot to have you all killed. When the Mercenary Order lets loose their strongest, she plans to watch as they slaughter the lot of you." Not the full story, but not untrue. It's only important to tell him which parts affect his kind.

"That can't be!" It is difficult to tell through his scraggly voice whether he is angry or shocked. "Kalma is still on the other side of the Alps, blissfully unaware. If she knew, we'd be worse than dead."

"I've seen her over here with my own eyes," I say. "Kalma is playing with you all. She gave you the opportunity for this escape so that she could watch you all get slaughtered. Her enjoyment is the only thing she cares about."

The Viisin mutters under his breath. Something about 'the others knew,' before he readdresses me. "If what you say is true, then we are doomed, regardless of choice. I'd prefer to take on thousands of your kind than risk Kalma's wrath."

The Viisin takes a step toward me, but stops at the same time I feel the earth quake. A glance backward reveals Tore a single step closer. The merminea gives up on approaching any further, but speaks in a hushed croak. "If Kalma is truly here, then don't expect your kind to remain untouched."

I give the Viisin a wry smile. "We know. And we plan to fight her."

"Fight her?" he repeats, as if he can't believe me. After meeting Kalma myself, I know exactly how unreasonable that concept might be.

"It's better than letting ourselves become her slaves and playthings, is it not?"

He doesn't respond. All he can do is stand there and either seethe or ponder my words. How he takes the insult to his race, I have no way to know. The dust still covers his features.

I return to Tore. It is unfortunate we cannot convince them to pull back on their invasion, but I still think it was worth the effort.

Now, we must go to the core of the pact nations. The Headquarters of the Mercenary Order. Hopefully, we won't be too late.

CHAPTER FIFTY-TWO

Chill

The Mercenary Order's headquarters sits at the far eastern border of Meja. Right in the center of the entire pact nations.

Well, the center of what used to be the pact nations. Now, so much ground has been lost that the headquarters may as well be on the front line itself.

I soar through the air in Tore's grasp once more. It's become more bearable to handle his unique form of transportation, but I would still prefer to fly under my own power. No matter how much faster this allows us to travel, I don't think I could ever truly be comfortable relying on someone like this.

It isn't even an issue of trust. I don't believe Tore would do anything to me. Not only because he's already helped me in the past, but because he has the power to do pretty much whatever he wants and I would have no way to resist. No, if I can do something, I would prefer to do it myself. And if I can't, I will improve until I can.

The earth passes below us too fast to make out many details, but some are simply too eye-catching to miss. A massive, ancient castle stands in the center of a city spanning tens of thousands of meters. Dozens of towers arranged in a spiral stand higher than the other the closer they are to the center. At the centerpiece of the city is an enormous spike of a structure that reaches higher than any other building I've seen.

It is an exquisite view as we pass overhead, but the sight of artillery and cannon fire detonating much of the land outside the castle's walls takes away from what would be a serene view. A ring of buildings around the castle are nothing but rubble. A constant barrage of explosions demolishes the city. Smoke obscures many of the outer regions.

The Meja Matriarchy is still holding out against the mermineae. Despite the rest of the city being taken, their castle is not so easily overcome.

I wonder if Imiha is down there, fighting for her people? I haven't seen her since we split over on the other side of the Alps. She was overbearing with her curiosity, as mages tend to be, but she was still a good person. I want to go down and help her fight off her attackers, but I can't.

It isn't a decision I'm happy to make, but we need to get to the Mercenary Order's headquarters and scare off the invaders before this war elevates. Tore is the only one who can do that. Only he has the strength to send the Viisin running with a glance. Only he can stop the ursu pushing in from the south.

If the world is reasonable, then the Mercenary Order's elite will be reasonable. They'll be unleashed upon their enemies and only kill those strong enough to put up a fight. They will listen to my warnings of a greater strength watching over all.

Unfortunately, I know the world isn't reasonable.

The chance that those elite will care is slim. My experience with the Beiths leads me to believe that there is little chance they will hold back. While Imiha is understanding, she is the only one. That fire mage I'd met a while back, I wouldn't trust to not burn everything he thinks he can get away with. I mean, he tried with me, and I'm an áed.

Spenne is my primary concern. As admittedly fun as my fight with him had been, all he cared for was the thrill of battle. If the elite share his views, his enjoyment of war, then there will be no persuading.

Soon, Meja's castle is out of view. Those still holding out are left on their own to defend what is left of their country. The rest of the Mercenary Order have pulled back, returning to defend the headquarters. As do we. I wish the best for Imiha. Hopefully, this war will be over soon.

Tore continues to fling us through the air. Every meter we travel without a sign of the defensive line is concerning. The mermineae have already pushed farther than I expected. It's strange; Spenne held off a few Viisin by himself. If only one of him could survive so long against that many, then how have the Beiths not been able to push back their offense? Considering each has similar abilities, how have the Beiths not slaughtered them all yet?

I can understand we were losing before the Mercenary Order gave the Beiths freedom to fight, but even after they entered the battles, the mermineae's encroach has not slowed. It is suspicious.

Is this Kalma's influence?

Do I even need to ask? This is obviously Kalma's influence. She admitted to preferring when both sides are even. But how has she controlled the mermineae's battle strength without giving them a reason to believe they are playing within her hands?

There are too many unknowns, but there isn't anything I can do about them. The only thing I can do is push forward and hope everything works out.

Actually, I hate that mentality. 'Hope everything works out'? No. Things never work out when you hope for the best. I need to do anything I can to achieve the best result. Even then, it might all go wrong, but as long as I'm alive, I can force my way forward.

I notice a chill in the air. Despite the Eternal Inferno resting high in the sky, the air just got a whole lot colder. Tore notices as well, but he must have felt something more, as his next leap angles us to the north. Far off our current heading.

The reason for our change in direction becomes immediately clear as we bound over the hilly terrain; we've finally reached the battlefield.

As we crash amongst the mermineae, the temperature becomes distinct. It is as cold as the snow-tipped mountains at the base of the Titan Alps. There is no snow, but as I look around, frost takes a grasp on the earth and spreads. The air continues to chill.

I have no issue anymore with this cold. My body is simply far too hot for the freezing temps to have an effect. It might be less efficient to stand around in this than a normal heat level, but the difference is so minuscule to me now, it's not even worth the effort to worry.

The battle is in full swing. Unlike the typical poke-and-prod method of offense the mermineae have adapted in the past months, they are attacking in full force. A few hundred meters away, a Viisin tears through mercenary teams. Explosions of dust rise with each attack. The mercenaries show excellent coordination, but they still struggle against the power of its decay.

Not far from the unopposed Viisin is a second locked in a brawl with a Beith. Somehow, the khirig doesn't decay on contact. It throws punches with antlers shining with markings. Each blow tears off limbs from the Viisin, but it always recovers. Their grappling and physical blows send the two all across the battle. Wherever they land, the earth strips clean, including all mercenaries, soldiers, and mermineae unlucky enough to be in their way.

We aren't too late. The battle is in full swing, but it hasn't yet reached the headquarters. If Tore can scare the mermineae off here, then we can plead with the higher ups of the Mercenary Order to cooperate with Tore to take on Kalma.

A gust brushes past me, sending a freezing chill through my body. The wind swirls slowly over the battlefield, almost casually as it casts an icy sheen across the earth.

I fling myself from Tore's grip, expecting him to dash forward and put a stop to all the fighting. He doesn't. Instead, I catch him gazing to the south, focusing on something other than the battle before us. What is he doing?

"I won't be long."

I don't even have the time to ask what he means. The shockwave of his leap sends me staggering. Tore is gone from sight within a few moments, bounding across the land far faster than when he held me.

He's leaving us? How am I supposed to scare the mermineae off now? How do I convince the Mercenary Order? I don't have the power to do this myself.

It's a terrifying thought, but even without him, I need to find a way. I clamp down on my writhing flames and straighten myself. This is my plan, and even without what is supposed to be the key piece, I need to move forward.

It'll be hard, but if I make an imitation of the Titan again with my flames, I might frighten off many of the weaker units on both sides. It worked back in the gulag; why shouldn't it work here? As long as I can get most of their forces to rout, I'll have just a little longer to convince the Order. Assuming they'll even listen to a fugitive.

Before I can spread my fires and start on my plan, the swirling icy wind accelerates. I take a step forward, only for the sleeve of my outfit to slice open. I stare at it for a moment, uncertain of what exactly attacked me. The blade passed through my arm so fast I didn't even register it.

It's a tiny, little cut in the cloth over my arm, but if I was flesh, I'd be bleeding right now.

A hiss no different from rain lifts my head to the sky, only for a tiny shard of ice to pierce right through my eye. The frozen fragment slices through the back of my head before it has time to vaporize. It stings a bit where it left, but otherwise it cut through so smoothly I hardly felt it.

The spiraling air converges. Thousands of minuscule blades of ice no bigger than a fingertip spin through the air with such speed I don't think I could have noticed had they not pierced me. The shards grow as the wind increases. A whirlwind of ice grows from the densest section of the battle.

The air howls as more ice forms from nothing. I stop suppressing my external heat. The icy blades disintegrate as they come close, creating a thin wall of mist that is dispersed by the ever-increasing wind. My snowsuit fits well, but even it whips around my body as the howl of wind becomes a scream.

Around the epicenter of the frozen twister, thousands drop dead. The shards slice through their bodies without resistance. Far more mermineae fall, but it is not exclusive. Mercenaries in the throes of battle collapse, almost regardless of rank. The only ones truly able to brush off the sharp icy wind are the two Viisin and the khirig Beith.

Every second I watch, the wind increases, centralizing around a twisting pillar of frost that has grown too dense to see through. Everything within range is shredded. As the tornado of ice condenses, the range that the shards reach extends, cutting down all as they attempt to flee.

I have no idea what's going on, but thousands fall as I watch. The ice disperses harmlessly into my heat. It's surprising; I would have expected it to hurt as the ice melts into water, but there's such little water content in the frost that it only stings as it whips against me.

Not long ago, I wouldn't have cared for all this death. I mostly still don't, but as these people, both mermineae and those of the pact nations die, I can't stop myself imagining how Leal or Grímr might react knowing I do nothing. I've already caused such immense pain to Leal that I struggle to see a day where I won't feel guilty about burning Morne and Calysta.

Unlike the ursu city, my killing of the mermineae has been entirely intentional. I have never cared about them, nor do I now, but they have been slaves to Kalma for who knows how long. I feel some sympathy for them.

It might not be the most beneficial thing I've ever done, but I spread my flames wide over the battlefield. I ease the freezing temperature and melt away the shards that continue to pelt the backs of those amidst a rout. My flames grow into an inferno empowered by the wind from the ice storm and spread farther than I could normally control.

Any of my fire that moves too close to the spiral of ice extinguishes immediately. I simply can't keep up the temperature to keep them burning with only my yellow flames, and I would rather not jump into the vortex to see how well my hotter fire handles.

It may not be much compared to the numbers I've killed in the past, but my flames give many of the mermineae and mercenaries enough time to escape the ever-growing storm.

Oh, how I wish for the battle to end here, but as I continue to shield the less enhanced from the incredibly unnatural phenomenon, the tornado of ice makes a drastic change. It condenses one last time before collapsing in on itself. The towering pillar of frozen wind crashes into a point and blasts outward.

The roar of rushing air is deafening. Wind and ice explode along the ground, expanding faster than I can witness. Within moments, the rushing opaque air tears through the battlefield, reaching the horizon and beyond my sight.

I thought it was cold before. Immediately after the blast, the air comes to a standstill. Even with my body as hot as it is, the world wants to slow my movement. Frost visibly grows over the fur of the mermineae adjacent to the path of the ice blast. Even my inferno barely heats the air enough that they don't freeze on the spot.

Spiky crystal formations line the edges of the blast zone. In the center of its path stands the body of the Viisin that only moments ago was butchering mercenary teams. Its body, frozen in place, has a million tiny fractures and holes through it. So too do the mercenary teams it was fighting. Nothing survived the explosion of frost. All that remains are the shredded, frozen corpses and a wasteland of ice.

This is far beyond anything any Beith I've met has been capable of. Even Spenne. The width of the icy path is consistent and not all that wide, but it has devastated all life it passed for leagues.

The shards of ice build up once more, carried along by the wind as the effect restarts. I turn to the center of the spiraling wind, and standing amongst the haze is an albanic shining with intense white markings.

We are too late.

CHAPTER FIFTY-THREE

Collateral Damage

Where has Tore run off to? If I had him by my side, this new mage wouldn't be a problem. Tore could stop them from inflicting so many casualties. As things are, I don't even dare approach. The air gets so much colder in the direct vicinity of the old albanic woman, that even at my hottest temperature, I'd be concerned.

If Tore were here, he would stop her with nothing more than his sheer presence. There would be no need for a battle. What is so important that he had to abandon me after we made it all this way? Could he not have told me what he was doing before he dashed off?

It's frustrating that the only solution for this entire mess has now up and left me.

The Mercenary Order have let loose their elite, and now the only one who has a chance against them has run off. How many more than this ice mage are unleashing equivalent damage across the defensive line?

Wait, did Tore figure that out the moment he felt that cold wind? Is that why he ran off? Has he gone to protect his kind from the Order's elite? If so, it would have helped if he'd dealt with this mage before rushing off.

This first showing of the Inner Circle is not promising. The mage is indiscriminate. Not only do the mermineae fall to the effects of her marking's spell, but no soldier or mercenary caught in the crossfire is spared the terrifying damage she inflicts.

Her whirlwind of ice builds up again, obscuring her from sight. I'd be glad such a devastating attack requires time to build up if the charge phase didn't cause widespread death. The air is considerably colder now than it was before; even with my inferno baking the land, anything not directly embraced by my flames struggles not to freeze in moments. Just how low will the temperature drop?

The khirig Beith tries to disengage from the sole remaining Viisin now that he knows the ice mage is here, but the Viisin doesn't let up so easily. The dust-covered merminea chases them across the battlefield as they run for the pact's defensive side.

Both notice the condensing chill right before another explosive blast of ice and wind tear across the earth. The merminea is fast, flinging themselves to the side as the air itself solidifies for an instant. Their rear leg, the only thing caught in the central blast, freezes immediately. The next step they take shatters the limb into a thousand shards across the earth.

The khirig with antlers able to withstand direct contact with a Viisin's decay is not so lucky. Their frozen corpse stands stiff in mid-sprint. Unable to escape the friendly fire in time.

The two came so close to bringing their fight within the line of mercenaries. Did the old mage decide to sacrifice the Beith to protect the thousands who would have died had the Viisin reached them?

She hadn't launched her beam of ice without care for the other fighter's life, right?

I'd like to believe she considered the alternatives and chose the option with the least lives sacrificed, but with the power she wields, I can't help but feel she could have done more. She simply didn't care if the Beith lived or died.

Are all the Order's elite like this?

The Viisin finally realizes how outmatched it is and flees on three legs. While the frozen leg has shattered, it refuses to regrow. The merminea bounds across the land with speed, and soon it is well off the battlefield, running amongst the rest of the fleeing mermineae.

The frozen wind gathers around the albanic mage again, this time not spinning in a vortex, but directly around her. The elite lifts off the ground, the razor-like wind lifting her with a gentleness not previously displayed. The wind carries the old albanic through the air, chasing after the Viisin with little care for any she tramples in her path.

The wind treats her gently, but only her. Icy blades shear through the earth as she accelerates forward, leaving the landscape frozen and shredded.

She is quick to pounce after the fleeing mermineae, but the battle isn't over. Everything near where she unleashed her storm is frostbitten dead land, but beyond the range of her icicle blade gusts, the invasion continues unabated. So focused on hunting down her prey, she's forgotten the purpose of her being here.

Nothing remains of each army for hundreds of meters. The earth morphed into a lifeless region of brittle, frozen soil and crystalline formations rising in ringed circles. Without the opaque wind to block my sight, it is clear she cared little for the other mercenaries. Some corpses remain standing, frozen and mangled, but most are nothing more than feet and the boots they wore, reaching up from the earth toward bodies that no longer exist.

I saved hundreds, but the effects of that ice storm extend further than my inferno could spread.

There is nothing blocking my path, so I bound forward. I can't let myself be distracted by the fighting here. The longer it takes to convince the Mercenary Order, the greater the battle will grow, the more unnecessary lives lost.

If it were possible for the elite to go forward and end this war themselves, a few lives lost now might not be the biggest issue. But it's not. Kalma won't let it end that easy. I don't know how the merminea assault will compete if there are even a few of these elite Inner Circle mercenaries. I only know they will compete. Whether Kalma herself enters the battle, or she does something else, only time will tell.

Time that I'm wasting by staying on this war front.

I sprint forward, blasting myself with the occasional burst of physical flame. By the time I push into the area where the ice mage once stood, the chilly wind threads through my core. This is colder than anything I've felt. It's like the very air refuses to move out of my way as I run. My white flames work overtime to heat the surroundings enough to stop the stiff air from holding me back.

I'm not the only one taking advantage of the hole in the battle line. The mermineae at my sides rush to fill the gap, to push their advantage and attack the flanks of the pact nations. Mercenaries hurry to fill the gaps, but they are slow compared to the mermineae's quadruped sprint.

The number of soldiers is immense. It is clear the Mercenary Order has thrown everything into this battle, but these numbers are concerningly large. I'm sure the death count for this war is already on unimaginable levels, so where exactly are they fielding these armies?

The only answer I can come to does nothing but push me to reach the headquarters faster.

With the air as unbelievably cold as it is, I almost miss the approaching heat signature flying toward my back.

I blast a jet of flame to the side and the Viisin's dust-covered claws miss me by a good meter. It has all four limbs, so it clearly isn't the one the elite went chasing after, but I still glance over my shoulder, just in case. This Viisin must have come in from the sides with the other opportunistic mermineae.

I don't have the time to sit around and fight. I dash off, pushing an immense amount of flames behind to give myself as much thrust as possible. The Viisin reacts instantly, hurtling after me. I'm forced to dodge again, sacrificing all my speed.

Fine, if you won't let me go, then I'll make this quick.

My flame jet reverses and I tear toward the Viisin before it can truly react. I crash through its side, incinerating its arm, head and much of its torso. It is painful, and I stagger as my feet hit the ground. The Viisin collapses, but its body is already recovering. I twist and try to cover the decaying merminea with my hottest flame.

I don't know if it knew the flames were coming, or if it simply tried to gain space, but the headless creature kicks the ground and launches away from my blaze.

My flames twist around me in frustration. I'd hoped to finish the Viisin with that, but it looks like it won't be so easy. I leap toward the merminea as its head finally recovers, but it is now wise to the danger I pose. As fast as jets of physical fire allow me to move, it can't beat the instantaneous speed the Viisin's legs provide.

In the aftermath of the ice storm, I give chase to the Viisin. Both its explosions of decay and my intense flames devastate the land further. While I'm sure the Viisin's damage is inflicted only because of a lack of control over its decay, I am not so limited, but I burn through the frozen land regardless.

While I could power my movement with physical flames created from my energy, it is still far more efficient, and rapid, to supply that physicality from what I might otherwise consume. Rock and soil may not be all that energy-filled, but they work well enough as a source for my thrust. The frozen earth only makes me work all the harder to burn it into something usable.

I launch forward again, barely scratching a leg with my inner flame. The Viisin is hurt, but it is still too fast for me. Mermineae swarm past us now. They leave themselves a safe distance to not get caught in the crossfire, but for some, it is in vain. Neither myself nor the Viisin stay still, and with how much faster the both of us are than the surrounding mermineae, it is unavoidable that some find themselves in our way.

The Viisin hardly shows any hesitation as a merminea explodes into dust after dodging my flames, but I am no different. Sometimes, I throw myself toward my opponent only to crash through a bystander. Under normal conditions, I'd be able to limit my flames from burning them, but in a fight like this, I can't hold myself back.

It doesn't help that they combust before my flames even touch them.

I don't have the time to waste with this. I can't kill the Viisin while it keeps avoiding me. Unfortunately, the idea that this fight would be quick had been far too hopeful. It knows to respect the heat of my flames now, so maybe it won't continue to chase me this time.

I pretend to attack again, but jet away instead. The mermineae have already taken hold of the open space between the mercenary's defense. There are some warriors filling in from the rear of the pact nation's defense, but not nearly enough to hold them back.

Despite my hopes, the Viisin continues to pursue. Why can't it just give up? My flames burn it faster than its decay can rip the energy from them, so it shouldn't bother with me. It should go for a target it can actually beat. Does it know how painful fighting it is for me, how much harder it is for me to recover from each attack compared to it? I thought I hid it well.

Maybe the last Viisin I fought—the one Tore scared off—told them of me. It would explain why this Viisin is so adamant about extending this fight. I can only win by taking it out in a single blow, but with how wary it is, I won't be able to get the jump on it again.

As the Viisin gives chase, I have an idea that might catch the dusty merminea completely off guard. I already have a head start, but the Viisin is closing the distance quick. Once he's within range, I'll only have a second to attack.

My tail already has hyper awareness of my actions, so turning as it strikes will not be effective, especially considering my flame jets don't give me instant speed. They allow me to accelerate incredibly fast when I lower my body weight, but they aren't an instant burst of speed like the mermineae's legs provide.

What I need to do requires a bit more . . . finesse. More than I've yet achieved.

My white flames, by their nature, are harder to control. Yellow and cooler fire spreads easily beyond a hundred meters under my control, but the distance in which I can create them from nothing, without a connection to myself or another flame, is far shorter. White flame is the same, though with a much narrower range.

My inner flame can only become about the equivalent size of my body in white fire. If I want that much, I cannot be spreading my yellow flame, even if it would be easier to encase the Viisin by covering everything. The Viisin won't ignore it and will disperse it before I have the chance to intensify it into white flame. It would make things incredibly convenient if I could simply use the flames I'm far more familiar with to spread my peak temperature, but the Viisin is far too cautious, dispersing the mild inferno before it can cling to its fur.

What I hope to achieve will take all my focus. I'll even have to ignore the portion of my mind I always leave on controlling my body.

The world fades away from my sight as I focus on two things: the thrust keeping me moving and the Viisin closing in. I choose a point between us, only a few meters behind myself, and focus intently on it. When the Viisin reaches that distance in relation to me, I'll have an instant to act. Multiple meters might sound like a lot, but with how fast the Viisin is moving, it isn't much to work with. But I don't trust myself to work at any greater lengths, not with my white flame, not without giving the creature time to react.

I gather my energy and push out a stronger burst of physical flame, enough to send me soaring through the air far enough I don't have to worry about the ground. My jet cuts off and I redirect that focus to the point behind me.

The world doesn't exist. It is only a thermal dot and the point it is moving toward. All my thoughts flee my mind with an almost impossible ease. No stress, no fear, nothing. There is only one thing I need to do, and I can be patient for the moment to come.

The heat moves over the point, and it ignites. Immense heat appears into existence, fully engulfing the other. As soon as it appears, the momentary burst of mental strain lessens and I can refocus my thoughts.

The first thing I notice is the scream, right before I slam face-first into the ground.

The energy in the white flame around the Viisin is nothing greater than what I usually wield, but to create so much of it remotely is painfully difficult. It's nostalgic, like I'm back with Auntie Kay, succeeding at remote fire for the first time. Only this time, I could focus my mind completely on the task. Something that makes me oddly proud, despite not truly understanding why.

I've created my white fire remotely before, notably when I threatened the Order executives, but there is a massive difference between making some fingertip-sized orbs over a few seconds, and a flame with all my capability in an instant.

The scream cuts off after only a second, and I witness the last of the being as it incinerates. There is no time for it to recover, nor make any last acts. It simply burns up into nothing but fuel for my fire.

Soon, nothing remains.

Nothing besides the dust remnants that had once flown freely off its decaying body. The ash swirls through the air where the Viisin once stood, moving in a breeze I cannot feel.

A disappointing feast for one so strong. The decay energy is not truly part of them.

I'm already far behind the pact nations' defensive lines and while there are still many mercenaries around, the numbers don't come close to the battlefield in the distance. Time is wasting, and while I really should hurry, something, a feeling, makes me stay.

The swirling dust flows inward, congesting at a point. A shape forms; a body.

I incinerated every part of the Viisin. It shouldn't be able to come back; there was nothing left.

Details of the body quickly become clear. This is no Viisin. It is too short. The two thin tails and large, sharp ears confirm it. I don't even need to wait for the creature's skin to take form to know who it is.

Kalma.

Her toothy grin is terrifying, but mostly infuriating.

CHAPTER FIFTY-FOUR

Reversal

That was a very cute attempt, trying to get these rodents to back down." Kalma walks out of the cloud of dust as it concentrates into the last of her skin. "I told you, didn't I? Doesn't matter what you say, there's no stopping this now."

The unsettling feeling of her voice eating my very being returns along with her hardly suppressed presence. Why is she here? Didn't she want to keep her involvement hidden? Her appearance has not gone unnoticed. All around us, both mermineae and mercenaries alike have frozen. Her pressure too great. The sheer, unhindered terror on the faces of the mermineae hides none of their thoughts.

Kalma twists her head from left to right. "Where's that big guy you brought with you? Wasn't he supposed to be the only hope you had?" Her grin grows vicious as she raises a hand over her mouth in mock surprise. "Oh! He hasn't abandoned you, has he? How sad. I was looking forward to watching him fight."

"Why are you here?" I seethe through gritted teeth. Tore should be here. She's shown herself so willingly and yet the only one with even the slightest chance of competing had run off. I'm not sure if I'm madder at Kalma's gloating or Tore for giving up this opportunity.

Does she have something to do with why he ran off? She clearly already knew he wasn't here when she showed herself. So what happened to Tore? Is he still alive?

"Well, after you killed one of my Viisin, I didn't want you to suddenly think you had a chance. Plus, this gives me the perfect view," she says as she turns to watch over the fleeing mermineae. Those that have broken from the shock of her presence bound away at a sprint. Unfortunately, they run right into the storm of the returning ice mage. Kalma's smirk remains plastered on her face even as countless mermineae fall before her.

How does she know I killed a Viisin? It's almost impossible to miss her presence, so how far can she see? Was she watching over my conversation with that Viisin I tried to convince as well?

With the old albanic mage back along the defensive line, the mermineae are quickly overcome. Kalma stands here, watching. The elite of the Order are enough to push back the entire invasion.

Even so, Kalma chuckles, as if pleased by the course of the war.

"The Viisin; you never thought the decay was *their* strength, did you?" she glances at me out of the corner of her eye while raising her clawed hands before her, and I already know I will not like what's about to happen.

She claps. A short, almost insignificant gesture. But as she does, the battlefield drowns in dust. Haunting, guttural screams create a chorus of suffering. Each instant that passes, the howls become more raspy, bestial, and hollow.

"What did you do?" The words escape my lips.

"It's not their power, it's mine. I just gave those with my touch a slight boost."

The dust settles and the mermineae are no longer being pushed back. Where there were none before, a hundred Viisin slaughter their way through the mercenaries with mindless intent.

I'd expected something like this to happen, but it's still hard to watch. It is too late to convince the Order to pull back their strongest. Doing so will only allow the mermineae to crush the pact nations.

"Every Forvaal across the battlefront now has the decaying body of a Viisin. Look to the north." Where she points, a large plume of dust rises into the sky from near the horizon. "Each Viisin, the few that remained, now enjoy their bodies falling apart at a rate I doubt they could have believed. Neither the former Forvaal or Viisin will survive long, but it'll be enough for them to drag the battle out."

Kalma says it so casually, but her words are horrifying. Thousands across the entire remaining border of the pact nations have their bodies tear themselves apart all at once. If she's not lying, then exactly how far can she control her decay?

Running toward the headquarters will not help anymore. That option has departed. With Tore gone, there is no option but to fight and limit the number of losses. There is nobody who can stop this from going forward, besides Kalma herself.

In a moment of frustration-fueled foolishness, I lash out. I guess it's no different from last time; I haven't learned my lesson, but this powerlessness hits me harder than any intent to keep others beside those I care for safe.

My entire reason for fighting for all these lives rests entirely on what my friends think of me. It's a flimsy reason at most, and I do feel bad that I'm apathetic to the thousands, hundreds of thousands, or even millions of lives that have or will be lost, but I simply don't have it in me to care for more than those close to me.

Despite all that, failing so totally, and then having Kalma twist the knife, rubbing water into the wound, is infuriating.

It is stupid; I know I have no chance, but I attack anyway. My flames roar over her body as my presence pushes against hers in futility. It doesn't matter if I'm outmatched. It doesn't matter that I'm putting myself in immense danger. All that matters is that Kalma burns.

She only snickers. "Quite the candle-flame you got there, but not nearly comparable to Ember's."

I falter before pressing further. "What do you know about Eldest Ember?" For Kalma to use her name only angers me further.

"Oh?" Kalma appears genuinely surprised, but for all I know, it is an act. "It's impressive she's still remembered after all this time. I'm curious, what is it you believe about her?" With the wave of a hand, she brushes my flames off with ease.

I don't stop. My flames engulf her once more, which only amuses Kalma. "Would you believe me if I told you she's been imprisoned for a millennium by one of those world-damning Titans?" She ignores the flames sticking to her skin, peering up at the midday moon with an expression other than arrogant amusement.

It's the first time she expresses anger, and I feel it through her presence. It overwhelms mine in an instant, and I hardly notice when I extinguish my flames. She stares up at the orb in the sky with such fury that my own flees me. I know Kalma doesn't treat this war as anything but a source of amusement for her, but I never truly understood how small we are in her eyes.

The venom of her tone as she curses the Titans rips through my core. Even to a being so intense and powerful as Kalma, the Titans still come out on top. Not even those considered gods can overcome living calamities.

Does she hate them because she can't beat them, or is it something more? And what does she mean about Eldest Ember being trapped by one? Her influence is visible every night, so she can't be imprisoned. Why would the Titans trap her, anyway?

Kalma lets out a sigh of frustration. "Well, that ruined the mood." She shakes her head and turns back to me, grin back in place, though not as toothy as usual. "The war can't be stopped now. You should find a nice place to watch the finale. Might as well experience some joy before the end of everything, right?"

Kalma turns back to the battle as the old ice mage carries her storm through the fighting, leaving none in her wake as she cuts toward the massive plume of dust in the distance. Even if Kalma has amplified her power through the Viisin, I should be glad she hasn't entered the battle herself.

The mermineae's god disperses in flakes of dust without another word.

The frustration of my inability to achieve anything is immense. My flames still cannot touch her, but I already knew there was little chance of that succeeding. The issue is that not only have my efforts up to now been pointless, but I have no plan for what to do now.

If I were still on the other side of the Alps, I'd probably take the risk and attempt to bring the Euroclydon after Kalma. How I would manipulate a Titan in any way, I don't know, but it would at least be an option.

Here? I have nothing to work with.

The mermineae, now emboldened by their empowered brethren, charge amongst the mercenaries with renewed vigor. I wonder if they'd still attack like that if they knew no matter how well they fight, neither side will survive?

The old mage lady has already taken her storm far to my south, the land between us a frozen wasteland that prevents any unenhanced from walking through without freezing.

The boosted Viisin, only noticeable by the immense dust cloud rising in the distance, moves to meet her. When they finally collide, the chilly wind can be felt even as far away as I am. An icy blast explodes upon the Viisin, arcing outward and taking much more of the land than the mage could have intended. Unlike before, the Viisin doesn't die to the mage's power. With Kalma's power pushing the creature far beyond its limits, it can stand toe to toe with the mage.

I head north, away from their fight as it reshapes the landscape. Anything that dares approach them will die. There is no doubt in my mind.

I truly must have been mad to attack Kalma. Only barely could I beat one of the Viisin before its enhancement; in no world could I burn such a being as they are now.

As I run through the battlefield, I hesitate to fight. There's not really any reason to, is there? I cannot stop the two sides from fighting, nor can I impact the battle enough for the pact nations to come out on top. Even if I could, Kalma would simply pump the mermineae with more energy until it is impossible.

I'd hoped to limit the losses on both sides, but if there's no more option, then I'll have to go back to burning mermineae. The safety of those in the pact nations is still my priority, no matter the futility Kalma's existence brings.

Even if it is impossible, I don't want to stand on the sidelines and watch as everything is torn down.

It's strange; a year ago I would have fled without hesitation. The pact nations are doomed and staying here will only open myself to more danger. I thought my survival and freedom was still the most important thing to me, but I guess not. Not now that my team will face such an insurmountable challenge. Not with my friends relying on our success.

A wry grin crawls over my face despite the circumstances. I wonder how they're doing?

Welp, no use complaining about our circumstances. I can't go for the headquarters anymore, so I might as well help trim the fat.

I rocket over the heads of a team of mercenaries. They are only barely holding off a Viisin's attacks due to the mage's defensive stone walls. It does little to block the creature's explosive attacks, but it gives them time to make space. Unfortunately for them, none of their attacks are effective. Two of their weapons have already lost their blades to the decaying skin of the Viisin.

I crash into the earth before the team and spread my flames. Before combating the creature, I want to separate it from the team clearly unable to handle it. I may lose the element of surprise, but I've fought with enough Viisin to know how hard it is to catch them unaware.

Instead of backing away at the sight of my white flames, the decaying mermineae lets loose a shout, and it is impossible to distinguish whether it's a scream of pain or a battle cry. It flings itself my way without hesitation.

I hardly need to move my flames. The creature dives into them and incinerates in moments. The pain is still there, but it's hardly much to eradicate a Viisin.

It looks and feels like a Viisin, but it certainly doesn't act like one. They aren't stupid. The Viisin know when they can attack and when to be wary. But this one attacked without thought. A mindless attempt that resulted in nothing but its own death.

Clearly, this is one of the new Viisin. The Forvaal Kalma forced her power upon. Are they unable to handle the immense decay through their bodies?

It is horrifying if they've become nothing but mindless beasts to the pain they endure, but I can't say I'm unhappy. Without their minds, these new Viisin will be easier to deal with.

Though, going through the sudden immense number of them is definitely not going to feel great.

I let out a breath and glance behind me, noting each mercenary is without significant injury. They give a quick gesture of gratitude, but are already moving off to support the others struggling against Viisin of their own.

None are faring well. Only Beiths seem to have definite methods to deal with the Viisin, so even mindless as they are, most mercenaries can only hope to delay until one appears. Unfortunately, the only Beith in the area was already killed by the Order's elite, who is also no longer around.

I guess it's all up to me then.

My flames push outward, quickly spreading over the battlefield. It's difficult, but I manage to use the airflow to spread my flames while keeping them under enough control that I don't burn through the unenhanced caught in my path. Resisting the urge to take all the breathable air for myself, I hold back and allow the air to flow freely. Wouldn't want to accidentally cause thousands to suffocate.

I could rely on my heat sense, but this simply makes my work more convenient. Not only can I see how the battle plays out around me easier, but it allows me to burn the Viisin as I find them. It's rather difficult to push a flame to its maximum temperature at my farthest range, but I don't plan to sit still.

As soon as my flames spread over a point where they cannot burn, I fly toward it. The newly minted Viisin enters my sight, and as soon as I'm on top of it, it burns to ash. Thankfully, they are all just as mindless as the first.

There are some annoyances within my flames across the battlefield. Some water mages cover themselves in deadly liquid, others try to put out my flames, even though they shouldn't be hurting them. I retract the fire from around them. It often leaves them exposed to the Viisin's attacks, but it's their fault for not wanting my help.

"I've finally found you."

So engrossed within my blaze, I never look toward the sky. Grímr lands in front of me, his talons crushing a Viisin I was just about to burn. Metal talons that I'm absolutely certain would have melted on contact with a Viisin's decay the last I saw him.

Glowing inscriptions line much of his metal feathered body. I can tell they are inscriptions rather than the markings of a mage; they follow too closely to the structure of the inheritance ritual Remus had me memorize. I can't tell what the inscription itself can do, but the components are the same.

I grin up at him. "I see you're doing better."

Solon

Grímr, you look different." Without a moment of hesitation, I'm already on top of him, inspecting the compact glowing markings that thread along his razor plumage.

He vibrates his feathers and they weave out of position, breaking the inscription and cutting the glow. When they lock back in place, another inscription illuminates, and a sudden gust launches me off his back.

I land on my feet as Grímr laughs an amused trill. "Yeah, Remus knew a guy," he says as I gape.

He can change the inscription by rearranging the formation of his plumage? That's amazing. Both inscriptions are incredibly detailed, almost to the extent of Henosis's experimental weapon. How many forms can the inscription take?

It's good to see Grímr fully recovered after our last fight with that Viisin. I'm not the only one that's grown the capability to combat the decay those creatures can inflict. His talons would have been pulverized if he'd tried the same thing last time, so I'm glad he has a means to defend his body now.

It is also relieving to see Kalma hasn't hurt him, or messed with him in any apparent way. Maybe she thought I was the only one who brought the centzon. That doesn't really make much sense, but I'm not about to question Grímr's good fortune.

"That's so cool. How many inscriptions can you make?" I ask.

Grímr stands tall, his beak rising high in the air at my praise. "It's just the two, but the Riparian said there was still room to fit another."

He flutters his feathers and returns the inscription to an inactive state.

"The first makes my metal resistant to decay and supposedly increases its toughness. The other doesn't help much in a fight, but it vastly improves my acceleration and maneuverability in the air," he says. "Hop on, I'll show you on our way to Remus."

I don't hesitate. There are still some Viisin in the area, but I've already killed so many of them and I need time to recover. The mindless creatures are nowhere near the difficulty they used to be to defeat, but it still takes it out of me to surpass their decay. At most, I can only kill a few before I need to sit aside for a dozen minutes.

My inner flames still have to be sacrificed to push past their decay, and it has become expensive on my energy reserves to recover. I've been trying to take what I can from each individual Viisin, but while I do feel my capacity increasing ever so minimally, the immediate energy I gain is not enough to recover my expenditure.

The wasteland that has become of the battlefield doesn't provide much fuel either. Everything has either been frozen beyond reason, or bombarded into dust. There are still remnants of artillery shells that remain scattered across the land, but even those are rare because of the swathes of land now scarred from the Viisin's involuntary decaying bodies.

I jump on Grímr's back again, and with hardly a flap of his wings, we are airborne. It's a far cry from the time it used to take. The glowing inscriptions over his body don't so much as create air, but redirect it around his massive body. It's somewhat similar to the manipulations I tried to do when I was carrying Leal, but clearly created by someone with a far better understanding of the principles than I.

Grímr tilts his wings and I'm almost crushed against his back as he turns at an unbelievably sharp angle. Even with the little weight I carry, I can barely make turns as fast as this. It reminds me of the first bird of prey to attack me over on the other side of the Alps; the enantiorn eagle.

The land below is a mess. It's hard to spot any speck of earth that remains untouched. I wonder what this place looked like before battle marred it? By the time I'd arrived, artillery bombardment already pockmarked the land. Since the arrival of the Order's elite mage, it has only grown worse.

The mercenaries and soldiers have been in retreat ever since the manifestation of the many new Viisin. Most flee in a disorganized mess, but there are plenty of more experienced and enhanced teams which hold the vanguard and protect their rear.

Those defending the retreat can't do much to fight off the Viisin, but their experience fighting creatures on the Titan Alps gives them the skill to hold the mindless Viisin's attention on themselves. Most teams have no method to beat them, but surviving long enough for the rest of the mercenaries to escape is possible.

It is possible, but even watching over the battle from the skies, I see many Luis mercenaries fall to the rapid movements of their opponents.

Grímr takes us north. He quickly reaches his previous maximum speed and surpasses it. We don't reach the same pace we did with Imiha's support, but it's an impressive improvement.

My portian friend favors the air above the pact nation's side of battle as we fly. The number of combatants thins in places, and rises in others over the distance we travel, but the advantage toward the mermineae's side is the same everywhere. The pact nations are pushed back no matter where I look.

At least, until we reach another section of immensely devastated land.

It looks like a herd of dahu went wild in the area. A massive forest of stone spikes, each the size of an ursu continae, spread for leagues outward in an arc. There is no sign of any mermineae in the area, or the mage who reshaped the land so totally. The only ones around are the mercenaries set up at the base of the expanse of towering stones.

This is the first place I've seen where the pact nations not only have the advantage, but have complete control. Though they hesitate to capitalize and push into the stone forest, and I can understand; the immense jagged stones won't make traversal easy.

Whatever mage inflicted such far-reaching damage is no longer around, but from how safe the people below are, it's encouraging to see the elite mercenaries might not all care nothing for mass casualties. Well, assuming there was nobody besides the mermineae caught in such a devastating rush of rock.

Grímr and I continue flying for a while. We never stop to help those barely holding on under the assault of the mermineae. Knowing Grímr, I'm sure he hates to ignore them, but returning to Remus must be more important.

Beiths help the mercenaries below with the Viisin, but there is clearly not enough to go around. If we hadn't lost so many to the other side of the Alps before this war ever started, there wouldn't be nearly as much of a problem. But what has come to pass cannot be changed. We can only make use of what we have and not regret what is lost.

"So, uh . . . you haven't heard what happened, have you?" I ask, unsure of how wide Kalma's effort to sabotage my coordination with the Mercenary Order has spread.

Grímr gives me a pitying side-eye glance. "I don't think there's a soul in the pact nations that hasn't heard," he says. "Remus filled us in about Kalma's involvement, but you should probably keep your distance from anyone you're not overly familiar with."

I melt onto Grímr's back. There was little chance it wouldn't have spread, what with how many mercenaries were there to witness, but I'd still hoped. Being considered a criminal by the entire pact nations is definitely not going to be fun. It was fine when it was Joiak, as I had no reason to respect them after how they allowed my friends to be treated, but my life is already too bound to the pact nations.

At least Remus believed my message. I'm thankful he's spread the word with Grímr and whoever else might be with him. Assuming they all believe him, I won't be walking into a bunch of spiteful mercenaries.

Honestly, I didn't even need to ask Grímr; I already knew the word had spread. The mercenary teams I've assisted have shown hesitation at my appearance, and while none have shown hostility—because that would be absolutely stupid with the power difference between us—they still didn't trust me.

"Also, you should apologize to Remus as soon as you see him. He doesn't like to show it, but he was pretty upset you didn't wait for him."

"Ah." Right. I completely forgot how I abandoned our meeting point in my rush to get Tore. And what a waste that was. That giant better be doing something important, because if he's not, I'll be pissed. I'm coming back to Remus empty handed. "I will."

We've been flying for not even an hour when Grímr drops our altitude. It wasn't a long flight, but with Kalma pushing the fight ever closer to its end, every minute we waste makes me stress.

In the distance, the iconic centzon war machines roll across the earth unopposed. There aren't nearly as many of them as there were across the Titan Alps, but even seeing them here means the centzon we left within the mountains made it across alive. A relief considering Kalma apparently destroyed their fortress herself.

"They've made more progress than I expected," Grímr comments as he comes in to land amongst the siege engines.

I jump off as soon as Grímr's talons touch the earth. Remus dismounts his moving machine to greet us. Jav, like he used to, rests on Remus's head with a determined stance. It's great to see him better. He hadn't exactly been in a great mental state the last time I saw him, so I'm happy to see him back to his normal self despite the circumstances.

"Solvei!" Remus cheers, his signature eye smile directed my way. "Hope you're not about to leave without a word again."

"Sorry about that." I cringe in regret. "I was in a hurry and I didn't know how long you would be."

Remus shakes his head with a chuckle. "Just be careful around Ossian when he finds out you burned the wall of his cabin. He might be unenhanced, but he knows how to hold a grudge."

Despite Remus's jovial tone, he sounds serious, so I nod in acknowledgment before raising my eyes to the small volan on his head. "I'm glad you look well, Jav."

He waves a small, artificially winged arm dismissively. "Don't worry about me. I'm done moping." He gives off an awkward chuckle. "My old man made sure of it."

With the four of us here, the team is almost back together. All we need now is Bunny, and we'd be back to how we started. I can't help but look around in anticipation of the off chance that she is here somewhere.

"She's not here," Grímr says, stepping up beside me. "Sorry, but Bunny's still defending her country from invasion on two fronts."

"Do you know if she's all right?"

"The Vanguard has held its ground through this entire war. Far from what can be said about the pact nations. There's little to worry about."

"Is this the one you told me about?" a voice completely unique to any I've heard before says. It sounds screechy, like the mermineae, but far too deep to be one of them.

I turn to face a strange three-eyed creature looking down on me from hardly a meter away. How did I not notice him? A quick check with my thermal sense shows absolutely nothing. I can't feel any heat coming from him.

I've never seen anything like him. He stands above two meters tall, but only because of a wooden brace holding his chest. Four symmetrical wooden legs extend out radially like a spider. The wood is absolutely brimming with dense inscriptions. A thousand individual lines carved into the wood glow with each tiny movement of the timber legs.

What is below his chest is obscured by the artificial appendages, but four arms extend from his brown leather-like torso. Each of the creature's hands has five long fingers and two thumbs.

"Solvei, this is my friend—" Remus starts.

"Friend?" Remus's apparently not-friend questions.

"Business associate," Remus tries, and the strange creature nods in acceptance. "Solon. He owes me a favor, so he'll be helping us. Solon is a Riparian and is one of the foremost experts on inscription engineering."

"Yes, yes. That's all very interesting, but I want to see if she can really do as you say."

The strange Riparian steps closer, his mechanical wooden legs moving in a way completely dissimilar to the centzon's machinery. Unlike the loud grinding and clanking of theirs, his legs move with a fluidity I would expect from something alive. But I can see the joints. I can see nothing but timber and the glowing engravings which relight with each movement.

"Solvei, can you show him the ritual?" Remus asks.

I'm uncertain why this Solon wants to see it, but I decide not to question it for now and do as asked. There're no corpses around, but he just wants to see me make the inscription with my flames, right? No need to actually do anything but show I can make it work.

The floating ritual comes together quickly. Surprisingly fast, even for me. My focus must have improved more than I'd thought since the last time I created this inscription. With no material to target, the ritual can't do much more than grasp at nothing, but it still operates properly.

"Satisfactory," Solon says as he turns back to Remus. "I can work with this."

"I still don't know why you refuse to work with an áinfean," Jav says. "We wouldn't have needed Solvei if you'd just accepted Spenne while he was here."

Solon says nothing, but Remus shakes his head. "Just leave it. Changing Solon's mind once he's made it is impossible."

I glance between them curiously. What exactly do they need me for?

CHAPTER FIFTY-SIX

Riparian Lesson

What is so important that you need me for?" I ask, unsure exactly who to direct my question to.

"You can create inscriptions at will," the Riparian says. "I would much rather inscribe it onto a plate for use, but I had to give up all my usual equipment to travel here." He slaps his artificial wooden legs. "Why else would I be donning this piece of junk?"

"So . . . you want to teach me an inscription? Like the ritual?" I ask. "What for?"

"I'm not clear on the finer details. Remus wants you to know this particular inscription for a reason."

I look to the dohrni, expecting some explanation, but he deflects instead. "I think now's a good time you told us exactly how Kalma is involved with this war. You weren't all too detailed in the message you left me."

I wince. "I guess I should start with how she's already impacted the war. The Forvaal and Viisin being pushed far beyond their limit; that was her influence."

"We already assumed as much. There are few other possibilities that could cause such a widespread change," Remus says. "As damaging a situation as she has put us in, it's not all bad. To do such a thing means she has a direct link with each of them. We can use that."

"We can?"

Remus smiles at me. "Why do you think I'm having you learn from Solon here?"

That still doesn't explain how we are going to make use of it. Even with some incredible inscription, what can it really accomplish in the face of Kalma's power?

This isn't the time to worry about that. Remus has a plan. That's more than I can say for myself after Tore's disappearance.

I don't want to waste much time, so I'll get through this quick. "Kalma's been manipulating things from the start. She invited the Beiths over the Alps to guide the mermineae and to thin their numbers. She takes enjoyment in both sides having even odds, and watches as we each kill the other off," I say. "Back when she destroyed the command center, she used some sphere to steal my flames and burn the city down."

Before I can continue, Solon interrupts. "A sphere? This sphere didn't happen to be a multi-layered inscription medium that gave her the capability to convert any input energy, did it?"

I stare up at the Riparian. "That's exactly what it did. It was my flames that burned the city, but she powered them with her energy. How did you know?"

Solon's three eyes harden as he turns to Remus. "If you can get that orb back for me, I'll owe you another favor. It is a stolen treasure of our clan," he says. "To think it would appear here."

Remus hums in affirmation. "Assuming we can find and beat her, it should be no problem to return the orb. I'll come find you should we succeed."

"Wait, you're not joining us?" I ask the Riparian. Considering he's already on the battlefield with us, I assumed he was going to stay.

"This is not my clan's war; I do not have the means to fight."

Well, that's unfortunate, but it's not like I really expected much from someone that uses wood as legs. It's like he's asking to be burned. Still, if he's good enough with inscriptions that Remus would ask him to come down at a time like this, he must be the one who inscribed Grímr's metal feathers. Even if he won't join our war, he's already helped my team.

"Now, I'd rather not waste time," Solon says as he pulls out a roll of parchment from a compartment in his wooden brace. "Let's make sure you can replicate the tracing design to an operable degree."

"Tracing?" I repeat, before spinning to Remus. "You plan to track down Kalma? But how can we beat her?"

"I've sent Doe to get in contact with members of the Inner Circle. A few of them owe me, and others will hopefully see the wisdom in taking the head off our enemy. Once we have the means to track her, we will group with those willing to help, then ambush Kalma. Let's see this supposed *god* survive the full force of the pact nations."

After seeing the power those Inner Circle mercenaries wield, it will be an impressive group, certainly. But I'm not sure it will be enough. Kalma is beyond anything, and I feel we need Tore to stand a chance.

Before I can voice my concerns, Solon grabs my arm and pulls me along behind him. The temptation to burn his hand off rises at the forced hold, but he's Remus's guest, so I overlook it for now. His grasp does get slapped off, though.

I'm led upon one of the centzon's war machines as the Riparian holds the wide parchment with his upper pair of arms. I spot Tzilac upon an adjacent siege engine and wave at him. It is a relief Kalma didn't kill the centzon and all his hunters as she made her way across the Alps. Though I wonder for the safety of those who'd been defending the fortress on the other side of the Alps.

It's surprising to see they have rebuilt such a large number of these machines. Last I'd seen them down in that cavern, they went without many, relying only on their handheld contraptions and a few higher mobility mechanisms that could traverse the vertical walls and the tight tunnels down in the depths of the Alps.

"Now, I know you are aware of the basic components within the general inheritance ritual, so I'll start off with the requisite components you don't yet know."

Solon places his parchment on a makeshift table on the back of the machine and pulls out another piece and scratches away with an ink dipped pen.

The large parchment he'd been holding contains a dense array of lines far more complicated than the ritual. Is this the inscription he wants me to learn? It took me ages to figure out how to get the ritual to work. We are already strained on time; there's no way I'll succeed.

I turn to what the Riparian is writing, and am surprised to find the entire sheet already filled. I don't think I've ever seen someone write so fast.

He flicks his pen, tossing the remaining ink over the siege engine, and slides it into a slot within his leg. Solon hands me the page and immediately dives into explaining each of the diagrams drawn, not even bothering to direct my attention toward the inscription he's supposed to be teaching me.

"Since you are already familiar with the hyle flow through the components used in the ritual, I'll start with the components that operate similarly." He points to the first of six relatively simple inscriptions on the page. "This is a combination of a sampler and a collector. It lacks two of its outputs to give higher efficiency on operational accuracy."

I stare at the drawing, completely at a loss for what he just said. "Sampler? Collector?"

"Ah, self-taught? No matter." He doesn't seem bothered that I didn't pick up on his explanation, instead he pulls out his pen and paper again and draws another series of inscriptions. This time, they are ones I'm familiar with.

"This is a sampler, and this is a collector. If you ignore the power aspect of the collector and incorporate it into the input of the sampler while feeding an output back into the input, you get a basic receiver," he says as he points back to the first on the original sheet.

That makes a lot more sense. It's still difficult to follow, but I'm pretty sure I understand what he's trying to get across.

"Make it."

"What? Right now?"

"You have the benefit of being able to experiment in real time. Use it. Most need to prepare the required materials and instruments to learn."

Seeing no reason not to do as he says, I create a flame above my hand and move it into the shape of the inscription. The easy part is done. Now, I need to make my flames act in a way that is expected by the lines. I try to replicate the effects they had in the two components I'm familiar with, but it doesn't work.

"You're not directing the hyle through the feedback loop correctly. Also, lower the intensity of your inputs," Solon comments.

"Can't you just make the inscription so that I can feel how it works? That's what I did last time."

"If I had the equipment and materials to achieve that, I would have simply made it for Remus."

My eyes fall to the densely glowing wooden legs of his.

Noticing my gaze, he speaks again, "These are a different category of inscription. The minimum material prerequisites are far lower than for the design I am trying to teach you."

There goes the easy method.

Well, it's not all bad. Unlike last time where I was left to memorize the inscription on my own and only had a single attempt to figure out what each part did, I actually have someone to guide me now. It's hard to believe I'll be able to get the inscription memorized within any reasonable length of time, but that doesn't mean I won't try.

I recreate the inscription component Solon calls a basic receiver and follow his instructions to bring it closer to its intended purpose. The first design takes me almost thirty minutes. Each subsequent component takes less time as I grow accustomed to his descriptions.

Compared to Solon, it is clear I have no idea what I'm doing. All I'm being taught are the direction, size, and effect my fire needs to exhibit in particular patterns. I still do not know how each part does what it does, nor what they are intended to achieve.

And not for lack of effort by my Riparian teacher; he gives me an in-depth explanation of each, but there's only so much I can do to comprehend phrases like: split-pathing energy quarantine, hyle noise suppression tactics, and high-power inscription shielding. So while it would be interesting to learn all about these inscriptions, I don't have the luxury.

For now.

Once I have time, I'm definitely going to learn everything I can. It is clear simply listening to Solon talk that there are limitless possibilities for inscriptions. I can't wait to see how they might improve my flames.

Until then, I'm stuck simply memorizing the inscriptions shown to me. And that is exactly what I do now. Solon finally directs me through the tracking inscriptions.

It's far simpler to achieve than learning the individual parts. The only difficulty is the sheer amount of focus it takes out of me. Compared to the inheritance ritual, it requires me to focus on four times the number of inscription components to complete. Not easy, but I manage better than I'd expected.

What makes constructing the tracing inscription harder is Solon stopping me from creating it part by part. I'm instructed to construct it all at once. No negotiation. He says there wouldn't be an issue with this inscription, but some could create unintended effects if created in a less than optimal order.

His first example of a sudden explosion hadn't worried me, but his second of an unintended hyle transition from fire to water did. Apparently, that is possible; how frightening.

After three full hours of effort, I can finally create the inscription with consistency. The only issue: it doesn't actually do anything.

The flaming inscription hovers a dozen meters across, larger than I need to make it, but it's easier to alter and practice when I don't need to concentrate my flames into such dense weaves.

"So why isn't it doing anything?" I ask as we both peer up at the thousand burning lines in the air.

Solon looks down at me. His gaze reveals nothing of his thoughts. "You should at least think the question through before asking."

I blink at him before returning my attention to the inscription above. I don't understand how each component affects the whole design, but there is one thing that's clear: there are two distinct pathways for hyle to flow, only connected via components which he has taught me allow separate energies to influence each other without directly interacting.

Of course, considering the entire thing is made of my flames, that separation between pathways means little, but it is clearly important to the design.

"It needs another energy." I follow the lines where one pathway enters an array of basic receivers. "Kalma's?" I ask.

"Precisely. You will need some of her energy to find her."

"But that's insane. Where are we supposed to . . . oh. Oh."

"That's right. And for a being like Kalma, it is likely she suppress her energy to a great degree. So, for the best chance, find one with as much of her signature hyle as possible."

Great. I wonder if the lesser Viisin will be enough?

Who am I kidding? I already know we need to go after one of the intelligent Viisin that can compete with an elite.

CHAPTER FIFTY-SEVEN

Ankor

So, how exactly are we going to meet up with those Inner Circle mercenaries you convinced to help us?" I ask atop Grímr's back.

We set out as soon as Solon gave his approval of my capability. Remus, Jav, Grímr, and I left without so much as a goodbye to the centzon. It's somewhat regrettable to leave Tzilac and his kin so soon after meeting them again, but the centzon hardly need us around to support them. Assuming none of the superior Viisin get in their way, nothing can threaten them with those war machines of theirs.

Solon stayed back with the centzon, but I don't imagine he'll stick around for long. He made it pretty clear in the short time I was with him he plans to return to Riparia's island as soon as he can.

Whether the Riparian doesn't enjoy being away from his home, or simply wants to avoid the war, I don't know. Maybe one day, should I survive this mess, I'll find him again. It would be nice if I could get him to teach me for more than a few hours, but something tells me that won't be so easy.

Regardless, I'm thankful for what he has taught me.

I realize now that my plan to get Tore to fight against Kalma was hasty at best. I'd been lucky not to have the giant kill me the instant I showed my face in New Vetus. But even with that luck, there was no plan to find Kalma. There had been an assumption that if I brought him to the battlefield, the two would find each other.

Kalma isn't self-indulging, though. Not when it comes to fighting personally. She would likely have just kept her distance and watched as the war brought everything down around us and let Tore flounder. It would have been nothing more than an extra source of entertainment for her.

I'm thankful Remus thought about it. Really, I should have stayed to talk to him properly.

There is no changing the past. It was the right action at the time, given what I knew. Unfortunately, it didn't bear fruit, but we have the opportunity before us to at the very least make things difficult for Kalma. Beating her seems all but impossible, but there's no point not trying.

"One of the Inner Circle is waiting for us to the south. We'll head toward him. I'm hoping he can subdue the Viisin long enough for you to tear out Kalma's hyle. After, we'll join the rest."

"Hoping?" I ask. "You don't know?"

"Oh, don't give me that." Remus's eyes roll in his head to look back at me. "The last time I saw the khirig fight was near a century ago."

"Shocking, isn't it?" Jav says. "There are actually people older than Remus." Jav effortlessly dodges the tentacle swatting at him. "Besides, they are the Inner Circle for a reason. Even if their . . . character can be called into question, each might as well be unbeatable in battle."

I'd love to believe that, but the ice mage clearly didn't have an easy time against the superior Viisin. How is one supposed to fight something that doesn't die even when its whole body is destroyed?

Though, I'm pretty sure I thought the same thing when I saw a Viisin for the first time.

"So you know where to find this khirig?" We've been traveling south ever since we left, following the battlefield from the sky.

Thankfully, much of the fighting has entered a sort of lull. Except for the mindless Viisin throwing themselves into teams of mercenaries, there is very little combating occurring. But we've only flown over areas mostly untouched by superior Viisin and Inner Circle mercenary, so while I can hope the entire battlefield is identical, it is unlikely. There's a good chance other places have been less fortunate.

"Nope," Remus says. "We're just going to keep flying until we find him. Don't worry though, if Ankor has been in a fight, we'll know about it."

I'm not sure how Remus can keep his relaxed attitude even in the middle of war, but I believe him. If there's anything the Inner Circle mercenaries have in common, it's the absolute devastation they leave behind them from their battles. I assume this Ankor will be no different, so tracking him down will be no issue once we find the remnants of his battle.

Once we find his remnants. The battlefront covers an immense section of land. How long will it take to find a hint of his passage?

I wonder if I can use my new inscription to find this khirig. It would need some inkling of his hyle to operate, and the only place we might find that is a battlefield he passed through, so it's not like it's all too helpful.

In no time, we pass the towering pillars of stone and reach the frozen battlefield again. There are more unfaltering paths of frost littering the landscape. The albanic mage hasn't been holding back with her icy blasts in the time I've been gone. She's nowhere in sight, and neither are either side of the battle. Whether they fled, or were killed in the crossfire, is uncertain.

I tried to support Grímr's flight with my flames, like I used to, but we are quick to discover it interferes with the operation of the inscriptions carved into his feathers and slows us down rather than amplifying our speed as intended.

We travel for an hour beyond the icy wasteland with no sign of the mercenary we're looking for. Nearly half of our flight passes over flooded land. A sign that one of the Inner Circle is a water mage. Not something I'm happy to learn.

There are a surprisingly disproportionate number of mages amongst the mercenary elite. Is the growth potential for a mage simply that much greater than one who relies on weapons and enhancement? Or is there some other reason for the bias? It's frustrating for me, as I know I'm far better suited to those who use physical attacks like bladed weapons and such. Those who have the power to influence the world around them are far more dangerous.

I guess I'm lucky New Vetus prefers a warrior's strength to a mage's capabilities. If either the warden or the commissars had been mages, my fights against them might have gone very differently.

The sight of what I assume to be a Luis mage a thousand meters below being overwhelmed by a lesser Viisin catches my eye. Despite their ability to wield water to their will, and the vast knee-deep sea of water around them, they still fail to effectively combat the decaying mermineae.

Then again, maybe I wouldn't have had much of a problem. Unlike with warriors, there is an obvious difference of talent and intelligence between them. Sure, physical warriors can exhibit skill in the way they wield their weapons, but most of the time, the only defining factor is the amount of enhancement one has achieved.

While it is probably wrong to say the same isn't true for a mage, Leal is an example of one that can hit far beyond what her enhancement should allow, simply because of her skill and understanding of markings. Elite mages must be the same; having reached where they are, not because of the amount of energy within them, but how effectively they wield that energy.

There are plenty of sections along the front where our defense clearly lacked any of talent, or at least suitable enhancement. The mermineae swarm through the undefended land as the lesser Viisin continue to chase down teams of mercenaries unable to fight back.

As we pass many such areas, my team plunges within a somber air. It is clear in the way Grímr's and Remus's eyes linger on the hopeless mercenaries below that they want to dive down and save each of them. Jav intentionally doesn't look, his eyes locked on the horizon ahead.

Despite their wishes, there are far too many occurrences for us to waste time on any single one. It's not an enjoyable circumstance, but on the off chance we can actually beat Kalma, her energy will no longer empower the mermineae.

Well, we don't know that for sure, but it's only one more assumption to add to the pile that needs to be fulfilled without issue for an optimal outcome to this war.

. . . We really are grasping at straws.

Glistening flashes of light amongst a cloud of dust in the distance is the first sign that we've found another Inner Circle mercenary.

Every so often, booming cracks resound through the air, increasing in volume as we fly closer. The obscuring dust cloud covers much of the battlefield to our south. The fight likely occurring within continually spreads ash through the skies without a chance to settle.

Occasionally, bright flashes of light shine from within the dust cloud. They only appear briefly, but with how the dust blows outward at each flash, I assume something within is moving incredibly fast.

"Oh, good!" Remus cheers. "I was worried we'd have to travel all the way to Vanguard to find him."

So this is Ankor? The elite who's agreed to help us? I'm surprised Remus can distinguish his identity simply from those brief lights, but he's the only one of us that's seen him fight, so I'll take his word for it.

As we close in on the battle, the area both Ankor and the Viisin have been becomes clear. Covering all is a thick layer of dust. It's like an ugly gray snow over the earth. But visible beneath the dust is scarred land with craters a hundred meters wide and sharp crevices cut into the earth at odd angles.

Unlike the other damaged landscapes, the only visible effect is the damage the ground below us has received. No elemental effects to give away what type of mage Ankor might be. Unless, like Tore, he's a physical only warrior.

Once we reach the outskirts of the dust cloud, the source of those light flashes becomes clear. Breaching the dense depths of dust is a heavy curved blade arcing through the air around a chain leading to the center of the ash. The weighted blade shines with inscriptions as it reaches the apex of its swing before it disappears back within the obscuring dust. A crack soon follows, the sound somewhere between the crack of a whip and grinding stone.

Within a moment of the first, another chain breaches the ash. This time, nothing more than a blunt weight is attached to the end. The weapon arcs high into the air before jerking back out of sight and exploding into the earth. The force smashes through each of us, along with a faceful of dust.

"So, I hate to be the one to ask, but how are we meant to approach?" Jav asks, and I have to share his hesitance. Those chained weapons weren't short, by any means.

It's clear Ankor is a weapon wielder rather than a mage, so out of the four of us, it would likely be safer for me to be the one to dive in. Though, the more I watch those glowing weapons break into view and the explosions of dust that must be the superior Viisin, my hesitance grows.

"We don't need to approach. We only need to get his attention," Remus says, to my relief. "Grímr, can—"

Without needing to be told, Grímr lets loose a shrill whistle loud enough that Jav has to cover his ears. It is far closer to a buzz of scraping metal than a typical bird's call, but it does the job.

A crash, followed by clanking of chains echoing through the dust is all the warning we have before a giant of a khirig tears out of the obscuring cloud. Half a dozen weapons follow in his wake, connected to his body by thick metal chains. Surprisingly, none of his antlers have inscriptions or markings on them. It's only his chains and their connected weapons that do.

Only after a few seconds of Ankor having cleared of the dust do I realize his fleshy inner body isn't actually any larger than the rest of his race. It is because his antlers extend so far from his body that he looks twice the normal size.

Each of his antlers grows outward, which is also not a common sight amongst the khirig. Usually, beside the antlers that make their arms and legs, they curve around the head and chest in a protective cage. Ankor's antlers grow in a way that would leave his chest exposed . . . if he didn't fill the gap with a web of chains.

As he moves through the air, the slightest jerk of one of those antlers sends the weapons trailing behind him spinning. The movement is enough to drastically alter his trajectory, which is fortunate, as the air itself disintegrates to dust.

A clear path of the remnants of decay leads back into the dust cloud. The instantaneous disintegration of air leaves a far thinner dust than what is left of the earth, and it disperses relatively quickly, but that was clearly an attack I've never seen before.

The superior Viisin have new tricks. Not good.

"You took your time, Remus." Ankor doesn't even look our way. Instead, he swings his pendulum blade through the dust behind him. The blade momentarily clears the decay in its path. It parts long enough to see the pendulum cut through the Viisin deep within. To my eyes, it's like the blade simply passes through a merminea-shaped bundle of ash without effect. The same way a blade might pass through me.

The moment of visibility soon disappears. Dust explodes out of the Viisin in enough quantity to block sight for a good hundred meters.

"Give me a few minutes to get ready. Deal with the fodder heading east until then."

He knows what we expect from him already. That's good. Remus must have told him the plan before he was sent out. I need him to hold the Viisin still long enough for the inscription to lock on, otherwise I won't be able to take Kalma's energy.

We follow Ankor's directions, and turn east. In the distance, there is a swarm of lesser Viisin pushing through an already defeated army of mercenaries. Looks like it's time to see just how good Grímr's new inscriptions are in a fight.

CHAPTER FIFTY-EIGHT

Horde

While Ankor continues fighting back the Viisin, the four of us fly toward the former Forvaal as they sprint into the now undefended land of the pact nations. The lesser Viisin leave very little sign of the mercenaries they must have only recently cut through, but the odd limb or discarded weapon is enough that there is no doubt of the slaughter they've left behind.

There have to be nearly a hundred of the fresh Viisin rushing along the land. With so many crowding so close together, it's no surprise whatever army of mercenaries stood in their way didn't last long. I can kill probably five or six—maybe I could reach ten if I really push myself—before I'd have to recover for a while.

With Grímr's new inscription-covered body, I'm sure he can fight some off himself, but my concern lies with the other two. Even without intelligence, these Viisin are just as fast and their touch as deadly as always. I distinctly remember my team struggling against normal Forvaal, before Kalma's boost. How are Remus and Jav fine to join us?

"Are you sure it's safe for you two to join?"

Remus laughs. "In a direct battle? Of course not. Jav and I don't plan to get close." He reaches a tentacle and unstraps a couple of packs from Grímr's side. "But Solon wasn't the only one I asked help from."

I'm curious as to what he means, but the old dohrni doesn't elaborate. He chooses to smile my way in infuriating silence.

Fine then, keep it a secret. I throw myself off Grímr's back, and finish my transformation to a falcon before rocketing ahead. If he wants to tease me like that, I'll kill the Viisin before he even has the chance to show off.

The decreased mass in this form helps a lot with mobility. My physical jets require far less energy or resources to achieve the same acceleration. It's a shame, but I haven't been able to use a spear in a while. Without the weapon to use, I don't really need to stay in my default form for any other reason than comfort. It might be useful if I was desperate enough to use my body's flames to fight the Viisin, like I did when I first pushed them to a white heat, but while it's possible to kill them with my inner flame alone, there is no point putting my life in such danger.

I soar forward, incinerating the first two I pass and intentionally gaining the attention of the rest. As expected, they simultaneously dash after me. If I hadn't already accelerated to an immense speed, there's no way I could have dodged them all.

I find some amusement in the way they crash into each other before throwing themselves after me. Many claw at their neighbor to give themselves more speed, unknowingly dismembering them. More than half fall behind, recovering as the fewer close in on me. One unfortunate soul dies completely at his brethren's hands.

If only I could replicate that a hundred more times.

I incinerate two more in an instant, but the strain it puts on my flames is hard to push through. Three more jump directly into balls of white flame, only for the blaze to engulf them and leave nothing left. Much of my inner flame disappears along with them, leaving nothing but an ache as replacement. As much as I wanted to show Remus up, it looks like there's only so far I can reach.

A metallic grinding screech rings out a moment before Grímr, in his huge glowing alicanto body, tears through the swarming Viisin. The inscriptions on his wings shine brighter as they shear through a dozen mermineae. He grasps a couple of Viisin in his taloned feet and carries them away from the horde before slamming them into the earth, crushing them under his entire weight.

The ones his wings cut through quickly recover, dashing after either of us, while those caught beneath him are gone for good. The crowd splits their attention between the two of us, and bound after us in a way that reminds me far too much of the chthonic my tribe fought so long ago. Their ample numbers, in addition to their mindless bloodthirst, mimic the first creatures I'd truly feared.

Grímr takes to the air long before they can reach him. He clearly doesn't want to get caught in a melee with the Viisin, and as I watch him gain altitude, I see why: an ever so slight trail of dust falls off his wings. It appears those inscriptions don't entirely make him immune to the effects of decay.

A Viisin leaps through the air, coming far too close for comfort. I burn it and take some more height. I'll need to wait around for a minute before I can try to take any more on. Most of the inner flame I can control at once is already gone. Unless I want to try using the flames of my body, I'm forced to ascend and wait until they reignite.

As Remus said, both he and Jav keep their distance. Remus reaches into a pouch and hands something to Jav. Though I'd rather not let him get his way over me, I am curious about what he's brought.

I don't have to wait long to find out. Remus wraps a tentacle around Jav only a moment before the small volan spears through the air with terrifying speed. Even if Grímr and I have grown immensely since we all fought as a team, the power Remus can put into his throws is still impressive.

In the blink of an eye, Jav has crossed hundreds of meters, soaring over the heads of the Viisin chasing me. I almost miss the capsule Jav tosses amongst the mermineae before it explodes into an intense flash. The crack of Remus's whip-like limb reaches my ears an instant before the thrumming blast does.

Shrapnel pelts me, surprisingly not melting as they impact my body. Below, a crater appears in the center of the swarm of Viisin. The blast completely erases some mindless creatures from existence, and blows away those further out.

So the centzon were able to create more of those bombs in the time they crossed the Alps. Remus didn't have many satchels with him, so I can assume we have about five more of those bombs left at most. I'm surprised the centzon gave even that many away. It's supposed to be a time consuming process to create both the oil and shrapnel used in the explosives.

Jav is already curving back to Remus, ready to pick up another bomb, but the Viisin are no longer ignorant of their presence. With me out of their reach, they unanimously turn toward the old dohrni.

Remus, after throwing Jav a second time, has the wisdom to move as fast as he can. He's already a good kilometer away, but if he's not careful, they'll catch up before he realizes. But I trust Remus to have the experience to keep himself safe.

Jav, on the other hand, has to get in real close to toss those devastating bombs. I know with his reaction speed and the velocity he moves, there's little to worry about, but he's still the most vulnerable. A single mistake, and it could be all over for him.

Grímr swoops, cutting through the group chasing Remus and leading his own pack into the rest just as Jav flings another bomb. The resultant explosion peppers Grímr with shrapnel, but with his inscriptions hardening the metal of his body, they clatter off like nothing.

Despite the strike being perfect, there are still so many remaining. Only the Viisin vaporized by the initial blast stay down. We've whittled down barely a quarter of the numbers they started with.

There are simply too many to fight in any way that isn't conservative. Grímr would be overwhelmed if he tried to take out any more than one or two at a time, and the duo have no choice but to keep their distance. Not to mention they are on a counter before they lose their only effective method to deal damage.

My fire is coming back, but far too slowly. Ankor has been fighting that superior Viisin for who knows how long now, so I hardly think there's any need to clear through these mermineae with any haste. But still, I'd rather my team not put themselves in danger while I'm simply watching from the sidelines.

. . . Okay, fine. I just don't want to lose out to them after I've grown so much. I want to show them up a bit. It's Remus's fault for winding me up at the start of the fight.

But I'll never keep up with their pace as it is. In the time it's taken me to regain enough flames to burn two Viisin, Grímr has already crushed six, and the other two have probably blown up over a dozen between them. As things are going, I'll lose in the kill count. I can't have that.

If I want to compete, I'll need to try something different. Simply burning them will waste the resources I have, but do I have any other options that will work?

Attacking them directly with my body should be a last resort. I highly doubt I'd be able to cook them alive by surrounding them; not only would it take too long for the temperature to rise to a level that might actually hurt them, but they're likely to jump into my flames before I can react, making the attempt pointless.

I could make my flames physical, to attack without touching them, but I'm still unable to add all that much weight to them. The best offense I'd be able to inflict is raising some rock high into the air and dropping it on their heads, but I don't even waste time on that idea. The Viisin tear through so much stone with each step, the size of the rock I'd have to lift would be so far beyond my capabilities that I'd have a better chance burning Kalma.

But, there is one thing I've not tried.

There has never been a need to test the other side of the range, as my inner flames are already immaterial. What could making a nonphysical fire more intangible possibly even accomplish? It's not something I've ever really needed to try. Not until now. The decay obviously interacts with my fire. Moreso when physical. It would be amazing if I could stop that interaction completely without extinguishing my flames.

Hundreds of meters in the sky—high enough that I can dodge any Viisin tempted to fling themselves up at me—I concentrate my inner flame around me. I take a grasp of their state, and ease the fire away from the physical form I use to carry things and thrust myself through the air.

It's a strange feeling. Surprisingly not even hard to achieve. My flames don't change visibly, still swaying with candescence, but there is a distinction that is hard to describe. It's less . . . present, and yet entirely still here.

I try consuming the air and find that while I can interact with it, doing so actually takes effort. In the future, I'll have to be careful never to push my entire body to this state—assuming I could ever push my body that far—it will be difficult to breathe.

Another explosion tears me out of my concentration. Those two should only have a couple of bombs left, so now is probably a good time to test whether this incorporeal flame is enough to combat the Viisin. I have recovered enough inner flame to incinerate three Viisin, which should be plenty to experiment with.

I swoop down, chasing the mermineae that have all but forgotten me in their chase after Remus. The dohrni is quick, and keeps his distance, but the Viisin are gradually catching up. I'm not worried, though. Should they get too close, I know Grímr will pick him up. It's good he has their undivided attention; I can play with a laggard.

A Viisin that only recently had its bottom half cut off by Grímr's large wings trails behind the rest of the pack of Viisin, rear legs regrowing. I fly in close, swirling my flames close around my chest.

Really, if they hadn't lost their mind from Kalma's forced enhancement, this would be a nightmare scenario. If they had even the slightest sentience left, they would split up and surround their targets rather than pointlessly chasing after them. Remus herds them with far too much ease.

The Viisin doesn't even see me coming. Something I know would have been impossible if it had intelligence. I could never catch a Viisin off guard before.

I wrap my flames around the creature, and to my relief, it doesn't hurt. Even through the dust, I can feel the Viisin's body. I watch as the flesh, bones and organs continue their rapid cycle of decaying and subsequent renewal. It's like my flames permeate its body without truly interacting with it.

Well, to say there are no effects would be a lie. The Viisin clearly notices the flames shrouding its body, and I can see the heat around the creature rising drastically.

It turns and launches itself at me. From the distance it does so, I have nothing to worry about. I simply burst a jet of physical flames from my side and alter my trajectory . . . but I don't move anywhere near as far as I expect, and I panic as the Viisin comes within a claw's breadth of striking me.

Okay, so creating a physical flame becomes multitudes more difficult when controlling ethereal flame. With a deep breath, I calm myself from the close call and vow to myself to be more careful.

My flames are still hot, but they aren't truly burning the Viisin, so I push them to consume. Like the air, it is a challenge to eat through the physical separation and scorch the creature's body. It works. Flesh incinerates far slower than normal, but the merminea still burns up in my grasp, and with hardly any pain on my end. I can feel the decay trying to combat my flames, to reduce them to nothing, but the decay simply has an immensely difficult time reaching through the ethereal barrier.

This new state I can reach has the added benefit of allowing me to reach within the creature's body before I burn it, so I don't need to struggle past the wall of dust before I can vaporize it.

The only downside is that while my normal flame could immolate a Viisin in an instant, this method requires a relatively lengthy amount of time to burn them. I have to push past their regeneration and slowly wear down its body from within. But even so, the rate at which I can kill Viisin is far faster than if I have to wait for my inner flame to recover every time.

Also, being able to fight without inflicting pain upon myself will be amazing.

My test subject is no more. Nothing but dust dispersing in the breeze. I can't help the smirk that sneaks its way over my face as I look over the many Viisin waiting to be incinerated.

Ha, Remus won't be able to show me up now.

CHAPTER FIFTY-NINE

Tracking Kalma

After killing my first play partner, another three volunteer themselves by pouncing toward me. Now that I know controlling ethereal flame influences my separate physical flames, I can dodge by adjusting the amount my jet thrusts. Each Viisin get a ball of fire to the face.

If capable of thought, I'm sure they would be relieved that their faces aren't scorched off on the spot. Unfortunately . . . or rather, fortunately, they do nothing but shriek in incoherent rage as they fall back to the earth.

A small flare stays attached to each of their bodies, even in their incorporeal state. Two of the volunteers find their bodies shrouded in flame before they even hit the ground. The other gets to wait a dozen seconds before it's their turn. I can only cover so much area with my white flames, so I'm limited to killing two at a time.

The two with flames burning right through their core must have some level of self-preservation remaining within them, as they jump up without delay, desperate to kill the one inflicting damage upon them. Of course, they don't come close. They even get another leap in before the heat is finally too much for them and my flames overpower their recovery. I have to wait a few more seconds after they are immobilized to actually kill them. If I were to let go early, they would likely recover within moments.

With the first two done, I focus on the other Viisin I tagged and spread the flame across their body. Grímr must have distracted them, as they now chase after him. As soon as the flames eat into its body, it shrieks and mystically turns its attention to me again. Strange. Maybe beneath the mindless fury, there's still some intelligence hidden within.

Well, nothing will change even if there is some remnant of themselves remaining. If anything, it's probably better to put them out of their misery.

While that Viisin burns, I fly low enough to spread the rest of my inner flame. I have to let my fires revert to their yellow heat to cover a wide enough area, but as I swoop over the heads of the remaining mermineae, the ethereal wisps cling to their bodies.

Not a minute passes before I'm back high in the air out of their range, watching as the creatures burn away two at a time. As soon as a pair fall to my flames, I incite the tiny lingering flares to consume their bodies and grow to the intense white flame.

Up here, they cannot reach me. There is nothing they can do except scream, flail, and die under my guided blaze. Never would I have believed I could control my flames from so far away, but here I am, manually spreading my fire from five hundred meters above.

It's definitely not easy; my control is pushed to the limit to do so, but it makes fighting the Viisin near leisurely. Not long ago, taking on a Viisin was far beyond my capabilities. Now, I believe I'd be able to take on an intelligent one without difficulty. Unless they have a way to stop my ethereal flame from attaching to them, they won't be able to defend themselves against me, regardless of how tactically they approach the fight.

Below, Grímr picks Remus up and carries him out of the range of the Viisin swarm. I burn through two at the front of the pack, having them stumble before they throw themselves on Grímr's wings. With the speed he's moving, it's unlikely they could catch up, but there's no reason I shouldn't be careful.

Remus and Jav no longer throw the centzon bombs. Whether they've run out or are saving the rest, I don't know. Now, they spend their time distracting the Viisin so Grímr and I can clear through them with ease.

Between the initial salvo of explosions, and both Grímr's and my efforts, we are now down to only a couple dozen remaining Viisin. Despite the initial kills from the bombs, I'm certain I've taken down the most Viisin now, but I'll need to wait until they are all dealt with to gloat.

"Remus, I'm ready!" Ankor's voice echoes across the land despite the thousands of meters separating us, intense like a war-horn.

I'm immediately reminded that our purpose here isn't to kill the Viisin. It seems whatever preparations Ankor needed to set up are complete, but we still haven't finished clearing out the Viisin.

I fly toward Remus, intending to help my team clear through the last before heading over to help Ankor, but the dohrni has a different plan. "Solvei, we can deal with the last of these. You get that inscription working." His eyes turn my way as Grímr drops him to the earth again. "Be careful and don't get too close."

With reluctance, I nod. I'd rather not leave them to fight the Viisin themselves, but I know they can take care of themselves. Before I've even turned to fly toward Ankor and the superior Viisin he's fighting, I've begun weaving the complex pattern of flame through the air before me.

I have to sacrifice all the flares I have attached to the mermineae around here, as this inscription requires all my focus to make sure I don't mess it up at such an important time. The flight toward the massive dust storm is short, mostly spent troubling over the perfection of the inscription.

"Are you ready?" the voice carries from within the cloud.

I can't tell exactly where they are, so I spread the inscription wide over the top of the dust. With myself flying over the center point, the weave of flames spread as far as I can reach, yet it still isn't enough to cover the entire cloud below.

"Yes," I shout down, adding my presence to my voice, hoping it will reach Ankor through the rough wind and consistent explosions within the dust.

Near as soon as I do, a roaring chorus of chains echoes out of the dust. Heavy grinding followed by loud clanks are the only signals that Ankor is acting. A guttural shriek wails through the air before the world falls quiet. The quiet remains for a few long moments as the dust finally disperses.

Within the clearing dust is a bundle of chains pulled taut toward a dozen points where the chains dig through the earth. The superior Viisin has been bound so tight that not even its dust can escape the confines created by the cage of chains.

I don't need Ankor to tell me to start. Without delay, the inscription activates. I guide it through the initial process before the components take over and enact the design's effects almost all on their own. With the smallest of alterations, I direct the inscription to target the creature within Ankor's chains. I have to manually filter out the hyle running through the inscriptions lining the chains and focus only on the Viisin.

It takes nearly thirty seconds for it to lock on, and by the time it does, dust is rapidly escaping from the binding of chains. I wait for the inscription to pull the energy from the Viisin, but it doesn't happen. We have a problem; while the inscription binds to the creature's energy, it isn't strong enough to pull it out of its body.

"I have a lock, but the energy won't come." I'm not sure what to do. If the inscription can't pull the hyle from their body, then what are we supposed to do?

"You've done fine," Ankor says. His voice closer than expected.

I turn to my side to see him still rising through the air not a few meters away. As he climbs higher, the chains reaching into the earth become taut. Right before the chains halt him from rising any higher, he flicks his arms and many of his antlers upward. The motion breaks his upward momentum and shoots all the dangling chains through the air, up past him.

It takes a moment for the force to ripple down the long chains. As one, they combine their force on the imprisoned Viisin, shredding every fiber from existence.

Without a body to hold it, there is nothing to stop the energy from flowing into my inscription. As soon as the section of the inscription that holds the energy takes on Kalma's hyle, I pull my own energy away. I needed mine there to keep the quarantined path from falling apart, but now that it is flowing in, I don't need to be concerned.

The amount of energy is immense. Likely far too much for me to handle, which makes it fortunate that the inscription does the work for me. It flows in slowly but steadily, wrapped within my woven flames.

Eventually, the last of the lingering decay hyle is absorbed. The energy compresses within the storage section of the inscription and gives off a transparent gray glow as it moves along its lines.

As soon as no more energy enters the inscription, it enters the next phase and immediately searches for the matching energy. I know where it's pointing long before a flame materializes to visually represent the direction of the energy link it has found.

The inscription points east. Not the direction I'd assume her to be, but it doesn't change that we now know where Kalma is. Once we gather the rest of Remus's contacts, we can follow her and challenge her.

I take my time to compress the inscription down to a far more manageable size while keeping its functionality intact. The small flame rising from the center continues to point east, remaining steady and straight in its heading. In no time, I have the inscription down to about a meter wide, and even that is almost too much for me. The decay energy stored within glows with a brightness that's hard to look at, but it stays contained without issue.

Slowly, I allow my focus to spread away from the inscription. Remus, Jav, and Grímr have clearly finished the last of the lesser Viisin, and now rest besides Ankor. The large khirig himself seems to have wasted no time tying his chains and their attached weapons over his extending antlers. He's quite the daunting figure with all his weapons tied around him like that.

"Any issues?" Remus asks as I fall beside them.

"No. It worked better than I expected," I say. "I can feel where Kalma is right now."

Immediately, the dohrni's eyes harden. "Then we best get moving. Ankor, are there any other Inner Circle we need to pick up on the way to our rendezvous?"

Ankor hums, or at least I think he hums. It's hard to tell through the constant jingling of chains. "El was sent to defend the west of Vanguard. Shouldn't be too far out of the way."

Looks like I'll be holding this tracing inscription for a while. I don't know enough about the inscription to isolate the contained energy and hold it for later. It shouldn't be an issue, but it will take a fair amount of my focus while we travel.

"So what can we expect from El?" Grímr asks as we move out together. Our team is together, and Ankor is somehow keeping up with some odd back-and-forth motion of his chain weapons. Can he alter the weights of his chains and weapons? It'd be the only way I could think of that would allow such movement.

"She's a skank. A genuine pleasure," Ankor says without hesitation. "But she's also my wife, so say nothing bad about her."

"Uh . . ." Grímr hesitates. "That's good to know, but I meant how does she fight?"

Ankor gives us a side-eye glance. "You know I'm not supposed to say, right?"

"Should I, then?" Remus asks.

"No, no." Ankor waves him off. "I'm surprised you haven't already."

Before they can continue their talk about this El person, a major reaction occurs from my inscription. The directing flame all but snuffs out. With my direct connection, I can feel what minimal remains of the tracer suddenly switch, going from east to west. It's as if Kalma's energy simply disappeared from the world, only to appear again somewhere completely different.

The brightness of the guiding flare doesn't return, and yet I feel as though Kalma is closer than she was before. Is she suppressing her energy now? She can't have noticed us tracking her, right?

"Hey," I say. "We have a problem."

Remus's eyes swivel to me through his body. Immediately, he seems to have guessed what is happening. "Cut the tracker. Now. Ankor, I'll need you to be ready."

The khirig simply nods, but doesn't make any motion to prepare.

I can feel Kalma clearly through the inscription now. She's closing in. I extinguish my flames, which disperses the decaying energy, but before the hyle is completely gone, Ankor flings his chains outward.

A web of chains forms in the air with an unbelievable amount of skill, and yet it's not enough to stop the wave of decay. Many of the chain links simply disappear. The same glowing metal that could stand up to the superior Viisin's power without issue.

The wave continues unabated, eating away much of Ankor's antlers and leaving many of the remaining chains smoking. The dust that rises from the decayed weapons suddenly rematerializes above our heads. We have no time to react as a wide plate of the same metal that once made Ankor's chains now falls on us from above.

I try to burn through the large metal disc, but even my hottest flames are slow to melt through. The plate of metal slams into all of us, dragging us down to the earth. I try to burn the metal and breach the top, but the ground reaches us far too soon.

We hit the ground so hard it stuns me, but it doesn't take longer than a moment to recover. Ankor, despite having lost many of the antlers covering one side of his body, recovers quicker, and is already in the motion of tossing the heavy metal away from us.

My team is relatively unharmed by the fall. The earth itself seems to have come out in far worse shape after having Grímr collide with it.

"Okay, it was entertaining while it lasted." Kalma walks up to us with a casual air that belies her words. "But this has become annoying."

CHAPTER SIXTY

Failure

Tracking me? Seriously? I thought you would have learned your lesson after last time." Kalma's presence washes over us, freezing my body in fear. No longer is it suppressed. She lets the pressure crush down on each of us as she closes the distance with casual steps. "I do not like people getting in my way."

The air weighs down on me with a heft I cannot fight. Unlike every other time I've seen her, Kalma does not have the same air of amusement. She doesn't yell, nor does she glare, but her blank face makes me more nervous than when she'd grin with viciousness.

I let my body revert to normal, an effort to fight off the crushing weight of her presence. Whether it works is difficult to tell, but at least I'll have two feet under me.

From the corner of my eye, Ankor moves. That he's able to push through this pressure is encouraging. With a motion of his antlers, Ankor sends innumerable chains flying. Many blast right toward Kalma, while others curve around to entrap her.

The khirig has no issue surpassing the body-halting, instinctual fear Kalma inflicts around her. Maybe he really will put up a fight. Hopefully long enough to let us run and find other Inner Circle mercenaries.

Kalma doesn't even acknowledge the powerful warrior. She continues her casual steps as the chains and their linked weapons tear through the air on their path toward her.

Without a motion to defend herself, the chains collide against her tough gray skin, only to collapse into dust. Despite what must be tons slamming into her, Kalma's steps go uninterrupted.

Ankor grunts at the failure of his attack and dashes forward. A deep glow appears over his antlers. The glow of markings that I hadn't seen until now. His antlers extend, creating chains of the same bone-like growths that are on his body. These new antler chains grow quickly and slam to the earth, leaving craters where they land. He dashes forward, his body spinning to launch a volley of these new, heavier antler chains.

Kalma still refuses to turn her head. One of her two tails lifts and flicks his way. A ripple explodes out from the appendage, air deteriorates as the attack overcomes Ankor in an instant. The khirig cannot dodge.

Nothing remains.

The air quickly clears of dust, but nothing remains in the path of her blast. I stare at the last place I saw Ankor, but he no longer exists, and neither does much of the earth that was behind him. The curve in the ground only grows the further it is from us, and now holds nothing but the dust remnants of what once was.

As I watch on, the dust gradually reverts to soil and stone within the void it was taken from. Even water fills in the space, recreated from a lake that was wiped from existence with her attack. None of the elements are returned to their original position, left to fight for dominance as they fall into the carved depression.

The only thing that doesn't reappear is Ankor.

"I see you were able to convince your little group that it wasn't you who burned down the city." Kalma ignores the rumbling of the earth as the recovered elements crash into the new valley as an enormous mudslide. Her large, impassive eyes focus on Remus. "I probably should have killed you back then to make sure the little áed knew not to make the same mistake twice."

Kalma turns to me, her gaze penetrating. I'd love to fight back, to burn her where she stands, but what can I do? I already know my fires aren't enough to hurt her and the attempt will just get us killed. Like Ankor.

Kalma opens her mouth to say something, but she's interrupted by Grímr. "You don't really think you can take on all the Inner Circle alone, do you?" he grinds out, anger lacing his words. "You have made your abilities more than clear for all. They'll have counters for you before the day is out."

Kalma laughs, a single huff before she breaks down in snorts and chuckles. Amusement trickles back into her voice. "Sorry. Sorry. I don't mean to laugh at your confidence, but I don't think you understand the scope of difference at play. Regardless, I don't plan to let them find me. It wouldn't be fun if I had to do the fighting myself."

Her eyes widen slightly as she stares at Grímr. "I recognize you. I'd assumed you died after the damage you took from one of my Viisin," Kalma says. "Huh, you're quite the unique creature. You control that body like a puppet. No wonder you survived. If you were a sapient alicanto, as was my guess, there's not a chance you would have lived."

"I guess you deserve a punishment as well." Kalma turns her attention back to me. "We have to make it fair after all. Oh, I might as well double it up; this one's punishment was nowhere near as effective as I'd hoped."

Kalma pulls the riparian's treasured orb into existence. "So, what do you say to finding your end at the flames of your collaborator?" She holds the orb out in front of her, as if inviting me to take it, her toothy grin back in place. "Go on, burn me. I know you want to."

My flames churn and fists clench. I want nothing more than to do exactly as she says and scorch her from existence, but to do so would achieve nothing but the deaths of Remus and Jav. I turn to the three, trying to find some answer to the situation.

Remus flings Jav through the air, the volan hundreds of meters away before the dohrni can shout. "Solvei, run!" At the same time, Grímr rushes Kalma.

A metal boulder crushes Grímr's beak into the earth, halting his short charge. Jav hasn't made it far either. His artificial wings collapse into dust and he falls to the earth with the entire momentum of Remus's throw. The dohrni himself now finds himself in a cage of metal. Clearly the same material as the Ankor's chains, there's no chance of escape.

What were we thinking, really? I've seen Kalma. I knew no matter how strong the Inner Circle mages, no amount of them would be enough to compete with Kalma. Even still, I let this whole situation occur. If I'd simply refused and dragged my friends away from the war, we might have gotten away safely. The pact nations would be destroyed, and I would likely lose the trust of my team, but those close to me would be safe.

Was it wrong to consider their opinions? Should I have just continued to prioritize myself and those I want to keep alive, regardless of the countless others that will die because I chose to run? Maybe things would have turned out better for us if I had acted on my selfish impulses, but I already know they wouldn't forgive me.

If I were to force my team into safety, if I were to take all my friends and run off somewhere safe and leave these lands to die, they won't forgive me. It would not differ from my team's betrayal of dragging me down into the Alps without my consent. No, it would be worse; there's no way to bring back the lives of those my friends care for. No way to repent for the deaths that would have been prevented.

There's not a chance they'd forgive me.

What I've done is the right thing, no matter how much I dislike it and no matter how terrible the situation has become. I don't regret working alongside my team to attempt to fix things, even if the chance we had to see this to the end has been ripped from us.

We might have lost, but the last thing I want to do is give Kalma what she wants. I won't power that orb so she can kill my team.

I glare up at the tyrant still holding the orb between us. "No." I need no more words to make my intention clear.

"Are you sure?" Her grin grows. "At least with your flames, their deaths will be quick. I can assure you, decay is a far more painful way to go."

I'm sure that will be the case, but death is death. If we are to go, then I will keep this slight against her. No matter how inconsequential my defiance, she won't get her way.

"If that's how you want to be." Kalma tosses the sphere into the air before catching it. "I was hoping you'd give me some more amusement, but I guess I'll have to settle for killing them myself." She tosses the orb again, catching it without looking.

Helplessness overwhelms me as she turns to Remus and Grímr. Thankfully, Jav is a fair way away, but I doubt that'll pose an issue for Kalma. There's nothing I can do. The only form of attack I have will simply power that orb and allow her to kill my team with my flames. If only I had some other method. Another avenue I could use to threaten her that wouldn't leave my friends as cinders.

Kalma lobs the orb once more, higher than before. The glowing inscriptions layering its surface spin as it curves through the air. Lines weave to the surface and back to its interior in a way that goes against what I've learned of inscriptions. Components exist in portions; something that should break the design, but clearly still works as intended.

The sphere falls, and even with my limited knowledge, I can grasp at why this is considered a treasure. The implementation is not something replaceable. Only a true master of the practice could hope to replicate it. The effect it creates isn't what makes it special, it's the application of an inscription in a volume rather than on a flat plane that places this so far beyond the two inscriptions I know. It is a three-dimensional design. Not even those of two dimensions folded and bent could come close to this complexity.

The orb hits the ground.

Huh?

A sudden blast knocks me clean off my feet and sends me flying a dozen meters before I crash on my back. The sound of the bang that follows is so intense my ears momentarily dematerialize.

I scramble with the earth as I roll backward, trying to halt my movement. After a few moments, I finally come to a stop. The orb lies on the earth, forgotten. Kalma is nowhere to be seen. What stands in her place is both as shocking as it is intimidating and a grin crawls across my face, along with a series of relieved, nervous giggles.

Tore stands with an outstretched fist. His massive, bulky figure is an incredibly awe inducing sight. Slowly, he lowers his hand, his attention far in the distance. His other hand grasps the enormous sword strapped to his back and pulls it free.

I can feel Tore's presence. No longer is it suppressed as per usual, and I shudder at the intensity of it. I'd never really considered how tight of a hold he might keep on it. Even when I approached him to gain his help, I didn't think he could come close to Kalma, but this feels equivalent to hers. I'm crushed under the weight, but it doesn't feel hostile nor does it eat away at me from the inside.

I follow Tore's gaze to the horizon, where much of the loose earth from Kalma's earlier attack has blown outward. A sky filled with shrapnel rains down on any soul unfortunate enough to be in range.

Tore lifts his blade and swings at nothing. Or at least what I thought was nothing. A small gray blob—too fast to see clearly—slams into the length of steel and rockets back the way it came. The earth rumbles as it smashes through the rubble once more. The blob bounces a few times, spraying mountains of stone through the air with each impact.

Tore inspects his blade and grunts in annoyance. On the otherwise sharp edge, a chunk of the sword is now gone. He reattaches the blade to his back and clenches his fists.

The gray blob returns, this time moving slow enough to see. It takes way too long to recognize Kalma, but her identity is clear when she slows to a stop only a dozen meters away from Tore.

The giant ursu stands ready with his fists tensed by his side. Neither attack immediately. They simply stare each other down. Their presences fight for supremacy, but I quickly feel Tore's cover me completely, holding back Kalma's. My own cannot compete with either.

Kalma is the first to break the silence. "Another corrupted by the Anatla, huh? And how many years have you let the Void's influence go uncontested?" Her eyes move to me, but I can tell she doesn't take her attention away from Tore. "One is already too many. Looks like I'm not the only one who's become complacent in their role with the coming Armageddon."

"Abandon these lands, and do not return." Tore's words thump through my chest with the intensity of an earthquake. It is clear he is not messing around.

Kalma laughs. "And give up the fun? No. We only have a short time left and I'm going to enjoy it."

Kalma's pressure explodes, overpowering Tore's. It floods my body with the feeling of being torn apart and forced back together in a vicious cycle. She grins and flicks a tail. The same blast that killed an Inner Circle mercenary in an instant rockets toward Tore, who doesn't yet know how devastating it can be.

CHAPTER SIXTY-ONE

Culmination

The wave of decaying air slams into Tore. His raised arms take the brunt of the blow, but his body is still encompassed by Kalma's all-consuming power.

Even as the blast continues on to destroy much of the land behind him, Tore stands tall, hardly affected by the decay effect which ended Ankor's life in an instant. A thin powdered dust wafts off his heavy arms, but he remains whole.

Kalma stands with wide eyes. Her grin stripped clean off her face. She bares her teeth and takes a step back, flicking both tails forward. The air around each ripples as two new waves of power shoot forward, combining their strength on their path toward Tore.

The giant ursu doesn't stand to take it again. He pivots to the side before rushing forward with speed that should be impossible for one so massive. It's hard to even focus on his movements with how fast he bursts forth, but somehow, I manage.

Tore punches away from me, yet the crushing power still sends a wave of pressure through my chest. Kalma barely dodges. Her jaw clenches as a hurried step takes her out of the path of the fist thicker than her torso.

Unfortunately for her, she cannot avoid the second attack. Tore's other fist collects her square in the face. Kalma's head gives no resistance. It annihilates as her body rips through the air, leaving only a booming crack of thunder in her wake. Tore doesn't wait around; he bounds after her already distant figure. She can't even hit the ground before he slams into her again, sending her crashing into the earth with even more force.

The world groans in complaint. Wind whips around us as the earth shakes beneath my feet.

I snap myself from my stupor and rush to Remus's side. The strange metal cage pins him tightly to the earth. My flames are quick to engulf it. I should be able to free him from his cage, but even with my candescent flame, the metal is resistant, so it won't be quick.

Grímr has already dug himself out of the earth, the metal boulder pinning him having already been tossed to the side.

"Grímr. Can you find Jav?" I say.

The portian stares toward the battle in the distance, each blow shared bounds through the distance like they occur right next to us. It's hard enough for me to stand upright with the amount of wind that blows through me with each thunderous explosion, so I can't imagine what it would be like for the tiny volan. Grímr doesn't reply, but does as asked. He flies toward where Jav crashed, sticking low to the ground and keeping an eye on the duo of incomprehensibly strong beings.

I turn to watch, only to see Tore barreling through the air. Smoke rolls off his body; the familiar sign of decay. Despite his initial success at blocking her attack, it seems he's not completely immune to the effect of her power. Tore lands on his feet near a thousand meters away, the impact flattening the surrounding earth. Before he can launch himself after Kalma again, she appears above.

Kalma curls into a tight ball and spins in place, gaining speed with each rotation. At once, she unwinds. Her tails flick out, augmented by the angular momentum and disintegrate as they fire off a wave of power. The tails recover quickly, but the same cannot be said for anything else in her path.

The blast slams over Tore, encapsulating the ursu in a cone of Kalma's power. He doesn't remain in sight long; the ground beneath him vanishing. A jolt runs through the earth beneath my feet as Tore leaps out of the hole. He collides with Kalma, sending her flying over Remus's and my heads. Tore himself has a dangerous amount of dust falling off him. It clears enough for bloody gashes over much of his upper body to become visible.

A tremor runs through me as Kalma impacts the ground, but it doesn't calm after a moment. Instead, the quaking beneath my feet only grows. I grab a hold of Remus's cage—which I've almost melted through—and hold tight as the earth continues its shuddering.

Despite my grip, a sudden feeling of weightlessness overcomes me. It only lasts a moment before the opposite happens and I feel crushed. A thunderous rumble overwhelms everything as the ground beneath me slants. The very earth itself tilts toward the hole Kalma made.

Looking around, I see we are now within a depression. Thousands of meters of earth now slide toward a central pit of vacant earth. I only keep my feet because of the training Bunny encouraged me to do whenever I could . . . and the metal bars holding Remus down.

I need to hurry and melt the metal. Kalma's attack must have wiped out an immense amount of stone beneath our feet. It's like experiencing the Titan all over again; nowhere I stand is safe. Each second I take, the faster our foothold falls, and the closer we are to being buried alive.

Movement catches my eye, and I watch as the inscription orb rolls past us, speeding up as the new slope continues to become more steep. Acting on impulse, I send out a rope of fire to catch it, and pull it into my hands. Some of my white blaze swirls into orbit around the orb, but Kalma doesn't control the sphere this time, so I can take my flames back with ease.

We can't stay here. The fight between these two monsters is tearing the world apart. All it will take is a stray attack, or simply the secondary effects those attacks inflict on the surroundings, and we'll be dead.

I can no longer see Grímr past the border of our sloped earth. All I can do is hope he and Jav are fine. For now, there's nothing I should focus on other than freeing Remus and getting us to safety . . . well, somewhere that isn't sliding into a pit who knows how deep.

Through the continual rumbling of the earth, a single clap reverberates. The sound clear. A gray mist spreads out, blanketing the sky as far as I can see. Thin dust particles fall around us. At first, nothing seems to happen, but as time goes on, a pricking sensation appears and intensifies into an all-encompassing pain.

I'm not the only one to feel it, either. Remus is good at hiding his pain, but his outer membrane is clearly dissolving. Both the air and rock around us experience the same. Whatever Kalma has done, it has covered a wide-spanning area in her decay. This can't be an attack on Tore; it would be pointless with the resistance he's shown. Is she really that spiteful that she would attempt to kill my team even while preoccupied with Tore?

I need to get Remus out. The metal restraints are so close to melting, but I don't know if I can free him before the decay grows any more intense. My flames spread over his body to protect him, but that only gives the decay more area to eat into my flames.

Each second I spend burning into the metal, the pain through my flames only grows more agonizing. I can stand it when fighting the Viisin because I only need to handle the pain for an instant before they're dead, but this is different. Constant. Deeper.

In a moment of weakness, I transition my flames into ethereal. The relief is immediate, but I fully expect the decay to breach through and take hold on Remus, so despite how difficult it is to do so, I gather myself and return my flames.

The pain that comes is somehow worse after my short break, but strangely, Remus's skin is no more damaged after I let him take the brunt of the decay.

Is it possible that my incorporeal flames still stop the decay even though they don't interact? I really want to let go again, and see if it's possible, but testing on Remus is not something I want to do.

While I continue to burn away the last of the metal clamping down on Remus, I convert only the flames around my body to their ethereal state, and am delighted to find I barely feel the effect of decay.

Immediately, the both of us are encapsulated in my nonphysical fire. Free from the agony of Kalma's power, I can finish cutting through the binding metal. Before I completely sever it, Remus flexes, snapping the red-hot material.

Not waiting a second, I cling to the dohrni's head and jet us out of the massive sinking pit. We still had a bit of time until the land we were stuck on would crash any further down, but there's something far more important on my mind.

"We need to get to Grímr and Jav, now!"

Remus, to his credit, is quick on the uptake. With the added thrust from my flames, he's able to skip us along the ground in the right direction.

The smoking form of Grímr is unmissable, curled up as he is. His inscriptions glow bright through the dust, but it is clear his body is suffering from the effects. Long before we reach them, my flames have already crossed the distance, covering the alicanto body in my protection.

As my fire spreads over his body, I find Jav pressed tight beneath Grímr. The volan is mostly unharmed by the decay, but he is not without injury. A massive gash runs along his arms and chest, likely from the horrid crash he endured.

Before Remus and I can reach them, a sudden explosion of air blows us back. Tore crashes between us, his massive legs lodged within the earth with a fissure newly torn across the surface. The crevice travels almost perfectly perpendicular to the location of my team.

I catch Tore glancing our way before returning his sight above. The earth didn't crater as it typically has upon his landings. Can he control the effect he has on the environment? Did he land the way he did so we wouldn't be hurt?

I don't even see where she comes from, but in the time it takes to blink, Kalma crashes into Tore. The ursu grapples her with a death grip, but the disproportionate size makes her look like a toy in his grasp. Kalma stands not even a quarter of his height.

Kalma grins down at Tore, whose hands smoke simply holding her. "So? Not going to attack? Worried about the little ones?" Her gaze moves first to Grímr and Jav, before pivoting to me and Remus.

Kalma's tails lift as she returns her gaze to Tore. Her smirk only widens. Suddenly, I feel we are in a terrible amount of danger. Tore seems to think the same.

Before she can act, Tore lifts her above him in one hand and pulls back his other. His fist moves too fast to see, but we feel its effects. The shockwave knocks us off our feet and the ground flattens around him.

It is clear from Kalma's disappearance that he just pelted her far into the sky.

Above, a tiny speck disappears amongst the blue midday sky. Kalma has gone too high to see. I look around, expecting her to reappear at any moment, but she doesn't. Instead, the sky above darkens. Where Kalma disappeared, the starry night returns, but it is far from natural. The night spreads across the blue sky like a growth of rot. Millions of tendrils reach out to cover ever more of the sky.

The growth-like night eventually slows to a crawl with a quarter of the sky overhead consumed, but not before piercing the Eternal Inferno. A single rotten tendril removes all light from the tiny section it covers, cutting the sun in half.

I can hardly believe what I'm seeing. There's no way Kalma could compete with the Eternal Inferno. It is impossible. The uncaring entity should be so far beyond anything else to be damaged by even one as strong as Kalma. Whatever this darkness is, it definitely isn't Kalma.

"You four need to run," Tore says, not taking his eyes from above.

"Are you insane!" Kalma's voice cracks through the air like thunder as she barrels down through the air.

Tore leaps to intercept her, knocking her away before she can bring the fight close to my team again.

"Are you trying to doom your people even before the barrier collapses?" Kalma's voice is clear despite the distance.

While amid her brawl, she shoots worried glances to the new dark patch of sky. To hear her panicking is music to my ears, even if the words themselves concern me. I peer up at the darkness now settled in place above. What exactly is it? What has her so terrified?

I'm pretty sure it's not the Void Fog. It doesn't move the same way, and this darkness shows the stars of night, not a pure black.

Whatever it is, it has sent Kalma over the edge in fury. Tore can hardly keep up anymore; her power overwhelms him each time he tries to attack. His thick hide peels in places and blood flows from numerous lesions.

If nothing changes soon, I fear for Tore. He's our best hope, and if he can't beat Kalma, then what chance does anyone else have?

The feel of smooth metal reminds me of the orb I still hold. I should really take my team and run. The longer we wait around, the more likely we'll fall victim to either Kalma's stray attacks or the crumbling landscape.

But what would that achieve? We would only delay the inevitable. Kalma has already shown she's no longer remaining passive. Should we run, Kalma will hunt us down as soon as she's done with Tore.

No. I need to stay. It might have a slim chance of success, but if I can support Tore, then it will be worth the risk.

I step away from Remus, leaving my flames shrouding both him and the others.

"Solvei?" Remus grabs my arm with one of his tentacles. "Don't. They are beyond us."

I look down at his limb holding me back, curious how it no longer sends my flames roiling in revulsion. Remus seems to misunderstand my gaze and snaps his tentacle away.

"Tore cannot win if this continues." I look him in the eyes. "I have a plan. Please trust me."

Remus is silent for a long moment before letting out a frustrated sigh. "Be careful," is all he says.

I nod and turn away, leaving him to take care of Grímr and Jav. My flames should stick to them and keep them safe from the decay, but they should really get out of the area while they can.

Kalma and Tore continue their fight, uncaring to the damage they inflict upon the world. The sky above remains blemished with night rotting away daylight.

I've resolved myself. Either this works and I'll give Tore a fighting chance, or I'll die.

Let's hope I'm lucky.

CHAPTER SIXTY-TWO

Molten Earth

'd love to say I've thought this through, but the truth is my *plan* isn't so much a plan as it is an idea. An idea that might be impossible to attempt while Kalma and Tore knock each other across the land.

There's no point in chasing them; I'll never keep up. So I settle with putting distance between myself and my team and hope for an opportunity to present itself.

The battlefield hardly looked like anything but a muddy wasteland even before the duo began their fight, but now it doesn't even look real. All flora had long since been wiped clear by artillery bombardment, leaving pockmarked land. Despite the damage, the hilly terrain remained the same. Now? The landscape has been flipped upside down. It's impossible to imagine what it might have looked like before.

The earth is carved away in unnaturally smooth valleys and pits, between them are craters and fissures. The ground shakes beneath my feet, and I watch on as the land Remus and I were stuck on finally crumbles into the pit.

Despite the initial attack only creating an opening a few dozen meters wide, the amount of land that has fallen has to be near five kilometers across. The depression in the earth takes up all my vision to the south. Just what is the limit to Kalma's decay? The sinkhole is hardly shallow, nearly as deep as it is wide, and the earth only continues to crumble.

None of her other attacks have been near as damaging as the one that caused this void in the earth, so we can probably be glad she hasn't used it more than the once.

Tore's giant body flies over my head, pelting me with a wake of intense wind before he lands in the deep hole. I realize too late where exactly that puts me; right between Kalma and her target. The wave of decay brushes past me before I can even turn to look.

Her power breaks through the yellow ethereal flames I have shrouded around myself without resistance, removing them from existence. Not a single step away, the earth has evaporated. The new valley cuts down into the pit. Any closer, and I would be dead.

I gulp, both from the immensely close call, and the knowledge that my less intense ethereal flames won't protect me from an actual attack from Kalma. Of course, it was too much to hope, but I hoped, regardless.

Tore leaps out of the sinkhole, passing me and blowing away the thick layer of dust. The ursu grapples Kalma, but his fingers just pass through without resistance, her body dispersing in dust before reforming behind each digit. Tore's momentum keeps him shooting through the air, but he's able to swing an arm around for a backhand swat that sends Kalma crashing to the earth.

Without leaving the surface, Tore rushes Kalma. Rather than climbing out of the hole Tore's strike buried her within, she simply appears out of the nearby dust. Casually, she watches the incoming giant. Each step brings him hundreds of meters closer.

Like what Kalma did with the metal before, she creates a cage of stone around the ursu in mid-sprint. The rock blows away as easily as air, but Kalma has already dissolved to dust. Tore stops, looking around for her.

When I spot her, I know it's now or never.

She materializes from the dust a hundred meters above. Her body defies gravity as she spins. Slow for now, but if I don't act immediately, it'll be too late.

I don't hesitate. The inscription orb rockets forward, pushed by as much physical flame as I can output at once. Any of my fire that gets caught in the blast is without doubt going to be obliterated, but I can't afford to not put in everything.

The orb carries through the air between Kalma and Tore just as she unleashes that massive conical blast of decay down on his head. I expected it, but the pain of losing so much inner flame at once is excruciating.

But . . . it works. The orb sucks in much of Kalma's decay wave, and my white flames come out in its stead. The world bathes in fire.

The flames continue downward with the same speed as Kalma's blast, vaporizing stone as it descends thousands of meters beneath the earth's surface. I can feel them all, and it's euphoric. The immense power flowing through these flames is unbelievable. Far too much for me to absorb. Thankfully, I don't need to; I only need them for this fight.

"What are you doing?" Kalma's irritated voice reaches me. "You think this will help you?"

I feel the flames move against my will. Kalma pulls my fire up through the earth, bubbling away rock and stone as white flames rise to the surface. It is still Kalma's energy powering the blaze, so of course she has some control over them.

But I'm an áed. Not even Kalma can strip me of my connection to fire.

I spread every sliver of focus I can into the flames, and tear back control. She fights me, not wanting to admit defeat to someone so obviously lesser to her, but it's a losing battle.

The ground melts around us. My feet sink. A wide pool of lava forms over the surface, growing hotter each moment she resists. Molten rock flows along the misshapen landscape, creating glowing rivers that fill into both the sinkhole and the new pit created with a mix of my flames and Kalma's energy.

I know I've won when she resorts to inflicting decay through my fire. She intends to do the same as when we first met, inflicting pain so I give up without resistance. But that won't work this time. Before she can eat through even a portion of my blaze, I force every last bit of it to transition to ethereal. Suddenly, her basic decay has no effect on me.

Kalma shouts in rage. A tail flicks a wave of power through my flames, but even that hardly affects me. I nudge my fire, and it needs no prompting to explode. The white flames, as compressed as they already are, experience an immense pressure deep beneath the earth. A mighty column shoots into the air through the narrow hole in the earth, overwhelming Kalma in an instant.

Fire spreads from horizon to horizon, swathing everything in intense heat and scorching light. It is overwhelming to my senses. I can feel all that fall within the blaze. Remus, Jav, and Grímr stand in awe, my flames leaving only them unmarred by the heat. Even while ethereal, my flames are hot enough to melt anything they come across.

Well, everything besides Tore and Kalma.

I'll admit I relish in a bit of satisfaction upon feeling my team's gazes. But disappointingly, they snap themselves out of it and continue moving away. I shake my head. No, it's better they keep focused, as should I.

My body bathes in an intense blast of decay, but I remain mostly unharmed. I wasn't about to leave my form as the only section of my flame unchanged. I, too, have become as ethereal as I can push myself. The decay still affects me, unlike my inner flame, but it is hardly worth concern. My inner flame protects me.

Kalma is furious.

It's quite the contrary sight; no longer does she remain calm and aloof, laughing as others fight around her. Now, there's no sign of any humor in her eyes. They hold nothing but anger, and I couldn't be happier.

Her presence presses down on me, but it's all she can do. She glares, a terrifying sight on such a powerful creature . . . had her attack not just failed. I smirk. An action that might not be the smartest, as her eyes narrow dangerously.

Kalma spins in the air again, ready to unleash another blast, my way this time. I don't have the orb to convert her energy, and I know this attack is far stronger than her others, so even with the immaterial flame that makes my body, will I be okay? I don't know.

Thankfully, Kalma loses her opportunity. In her blind fixation on me, she completely ignores Tore. The ursu slams into her, ripping her out of her stationary position. In one smooth motion, Tore tears her chest from her lower torso.

He tosses her connected legs and tails far past the horizon, but holds what remains of her upper body tight. As he falls back to the earth, he throws her into the lava below. She doesn't have time to do much more than impact the surface before Tore's fist crashes down on her.

My flames permeate the lava, so I can feel intimately as the strength of his blow solidifies the molten rock, despite remaining far beyond its melting temperature. The solidified lava sinks, taking Kalma with it.

As much as I'd love to believe this is the end of her, I know that hope is too optimistic. Plus, I can already feel her decaying within the magma pit.

I jump on Tore's back, nestling myself beside his massive sword. The giant ursu's feet ever so slowly sink into the lava, but he doesn't pay it any mind. Tore's attention is instead on me. His head twisted back to look at me with a raised eyebrow that I just know he's asking, *What are you doing?*

"Ignore me and keep beating her up as you've been doing," I say, getting comfortable. "I'll protect you from her decay."

I'd prefer to sit back and let them fight it out without me, only shrouding Tore in protective flame from a distance, but even with this intense white firestorm that spreads as far as I can see, Kalma will simply take the fight elsewhere. By tying myself to Tore, I can make sure my flames follow and protect him no matter how far the battle takes us. Unfortunately, that means putting myself in the most dangerous position, but that's a risk I have to take.

As long as Kalma doesn't have any hidden attacks greater than that spin blast, I'll be fine.

Kalma walks out of thick dust layered air, completely unharmed, as if she was never wrenched in half. "You know, I would have been fine to leave you both to your fate, but waiting for the Anatla will be far too unsatisfying." Her eyes harden. "I really hate people getting in my way."

A blast of energy slams through us, my flames do their job and prevent the decay from eating into Tore. I peek over the ursu's shoulder, only to find Kalma missing. Another wave collides with us from behind. I turn to the source, but before I can, Kalma appears from dust off to the side. Her tails whip forward before her body disperses again.

Her pace picks up and soon she's teleporting around us and striking out a dozen times every second. It's an intense experience and even with the added protection from my flames, I still feel woozy.

What is Tore doing? He's simply standing here, taking the attacks head-on. I'm glad he's impressed by my ability to stop her decay, but I'd rather he didn't leave us in the epicenter of her attacks.

My body jerks upon Tore's sudden movement. Only with my flames engulfing everything do I know that we've crossed a hundred meters in an instant. Within Tore's clenched fist, is Kalma. Blood trickles from her eyes and the corner of her mouth. At least it does before she decays into nothing within his grasp.

Tore inspects his hands, covered in my flame and no more damaged than before. He hums in satisfaction, but not before we are hit with another of Kalma's attacks from above. The lava covered in white fire no longer dissolves, protected as it is.

Tore reaches his hand back over his shoulder, and I have to wonder if he's trying to grab me. His hand lands on the hilt of the blade he hasn't used since he showed up. Does he finally intend to use it?

"Keep the blaze dense. I care not for myself; prioritize my sword."

I do as he says and coat the blade with as dense a flame as I can manage as he pulls it from the straps on his back. With how far-spanning this Kalma-gifted inferno is, there's no need to worry about running out of energy to keep the ursu protected as well, so he gets just as dense a coating.

Belatedly, I realize Kalma hasn't reappeared in the past few seconds. Looking around, I can't miss the massive accumulation of dust in the air above. The sky, both the blue and the night, disappears behind a thick curtain as swathes of the decay remnants rise high.

At once, it all materializes. The thin light that broke through the thick dust no longer breaches; everything is shrouded in shadow. I'd realized it back when Kalma recreated the metal of Ankor's chains; she can recreate what she decays. Only I never thought she'd be able to do so on such a large scale.

Kalma has created a mountain to block out the sky.

Of course, there would be no point doing such a thing if it weren't intended to kill us. The mountain falls without delay. Long before it reaches my inferno, the bottom surface glows with heat as it gains speed.

It falls slowly, and although it is incredibly wide, I don't think we would have too much issue running out of the way, but I feel that leaving such an enormous mass to crash into the earth will be catastrophic. Tore holds his blade in front of him, the massive chunk of metal appearing far too small in his grip, and yet he still wields it in a way I can only describe as affectionately.

Looks like Tore is of the same mind; we need to destroy that before it hits the ground.

CHAPTER SIXTY-THREE

Epoch

Without a second's delay, Tore leaps into the air. The pressure slams through me at his sudden movement, and it's only due to the ethereal flame latching onto the hide of his upper shoulders that I stay with him.

Allowing my body to become this intangible has some strange effects. My fingers seem to phase through his fur, binding me in place the same way my inner flame could when burning inside those Viisin bodies. Unlike those Viisin, I'm unable to penetrate his skin. Only hairs allow me to hold on. Most likely, it's because of his overwhelming enhancement that I can't push my fingers into his flesh.

In this state, the air hardly bothers me; as we rocket into the air at insane speeds, it simply passes through me, but the force of Tore's jump still hits me with full force.

The ursu holds his sword over his shoulder as we rise well over a thousand meters to meet the mountain falling from above. The slab of steel feels slightly stronger than normal, but not by much. If I were to let my flames cook the metal, it would melt without issue. The missing edge from the beginning of his fight with Kalma makes it clear enough why he hasn't used his blade until now.

In no time, we reach the massive rock falling above. Tore swings down his blade, slicing through with ease. The impact sends a quake through the mountain, opening a large fissure along the path of his blade.

It's an immense, devastating attack that leaves a deep crevice in the mountain . . . but that's all it does. The rock doesn't break; it doesn't even come close to slowing it. At most, the strike is only good for sending us back to the earth. Despite all the power I know resting within those thick arms, the mountain remains unhalted.

His blade is nothing more than hardened steel, and yet Tore can still inflict such damage without the weapon breaking. With my flames interwoven through the metal, I can feel how, as he swings the sword, a strange densification occurs, enhancing the blade's hardness and strength for the brief time.

I guess even Tore relies on more than brute strength. Neither his body has markings nor does his sword have inscriptions, so I wonder how he achieves such a thing?

Tore bounds off the earth, sending us upward once more.

The falling mass hasn't moved far, but it is gaining speed. Wind whips around us. The air trying to flee out of the mountain's path. The lower surface has gone from glowing rock to near molten in the few seconds since it began falling. While my inferno spread across the earth is sweltering, it can hardly be giving off enough heat to burn rock from so far away.

As strange as the effect is, it makes for a great invitation for my fire. While Tore prepares to strike into the fissure, I carry the inferno behind me. I can't lift all of it at once. There are kilometers of it, far too much to control with haste, and especially not through the sky where there isn't anything but air to consume. So I use myself as a conduit. The fields of fire rush inward before blasting past me.

The wide fissure overflows with fire before Tore's blade gouges through the stone once more. His blow jerks us back downward, but it is enough. The fissure spreads through the mountain. My flames spread through the cracks as they spread with each quake.

The mountain splits.

But that doesn't really solve the problem.

A pillar carries my flame to the now two mountains in free fall. The semi-molten lower surface of both allow my flames to spread across them rapidly, and without delay, the immense rocks are set ablaze.

The surface of the fractured mountain is easy to spread across, but with ethereal flame I can push through the hard rock before it even melts. Though, piercing takes time. Time we don't have.

Considering the rate it's falling, we have a little over ten seconds before it hits the ground. Definitely not enough time for me to burn through. It's crazy I'm even able to cover such distance with my flames. Maybe I should thank Kalma for her donation? I'm sure she would take that well . . .

With his next blade swing, Tore sends us bounding between each rock. Each ricochet fractures the mass of stone slightly more, along with spreading them further apart. Soon, we have four, then eight masses falling in unison. It doesn't stop the threat they pose, but it makes it much easier for my fire to spread through.

Each surface exposed to air is already dripping with molten rock. If the mountains weren't falling, I'm sure the lava would be raining down on anything below. Actually, they hardly look like mountains anymore. The deeper my flames breach through the rock, the more the accumulation of stone appears like a flowing blob of magma.

Below, the ground is approaching far too rapidly. It has passed the halfway point in its fall, but that means we only have a few more seconds before impact. Tore shreds through the rock, making my time eating through it all far easier, but it will still be close.

For a moment, I lament the waste of resources. I'm consuming far more than I could ever need. It may be only rock, but with this immense quantity, even rock fills me beyond belief.

Through the gap in falling mountains, I can see the sky again. The rotten growth of night across the midday blue remains a blemish. But far overhead, barely visible on the border between day and night, is Kalma. She remains still. Floating in the air, eyes closed and hands hanging wide, Kalma breathes out and a shiver runs through me.

I pull all the flame I can around us, but that won't be enough. Tore doesn't seem to realize the danger we're in; he swings his sword at the mass of rock like the last twenty times, unaware of Kalma looming above.

The falling mountain wasn't her attack; it was a distraction.

When Tore's sword impacts the rock, I blast us with every fraction of flame it holds. I focus everything I have on converting the flame to physical and pushing us away. Tore's swing would have had us going toward the next rock to break, but I couldn't have him swinging again. My flames add to our speed, but push us away from any of the other mountains of stone.

Tore is heavy, but with such an immense blaze at my call, it is possible to accelerate us away. I have to pull every fire away from burning through the mountain to get us even the slightest bit further away.

A second passes with nothing happening and doubts enter my mind. We still haven't reached the end of the pieces of mountain, but because of my action, there's no chance we'll be able to stop it now. If Tore and I continued cutting and melting as we had, it would have been possible to stop it, but not anymore.

I calm my writhing flames. No. I trust my instincts on this. With no more hesitance, I thrust us as far away as I can before it's too late.

Tore was a man defined by respect. He dedicated his life to the leader whose wisdom, charisma, and drive were leagues beyond any that came after; the man he respected most.

Tore did not give respect freely, so it was no small feat that such a young child could gain it.

And it is only because of that respect that he did not strangle that young áed as they sped through the air.

Between the two of them, the destruction of the restructured earth above was possible, if not assured, but the girl ruined their chances. Did she not realize the potential damage the impact would cause? It was not the immediate damage that concerned Tore—on such a devastated battlefield, even if the blast was wide, the number of lives it would take would be minimal—no, it was what would come after that would kill the most.

Ash-filled skies would leave the land inhospitable. Tore knew better than anyone just how fragile the average life was. Such a massive disturbance in the earth would bleed smoke and ash into the sky for years, cutting all sunlight and sending the land into a long winter. Famine and disease would spread. Only those fortunate to flee would survive.

Tore was intimately familiar with how things would play out. He had lived it. The Titan Cipactlteteo, disturbed from its slumber, had toppled the island of Vetus's tallest mountain. Back then, he had been nothing more than a child. Now, he was the only ursu to have seen their homeland.

The áed, Solvei, as much as it is because of her he finally had the will to go against a legacy of Chairman Torben, has now doomed his people to a repeat of two and a half centuries ago.

At least, that's what he believed until everything behind them disappeared.

The mountain above and the earth below, Solvei's flames and the air itself; nothing remained. Not even a sound reached them until gale winds ripped into the absence of air.

Tore's eyes widened. He hadn't felt it coming. Each of his opponent's attacks always came with the slightest sensation before it hit that he had used to gauge the strength and distribute his defenses appropriately. But this attack had none of that. There was not even the slightest warning before it hit.

Tore glanced over his shoulder. How had she known?

A short gasp escaped Solvei, and Tore felt her grip tighten on the thick hide of his back. The flames that pushed them through the air were gone, so they plummeted with all the built-up speed Solvei had managed.

Tore landed as gently as he could after coming in so fast. But even as he slid through the dry earth like it was mud, the pressure wave that blasted through his back was too great to ignore; strong enough to burst the eardrum of any unenhanced.

Behind them, an explosion of glowing red ash shot outward. The peripheral of the falling mountain had been left untouched by Kalma's attack and impacted the earth with a force thankfully nowhere near what it could have been, but the damage had been done. Cinders and black dust rose high through the air.

"I'm sorry for doubting you," Tore said.

The young áed let out a nervous chuckle. "Don't worry, I doubted me too."

Tore lifted his weapon, the blaze burning across its edge the only reason he could use it. Now wasn't the time to deliberate over scars of his past. The ash may spread, but that was no reason to turn his eye from an opponent. It was a mistake that almost cost Tore not only his victory, but also the life of his charge.

A mistake he would not repeat.

Tore readjusted his grip, holding his sword wide before leaping through the air. No matter the danger that should face the world, he would not take his eyes from the threat before him.

Tore's opponent was strong, far greater than any other he'd fought, yet his carelessness nearly cost them. He had grown complacent. So many years had passed since his strength was last challenged. Kalma was a threat he could not ignore, not even for a second, and so he would treat her as such. It was time to end this.

Tore breached through the thick, hot ash and found himself over nothingness. For dozens of kilometers, there was no land below, only depths which ate all light that entered. All around the rim of this pit were sections of smoking earth crumbling into the darkness.

The flames around them spread wide, forming hundred-meter-wide wings that sped them toward Kalma. Much of the áed's inferno was obliterated alongside the falling mountain, but it seemed she still had enough under her command to lift Tore's immense weight.

Kalma didn't flick her tail, nor make any other clear actions to indicate an attack, but Tore felt it coming regardless. Solvei did too, as her flames lost their weight before the blast of decay overcame them. The impact passed without issue, and Tore felt the lift from the áed's flames return.

They rose toward Kalma. The being suspended high above unleashed an onslaught of decay, and Tore felt the flame around him switching states to push them closer with each window of opportunity.

Tore readied his blade to strike. Solvei had done her part masterfully, but it was time for him to do his.

He focused his presence and compressed it the moment before his blade pierced his opponent. It had been a long time since he learned that one's presence could be used for more than just intimidation. Mostly, Tore only used it to keep his sword from shattering under the force of his blows, but against Kalma, he needed to be more creative.

Tore thrust the blade through Kalma's chest. As her body decayed, he unleashed his presence upon her. His opponent's eyes widened in shock, clearly feeling the effect. She immediately stopped the decay, recovering the body she'd already melted away, but Tore's sword stayed lodged in her chest, from navel to the bottom of her neck and piercing out her back.

Kalma flailed, unable to escape because of Tore's pressure. She flung wave after wave of decay over them as they fell many thousands of meters, none penetrating the engulfing flames. Each opportunity given to her, Solvei applied thrust to their fall, accelerating them down faster.

The pillars of ash encircling them soon made way for cliff faces as they descended below what once was the surface. They fell, continuing to speed into the earth, but the ground never met them. The sky above shrunk until it was nothing more than a speck of light, and yet they still fell.

Tore held his blade tight and pressure tighter as his opponent's struggles only intensified. An entire minute passed before Tore caught sight of something below. In the near nonexistent light of this abyssal hole, Tore planted his foot on his opponent's torso before kicking away with all his capability and tearing his sword from the cavity in her chest.

Despite the power of his kick, and the sudden reverse thrust from his little passenger, Tore still hit the slanted surface with enough force to shatter his arm. The earth did not even budge under the excessive momentum he'd built up and so Tore rolled down the slope until he got his feet under him.

The injury was severe. The worst he'd had in a long time. But his primary sword arm was fine to continue the battle. Even now, he could feel Kalma fighting his pressure, trying to teleport away with hysterical urgency. The fall hadn't killed her, but she was weak; her attempts came nowhere close to breaking his hold. She lost her composure. Unless she regained it, she had no chance against his presence, and Tore wasn't about to let her regain it.

He charged forward, flaming sword slicing through her head. It regrew quickly, but her recovery was unstable. Slow. Her eyes narrowed and, expecting an attack, Tore twisted his blade, knocking his opponent into the air. He jumped forward, but the expected attack didn't come. Kalma, inexplicably terrified, canceled her attack.

Tore didn't question it. He simply swung his blade, slicing her from neck to tails. Each time his blade would connect, she would recover, but each recovery was slower than the last. All he needed to do was wear her down.

He soon found that whenever the smooth, sloped ground beneath his feet was in the path of her attack, she would pull back, unable to even make the attempt. Tore was quick to make use of this, keeping her above him. Not once did she stop trying to flee, but as the battle wore on, her focus only deteriorated.

Solvei's flames illuminated the dark pit. The ground was a perfectly flat surface set at a consistent angle that shone under the illumination, like an amber diamond. What was more strange about the bottom of this pit was the air itself. Tore couldn't see the walls despite the áed's bright light, but occasionally, from the corner of his eye, he was sure he saw something, only for it to disappear when he looked closely.

At one point, Tore swore he saw himself, a reflection bathed in the candescent glow. He would have assumed it was the flickering of Solvei's flames casting illusions if he weren't so sure of his sight.

"Bastards." Kalma coughed up blood. Healing even that was too much for her now. "Enjoy damnation. The Anatla won't be merciful to your souls."

Kalma let out a sound indistinguishable between a cough and a laugh before she made it clear she was preparing another attack. Tore didn't give her the chance. His blade thrust through her head and she toppled to the ground. Kalma bled out. She didn't decay, nor did she recover. Blood slid down the slope beneath her.

Kalma was dead.

CHAPTER SIXTY-FOUR

Deep

Kalma is dead.

There's no denying it. Her body lays headless and limp on the sloped amber ground. My flames crawl over her, and I don't feel any response. The natural heat of her body slowly leaves her.

I try to eat her, but even dead, my hottest flames cannot burn her flesh. Instead, I cast the inheritance ritual inscription above myself and Tore. I can't ignore my tribe's teachings. Especially when a body so nutrition rich like Kalma's is in question. Leaving her to rot would be a waste of unthinkable proportions.

I feel Tore's fingers wrap around my chest. I'm lifted off his back and placed on the ground before he walks out of the inscription's range. He doesn't want any? Well, I won't complain. More for me.

As soon as the ritual starts, I realize it's going to be a long time before I'll get through her. Even in death, Kalma doesn't want to be cooperative.

While her energy slowly flows into me, gradually enhancing my capacity with the lackluster efficiency of the ritual, I cast my gaze around the cavern we find ourselves in. I don't know whether to call it creepy or intriguing. My eyes tell me an incredibly different story than the flames spread throughout.

Visually, the space looks normal, if you ignore the strange illusions that appear any time you move. But to the touch of my flames, it's as if we've stepped into an entirely different world. Connected flames less than a meter apart are also somehow on opposite sides of me, separated by dozens of meters. Other instances will have my flames overlapping each other to my senses, but never touch.

I watch Tore carefully as he walks away. For the first twenty or thirty meters, nothing seems off, but beyond that, the strange visual inconsistencies grow. The air warps, making his body appear distorted with each sway and step. I send a wisp of fire toward him, but despite traveling in a straight line to my eyes, I can feel an almost constant change in its heading. It's impossible to pinpoint exactly where that wisp is even while looking at it directly.

Tore turns to the side and pivots, no longer walking directly away from me. In an instant, his body flattens, disappearing from sight. I keep my eyes toward the area I lost him, but he doesn't reappear. I send my wisp off its straight path as well, and like Tore, it leaves my sight.

My eyes land back on the barely processed body of Kalma. Should I leave her for now and chase after him? Through the brightness of my flames, the light coming from above looks like a tiny star in the distance. We fell a damn long way, so I'd rather not be stuck down here alone.

Tore makes his appearance again, walking through the flames behind me. I turn, and sure enough, he's there, just coming within range of my thermal sense.

The space here is strange. And only grows stranger by the second.

I fall to my back within the ritual. It's hard to imagine Kalma is actually dead. The amount of destruction she's caused upon the world has been immense. And for what? Some end of the world only she knew about?

Now that she's dead, I regret not asking about it. About what she knew of Eldest Ember. About anything, really. She left us with nothing but doubt of what's to come. Do we have any way of knowing she wasn't simply delusional?

Well, at least she won't be able to cause any more damage than she already has. We'll need to make our way back up to the surface soon, but for now, I just want to relish in the feeling of victory . . . and the growth provided by Kalma's corpse.

The flames I left attached to my team are well and truly out of my range now. I hadn't been paying them too much attention during the fight, but I hope they are okay. I want to make sure none of Kalma's attacks reached them.

I pass my hand over the smooth surface below me. It's warm to the touch. The amber earth does a good job of reflecting the heat of my flames, almost doubling the heat as I bathe in the flames I refuse to extinguish. As soon as they're gone, I won't be able to create them again. Though, with only air to consume, they'll run out of energy soon. The ground is impenetrable to my flames.

A heavy rumble echoes down from above, followed by a shower of dust. The rumbles only grow louder in the next few seconds. A thousand impacts blended into one continuous sound.

Are the falling mountains only now reaching us? The crunch of a stone slamming into the amber surface beside me is all the answer I need.

"We should make our way up." Tore beats me to it.

I reluctantly disperse my floating inscription and climb into Tore's offered hand. He lifts me to his shoulder before reaching down and picking up Kalma's corpse, tying her to his waist by her tails like one would game after a hunt. Tore favors his right hand, not using his left when it would have been easier.

Did he injure it during the fight? It must have been when we crash landed. Even incorporeal, and having the ursu take the brunt of the fall, that had hurt. I can't imagine what it might have been like for Tore.

I'd love to help him, but there's not much I can do. Tore shrugs off the injury as if it were nothing, and hopefully it is to him. Maybe if we meet Imiha, she can heal him? It'll be a long time before that, though.

Not only is the climb above us daunting, but we have no way of knowing what we might find once we reach the surface. I'd rather not join another battle once we return.

Tore leaps through the air, grabbing the wall as a large crash quakes below. Rock and gravel buries that strange amber surface once more. We can't stay down here any longer. There are people waiting for us above.

It took over an hour of climbing to breach the surface. With gravity working against us, the difference is staggering. Tore would leap up the wall with incredible speed, but the falling debris far too often slowed our progress. Most of the time, Tore would use the falling stone as a platform to jump higher, but a few times I had to thrust us into the wall for the giant to recover.

At one point, a mist beat down on my flames. The water thin enough to evaporate without too much issue. As we rose higher, the mist condensed into a waterfall, which was thankfully much easier to avoid. It was only when the sky was fully visible above that the source of the water was discovered; some underground stream that flowed into the voided space.

Tore crashed through the veil of smoke surrounding the immense pit and brought us in to land. Despite our success and escape, Tore's eyes linger on the rising ash above. It has spread far to the horizon now. Is he worried about it being the same as the decay dust Kalma created? Does he think it will reform like how she could with that massive mountain?

I go to say that it's just normal ash when I think of a better way to reassure him. The remaining white flames spread into the sky, eating away the pillars of ash rising from the impact ring before rising with the smoke and burning outward through the sky. It takes a while, but eventually the sky is clear again.

Tore glances over his shoulder, giving me a flat look. What? Should I not have burned it away?

The rotten growth of night in the sky remains unchanged after Tore threw Kalma too far to see. I noticed after that neither side tried to rise that high again.

"Hey, Tore? What is that?" I ask.

He follows my gaze. "I don't know."

He doesn't? Kalma acted like it should be common knowledge. "You think the sky will return to normal?"

"Eventually." Tore nods with a certainty that's strange for someone who doesn't know what the phenomena is. I guess those warnings to never fly too high weren't without basis.

I watch the strange sky for a while. "Why did you leave when you did?"

"My people were in danger," he answers simply.

"You know, she appeared almost as soon as you left. We could have fought her then."

Though we might have been able to fight her had Tore stayed, actually beating her was impossible. If I hadn't had the time to alter my flames to defend against her decay, we'd be dead and Kalma would be watching the fall of the pact nations right now.

Though if we'd killed her earlier, the damage would have been less severe. Ankor, alongside countless others, would still be alive.

"If you want to come with me and my team, we can take you somewhere to treat your arm," I offer. The first thing I want to do is meet with my team, then find out the state of the war, but helping Tore comes in a clean third place in my priorities.

Despite our success, he did leave it to the last possible moment to help.

"No, I should return to mine. There are those that still fight." He drops me beside him, then allows Kalma's corpse to fall unceremoniously to my feet. "I will be busy for a while, but New Vetus will welcome you. I'll assure it."

Tore doesn't wait around. He bounds across the land and is quickly out of sight. No time to celebrate then? Well, if he's this dedicated to the ursu, then I'm sure they'll prosper under his leadership. I'm relieved Leal won't have to suffer anymore.

Before I head off to find my team, I can't help but stare at the immense transformation that has overtaken the terrain during the battle. It's like a Titan went on a rampage. Only, if that were truly the case, how far-reaching would the effects be?

If there was to be a fight between Titans, then how could any unenhanced species survive?

"You knew a Riparian and never told me?" As soon as I hear the familiar voice carried on the wind, I pick up speed, throwing in a bit of thrust for the boost.

Standing amongst my team, along with a dozen other albanics, is Bunny. She has yet to notice me, so I take the opportunity. My wings clamp to my side and I barrel through the air into her back. She twists at the last moment, but too late. I slam into her, nearly knocking her off her feet.

It's been such a long time since I'd seen her. Even when I'd made it across the Alps, Bunny had already gone to Vanguard and stayed there for the entire duration of the war.

The unfamiliar albanics all wearing similar armor as Bunny panic. A few step forward to separate me from my team member, while the others ready their weapons. Bunny, on the other hand, seems to have finally noticed my scorching feathers, and while the white fire is definitely different from what she would remember, she is quick to recognize me.

"Solvei?"

She doesn't have her bag of weapons with her anymore. Instead, she carries only a long halberd that shines with the distinct glowing lines of an inscription. With the flat of the blade, she swats away two of her compatriots so she can pull me close while I slowly return to my normal form.

"I'm glad you're all right."

"How are you here? I thought you were stuck in the war against the Theocracy?" I ask as I fall to my feet. My changes have been getting much faster as of late.

"The cowards backed off after I killed one of their presbyters. It gave me the chance to return." Bunny's eyes land on the other albanics with their weapons still raised. "Oi! Drop them already!" she snaps.

Though they watch me closely, they do as she says.

"I had to fight through a horde of Viisin on the way here, but a short while back, they all dropped dead."

Oh? So there's no need to worry about the merminea invasion any longer. Without the decay powering them forward, they won't be able to compete against the pact nation's mercenaries.

"Kalma's gone then?" Grímr asks, stepping forward.

"Oh, yeah. That reminds me." I turn to the flame carrying her corpse behind me. "I haven't eaten much yet. Want to share?"

I'll never forget my team's expressions as the headless corpse landed before them.

Drinks

Remus and Grímr try to turn me down, saying I should have Kalma's energy for myself, but I won't have it. Bunny and Jav agree readily, but these two remain resistant, so I grab them with hands formed by physical flame and hold them to the ground while I begin the ritual. Of course, they could break out any time they want, but they admit defeat and allow me to share.

The group of albanics try to join in, but I hold them off with the threat of fire hot enough to melt skin should they come too close. I'll share with my friends, but not those I don't know.

Bunny simply grins at them, silently boasting as the similarly dressed men and women stare with apprehension at my flames and envy at the powerful corpse they'll miss out on.

"This will take a while, won't it, Solvy?" she asks, and I nod in return. "So I think you guys should head on home," she says to the group.

An albanic steps forward. "But Tetsu, we—"

"I've reunited with my team, so there should be no need to remain together, right?" she says. "And it looks like the pact won't need you, after all."

The man at the front sighs in defeat. "Understood. I'll be sure to let your uncle know you sent us away as soon as you could," he says before leading the group that continues to throw longing gazes toward the inheritance ritual.

Bunny's smile becomes strained, but she stands firm.

"So, that was quite the battle back there," Remus says, no longer being pinned by my flames. "What happened to Hund?"

"He was in a hurry to return to the ursu. It's a shame; I would have liked to introduce you all."

"Hund is near Kalma's strength, right?" Jav says. "Shouldn't we be worried about New Vetus's invasion if he's supporting them?"

"I don't think so." I incline my head, thinking about what the massive ursu might do when he reaches his kind. "Tore will make them retreat." Though whether they give up the land they've already acquired is another thing.

"Don't even worry about it, Jav, I'm sure we'll know about it soon enough if a problem arises," Remus says. "Besides, we have a little hero to celebrate."

Bunny hums in agreement. "I want to hear everything."

* * *

Hours later, we've still barely made a dent in Kalma's body, and yet the growth of my capacity has been immense. So much so that I can only imagine the benefit to my teammates' enhancement.

We spend most of the time sharing stories and relaxing. Relishing in relief and victory. The air over our group becomes rather somber when deaths are mentioned, but those moments are short-lived. Mostly by an intentional effort to keep the mood positive and joyous by those older than I.

Bunny tells of her battles against the Theocracy. Obviously embellished stories that have the rest of the team watching her with doubtful expressions. I still like them, though. The halberd she carries was apparently once her father's. A weapon created by Riparian craftsmen.

"That's right!" Bunny turns on Remus. "You knew a Riparian all this time and never told me? I've been trying to get my hands on their weapons for years now, and you know it."

"Solon only owed me one favor," Remus says. "I was only going to request his aid in an emergency." The dohrni turns to me. "On that, what happened to that treasure of his?"

I freeze, not wanting to admit I completely forgot about the orb until now. "Uh, either destroyed, or a couple hundred thousand meters underground." I try my best to look innocent, but I'm not sure if I succeed considering the look he's giving me.

"A couple hundred thousand?" he repeats slowly.

"Yeah . . . it was a pretty long fall."

"What about the sky?" Grímr interjects. "Do you know what caused that?"

I look up to where it should remain in the sky, but sunset has long since passed, so the sky has returned to consistency. Whether the rotten night will return in the morning, I don't know.

I know Grímr was there to see Kalma whacked into the air, so he must mean more specifically. "I don't know. Tore didn't either."

Turning my head to see if anyone else on my team knows what it is—specifically Remus—but none put forward any explanation.

"Do you think the Mercenary Order will still see me as an enemy?" I ask. Kalma's influence is revealed now, so I should get off without issue, right?

"That might take some time to get your traitor status removed. It'll probably be best you stay in hiding for a while until I can clear your name," Remus says.

"Oh." I drop my head in disappointment. "I'd been hoping to see my friends now that everything is over."

It's been what? A year? More? Since I last saw them. We left them back in Baansguard as I joined team Luis-Eight across the Alps. Long before the war started. Ever since my return, I've wanted to meet them again to make sure they're doing well, but the war kept me from doing so. I guess I'll have to wait a bit longer to see them.

"Though . . ." Remus continues. "The Mercenary Order will go through a period of major restructuring for the next few months. The response to this invasion has appalled the state leaders. They will be overseeing the reform after the official declaration of victory." Remus gives his signature mouthless smirk. "As long as nobody is given a reason to suspect anything out of the ordinary, just about anyone could travel freely in this confusion."

I jump to my feet, ready to rush off right now. If Remus has said it will be fine, then there should be no issues. I'll need to keep myself hidden as an albanic like I did when I first met them back in Zadok, but that's hardly difficult. I can even hide the flames in my bird form now, so flying there shouldn't be a problem either.

"Wait up, Solvei," Jav says. "You can't go yet; the war hasn't officially ended. Plus, you still need to celebrate with us." The little volan turns to Remus with a grin. "I know she's young, but what do you say to getting some alcohol in her?"

Remus smirks in return, clearly agreeing, but Grímr is of a different opinion.

"I don't think that's a good idea. What about the water content?"

"We've seen her burn through skin and blood," Bunny says. "Just get her strong spirits and she will be fine."

It took a while, but my team soon places a small glass with a clear liquid on the wooden counter before me. I stare at the liquid hesitantly. It looks far too much like water for me to be comfortable. The rest of my team watch on with expectant eyes, waiting for me to try it.

We sit in an empty bar deep within the formerly merminea-controlled land. There is plenty of damage to the front door, and all the food has been ransacked by the mermineae, but most of the bottles along the wall remain intact.

After Remus met with some people in the nearest lived-in city and sent many letters, we flew out over the now uninhabited land for some privacy while we celebrate. The mermineae have gone. Run back to the mountains after losing their strongest fighting force.

As much as Kalma abused them, it was her power they relied on against the greatest of threats. I think it would be good if they are given their space. Hopefully, the pact nations won't chase them down to slaughter all that remain.

"Go on, just a little taste," Jav encourages. "If it stings or you don't like it, you don't need to have any more." He takes his own glass, shows it to me, then downs the liquid in an instant.

Hesitantly, I lift the glass and take a sip. It doesn't sting at all. In fact, it burns with a rather pleasant heat in my mouth. My eyes drop to the rest of the liquid sitting in the tiny cup, now on fire. I'd been a bit too ready to vaporize it had it been similar to water.

I extinguish the flame and drink. It's not nearly as intense as that oil the centzon gave me, but it still gives a similar hot feeling as it slides down my throat. It flows more smoothly than the oil too, giving a strange experience of tasting the texture of a liquid without it hurting.

"Hey, this is actually pretty good," I say. "Are you sure there's water in this? I can't feel it at all."

"There is, but it's a tiny amount. Usually, one wouldn't drink such pure alcohol straight, but you are an exception. Any juice, sweeteners, or other compliments would only increase the percentage of water and take from the taste," Remus says. "Some dehydrated snacks could go well with the drink, but I don't have any on me."

I take the offered bottle and pour myself another glass. Grímr watches on from the side, crouched low to avoid scraping the roof, casting concerned glances my way. Bunny instead eyes me with anticipation, as if she's waiting for something. Remus simply smiles as his eyes follow my teammates.

They each have a drink of their own, looted from behind the bar counter. None share the same type that me and Jav are drinking. Now that I think about it, Jav hasn't had another after his first. I look down to my side and sure enough, his glass is still empty. So, of course, I fill it.

Jav stares at his drink. Then he tilts his head to me. His eyes waver, as if flickering in a hundred directions at once, undecided where they want to focus. Does he not want the drink? But it's so good?

Jav whimpers, grabs the glass, and swallows its contents in one gulp. He goes to slam the small cup back on the wooden counter, but misses. Nearly faster than I can observe, his tiny hands grab for the falling glass, only to fumble and miss a dozen times before he finally gets a hold of it with both hands.

Remus bursts out laughing and Bunny grins, though I'm not exactly sure why. Is dropping his glass that funny?

"Do you want more, Jav?" I ask, offering the bottle. He drank it so quick, he must love it.

Instead, he shakes his head with vigor. Well, if I'm the only one to drink it, then there's no point in pouring into my glass every time. I drink straight from the bottle. I don't incinerate it all immediately, so the burning liquid pools in my chest with a comfortable warmth. The unique flavor is like nothing else.

Bunny's gaze morphs into a mixture of confusion and growing worry as I down the entire bottle. Grímr looks like he just saw someone eaten alive. Both rise to their feet immediately, Grímr crashing the back of his head through the roof.

I simply watch them in confusion as Remus lets out another burst of laughter, chuckling as he relieves their concerns. "Sit down. Don't worry. Alcohol doesn't affect the áed the same way it does us. She can't get intoxicated." Remus turns to Jav. "She's not the one we should be worried about."

Almost as soon as he says it, I hear a thump beside me. On the floor, to my side, Jav has collapsed.

"He really should have known better." Remus shakes his head.

I drop to Jav's side and shake him. What's happened? He's still breathing, but he's passed out.

"Don't worry, Solvy," Bunny says as her hand lands on my back. "He just drank too much."

"Volans aren't good with alcohol. Jav will be fine because of his enhancement, but he should never have drunk such intense shots straight." Remus chuckles. "But he wanted to assure you it was safe to drink, and who are we to stop him?"

"He was already done after the first," Grímr grumbles, glaring at the hole in the roof. "Why'd he take the second?"

"Losing to a first-timer would be shameful." Bunny nods in understanding. "I was getting worried after her third glass, but I guess it doesn't really count when the first-timer can't even get tipsy."

I'm not really sure I understand the pitying gaze Bunny sends my way, but I'm glad I'm not affected the same way if it means I'd be on the ground beside Jav.

Remus wraps the volan in a tentacle before depositing him on top of his head. Jav seemingly finds the spot comfortable and curls up in his sleep.

As weird as the effects are on my teammate, the taste is too good to pass up. My bottle is empty, so I pull another off the shelf with a quick application of physical flame.

I spend the night celebrating with my team, drinking from glass, and looking forward to what is to come.

EPILOGUE

The east of the pact nations cannot support the influx of population in the long term. If not for particular clauses in the pact between nations, many people would have starved or gone without shelter. Well, more than what already has. Each city east of the Mercenary Order Headquarters now supports up to twice their original populous, and are eager to send them packing now that the war is over.

Unfortunately for the cities facing intense overpopulation, the first refugees they may send off are the skilled workers and laborers. The type of residents most important for reconstruction, but also the ones a nation would rather keep hold of.

I fly over the railway station as thousands board trains ready to return home for the arduous task of rebuilding what was lost. Unlike the past, I can land on the roof of a nearby building and not a soul will bat an eye. I can hide my flames just as easily as with my normal form when I am familiar with the shape I take. My falcon form is the only real alternative I can take for now, but that only means I need to become familiar with other physiques. Maybe a dohrni or volan body will be useful.

According to Remus, I don't have to worry about my friends being on this train. They'll be amongst the next wave in a week. Along with all the other apprentices and youth able to work.

After a brief glance over those boarding the heavy metal cylinder to confirm Remus's words, I take off again. It shouldn't be hard to find Ash and the others. The section of the city housing the majority of the refugees is the same everywhere; rushed, poor quality housing and tents with enough people walking around to make it look more like an ant mound.

It's not an ideal situation for anyone involved, but there's little one can do in a crisis. My only hope is my friends are in a better state than I found them under Mr. Marshall. I promised Remus I'd remain undiscovered, but if I find them mistreated again, I don't know if I'll be able to hold myself back.

I shake my head. No, I shouldn't even think that way. There are other ways to deal with situations than slaughter. Between Morne and the city Kalma burned, I've learned that resolving my problems with indiscriminate murder will only come back to bite me.

Maybe if I'd dealt with Mr. Marshall and his mill differently, Joiak would have been willing to ally immediately, and be ready for the invasion from New Vetus. In a very loose sense, I hold responsibility for the fall of Joiak and its people. I don't feel guilty, but it is rather unfortunate.

Then again, Joiak was a horrible nation, so I'm happy it's gone.

I circle above, scanning through the crowds in search of any familiar face. A nervous shiver runs through my wings. A lot has happened since our last meeting; I've catapulted in strength, the war has changed everyone's lives, and the Mercenary Order branded me a traitor. How far has word spread? Will my friends think differently of me when we meet?

Eventually, I find Ash. I almost don't recognize him at first; he's a lot taller than I remember. With a paper in hand, he rushes through the refugee district, which is surprisingly still better than the city I first found him. Without making my presence known, I follow him.

Ash leads me to an old stone building. Likely, it was once a theater or performance hall of some kind now repurposed to house hundreds. He walks through the front double doors, but there are far too many people walking around to fly in behind him without causing a ruckus.

I could try to change without being spotted, but as I look around, there isn't really anywhere nearby that would give me enough privacy. The moment my flames become visible, people will know I'm here. Really, this would be so much easier if any áed besides myself traveled outside the wastelands.

On the second floor of the building there are a few balconies. Even those are occupied. I can wait for someone to return inside and follow without being seen. If I can find a place inside to change, the merminea fur of my outfit will let me walk around without issue.

I land silently on the roof above a khirig who holds a burning stick to their mouth. She doesn't seem to be in any rush, and within a few seconds, I'm already getting impatient. The mix of crushed plant leaves burns far too slow. I'll be waiting ages if she only goes inside after burning through it all. So, there's only one thing I can do.

I give a little nudge to the cinders. In moments, the herbs incinerate. The khirig chokes, unleashing a chain of coughs as if she swallowed something nasty.

Oops.

Regardless, she stumbles her way back inside, unaware of the bird following through the open door behind her. The khirig wheezes and gasps, finally regaining her breath, but I've already moved on.

I land on a secluded ledge overlooking the main floor below. The hall is divided into countless sleeping quarters with cloth separators. Immediately, I spot my friends within their own division. Ash has already arrived amongst them, speaking animatedly while throwing the paper to the others.

For a moment, I simply watch. It's comforting to know nothing terrible happened since we last met.

A volan flies across the hall, from the balcony across from me to where I assume the front doorway is. Nobody pays them even a glance.

Right, if I'm quick, everyone will just assume I'm a volan.

Next thing I know, I'm landing on Leslie's shoulder. I'd thought Ash had grown tall, Leslie is another thing entirely. If she has more growth ahead of her, she might grow taller than Bunny when she's an adult.

I feel her flinch, then freeze under my taloned feet. The others stop their chatter and stare. I eye each of them for a few moments, locking eyes with Leslie for just that extra bit longer as she grows increasingly uncomfortable with me using her as a resting post.

Once they've had enough time to stew in confusion, I let out a laugh and wave a wing at them.

"Solvei?" Kerry is the first to realize.

"Hi," I say.

Before I can continue, I'm flipped from my perch. I squawk as Leslie pins me beneath her arm. "Fuck, girl, I thought I was about to lose an arm."

I struggle in her grip, trying my best not to revert to flames where those looking down from above could see me clearly.

"Hey! Let me go!"

"Why should I? I've got the 'traitor of the pact' right where I want her," Leslie says, then turns to show me off like a prize. "What do you think? Do you think she's got a bounty?"

"Leslie, that isn't something you should joke about," Ash says.

"Oh, loosen up. I'm just getting her back a little."

Leslie finally releases me, and I flip to land on my talons. I don't even need to see the tall girl to know she's disappointed I didn't fall head first.

"It's great to see you all again, but is there somewhere I can change without getting spotted?" I ask, motioning to the balconies able to look in on us.

The twins, quiet as ever, jump up. Demi tugs on a curtain, closing the pseudo entrance, while Medi grabs a sheet and ties it over our heads with ropes. The small space becomes closed off in a matter of seconds. It's clear they've done this plenty of times before.

Now obscured from any unwanted eyes, I let my form relax. White flame blinds each of my friends until the short, sub-minute transformation is complete. I'm sure I've grown plenty in the past year, but standing next to Ash and Leslie, it sure doesn't feel like it.

Before I can get right into asking how they've been, some albanic woman flips open the cloth divider. "What are you lot doing in here? What was that awful bright light?"

I guess the cloth wasn't enough to hide the glow of my body. Maybe I should've cooled to a yellow or red while changing. Eh, too late now. Thankfully, as this woman looks amongst us, her eyes don't immediately land on me, so she shouldn't have caught me as the source of light. When she isn't able to find anything out of the ordinary, she finally notices me amongst the other teenagers.

"Are you new? I don't think I've seen you before."

Kerry jumps in before I can say anything. "She's a friend from work."

"Right," the woman says as her eyes drift to my hair. Even outside Zadok and the Theocracy, my hair must stand out. "Well, don't do whatever you did again. I don't want to search your belongings for things you shouldn't have." With a shake of her head, we are alone once more.

My friends don't wait two seconds before they dive into questions. Their voices hushed, but not enough for any who might really want to listen in.

"That was you, yeah? Ten days ago, the skyline burned like a second sun. Your fire is the same white."

"You could see that from here?" I'm surprised, considering how far away we are from where the battle took place.

"See it?" Ash repeats. "We could hear it. Feel it. Whatever exploded must have been huge. Who could miss the sky tearing apart?"

Thankfully, the rotten night that grew across the sky had receded by the next morning. It's worrying that they could feel the effects of Kalma's falling mountain even after the majority of it was obliterated in her proceeding attack.

"What about that destroyed city they tried to blame on you? What's the truth behind that?" Kerry asks.

I hesitate for a moment, thinking she's talking about Morne, but quickly realize that's not the city they're talking about.

"That was Kalma," I say. "She framed me after killing everyone at the command center." No need to mention that I killed those executives before Kalma arrived.

"Huh," Ash says. "Everyone kinda assumed the Order was trying to pin the blame on you to save face. Wait, is Kalma the leader of the mermineae?"

"Sort of; she manipulated them into attacking rather than ordering them."

"Tell us of the ursu ambush. How'd you get out alive?"

"I met an old friend. How do you know so much?"

Leslie throws the paper I'd seen Ash running with into my hands. "I'm surprised you don't know. You're a damn celebrity now."

On the front page, in bold letters, is the title 'The War Ends,' but below that, Leslie points to the bottom half of the page where another passage titled 'Lies of the Order: Incendia Is Innocent!'

"Incendia?" I ask.

Leslie chuckles and the rest of the group smirk. "That's the nickname the papers gave you. The way you fight attracts a lot of attention. 'Maelstrom blazes banishing foes and saving thousands.' Journalists love you."

I sigh in relief. "I was kinda worried you guys would think I burned that city as well."

"You don't need to worry about anyone thinking that," Kerry says. "People have been enraged by the Mercenary Order's performance through the war, and the papers have been questioning every statement they've released. It's honestly surprising that it was Kalma and not the Order itself that set you up."

That is . . . far better news than I'd been expecting. Do I not have to worry about hiding myself?

"Though, saying that," Ash says. "The Mercenary Order still lists you as one of their most wanted, so please be careful. Most will take your side, but there are exceptions."

Nothing changes then. I have to wait until Remus can rescind that wanted status before I can wander the pact nations freely.

"What about you?" I ask the group. "Things haven't been too hard?"

I stay and talk to them well into the night, trading stories and experiences. For the next week, I'll follow them as they return to Baansguard to make sure nothing bad happens during their journey.

The safety and prosperity of these friends was a central motive to enter the war as I had. If not for them, I might have simply run away. Returned to the wasteland to look for my kind. Thousands, maybe millions more would have died if I'd chosen that path. I found success where I never thought I could.

I overcame my fears and grew strong enough to stand by Tore's side.

As Remus said, it will take a while to clear my name, so now is perfect to return home. It's about time I retrieved my mom's spear. It's about time I find the Agglomerate.

But for now, I just want to enjoy some time with friends.

About the Author

J. B. Oro is the author of the Young Flame series, originally released on Royal Road. He is a massive progression fantasy and xenofiction fan. Oro finds that the more unassuming and visibly contradictory to their strength characters are, the better.

JOIN THE FELLOWSHIP

follow us on our socials

 podiumentertainment.com

 @podiumentertainment

 /podiumentertainment

 @podium_ent

 @podiumentertainment